The Green Years

Born in Cardross, Scotland, A. J. Cronin studied at the University of Glasgow. In 1916, he served as a surgeon sub-lieutenant in the Royal Naval Volunteer Reserve and, at the war's end, he completed his medical studies and practised in south Wales. He was later appointed to the Ministry of Mines, studying the medical problems of the mining industry. He then moved to London and built up a successful practice in the West End. In 1931, he published his first book, *Hatter's Castle*, which was compared to the works of Dickens, Hardy and Balzac, winning him critical acclaim. Other books by A. J. Cronin include *The Citadel*, *Three Loves*, *The Green Years*, *Beyond This Place* and *The Keys of the Kingdom*.

Novels

Hatter's Castle
Three Loves
Grand Canary
The Stars Look Down
The Citadel
Vigil in the Night
Beyond This Place
The Valorous Years
The Keys of the Kingdom
The Green Years
Adventures of a Black Bag
Shannon's Way
The Spanish Gardener
Crusader's Tomb aka *A Thing of Beauty*
Northern Light
The Judas Tree
A Song of Sixpence
A Pocketful of Rye
The Minstrel Boy
Desmonde
Lady with Carnations
Gracie Lindsay
Doctor Finlay of Tannochbrae

The Green Years

A. J. Cronin

PAN BOOKS

First published 1960 by Gollancz

This edition first published 2025 by Pan Books
an imprint of Pan Macmillan
The Smithson, 6 Briset Street, London EC1M 5NR
EU representative: Macmillan Publishers Ireland Ltd, 1st Floor,
The Liffey Trust Centre, 117–126 Sheriff Street Upper,
Dublin 1 D01 YC43
Associated companies throughout the world

ISBN 978-1-0350-6957-6

Copyright © A. J. Cronin 1960

The right of A. J. Cronin to be identified as the
author of this work has been asserted in accordance
with the Copyright, Designs and Patents Act 1988.

All rights reserved. No part of this publication may be reproduced, stored in
a retrieval system, or transmitted, in any form, or by any means (including,
without limitation, electronic, mechanical, photocopying, recording or
otherwise) without the prior written permission of the publisher.

Pan Macmillan does not have any control over, or any responsibility for,
any author or third-party websites (including, without limitation, URLs,
emails and QR codes) referred to in or on this book.

The text of this book remains true to the original in every way and is reflective of the language
and period in which it was originally written. Readers should be aware that there may be
hurtful and harmful phrases and terminology that were prevalent at the time this novel
was written and in the context of the historical setting of this novel. Macmillan believes
changing the text to reflect today's world would undermine the authenticity of the
original, so has chosen to leave the text in its entirety. This does not, however,
constitute an endorsement of the characterization, content or language used.

1 3 5 7 9 8 6 4 2

A CIP catalogue record for this book is available from the British Library.

Printed and bound in the UK using 100% Renewable Electricity by CPI Group (UK) Ltd

This book is sold subject to the condition that it shall not, by way of
trade or otherwise, be lent, hired out, or otherwise circulated without
the publisher's prior consent in any form of binding or cover other than
that in which it is published and without a similar condition including this
condition being imposed on the subsequent purchaser. The publisher does not
authorize the use or reproduction of any part of this book in any manner
for the purpose of training artificial intelligence technologies or systems.
The publisher expressly reserves this book from the Text and Data Mining
exception in accordance with Article 4(3) of the European Union
Digital Single Market Directive 2019/790.

Visit **www.panmacmillan.com** to read more about
all our books and to buy them.

Book One

Book One

Chapter One

Holding Mama's hand tightly, I came out of the dark arches of the railway station and into the bright streets of the strange town. I was inclined to trust Mama, whom, until to-day, I had never seen before and whose worn, troubled face with faded blue eyes bore no resemblance to my mother's face. But in spite of the bar of cream chocolate which she had got me from the automatic machine, she had so far failed to inspire me with affection. During the slow journey from Winton, seated opposite me in the third-class compartment, wearing a shabby grey dress pinned with a large cairngorm brooch, a thin necklet of fur, and a black-winged hat which drooped over her ear, she had gazed out of the window, her head to one side, her lips moving as she maintained a silent yet emotional conversation with herself, from time to time touching the corner of her eye with her handkerchief as though removing a fly.

But now that we were out of the train she made an effort to put away her mood; she smiled at me and pressed my hand.

"You're a good man not to cry any more. Do you think you can walk to the house? It's not too far."

Anxious to please, I replied that I could walk, so we did not take the solitary cab which stood outside the arches, but set off down the High Street, Mama attempting to interest me in the points of importance which we passed.

The pavement kept lifting and falling; the rough seas of the Irish Channel were still pounding in my head; I felt a little deaf from the thrumming of the *Viper's* propellers. But opposite a handsome building, with polished granite pillars, set back from the street behind two iron cannon and a flagstaff, I heard her say, with gentle pride:

"These are the Levenford Municipal Offices, Robert. Mr. Leckie ... Papa ... works there, in charge of the Health Department."

"Papa," I thought, giddily. "That is Mama's husband ... my mother's father."

My footsteps were already flagging and Mama was looking at me with solicitude.

"It's too bad the trams are off to-day," she said.

I was much more tired than I had thought; and rather frightened. The town, harshly lit by the grey September afternoon, was full of cobblestones and sounds far less reassuring than the familiar, steady hum of traffic flowing past the open window of my home in Phœnix Terrace. A great ra-ta-tap of hammers came from the Shipyard, and from the Boilerworks, which Mama pointed out with a cracked gloved finger, there arose terrifying spurts of flame and steam. They were re-laying tramway lines in the street. At the corners little gusts of wind eddied up the dust into my swollen eyes, started off my cough.

Presently, however, we left the noise and confusion behind, crossed an open common with a pond and a circular bandstand, entered a quiet suburb which seemed part of a small country village very pleasantly situated beneath a wooded hill. Here were trees and green fields, a few old-fashioned little shops and cottages, a smithy with a horses' drinking trough outside, and prim new villas with painted cast-iron railings, neat flower beds, and proud titles like HELENSVILLE and GLENELG lettered in gilt on the coloured glass fanlights above the front doors.

We stopped at last, halfway along Drumbuck Road, before a tall semi-detached house of grey sandstone with yellow lace window curtains and the name LOMOND VIEW. It was the least imposing of the houses in the quiet street—only the facings of the doors and windows were of masoned stone, the rest had been left rough, an appearance vaguely unprosperous, yet redeemed by a front garden surprisingly aglow with yellow chrysanthemums.

"Here we are, then, Robert." Mrs. Leckie addressed me in that same tone of anxious welcome, heightened by a sense of arrival. "A beautiful view of the Ben we get on a clear day. We're nice and near Drumbuck village too. Levenford's a smoky old town but there's lovely country round about. Wipe your eyes, there's a dear, and come away in."

I had lost my handkerchief throwing biscuits to the gulls, but I followed obediently round the side of the house, my heart throbbing anew with the dread of things unknown. The matronly yet misguided words of our Dublin neighbour, Mrs. Chapman, as she kissed me goodbye that morning at the Winton docks, before surrendering me to Mama, rang in my ears: "What'll happen to you next, poor boy?"

At the back door Mama paused: a young man of about nineteen, working on his knees in a newly turned flower plot, had risen at our approach, still holding a trowel. He had a ponderous and stolid air, heightened by a pale complexion, a bush of black hair, and large thick spectacles which condensed his nearsighted eyes.

"You're at it again, Murdoch." Mama could not restrain an exclamation of gentle reproach. Then, bringing me forward: "This is Robert."

Murdoch continued to gaze at me heavily, framed by the trim back-green with iron clothes poles at the corners—a bed of rhubarb at one side; on the other, a rockery of honeycombed grey lava, spread with soot to kill the slugs. At last, with great solemnity, he expressed his thought.

"Well, well! So this is him, at last."

Mama nodded, nervous sadness again touching her eyes; and a moment later Murdoch held out to me, almost dramatically, a large hand, encrusted and stiff with good earth.

"I'm glad to meet you, Robert. You can depend on me." He turned his big lenses earnestly upon Mama. "It's just these asters I got given me from the Nursery, Mama. They didn't cost a thing."

"Well anyway, dear," Mama said, turning, "see you're washed up before Papa comes in. You know how it riles him to catch you out here."

"I'm just finishing. I'll be with you in a minute." Preparing to kneel again, Murdoch further reassured his mother as she led me through the doorway. "I set the potatoes to boil for you, Mama."

We passed through the scullery to the kitchen—arranged as a living-room with uncomfortable carved mahogany furniture, and diced varnished wallpaper which reflected the furious echoes of a "waggity" clock. Having told me to sit down and rest, Mama removed the long pins from her hat and held them in her mouth while she folded her veil. She then pinned hat and veil together, hung them with her coat in the curtained recess and, putting on a blue wrapper that hung behind the door, began with greater confidence to move to and fro over the worn brown linoleum, giving me soft encouraging looks while I sat, stiff and scarcely breathing in this alien house, on the edge of a horsehair-covered chair beside the range.

"We're having our dinner in the evening, dear, seeing I was away. When Papa comes in, try to not let him see you crying. It's been a great grief for him as well. And he has a lot to worry him—such a responsible position in the town. Kate, my other daughter, will be in any minute, too. She's a pupil teacher.... Maybe your mother told you." As my lip drooped she went on hurriedly: "Oh, I know it's confusing, even for a big man like yourself, to be meeting all his mother's folks for the first time. And there's more to come." She was trying, amidst her preoccupations, to coax a smile from me. "There's Adam, my oldest son, who is doing wonderfully in the insurance business in Winton—he doesn't stay with us, but runs down when he can manage. Then there's Papa's mother.... She's away visiting some friends just now ... but she spends about half of her time with us. And lastly, there's my father who lives here always—he's your great-grandpa Gow." While my head reeled with this jumble of unknown relatives her faint smile ventured forth again. "It isn't every boy who has a great-grandpa, I can tell you. It's quite an honour. You can just call him 'Grandpa,' though, for short. When I have his tray ready you can take it upstairs to him. Say how do you do, and help me at the same time."

Beside laying the table for five, she had, with a practised hand prepared a battered black japanned tray, oval-shaped and with a rose painted in the centre, setting upon it a moustache cup of ribbed white china filled with tea, a plate of jam, cheese, and three slices of bread.

Watching her, I wondered, aloud, rather huskily: "Does Grandpa not eat his food downstairs?"

Mama seemed slightly embarrassed. "No, dear, he has it in his room." She lifted the tray and held it out to me. "Can you manage? Right up to the top floor. Be careful and not fall."

Bearing the tray, I climbed the unfamiliar stairs shakily, confused by the steep treads and the shiny, waxcloth "runner." Only a fragment of the dwindling afternoon was admitted by the high skylight. On the second landing opposite a boxed-in cistern, I tried the first of the two doors. It was locked. The other, however, yielded to my uncertain touch.

I entered a strange, interesting, dreadfully untidy room. The high brass bed in the corner, with its patchwork quilt and lopsided knobs, was still unmade; the bearskin hearthrug was rumpled; the towel on the splashed mahogany washstand hung awry. My eye was caught by a black marble timepiece of the "presentation" variety lying upon its side on the littered mantelpiece with its inside in pieces beside it. I felt a queer smell of tobacco smoke and past meals, a blending of complex and intricate smells, forming, as it were, the bouquet of a room much lived-in.

Wearing burst green carpet slippers and dilapidated homespun, my great-grandpa was sunk deeply in the massive ruin of a horse-hair armchair by the rusty fireplace, steadily driving a pen over a long thick sheet of paper which lay, with the original document he was copying, on the yellow-green cover of the low table before him. On one hand stood a formidable collection of walking sticks, on the other a box of newssheet spills and a long rack of clay pipes, with metal caps, filled and ready.

He was a large-framed man, of more than average height, perhaps about seventy, with a pink complexion and a mane of still faintly ruddy hair flying gallantly behind his collar. It was, in fact, red hair which had lost a little of its ardour without yet turning white, and the result was a remarkable shade, golden in some lights. His beard and moustache, which curled belligerently, were of the same tinge. Though the white of his eyes were peculiarly specked with yellow, the pupils remained clear, penetrating and blue, not the faded blue of Mama's eyes, but a virile and electric blue, a forget-me-not blue, conspicuous and altogether charming. But his most remarkable feature was his nose. It was a large nose, large, red and bulbous; as I gazed, awestruck, I could think of no more apt simile than to liken it to a ripe, enormous strawberry, for it was of the identical colour, and was even peppered with tiny holes like the seed pits of that luscious fruit. The organ dominated his entire visage; I had never seen such a curious nose, never.

By this time he had ceased to write and, bestowing his pen behind his ear, he turned slowly to regard me. The broken springs of the seat, despite the brown paper stuffed around them, twanged musically at the shifting of his weight, as though ushering in the drama of our acquaintance. We stared at each other in silence and, forgetting the momentary fascination of his nose, I flushed to think of the wretched picture I must make for him standing there in my ready-made black suit, one stocking falling down, shoelaces loose, my face pale and tear-stained, my hair inescapably red.

Still silent, he pushed aside his papers, made a gesture, nervous but forceful, towards the cleared space on the table. I put the tray down on it. Barely taking his eyes off me, he began to eat, rapidly, and with a sort of grand indifference, partaking of cheese and jam indiscriminately, folding over his bread, soaking his crusts in his tea, washing everything down with a final draught. Then, wiping his whiskers with a downward sweep, he reached out instinctively—as though the business of eating was a mere preamble to tobacco, or even better things—and lit a pipe.

"So you are Robert Shannon?" His voice was reserved, yet companionable.

"Yes, Grandpa." Though my answer came strained and apologetic, I had remembered the instruction to omit his "great."

"Did you have a good journey?"

"I think so, Grandpa."

"Ay, ay, they're nice boats, the *Adder* and the *Viper*. I used to see them berth when I was in the Excise. The *Adder* has a white line on her understrake, that's how you tell the difference between them. Can you play draughts?"

"No, Grandpa."

He nodded encouragingly, yet with a trace of condescension.

"You will in due course, boy, if you stay here. I understand you *are* going to stay."

"Yes, Grandpa. Mrs. Chapman said there was no place else for me to go." A forlorn wave, warm with self-pity, gushed over me.

Suddenly I had a wild craving for his sympathy, an unbearable longing to unbosom myself of my terrible predicament. Did he know that my father had died of consumption, the spectral family malady which had carried off his two sisters before him—which had infected and with terrible rapidity, destroyed my mother—which, it was whispered, had even laid a little finger, beguilingly, on me . . . ?

But Grandpa, taking a few musing puffs, looking me through and through with an ironic twist of his lips, had already turned the subject.

"You're eight, aren't you?"

"Almost, Grandpa."

I wished to make myself as young as possible, but Grandpa was implacable. "It's an age when a boy should stand up for himself. . . . Though I will say there might be more of ye. Do you like to walk?"

"I've never tried it much, Grandpa. I walked to the Giant's Causeway when we went on our holidays to Portrush. But we took the miniature railway back."

"Just so. Well, we'll take a few turns, you and me, and see what good Scottish air does to us." He paused, for the first time communing with himself. "I'm glad you have my hair. The Gow ginger. Your mother had it too, poor lass."

I could no longer hold back that warm tide—almost from habit I burst into tears. Ever since my mother's funeral the week before the mere mention of her name produced this reflex, fostered by the sympathy it always brought me. Yet on this occasion I received neither the broad-bosomed petting of Mrs. Chapman nor the snuff-scented condolences which Father Shanley of St. Dominic's had lavished upon me. And soon the consciousness of my great-grandpa's disapproval made me painfully confused; I tried to stop, choked, and began to cough. I coughed and coughed, until I had to hold my side. It was one of the most impressive bouts I had ever had, rivalling even the severest of my father's coughs. I was, to be truthful, rather proud of it and when it ceased I gazed at him expectantly.

But he gave me no solace, uttered not a word. Instead he took a tin box from his waistcoat pocket, pressed open the lid, selected a large flat peppermint, known as an "oddfellow," from the number within. I thought he was about to offer it to me but to my surprise and chagrin he did not, placing it calmly in his own mouth. Then he declared severely:

"If there is one thing I cannot abide, it is a greeting bairn. Robert, your tear-bag seems precious near your eye. You must pull yourself together, boy." He removed the pen from his ear and threw out his chest. "In my life I've had to contend with a wheen of difficulties. Do you think I'd have won through if I'd laid down under them?"

Grandpa seemed about to launch forth on a profound and rather pompous dissertation; but at that moment a hand-bell tinkled on the ground floor. He broke off—disappointed, I thought—and with the stem of his pipe made a wave of dismissal, indicating that I should go below. As he resumed his writing, I took up the empty tray and crept, abashed, towards the door.

Chapter Two

Downstairs, Mr. Leckie, Kate and Murdoch had come in and, with Mama, were awaiting me in the kitchen, their sudden silence, which immobilized the room, indicating that I had been the subject of their conversation. Like most solitary children I had a painful shyness, exaggerated in my present state, and, with a confused understanding of the deep estrangement which had existed between my mother and Papa, I shrank into a kind of daze when, after a pause, he limped forward, took my hand, held it, then after a moment bent down and kissed me on the brow.

"I'm pleased to make your acquaintance, Robert. No one regrets more than I that we haven't met before."

His voice was not angry, as I had vaguely feared, but subdued and depressed. I told myself I must not cry, yet it was hard not to, when Kate also bent down and kissed me, awkwardly, but with generous intention.

"Let's sit in then." Mama, showing me to my place, again put on her veneer of brightness. "Nearly half-past six. You must be famished, son."

When we were seated, Papa, at the head of the table, lowered his eyes and said grace: a long, strange grace which I had never heard before, and he did not bless himself either. He began to slice the steaming corned beef in the oval ashet before him, while Mama served the potatoes and cabbage, at the other end.

"There!" Papa said, with the air of giving me a nice piece, his movements precise and correct. He was a small, rather insignificant man of forty-seven, with a narrow face, pale features and small eyes. His dark moustache was waxed out straight and his hair streaked over his scalp to conceal his baldness. His expression was marked by that faint touch of resignation seen on the faces of people who know they are conscientious and industrious yet have not been recognized or, in their own opinion, adequately rewarded by life. He wore a low starched collar, a made black tie, and an interesting, if unexpected, double-breasted suit of blue serge with brass buttons. A uniform cap, with a glazed peak, not unlike a naval officer's, lay on the chest of drawers behind him.

"Eat your cabbage with the meat, Robert." He leant forward and patted me on the shoulder. "It's very nourishing."

Under all these eyes I was finding it difficult to manage the strange bone-handled knife and fork, much longer than my own, and very slippery. Also, I did not like cabbage; and my small slice of beef was terribly salt and stringy. My father, in his gay style, had insisted that "nothing but the best" should appear on our table at Phœnix Crescent and he often came home from the office with some extra delicacy like guava jelly or Whitstable oysters—indeed, I was a thoroughly spoiled child, my appetite so pampered and capricious that often in the past six months my mother had bribed me with sixpence and a kiss to eat a slice of chicken. Yet I felt I could not displease Papa; I choked down some of the watery vegetable.

With my attention apparently diverted, Papa looked down the table at Mama, reverting, guardedly, yet in a worried fashion, to their interrupted conversation.

"Mrs. Chapman didn't ask anything?"

"No, indeed." Mama answered in a lowered tone. "Though she must have been out of pocket over the fares and what not. She seemed a good, sensible woman."

Papa exhaled a little breath. "It's a relief to find some decency left in the world. Did you have to take a cab?"

"No ... there was nothing much to bring. He has grown out of most of his things. And it seems *the men* took everything."

An inward spasm seemed to grip Papa, he stared at a painful vision in the air, murmuring: "One extravagance after another. Small wonder there was nothing left."

"Oh, Papa, there was such a lot of illness."

"But not much common sense. Why didn't they insure? A good sound policy would have taken care of everything." His hollow eye fell upon me as, with growing languor, I tried hard to clear my plate. "That's a good boy, Robert. We waste nothing in this house."

Kate, who sat across the table moodily viewing the twilight through the window as though the conversation were devoid of interest, gave me an odd sustaining kind of smile. Though she was twenty-one, only three years younger than my mother, I was surprised how little she resembled her. Where my mother had been pretty she was plain, with pale eyes, high cheekbones, and a dry, chapped, florid skin. Her hair was colourless, as if caught in a neutral state between the Gow red and the Leckie black.

"You've been to school, I suppose?"

"Yes." I flushed, simply from being spoken to; speaking was a great effort, "To Miss Barty's in the Crescent."

Kate nodded understandingly. "Was it nice?"

"Oh, very nice. If you made a good answer, at Catechism or General Intelligence, Miss Barty gave you a sugar dragee out of the bottle in the cupboard."

"We have a fine school in Levenford. I think you'll like it."

Papa cleared his throat. "I thought the John Street Elementary ... with you, Kate ... would be very suitable."

Kate removed her eyes from the window and gazed directly at Papa—resistant, almost sullen. "You know John Street is a wretched little school. He must go to the Academy, where we all went. In your position you can't do otherwise."

"Well..." Papa's eyes fell. "Maybe ... but not till the half term. ... That's October fourteenth, isn't it? Give him some questions and see what standard he's fit for."

Kate shook her head shortly.

"At this moment he'd dead with tiredness and ought to be in bed. Who is he sleeping with?"

Startled out of my growing drowsiness, I blinked at Mama while she meditated, as though her perplexities had prevented her from considering the matter before.

"He's too big a boy for you, Kate ... and your bed is very narrow, Murdoch ... besides you're so often up late, studying. Why don't we put him in Grandma's room, Papa? While she's away, I mean."

Papa dismissed the suggestion with a shake of his head. "She pays good money for her room. We can't disturb it without consulting her. And she'll be coming back soon."

So far Murdoch had been silent, eating stolidly, scrutinizing his food closely, inspecting each slice of bread like a detective, and from time to time picking up a textbook that lay beside his plate, holding it so close to his face he almost seemed to smell it. Now, he glanced up with a practical air.

"He must go in with Grandpa. It's the obvious solution."

Papa made a sign of agreement, though his face clouded at the mention of Grandpa's name.

It was settled. Half asleep though I was, my heart sank at the awfulness of this new prospect, this fresh link in the chain of my miseries, binding me to that strange and intimidating personality upstairs. But I was afraid to protest, too weary even to hold up my lids as Kate pushed back her chair.

"Come then, dear. Is the water hot, Mama?"

"I think so. But there's the dishes. Don't run off too much."

In the cramped bathroom Kate helped me to take off my clothes, her face flushing queerly as I reached a state of nakedness. There were only six inches of tepid water in the boxed-in bath which was yellowish at the waste and rough from re-enamelling. She stooped to wash me with the cloth and the block of gritty yellow soap. My head was nodding; my eyes were too heavy to exude further tears. I submitted as she dried me and again put on my day shirt. The bolt on the bathroom door clicked. We were going upstairs. And there, on the landing, looming out of the haze, the waves, the ship's vibration, the roar of tunnels, holding out his hand, to take me, was Grandpa.

Chapter Three

Grandpa was a difficult sleeper, snoring loudly, tossing on the lumpy flock mattress, squeezing me flat against the wall. In spite of this, I slept heavily, but as dawn came I had a bad dream. I saw my father in a long white nightshirt, breathing in and out of his green tea inhaler, that little brass tank with red rubber tubes which one of his business friends had recommended to him when the other medicines did no good. From time to time he paused, his brown eyes full of fun, to laugh and joke with my mother, who stood watching him with her hands clasped feverishly together. Then the doctor entered, an elderly man with a grey unsmiling face. A moment later there came a clap of thunder, a great black horse with nodding black plumes charged into the room, and I hid my face in grief and terror as my mother and father mounted upon its back and galloped off.

I opened my eyes, perspiring, my heart quivering in my throat, to find the morning sun streaming into the room. Standing at the window, almost dressed, Grandpa was rolling up the creaky blind.

"Did I wake you?" He turned. "It's a grand day, and high time you were up."

As I rose and began to pull on my clothes he explained that Kate had already set off for her teaching and Murdoch was on his way to get his train for Sherry's College in Winton—where he was preparing for a position in the post office branch of the Civil Service. Whenever Papa departed for his work the coast would be clear for us to go down. It came to me as a mild shock when Grandpa told me that Papa, despite his fine uniform, was only the district Sanitary Inspector. Papa's great ambition was to be

Superintendent of the Waterworks, but his present duties—Grandpa smiled indescribably—were to see that everybody kept their garbage cans and water closets in good order.

Almost immediately, we heard the slam of the front door; Mama came to the foot of the stairs and called us.

"How did you two get on?" She greeted us with a faint confederate's smile on her troubled face, as though we were schoolboys, up to all sorts of tricks.

"Nicely, Hannah, thank you." Grandpa answered courteously, seating himself in Papa's chair, with the wooden arms, at the head of the table. This morning meal, I soon learned, was the only one he took outside the confines of his room and he set much store by it. The kitchen was cozy from the range fire; there were crumbs and stains at Murdoch's place; a sense of intimacy bound the three of us as Mama spooned out cocoa into three cups from the Van Houten's tin and poured in boiling water from the big black-leaded kettle.

"I was wondering, Father," she said, "if you'd take Robert with you this morning?"

"Certainly, Hannah." Grandpa answered politely, but with reserve.

"I know you'll help all you can." She seemed to speak for his ear alone. "Things may be a little difficult at first."

"Tuts!" Grandpa raised his cup with both hands. "There's no need to meet trouble halfway, my lass."

Mama continued to gaze at him with that sad, half-hidden smile, a particular expression which, equally with that half-shake of her head, I saw to be the mark of her fondness for him. As we finished our breakfast she went out for a moment, returning with his stick and hard square hat, and the documents which I had seen him copying the day before. She carefully brushed the hat, which was old and faded, then retied more securely the thin red tape which bound the papers.

"A man of your parts shouldn't be doing this, Father. But you know it helps."

Grandpa smiled inscrutably, got up from the table and put on his hat with an air. Mama then saw us to the door. Here she came very close to Grandpa and gazed deeply, meaningly, with all her anxious heart, into his blue eyes. In a low voice she said:

"Now you promise me, Father."

"*Tch*, Hannah! What a woman you are to fash!" He smiled at her indulgently and, taking my hand in his, set off down the road.

Soon we reached the tramway terminus, where a red tram stood waiting, the conductor swinging the trolley-pole, making contact with the overhead wire amidst a crackle of blue sparks—still quite a novelty in that year. Grandpa led me to the front seat on the open upper deck. I held his hand more tightly and he gave me a side glance of communicative ardour as we slid off with gathering momentum down the slight incline from the Toll, making swift and bounding progress through the morning air towards Levenford.

"Tickets, please. All tickets, please." I heard the *ping* of the conductor's punch approaching, the rattling of the coins in his bag, but Grandpa, staring ahead, with his chin on his stick and his hair flying in the wind, had fallen into a kind of trance from which my appealing look, and the official's demand, entirely failed to rouse him. Such was his absorption, so statuesque his attitude, that the conductor paused doubtfully beside us, whereupon Grandpa, without a movement of his position, infused into his immobile countenance such a protestation of good-fellowship and secret understanding, topped off by a wink so full of complicity and promise, that the man broke into a kind of sheepish grin.

"It's *you*, Dandie," he said, and, after a moment's hesitation, brushed past us.

I was overcome by this example of my grandpa's prestige, but presently I recognized that we were in the High Street, opposite the Municipal offices. Here Grandpa descended, with dignity, and led the way towards a low building with a short outside flight of steps and a big brass plate, the name almost polished away: DUNCAN MCKELLAR, SOLICITOR. The windows on either side of the door were half screened by a kind of gauze, the one bearing, in faded gilt letters, the title LEVENFORD BUILDING SOCIETY, the other ROCK ASSURANCE COMPANY. As Grandpa entered this office much of his swagger was replaced by a sort of limpid humility, which, however, did not prevent him from throwing me a comical grimace when an unprepossessing woman with glossy cuffs put her head through a hatch and told us severely that Mr. McKellar was engaged with Provost Blair and that we must wait. I was soon to learn that sour women always disagreed with Grandpa and made him pull this face.

After about five minutes the inner door opened and a prosperous, dark-bearded man came through the waiting room, putting on his hat. His attentive glance confused me; and suddenly, with a disapproving frown at Grandpa, he drew up before us.

"So this is the boy?"

"It is, Provost," Grandpa answered.

Provost Blair stared me through and through, like a man who knew my history better than I did myself, so manifestly reviewing in his mind events connected with me, incidents of such a terrible and discreditable nature, that I felt my legs shaking beneath me from shame.

"You won't have had time to make friends with boys of your own age?" He spoke with reassuring mildness.

"No, sir."

"My boy, Gavin, would play with you. He's not much older than you. Come over to the house one day soon. It's quite near, in Drumbuck Road."

I hung my head. I could not tell him I had no desire to play with this unknown Gavin. He stood for a moment rather indecisively stroking his chin, then, with another nod, he went out.

Mr. McKellar was now free to give us his attention. His inner office, although old-fashioned, was very handsome indeed with a mahogany desk, a red-patterned carpet into which my feet sank, several silver cups on the mantelpiece and, on the dull green walls, framed photographs of important-looking men. Seated in his swivel chair, Mr. McKellar spoke without looking up.

"They've kept you cooling your heels, Dandie. Have you the work done? Or is some poor lass suing you . . ." Raising his head he noticed me and broke off as if I had spoiled his joke. He was a solid red-faced man of about fifty, clean-shaven, close-cropped, and sober in his dress. His eyes, beneath sandy tufted brows, were dry and penetrating but there was the hint of good nature behind them. His red underlip, naturally full, protruded judicially as he took the papers which Grandpa handed him and cast a glance over them.

"God help us, Dandie, but you're a bonny writer. Fair copperplate. I wish ye'd made as good a job of yourself as ye have of this deed of transfer."

Grandpa's laugh sounded a trifle forced. "Man proposes and God disposes, lawyer. I'm grateful for the work you give me."

"Then keep away from the demon." Mr. McKellar made a note on the book before him. "I'll credit this with the rest. Our friend Leckie," his tongue went into his cheek, "will get the cheque the end of the month. I see you have the new arrival."

He sat back, his eyes resting on me perhaps more shrewdly than the Provost's. Then, as though admitting a fact against his better judgment, as if implying, indeed, that he had expected some fearful and distressing freak to stand before him as the result of that horrible chain of circumstances which had passed before his vision, he murmured: "It's a nice enough boy. He'll not have his troubles to seek, or I'm much mistaken."

With due deliberation he selected a shilling from the loose change in his pocket and handed it across the desk to Grandpa.

"Buy the little son of Belial a lemonade, Dandle. And away with you. Miss Glennie will give you another deed. I'm rushed to death."

Grandpa left the office in excellent humour, inflating his chest as though savouring the breeze. As we came down the steps, he directed my attention to the other side of the street. Two tinker-women were making the rounds with baskets and wickerwork. One, the younger, stalwart and brown-faced, with that flaming orange hair so often seen amongst the roving Scottish gypsies, was carrying her burden on her head, swaying a little as she walked, her upstretched arms making firmer her strong bosom.

"There, boy," Grandpa exclaimed, almost with reverence. "Is that not a pleasant sight on a fine fresh autumn day?"

I could not follow his meaning—indeed, the two beshawled gypsies seemed to me quite beneath our notice. But I was very much cast down by certain obscure implications of the scene in the lawyer's office and, feeling myself more of a mystery than ever, I did not press the matter, but wrinkled my forehead in thought as we began our leisurely return. Why was I such a curiosity to all these people? What made them shake their heads over me?

The truth, though I could not guess it, was simple. In this small, prejudiced Scots town it was accepted history that my mother, a pretty and popular girl "who might have set her cap at anyone," had thoroughly disgraced herself by marrying my father, Owen Shannon, a stranger whom she had met while on vacation, a Dubliner, in fact, who had no family connections, held only an unimportant post in a firm of tea importers and had nothing to recommend him but his high spirits and good looks—if indeed such attributes could be considered a recommendation. No account was taken of the years of happiness which ensued. His death, followed so sensationally by hers, was regarded as a just retribution; and my appearance on the Leckie doorstep, without means of support, as certain evidence of the judgment of Providence.

Grandpa took the "Common way," which afforded us a view of the pond, and at the end of half an hour brought us, by an unexpected twist, to Drumbuck village—which Mama and I had skirted the day before—just as the noon hooter sounded musically from the now distant Works.

It was a pretty place, set beneath a slow rise of woods and traversed by a brook which ran beneath two stone bridges. We passed a little sweetshop filled with "lucky bags" and "bouncers" and liquorice straps, with the sign TIBBIE MINNS, LICENSED TO SELL TOBACCO above; then the open door of a cottage where a weaver sat working his loom. Across the road I could see the blacksmith shoeing a white horse, bent, with the hoof in his leather apron, a glow of red in the dark forge behind, a delicious smell of singeing horn wafting over.

Grandpa seemed to know everyone, even the hawker selling finnan haddies from a barrow and the woman who cried: "Rhubarb, jeelie rhubarb! Twa bawbees the quairter stane!" In his passage of the village street he gave and received most cordial salutations—I felt him to be a really great person.

"How do, Saddler!"

"How's yourself, Dandie?"

The stout red-faced man standing in his shirt sleeves on the step of the Drumbuck Arms was so especially friendly in his greeting that Grandpa stopped, pushed back his hat and wiped his brow with an air of pleasurable anticipation.

"We mustn't forget your lemonade, boy."

While he entered the Arms I sat on the warm stone step of the open side door, watching some white chickens pecking at spilled corn in the dusty yard with the greedy haste of intruders, conscious of the drowsy noontime peace of the village, and of Miss Minns, guardian of the sweetshop, peering across at me from behind her sea-green window, her dark shape dim and a little distorted by the blown glass so that she looked like a small marine monster swimming in a tank.

Presently Grandpa brought me a tumbler of lemonade which fizzed over my tongue, thickening my saliva deliciously. I watched him as he returned to his place amongst the midday gathering in the cool dim interior, first emptying a small thick glass with a single expert tilt, then, while he talked very prosily and importantly with the others, drinking from a big foamy tankard, in slow draughts, washing in and consolidating that first superior golden liquid.

At this point I was distracted by the cries and evolutions of two little girls who were bowling their hoops upon the village green across from the inn. As I was lonely, as Grandpa looked settled for a very long time, I rose, and in a gradual and indirect manner approached the edge of the green. I might not care much for strange boys but most of Miss Barty's pupils had been girls and I was almost at ease with them.

While her companion continued to strike her hoop furiously in the distance, the younger of the little girls had paused in her exertions and seated herself on a bench. She was about my own age, wore a tartan skirt with shoulder straps and was singing, singing to herself. While she sang I placed myself, unobtrusively, upon the extreme edge of the bench, and began to examine a scratch on my knee. When she had finished, there was a silence; then, as I had hoped, she turned to me in a friendly and inquiring fashion.

"Can you sing any songs?"

I shook my head sadly. I could not sing a note, indeed the only song I knew was one my father had tried to teach me about a beautiful lady who had died in disgrace. Still, I liked this little girl with brown eyes and curly dark hair pressed back from her white forehead by a semicircular comb. I was anxious not to let the conversation die.

"Is your hoop made of iron?"

"Oh, of course. But why do you say 'hoop'? We call it a 'gird.' And this stick we guide it with is a 'cleek.'"

Ashamed of my ignorance, which had revealed me so quickly as a stranger, I glanced at her companion, now attacking her gird to drive it towards us.

"Is that your sister?"

She smiled, but quietly, and with kindness. "Louisa is my cousin, visiting me from Ardfillan. My name is Alison Keith. I live with my mother over there." She indicated an imposing roof, embowered by trees, on the far side of the village.

Humbled by my fresh mistake and the sense of her superior dwelling, I greeted the bouncing arrival of Louisa with a defensive smile.

"Hullo!" Arresting her gird with great skill, Louisa, rather short o breath, looked at me askance. "Where did you spring from?"

She was about twelve, with long flaxen hair, which she tossed about with a bossy importance, which made me long to shine before her, for my own and Alison's sake.

"I came from Dublin yesterday."

"Dublin. Good gracious!" She interpolated in a singsong voice: "Dublin is the capital of Ireland." Then paused. "Were you born there?"

I nodded my head, warmly aware of the interest in her gaze.

"Then you must be Irish?"

"I'm Irish and Scottish," I answered rather boastfully.

Far from impressed, Louisa considered me with a patronizing air.

"You can't be two things, that's quite impossible. It all sounds most peculiar." A sudden thought seemed to strike her, she grew rigid, gazing at me with the sharp suspicion of an inquisitor.

"What church do you go to?"

I smiled loftily—as if I did not know. "To St. Dominic's," I was about to answer, when suddenly the gleam, the burning, in her eye awoke in me primeval instincts of defence.

"Just an ordinary church. It has a big steeple. Quite near us in Phœnix Crescent too." Flustered, I tried to dismiss the topic by jumping up and beginning to "burl the wilkies"—my sole physical accomplishment, which consisted in turning head over heels three times.

When I got up, red-faced, Louisa's disconcerting stare remained upon me and her tone held an artlessness more cruel than any accusation.

"I was beginning to be afraid you were a Catholic." She smiled. Redder than ever, I faltered: "What ever put that idea in your head?"

"Oh, I don't know. It's lucky you're not."

Overcome, I gazed at my shoes, more painfully embarrassed by the fact that Alison's eyes were reflecting something of my own distress. Still smiling, Louisa tossed her long hair back.

"Are you going to stay here?"

"Yes, I am." I spoke from between stiff, unwilling lips. "I'm going to the Academy in three weeks if you want to know."

"The Academy! That's *your* school, Alison. Oh, my goodness, it's lucky you're not what I thought. Why, I shouldn't think there's a single *one* in the whole Academy. Is there, Alison?"

Alison shook her head, with her eyes on the ground. I felt my eyelids smart; then, with a plunging movement, Louisa laughed gaily, finally.

"We must go for lunch now." She took up her gird primly, crushing me with her bright compassion. "Don't look so miserable.

You'll be quite all right if what you've said is *true*. Come along, Alison."

As they departed, Alison winged to me, over her shoulder, a look filled with sorrowful sympathy. But it did little to lift me, so overwhelmed was I by this terrible and unforseen catastrophe. Frozen with mortification, I stood watching their dwindling figures in a kind of daze until I became aware of Grandpa calling me from the other side of the street.

He was smiling broadly when I went over, his eyes bright, his hat cocked at a jaunty angle. As we started off in the direction of Lomond View he clapped me approvingly upon the back.

"You seem very successful with the ladies, Robie. That was the little Keith girl was it not?"

"Yes, Grandpa," I mumbled.

"Nice people." Grandpa spoke complacently, with unsuspected snobbishness. "Her father was captain of the P. and O. *Rawalpindi* ... before he died. The mother is a fine woman, though not overstrong. She plays the piano something beautiful ... and the little girl sings like a lintie. What's the matter with you?"

"Nothing, Grandpa. Nothing at all."

He shook his head over me, and to my acute embarrassment started to whistle. He was a beautiful whistler, clear and melodious, but quite careless of his own loudness. Approaching the house, he fell into a sort of hum:

"Oh, my luve is like a red, red rose,
That's newly sprung in June ..."

He put a clove in his mouth, murmuring to me, with a confidential air:

"You needn't mention our little refreshment to Mama. She's an awful one to fash."

Chapter Four

I think it was Mama's strategy, at this early stage, to keep me out of the way of the other members of the household. Often I did not see Papa until the evening, for, when he had a "smoke test" or a "milk prosecution" on hand, he did not return for lunch. His devotion to his work was exemplary; even at night he seldom relaxed, seating himself in his corner chair with an official report on plumbing or adulterated foods. He went out only on Thursday evenings to attend the weekly business meeting of the Levenford Building Society.

Murdoch was away most of the day at college. When he came in he lingered as long as possible over his supper; then, although he often seemed to want to talk to me, he spread his books all over the table and placed himself, with an air of heavy resignation, before them.

Kate reappeared from her teaching for the midday meal, but she was oddly uncommunicative and in the evenings she rarely joined the family circle. If she did not go out to visit her friend Bessie Ewing, she retired to her room to correct exercise books or to read, banging the door behind her, those queer bumps on her forehead standing out plainly as evidence of her inward turmoil.

It was not surprising that, while awaiting my beginning at the Academy, I fell more and more into Grandpa's hands. Apart from his copying he had little to do, and although he pretended to regard me as a nuisance he did not altogether disdain my awed companionship. Most afternoons when it was fine he took me to Drumbuck Green to watch him win at "the marleys," a game of china bowls which he played majestically with two friends: Saddler

Boag, a stout short-tempered gentleman who had kept the village harness shop for thirty years, and Peter Dickie, a small and sparrowy ex-postman who told me that in his time he had walked a distance equal to halfway round the world, and who was now deeply interested in Halley's Comet—which, he feared, might strike the earth at any moment. Grandpa's bowls were pale pink checked with brown. How wonderful to see him raise his last bowl to his eye with a calm ironic smile and "scatter the white" when Mr. Boag, who hated to lose, was "lying three"!

On other days Grandpa took me to inspect the Public Reading Room, to view a practice of the Levenford Fire Brigade—of which he was severely critical—and once, when Mr. Parkin, who hired out the boats, was away, for a lovely free row on the Common pond.

Sunday, which in any case gave me a peculiarly hollow feeling in my stomach, brought a different programme. On that day Mama always rose earlier than usual and when she had brought Papa a cup of tea in bed, she put the roast in the oven, and laid out his striped trousers and tail coat. Then began the general scurry and confusion of getting dressed, Kate running up and down stairs in her slipbody, Mama trying to get her fingers into gloves which had washed too tight, Murdoch at the last minute, in shirt and braces, putting his tousled head over the banisters and calling, "Mama, where did you put my clean socks?"—while Papa, his stiff collar hurting his neck, champed, watch in hand, in the lobby, repeating: "The bells will start any minute now."

More than ever conscious of myself as an acute embarrassment to these good people, I kept out of the way in Grandpa's room, until the distant bells began caressing the still morning air, those sweet importunate bells which always increased my loneliness. Grandpa never went to church. He seemed to have no desire to go; besides his clothes were not good enough. When the others had set out for the Established Church on Knoxhill, where the Provost and the baillies of the town attended service, he gave me a kind of privileged sigh with his eyelid that permitted me to accompany him while he "slipped across" to pay a forenoon visit to his friend Mrs. Bosomley, the lady who owned the house next door.

Mrs. Bosomley was the widow of a pork-butcher and had once been a leading member of a touring dramatic company, her most notable performance being that of Josephine in "The Emperor's Bride." She was about fifty, quite stout, her brown hair frizzed by tongs, with a broad face, small good-natured eyes which vanished when she laughed and tiny red veins on her cheeks. Often, peering through the privet hedge, I would see her pacing up and down her little garden, followed by her yellow cat, Mikado, and stopping to strike an attitude and recite something out loud. Once I distinctly heard her say: "Strike for the green graves of your sires! Strike for your native soil!"

Levenford was not her native soil; her origin and early life were obscure, and later on boys at school hinted to me that she had not really been on the stage but had travelled with a circus and was tattooed upon her stomach. I shall speak of Mrs. Bosomley again; now it is enough to say that her hospitality made a sharp contrast to the Spartan economy next door. In her front room she gave me milk and sandwiches while Grandpa and she drank coffee; and she startled me dreadfully by smoking a cigarette—the first time I had seen a lady do such a thing—that to this day the name of the brand upon the flat green packet remains printed on my memory. It was "Wild Geranium."

On Sunday afternoon while Papa, with his collar and tie unloosed, took a nap on the sofa in the cool depths of the parlour and Murdoch departed with Kate to teach in Sunday school, Grandpa again gave me his sign and sauntered off with me in the direction of the village, now steeped in digestive torpor. Turning up the lane beyond the Green he paused, with a detached and purposeful air, outside the hawthorn hedge of Dalrymple's market garden.

This was a beautiful garden, with the sun-blistered sign A. DALRYMPLE. NURSERYMAN spanning the gate, kale and cabbages and carrots sprouting in rows, the orchard still heavy with pears and apples. Grandpa, having first surveyed the deserted lane, peered carefully over the hedge; then, with his tongue, made a clicking sound of regret.

"What a pity! The dear man's not here." He turned, took off his hat and handed it to me with an urbane smile. "Just nip through the hedge, Robert; it'll save you a walk to the gate. Take the honey pears, they're the best. And keep your head down."

Following his whispered instructions I crept through, and filled the hat with ripe yellow pears, while he stood in the middle of the lane carefully scrutinizing the landscape and humming.

When I rejoined him and we began to eat, the juice running down our chins, he remarked gravely:

"Dalrymple would give me his last gooseberry. He's just devoted to me, the dear man."

Although I was a melancholy child I will not deny that I found great, if temporary, comfort in Grandpa's society. There was, unhappily, one odd detraction from the pleasure of our expeditions which shocked and baffled me. Grandpa, cordially saluted, everywhere acclaimed, was greeted by a certain juvenile section of the community with shouts of unbelievable derision.

Our tormentors were not the Academy boys, like Gavin Blair, whom Grandpa had pointed out to me across the street, causing me to redden furiously, but the small village boys who gathered at the bridge to catch minnows with their caps in the stream. As we went by, these boys stared at us rudely and jeered:

"*Cadger Gow! There he goes!*
Where did he get that terrible nose?"

I turned pale with shame, while Grandpa stalked on, his head in the air, pursued by the awful chant. In the beginning I pretended not to hear. But at last, my curiosity conquered my dismay. I besought him with wide eyes:

"Where *did* you get that nose, Grandpa?"

A silence. He glanced at me sideways, aloof and very dignified.

"Boy, I got it in the Zulu War."

"Oh, Grandpa!" My shame melted in a quick flood of pride, of anger against these ignorant little boys. "Tell me about it, Grandpa, please."

He gave me a guarded look. Although reluctant, he seemed flattered by my interest.

"Well, boy," he said, "I am not one to brag . . ."

While I trotted spellbound beside him, a great troopship glided out amidst the weeping of beautiful women, and made stealthy landfall of an arid shore bearing a gentleman cornet in that exclusive brigade, Colonel Dougal Macdougall's Scottish White Horse. Swiftly promoted, through a daring sortie against the Matabele, Grandpa soon had risen to be the Colonel's righthand man and was picked to carry dispatches from the beleaguered garrison, when the White Horse were cut off. I scarcely breathed as, in the darkness of night, a revolver in each hand, a knife between his teeth, he crawled over the rocky veldt. He was almost through the enemy lines when the moon—oh, perfidious moon!—sailed out of the clouds. Instantly the savage horde was upon him. *Pim! Pam! Pim!* His smoking revolvers were empty. Planted on a boulder, he slashed away with his knife. Bloody black writhing forms lay all around him, he whistled musically, and out of the night bounded his favourite white charger. Oh, the stark suspense of that midnight ride. After him came the fleet-footed Zulus. Flights of assagais darken the air. *Whish! Whish!* But at last, faint and bleeding, clinging to his horse's neck, he reached the cantonment. The flag was saved.

I drew a long breath. Excitement and admiration gave me starry eyes;

"Were you badly wounded, Grandpa?"

"Yes, boy, I'm afraid I was."

"Was it then that you got . . . your nose, Grandpa?"

He nodded solemnly, caressing the organ with reminiscent tenderness. "It was, boy . . . an assagai . . . poisoned . . . direct hit." Tilting his hat over his eyes against the sun, he concluded reminiscently: "The Queen herself expressed regret when she decorated me at Balmoral."

I contemplated him with a new awe, a new tenderness. Wonderful heroic Grandpa! I held his hand tightly as we returned from the Drumbuck Arms to Lomond View.

When we entered the house Mama was in the lobby, studying a postcard which had just come in, that first day of October, by the afternoon delivery.

"Grandma is coming back to-morrow." She turned to me. "She's looking forward to seeing you, Robert."

The news affected Grandpa strangely. He did not speak but gave Mama his particular grimace, as though he had swallowed something sour, and began to climb the stairs.

With her face upturned Mama seemed to offer consolation. "Would you like an egg to your tea, Father?"

"No, Hannah, no." The intrepid fighter of Zulus spoke despondently. "After that, I couldn't eat a thing."

He went upstairs. I could hear the melancholy twang of the springs as he flung himself into his chair.

Whatever Grandpa's reaction, mine was one of expectation. On the following day, which was Saturday, the dramatic sound of a cab drew me, running, to the window.

Excitedly, I watched Grandma lower her head and, treasuring her purse against her black-beaded cape with one hand, pulling her skirt from her elastic-sided boots with the other, climb carefully from the cab. The driver seemed out of humour. When Grandma paid him he flung up his arms; but at last, as though acknowledging defeat, consented to carry in the carpet bags. Grandpa had departed for a walk, silently, at an unusual hour, but Kate and Murdoch came out deferentially to welcome her. In the lobby Mama was calling: "Robie! Where are you? Come and help your great-grandma with her things."

I ran out and, in the general confusion, began to carry the lighter packages to the top landing, glancing hurriedly yet with shy interest at Grandma. She was a big flat-footed woman, bigger than my grandpa, with a long, firm, yellowish, deeply wrinkled face, nicely set off by the immaculate white frill which lined her black mutch. Her hair, still dark, was parted in the middle, and at the corner of her long, seamed upper lip was a brown mole stain from which sprouted a tuft of crinkling whiskers. As she talked to Mama, relating the events of her journey, she displayed strong, discoloured teeth which, however, were somewhat unmanageable and made little clicking noises.

Upstairs the secret door was open and while Grandma refreshed herself with a cup of tea downstairs, I sat on a bag in the doorway, satisfying, the curiosity which I had so long experienced. It was a neat and well-ordered room, smelling of camphor and beeswax, two hooked rugs making oval islands upon the stained boards, and between them a heavy mahogany bed with turned legs and thick magenta eiderdown, a gleaming chamber pot discreetly tucked beneath. In one corner was the sewing machine; a plush-backed rocking chair draped with an antimacassar waited expectantly at the window. Three coloured lithographs, magnificent and terrifying, hung upon the walls: "Samson Destroying the Temple," "Israelites Crossing the Red Sea," "The Last Judgment." In a lugubrious ebony frame shaped like a tombstone, and near the door, where I could read it, hung a black-bordered poem, entitled "Auspicious Day," praising Abraham for having taken Samuel Leckie to his bosom and inflicting such heavy sorrow on Samuel's bereaved and beloved spouse.

Grandma came up slowly, but steadily, pressing each stair firmly into its place, while I hung about against my will, magnetized, rather in the manner of those small fish which, by instinct rather than desire, gravitate submissively to escort the leviathans of the deep. She was inspecting her room to see if anything had been disturbed, moving the chairs a fraction of an inch, testing the treadle of the sewing machine with her foot, and all the time observing me with a serene yet penetrating eye.

At last, not wholly satisfied, she shook her head and, opening her Gladstone carrying-bag, took out her spectacle case, a Bible, and a number of bottles of physic which she arranged, with the utmost precision, on the little table, covered with a lace doily, beside her bed. Then she turned and addressed me in her broad "country" accent.

"Have you been a good boy while I was away?"

"Yes, Grandma."

"I'm glad to hear it, dear." Her soberness yielded to a warmer note. "You may as well help me to get things straight. I cannot leave this place a day without someone tampering and tinkering with it."

I helped her to unpack while she put away all her folded and laundered garments in a deep cupboard. Then handing me a flannel, and remarking that cleanliness was next to godliness, she set me to rub the fire brasses while, with a feather duster, which she took from the same cupboard, she began to flick the china dogs upon the mantelpiece.

Pleased with my activity, Grandma further relaxed her strictness and bestowed on me a look of deep and meaningful solicitude. "You *are* a good boy, in spite of all. Your grandma has something nice for you."

From the top lefthand drawer of her chest she brought out a handful of the hard peppermint sweets known as "imperials," took one herself, and pressed the rest on me.

"Suck, don't crunch," she advised. "They last longer that way." She stroked my brow protectively: "You're going to be your grandma's boy. You bide with me, my lamb. I'm taking you out for your tea."

True to her promise, Grandma kept me with her most of the day, conversing with me from time to time, even telling me something of herself. She came of a good country stock: the nephew with whom she had been staying was an Ayrshire potato farmer. Her husband had been the head timekeeper at the Levenford Boilerworks, a "saint" who had helped her to find grace. One never-to-be-forgotten day, as he crossed the yard, a ton of steel had dropped from a travelling crane on to his head. Poor Samuel! But he had gone to the Lord, and Marshall Brothers had behaved most handsomely: she drew a pension from the Works every quarter-day in life. She was independent, thank God, and could pay decently for her board and lodging.

At four o'clock in the afternoon, she told me to wash my face and hands. Half an hour later we set out for the village of Drumbuck.

By this time Grandma's austere and Christian spirit was having its effect on me, and in my desire to win her approbation I became serious, old-fashioned, even began primly to imitate her way of nodding her head. I was filled with a godly sense of importance as I walked beside her in all her "braws," for, although the day was warm, she had resumed the full state robes of her arrival, carrying, like a sceptre, her long tightly rolled umbrella with a gold and mother-of-pearl handle. No one dare shout after *her*.

"Remember, dear," she warned me as we drew near the little sweetshop between the horse trough and the smithy. "You are to behave nicely. Miss Minns is my bosom friend—we go to the same Meeting. Don't make a noise when you drink your tea, and speak up when you are spoken to."

Little had I dreamed, when I pressed my face longingly against Miss Minns's low greenish windowpanes, that I would so soon have the honour to be her guest. The door went *ping* as Grandma pushed and I followed in her wake, stepping down to the delightful dim interior of the little cave which smelled of peppermints, aniseed balls, scented soap, and tallow candles. Miss Minns, a small bent woman in black bombazine with steel spectacles on her forehead, was seated behind the counter at her knitting; but, as we entered, taken unawares, she gave out a startled exclamation of affection and surprise.

"Good sakes, woman, you're not back!"

"Aye, aye, Tibbie, it's me and no other."

Delighted to have caught her friend unprepared, Grandma, with unsuspected playfulness, submitted to, and returned, an affectionate greeting, interspersed with many effusive cries from Miss Minns.

Then, hobbling from her rheumatism, Miss Minns led the way into the back shop where, very quickly, she laid out cups and saucers on the round table and set the kettle upon the fire, all the time giving her close attention to the account Grandma had launched into of her visit to Kilmarnock, which pertained largely to the "Meetings" she had attended.

"Yes, woman." Miss Minns sighed at the conclusion in resigned and subtle flattery. "You have had a profitable time. I wish I had heard Mr. Dalgetty. But better you nor me."

Pouring the tea, she began to relate to Grandma everything which had taken place in her absence: the births and the burials and, though I did not then suspect it, the various pregnancies which had occurred. But presently, when these secular trivialities had been disposed of, there came a veiled silence, they glanced at me with the expression of two gourmands who, having exhausted the light dishes, now turn, with whetted appetites, to the main item of the repast.

"He's a fine boy," Miss Minns said, openly. "Take another piece of cake, my big man. It's very wholesome."

I could not but feel complimented by this extra attention. Miss Minns had already given me, all to myself, a plate of Abernethy biscuits and an extra cushion for my chair, to raise me to the table. Then, finding that I did not drink my tea, she had fetched from the shop a bottle of delicious yellow aerated water named Iron Brew, with a label showing a strong man in a leopardskin lifting dumb-bells of tremendous weight.

"Now, dear," she said kindly. "Tell your grandma and me how you've been getting on. You've been with your grandpa a good deal?"

"Oh, yes, indeed. I was with him nearly all the time."

A meaning, mournful glance between the two ladies; then, in a tone which seemed to veil the forebodings of her spirit, Grandma asked:

"And what did you do nearly all the time?"

"Oh, lots of things," I said rather grandly, reaching of my own accord for another Abernethy. "Played bowls with Mr. Boag. Hunted the Zulus. Gathered fruit in Mr. Dalrymple's Nursery.... Grandpa had permission, of course, to send me through the hedge." Flattered by their attention, I paid full homage to my grandpa, not forgetting our visits to the Drumbuck Arms, even mentioning the two tinkers whom Grandpa had liked in the High Street.

In the pause which followed Grandma continued to regard me

with unaffected commiseration. Then, with great discretion but firmly, as though resolved to know the worst, she began to probe into my more distant history, drawing from me an account of my life in Dublin. So tempered was her approach, I soon found myself giving forth, without a qualm, the full record of my upbringing.

When I concluded the two women looked at each other, charged with a strange silence.

"Well," Miss Minns said at last, in a suppressed voice. "You know where you are, woman."

Grandma gravely inclined her head and glanced towards me. "Robert dear, run out and play a minute by the door. Miss Minns and I have something to discuss."

I said good-bye to Miss Minns, then stood by the horse trough in gathering uneasiness, until Grandma rejoined me. She did not speak during our return; although she held my arm with a kind of sober pity. Leading me immediately to her room, she closed the door and removed her cape.

"Robert," she said. "Will you say a prayer with me?"

"Oh, yes, Grandma," I assured her with nervous fervour.

As though her heart bled she took my hand, guided me to my knees, then got down heavily beside me, amidst the growing darkness of the room. Her supplication, full of confidence and devotion, was for my welfare. Agitated, my face drawn by anxiety, I was nevertheless moved by the steadfast and personal quality of the prayer, and my eyes filled with tears when Grandma, having begged forgiveness for a sinner, and unceasing patience for herself, commended me tenderly to Heaven. When she concluded she got up, smiling cheerfully, drew the blinds and lit the gas.

"That suit you're wearing, Robert ... it's a pure disgrace. What they would think of you at the Academy I do not know." Summoning me, she deprecated the frayed shoddiness of the material between her finger and thumb. "To-morrow I'll begin to run you up something on my machine. Fetch me the inch tape from my drawer."

While I stood very still she measured me from every angle, jotting down figures with a moistened stub of pencil on a brown paper pattern which she took from a copy of *Weldon's Home Dressmaker*.

Then she opened her cupboard, reflecting aloud: "I have a good serge petticoat somewhere. Just the thing!"

While she rummaged there came a tap on the door.

"Robie." It was my grandpa's voice outside. "Time for bed."

Grandma turned from the cupboard.

"I will put Robert to bed."

"But he sleeps with me."

"No, he is sleeping with me."

There was a pause. Grandpa's voice came through the door.

"His nightshirt is in my room."

"I will provide him with a nightshirt."

Again silence, the silence of defeat, and in a moment I heard the sound of Grandpa's slippers in retreat. I was now thoroughly alarmed, and must have shown it in my pallid face, for Grandma's manner became calmer and more protective still. She undressed me, poured water from her ewer and made me wash, then, wrapping me in a flannel bodice, she helped me into the high bed. She sat down beside me, stroking my brow, as though facing a disagreeable task.

"My poor boy." She sighed with genuine compunction. "I want you to prepare yourself. Your grandpa never fought in any war. He has never been fifty miles beyond the county of Winton in all his life."

What was she saying? My pupils dilated in shocked incredulity.

"It's not my nature to speak ill of anyone," she continued. "But this is a solemn duty which affects your future." As her voice went on, my whole being revolted, I tried not to hear what she was saying, yet the words, from time to time, broke through relentlessly. "... A failure in all he did ... thrown out of every situation ... exciseman in the bonded warehouse ... hand-to-mouth for years. ... It was the end of his poor wife. ... And then the drink ... see it in his face ... his nose. Even the company he keeps ... Boag, three times a bankrupt, and Dickie, one foot in the poorhouse. ... Now not a penny to his name ... dependent on the charity of my son..."

"No, no," I cried, covering my ears with my hands and thrusting my head into the pillow.

"You had to know, Robert." She straightened the bedclothes. "He's not the right influence for a growing boy. Don't cry, my lamb. I'll take care of you."

She waited patiently till I was composed, then rose, and declaring that she, too, was tired, she quoted: "Early to bed, early to rise, makes us all healthy, wealthy, and wise," then proceeded to take her clothes off.

Fascinated, despite my desolation, I could not help but watch her. She began by removing her black mutch: the little black bonnet which sat on her bun of still brown hair. Then from her bosom she unpinned her thin gold watch, which she wound, carefully, and hung on a hook above the mantelpiece. Next to come off was the white shawl which kept warm her shoulders. A pause for unbottoning the front of her tight long-sleeved black bodice, then this, too, lay folded on the rocking chair. The slipbodies followed, white strips of cambric, perhaps four of them, the ends tired with tapes, until Grandma was seen to be encased in dark stays, which encircled her and rose high to the dark hollows of her armpits.

At this point she paused to remove her teeth, with one swift, almost magical pass of her left hand, a feat of legerdemain which caused her face to collapse in staggering fashion. Her austere features sank into an agreeable softness. However, once the teeth had been placed in a tumbler of water by the bed, Grandma put on a white bed-cap, the ribbons of which, tied tight under her chin, seemed to restore, partly, the rigidity of her facial structure.

Now she dropped and stepped out of her skirt, a process repeated with all her petticoats. The number of petticoats that Grandma wore became one of the great perplexities of my early life: first, a black alpaca, then three of white cotton, two of creamy flannel . . . but I never solved the ultimate and elusive mystery for at this point Grandma looked at me, sternly yet coyly.

"Robert! Turn to the wall."

When I obeyed, I heard more stepping out, the snapping of whalebone; other sounds; then the gas went out and Grandma was in beside me. She was a quiet and peaceful sleeper, but her feet, which she immediately placed against me, were very cold. Lying on my side in the darkness I fearfully studied her teeth as they grinned luminously at me from the bedside table: a heavy double set, of greenish colour, old-fashioned but immensely strong, with a powerful connecting spring. Grandpa had no such teeth; but I longed—oh, despite his wickedness I longed suddenly with all my heart to be back beside him.

Chapter Five

The old greystone Academy, with its high square clock tower, worn stone steps, long damp corridors, and hot classrooms filled with the smell of chalk dust, children, and illuminating gas, had for more than a hundred years exposed to the High Street its deep, dark archway, an entrance comparable, by my nervous fancy, to the opening in the mountain of Hamelin.

On the very morning that I must pass through that opening, when I woke up filled with anxiety and excitement, Grandma informed me that my suit was ready. She led me, complacently, to the window where it was laid out, complete, on tissue paper, to surprise me.

The first sight of my new suit, to which I had looked forward, so took me aback that I scarcely knew what to say. It was green, not a dark subdued green, but a gay and lively olive. True, as she treadled, I had seen this material piled on Grandma's machine, but, in my innocence, I had assumed it to be the lining.

"Slip it on," she said, with pride.

It was large, the jacket engulfed me, the wide breeches fell in straight lines like a pair of long trousers amputated below the knee.

"Fine, fine." Grandma was patting and pulling me here and there. "It covers you well. I made it for your growth."

"But the colour, Grandma?" I protested feebly.

"Colour!" She removed a white basting thread, speaking from lips which compressed a pin. "What ails the colour? It's wonderful stuff, stands by itself. It'll never wear out."

I blenched. Looking closely at my sleeve I now perceived in the material a faint stripe, composed of little raised whirls: oh, heavens, a pattern of roses, beautiful for Grandma's petticoat, but scarcely the thing for me.

"Let me put on my old suit for this morning, Grandma."

"A pack of nonsense! I cut it up for dusters last night."

Grandma's praise of her creation sent me from the room partly convinced, but immediately Murdoch dashed me to the ground. Meeting me on the stairs he stopped in mock terror, shielding his eyes, then lay back against the banisters with a wild guffaw. "It's come! It's come at last!"

In the kitchen Mama's odd silence, her air of extra kindness as she handed me my porridge, did not reassure me.

I went out into the cold grey morning, unnerved, conscious that on the whole of that drab, wintry Scottish landscape there was one strange vernal note: myself. People turned round to gaze after me. In my timid shame, I shunned the main street and took the "Common way," a quieter but longer road, which made me late for school.

After some difficulty, having lost myself in the corridors, I found the second standard—to which, on Kate's recommendation, I had been assigned. The partition was thrown back, the double class assembled, as I entered; and Mr. Dalgleish, at his desk, had already given out the first lesson. I tried to edge, unobserved, to a vacant desk, but the master stopped me in the middle of the floor. He was not, as I discovered, a habitual tyrant, for he had days of splendid affability when he dowered us with a wealth of interesting knowledge; but there were other spells, dark and bitter, when a glowering devil seemed to rage within him. And I now saw, with dismay, from the manner in which he chewed the corner of his moustache, that his mood was unfavourable. I expected a reprimand for my lateness. But he did not shout at me. Instead he climbed down from his desk and walked round me in a leisurely fashion, with his head slightly to one side. The class sat up, startled and excited.

"So!" he said at last. "We are the new boy. And it appears we have a new suit. The age of miracles is not over."

A titter of expectancy went round. I was silent.

"Come, sir, don't sulk at us. Where did ye buy it? Miller's in the High Street or the Co-operative Stores?"

Pale to the lips, I whispered: "My great-grandma made it, sir."

A roar of laughter from the class. Mr. Dalgleish, his blood-threaded eye unsmiling, continued to walk round me.

"A remarkable colour. But appropriate. We understand you are of Hibernian extraction?"

Great laugher from the class. In all that amphitheatre of grinning faces, magnified by my shrinking sensibilities to the vastness of a colosseum, yet seen minutely, vividly, there were only two that did not smile. Gavin Blair, in the front row, was gazing at the master with a kind of cold contempt; Alison Keith, across her lesson book, kept her brown, troubled eyes steadily upon me.

"Answer my question, sir? Are you or are you not a disciple of Saint Patrick?"

"I don't know."

"He does not know." The sneering tone took on amazement, a more leisured deliberation; the class rolled about the benches with merriment. "He bursts upon us, garlanded, as it were, with shamrocks, the walking apotheosis of that heart-moving ballad 'The Wearing of the Green,' yet he blushes to admit that the holy water still bedews his brow ..."

This continued until, suddenly, he turned and, with a cold stare, stilled the class. Then he spoke to me in his natural voice.

"It may interest you to know that I taught your mother. It looks now as if I wasted my time. Sit over there."

Trembling and humiliated, I stumbled to my place.

I hoped that this might end my suffering. Alas, it was only the beginning. At playtime I was surrounded, by a crowing, jeering mob. Already I had been marked as someone different from the others, now I was confirmed as a freak amongst the herd.

Bertie Jamieson and Hamish Boag were my worst tormentors.

"Green's the colour! Blue's its mother." The wit was cruder than Mr. Dalgleish's, but it followed the same pattern. The unhappy petticoat of an old woman had stirred racial and religious hatreds to their dregs. At the lunch hour I locked myself in one of the cubicles of the lavatory, my piece of bread, spread with rhubarb jam and wrapped in paper, resting untouched on my knees. But I was discovered and forced out to the light of day.

That afternoon we had drill, which was conducted in the school hall by the janitor, an ex-sergeant of the Volunteers. Here, as I removed my jacket with the others, Bertie Jamieson and Hamish Boag approached me with a threatening air. Bertie was a loutish boy with a bulging forehead who was always running and scrambling with the girls. He said: "We're going to give it to you after."

"But what for?" I faltered.

"For being a dirty little Papist."

During the next hour, I excuted my "arms raise" and "knees bend" in shivering foreboding. Whenever the exercises were over and the janitor had gone I was crowded back into the hall cloakroom. Most of the bigger boys were there, and when I had been pushed and kicked into a corner, Jamieson, catching hold of my arm, began to twist it painfully behind my back. In trying to escape I slipped and fell. Immediately, while Hamish Boag collared my legs, Jamieson sat on my chest and began to bang my head on the floor.

"Give it to him, Bertie," cried several voices. "Knock the stuffing out of him."

This gave Jamieson an idea. He released my hair and exchanged a glance with the others. "Who's got a knife? We'll see if he's green inside as well as out."

"No, Bertie, no," I cried. I could scarcely speak for the frightened beating of my heart. Suddenly the bell rang and they were obliged to let me up. As I reached the corridor, from which we were to march to the classroom, Mr. Dalgleish, waiting, with his hand on the tongue of the bell, gazed at my dusty dishevelled form.

"What's all this?"

The others answered for me—a sycophantic chorus: "Nothing, sir." Then little Howie, pert as a squirrel, cried out from behind: "We were just admiring Shannon's new green suit, sir."

Mr. Dalgleish smiled sourly.

All that week I felt the full misery of life. There was no end to the violations committed upon me. After school, opposite the Church of the Holy Angels, which stood quite near the Academy, there was usually collected a predatory band. Though I had never put foot within the edifice I was ribaldly urged to nip in and have my sins forgiven, to rifle the poor box, to kiss the priest's toe—and other portions of his anatomy. My tormentors were merciless and when, in desperation, I struck out at them I was always overwhelmed by the mob.

To avoid them, constantly on the lookout and ready to run, I took circuitous and unfrequented paths—especially the "Common way," which led past the Boilerworks; yet even here I was not immune—that dreadful suit was on my back and the young engineers and fitters from the works would shout: "Hey! Green Breeks! Does your mother know you're out?" Their remarks were good-natured, yet, by now, I was too cowed to know the difference between humour and abuse. I sank deeper into despair, I made a bungle of my homework, blotted all my copy-books in class, I was behaving like a halfwit. Once when Mr. Dalgleish asked me to stand and recite a poem we had learned I hesitated so long he shouted: "What are you waiting for?" I answered absently, vacantly: "Please, sir, for my green suit." Stupefied silence. Then a great howl of laughter.

I could endure it no longer. That evening I burst into Grandpa's room. The first whiff of the familiar fusty yet beloved smell—tears gushed from my eyes. Since Grandma had adopted me our estrangement had been complete, and though I had been prepared to offer him my forgiveness, he had passed me with his head in the air, wearing his chilly, aloof, disdainful smile, meeting my stammered explanation with the indifferent remark: "Sleep with who you like, my boy." Now, he was seated, philosophically, yet with a certain air of apathy, doing nothing.

"Grandpa," I wept.

He turned slowly. Was I mistaken? Or did his eye brighten at the sight of me? A pause.

"I thought ye'd come back," he said, simply; then, unable to resist his dreadful sententiousness, he added: "Old friends are better than new."

Chapter Six

Calmed at last and seated on Grandpa's knee—joyful proof of our reconciliation—I poured out my heart. He listened to me in silence. Then, with a firm hand, he took a charged pipe from his rack.

"There's only one thing to do," he said, in his most reasonable voice—and oh, how, after days of bedlam, I blessed its tranquil logic. "The question is, will ye do it?"

"I'll do it," I cried fervently. "I will, I will, I will."

He lit his pipe and took a few calm puffs.

"Who is the strongest . . . sturdiest . . . stubbornest boy in your class?"

I need reflect only an instant: there was but one answer to that question. Unhesitatingly I declared: "Gavin Blair."

"The Provost's son?"

I nodded.

"Then——" He took his pipe from his lips. "You must fight Gavin Blair."

I stared at him, appalled. Gavin was not really one of my tormentors. He had kept himself contemptuously aloof from the whole miserable disturbance. Indeed, at the Academy, he had only spoken to me twice. He was a superior boy: bright yet self-contained, the top boy of the class, a favourite even with Dalgleish. In all the games he was the best; it was acknowledged that he could beat Bertie Jamieson with one hand behind his back. I tried to explain this to Grandpa.

"Are you feared?" he asked.

I hung my head, thinking of Gavin's wiry figure, small yet

determined chin, his clear grey eye. Unlike the heroic boys of the fiction which had come my way, I was painfully afraid.

"I don't know how to fight."

"I'll learn you. I'll take a week and learn you. It's not size that counts but spirit." He shrugged his shoulders. "We'll write a letter to Dalgleish if you like, asking him to speak to the boys. But they'll scorn ye all the more for it. It's a matter of principle, to go in and whip the best of them. Will ye do it?"

I shivered; yet, strangely, in my extremity I found a certain resolution: perhaps the sort which makes suicides jump off high buildings. I gulped an incoherent: "Yes."

My training began that same evening after I had dried the dishes for Mama. It was agreed that Grandma should be kept in complete ignorance of our design. Grandpa placed me in a series of stiff and uncomfortable attitudes with my knuckles advanced and my chin so drawn in I could see nothing but my own boots. Facing me in a corresponding pose, he then commanded me to "let go with my left," which I did with such precipitancy I caught him full in the midriff, doubling him up, gasping, in his chair.

"Oh, Grandpa," I cried, shocked. "I did not mean to hurt you."

He was very cross. I had not in the least hurt him, it was merely that I had taken a most ungentlemanly advantage in striking him in a region known as "below the belt." When he had got his wind back he lectured me severely on foul blows, then sent me out to run to the road end and back to improve my legs.

In the days which followed he strove hard to advance me in the noble art of self-defence. He told me bloody and inspiring stories of Jem Mace, Gentleman Jim, and Billy the Butcher, who had fought eighty-two rounds with a broken jaw and one ear hanging off. He bade me drink no water, or as little as I could, to toughen my skin. He even sacrificed his dinnertime cheese, the one food he cared about, making me eat it slowly as I stood before him while a bead of saliva ran down his whiskers.

"There's nothing like Dunlop cheese, boy, to put real pith in you." I did not doubt him, but I suffered dreadfully from heartburn.

On Saturday afternoon he took me along with him to the cemetery and demonstrated me to his friends. As I struck my pugilistic postures before them he explained, darkly, the reason for the coming conflict. I heard the Saddler laugh offensively.

"What about your grand ideas now, Gow? You're aye talking about live and let live, and yet you start a fight."

"Saddler," Grandpa answered stiffly, "sometimes it is necessary to fight so that we *can* live."

This silenced Mr. Boag but I could see he held a poor view of my prospects of success.

The fateful day dawned. Grandpa called me to his room as I crossed the landing and solemnly shook me by the hand.

"Remember," he said, looking me in the eyes: "Anything . . . but don't be feared."

I felt like bursting into tears—despite Grandpa's cheese the soft and tender years at my poor mother's apron strings were not entirely undone. What made it worse was that, although my persecution had not abated, Gavin had lately shown signs of taking my part: he had cuffed Bertie Jamieson for shouldering too roughly in a game of Hopping Charlie, and once, in class, seeing me in need of a rubber, had silently pushed his own across to me. But I had given my word to Grandpa, and nothing, nothing must hold me back. The hour selected for me by my mentor was four o'clock, immediately following the dismissal of school. All day long, in a continuous tremor, I sat watching Gavin's calm, intent, intelligent face across the classroom. He was handsome, with deep-set dark-lashed eyes, a short proud upperlip: it was a Highland face, for his father was from Perth and his dead mother had been a Campbell from Inveraray. To-day, perhaps because he was going out with his grown-up sister that evening, he wore his kilt, the dark Blair tartan, austere leather sporran, black brogues. Once or twice his eyes touched mine, which must have seemed strangely pleading. My heart lay heavy in my side. I felt almost that I loved him. Yet I must fight him.

Four strokes from the old clock in the tall grey tower of the Academy . . . My last hope that Mr. Dalgleish would keep me in had vanished. I was dismissed with the others, I was even crossing the playground, Gavin striding ahead of me, his satchel slung carelessly across his back. The need for urgency—if I were not to return to Grandpa a pitiful failure—goaded me beyond my senses. Suddenly, I ran forward and pushed Gavin hard. He spun round to find me confronting him with my fists arranged one on top of the other, rather as though I were holding a candle in a procession.

"Knock down the blocks." I croaked out the phrase, which, in case it is not fully recognized, is the traditional invitation to combat in Levenford. Immediately a shout, between wonder and expectation, went up from the other boys. "A fight! Gavin and Shannon. A fight! A fight!"

Gavin flushed—his fair skin coloured easily—and he glanced in annoyance at the ring of boys who already swarmed round us. He must accept the challenge, feeble though it was. With the palm of his hand he slapped my fists apart. Immediately I set them up again, holding them sideways from my body.

"Spit over the blocks."

Gavin spat expertly over the blocks.

I proceeded with the ritual. With boots that seemed dissevered from my fluid legs I traced a wavering line on the gravel surface of the playground.

"I dare ye to step over it."

Gavin, I perceived with dread, was growing angry. He promptly stepped over it.

I trembled in all my bones. Only the final act remained. Dead silence from the surrounding boys. With dry lips I whispered: "Give the coward's blow."

He rapped me, without hesitation, on the chest. How hollow my breastbone sounded—as though made of cardboard! How pale I felt myself to be! But there was no retreat. I clenched my chattering teeth and rushed at the beloved Gavin.

I forgot everything Grandpa had taught me, everything. My thin arms flailed the air in wild circular sweeps. I hit Gavin often, but always in the hardest and most resistant areas, like his elbows, his cheekbones, and especially the square metal buttons of his kilt. The unfairness of these dreadful buttons moved me to a surging bitterness. Always when I struck him I seemed to hurt him much less than I hurt myself. While his blows, on the contrary, sank painfully into my softest places.

He knocked me down twice, to the accompaniment of cheers. I had never before recognized in myself the capacity for rage. These base cheers helped me to discover it. Yes, surely the basest of all human beings were those who, while standing by, drew enjoyment from the strife and anguish of their fellow creatures. Fury against my real enemies welled out from my very marrow; their blurred yet grinning faces incited me to show them what I was made of. Rising from the gravel I rushed again at Gavin.

He went down before me. Deathly stillness. Then, as Gavin got up, the voice of little Howie, the squirrel: "You only slipped, Gavin. Give it to him! Give it to him!"

Gavin was more cautious now. He circled a good deal and did not appear to enjoy my rushes. We were both the worse for wear, and breathing like steam engines. I was flushed and warm, the clammy coldness had left my skin. I observed with strange wonder that one of his eyes was of a purplish hue and closing fast. Had I really inflicted such a mischief, on such a hero? Then, through the haze, the tumult, the confusion, a voice fell deliriously on my ear. One of the "big" boys, from the upper forms ... A group had stopped on their way to the gymnasium.

"By God! Green Breeks is making a fight of it!"

Joy and ecstasy! I was not disgracing my grandpa. I was not such a coward as I had feared. I rushed again at my dear Gavin, as though ready to embrace him. Suddenly, but without intention, as we wrestled about, he raised his head.

I received the stunning impact of his skull upon my nose.

It began to bleed. I could taste the warm saltiness in my mouth, feel the river running down my nostrils, splashing all over my front. Heavens! I never knew there was so much blood in my puny body. I was not in the least inconvenienced. My brain, indeed, was more and more clear, though my legs, once again, had ceased to belong to me. Dizzily, I landed my knuckles once again on Gavin's buttons. Dazzling lights, shouts, rockets in the sky ... Halley's Comet, perhaps! I was still swinging my arms when I discovered that someone was holding me back. Another of the big boys had Gavin by the collar in like fashion.

"That's all, youngsters, for the time being. Shake hands. It was a dam' good scrap. Now run in for the hall-door key, somebody. This little brat is bleeding like a pig."

I lay flat on my back on the playground with the huge cold key pressed in at the back of my neck while Gavin knelt beside me with a smeared, concerned face. My clothes were sopping, the big boys were worried that the bleeding did not stop. At last, by plugging my nostrils with shreds of a torn-up handkerchief soaked in salt and water, they were successful.

"Lie still for twenty minutes, young 'un, and you'll be right as the mail."

They went away. All my classmates had gradully drifted off, all except Gavin. We were alone in the strangely empty playground, a battleground, stained, scarred and kicked up by our feet. Dreamily, I tried to smile up at him, but my plugged nose and the stiff film on my face prevented me.

"Don't move," he said, softly. "I didn't mean to hit you with my head. It was a foul."

I shook my head in disagreement, almost starting the bleeding again. Somehow, I managed to smile. "I'm sorry your eye got closed." He explored the shut optic tenderly, then smiled, his warm beautiful smile, which radiated through me like sunshine.

Carefully, when the little tails of handkerchief hanging from my nose ceased to drip, he pulled them out. Then he helped me to my feet. Together in silence we began our pilgrimage to Drumbuck Road.

Halley's Comet still flashed about the sky. Opposite his house he paused. "You can't go home like that. Come in and have a wash."

I accompanied him diffidently between the twin entrance lamp-posts, insignia of the Provost's residence, each with the town coat of arms painted on the glass, then up the carefully raked drive, with shrubs on either side. The garden was large and splendidly maintained: a handyman was working beside a wheelbarrow in the distance. At the back of the villa we approached a large coach-house with an outside water tap. As we started to get the worst off, a maid in a neat black-and-white uniform viewed us nervously from the window and, presently, a lady in a brown dress came hurrying out.

"My dear boys. Have you had an accident?" She was Julia Blair, Gavin's grown-up sister, who had kept house for his father since his mother died. After her first inquiring glance she stopped asking questions. She took me up to Gavin's room—a beautiful room of his own full of photographs, rods and fishing tackle, and fretwork pieces he had made himself. There she made me strip off my clammy garments and, while the maid took these away, not without disgust, to wrap them in a brown paper parcel, she made me put on a good grey tweed suit of Gavin's.

"I knew your mother very well, Robert," she said in her kind, matronly voice. "Why don't you come round to see Gavin when . . ." She glanced round, but he had been detained in the kitchen to have treatment for his eye. "When you're both better." Downstairs, as she handed me my parcel at the front door, a flush came over her mature, earnest face. "We certainly don't want Gavin's suit back, Robert. He has quite grown out of it." She stood alone on the steps for a considerable time watching me vanish into the dusk.

I came up the road slowly towards Lomond View. Now I felt my full weariness. I ached all over, my head was whirling, I could scarcely move my dragging limbs. And with this growing lassitude, my spirits also drooped. Gavin's grand house had depressed me. That peculiar despondency which, in my later life, was to follow swiftly, and thus spoil, even my most apparent successes now began to gnaw at me. From the standards of perfection I viewed my recent performance with increasing dissatisfaction. After all—if the big boys had not stopped the fight . . .

I reached the gate and there, alone, waiting for me, was Grandpa.

A long pause. His look encompassed my pale strained features. His voice was gentle.

"Did ye win?"

"No, Grandpa." I faltered. "I think I lost."

Without a word he took me to his room, and seated me in his own armchair. I broke out:

"I wasn't feared ... not after we had started ..."

He drew from me, haltingly, the story of the fight. I could not understand his excitement. When I had finished, he shook me, in a kind of exaltation, by the hand. Then he rose and, taking the brown paper parcel which contained the cause of my misery, cast it square upon the fire. My green suit took an awful time to burn and made a bad smoke in the room. But at last it was gone.

"You see now," said Grandpa.

Chapter Seven

In the wintry weeks which followed, with hard frost and long dark evenings, the feud between my two great-grandparents, which had its origin in different viewpoints and unequal privileges, continued to manifest itself in a silent struggle for possession of me.

Grandma was very cross indeed about the change of suits; she gave me a good slap and, at night, as we lay in bed together, lectured me soundly on the baseness of ingratitude, telling me I must do much better if I wished to remain "her boy." Her fears for my health, always grave, seemed to deepen, and I could not sneeze without her endowing me with an inflammation of the lungs against which she dosed me freely with a dark horehound-and-senna physic of her own compounding. In spite of this I was happier than I had been before.

At the Academy, my fight had helped me greatly; perhaps less my fight than my Homeric loss of blood. This threatened to become historic, for already boys spoke of events in relation to it: as before, or after, "the day Shannon had his nosebleed." At all events, decently clad in grey, for which I blessed Miss Julia Blair, I was no longer derided. Indeed, Bertie Jamieson and his allies went out of their way to offer me signs of their regard. It was recognized that Gavin was my friend.

Gavin, as I have implied, stood apart from the other boys, not in a snobbish sense because he was better off than they—his father had an old-established corn-chandler's business—but in his character and disposition—really, in his interior life. He played all the ordinary games skilfully, yet sparingly, for he had other tastes and recreations far beyond the common lot. In the bookcase of his cozy room were volumes of natural history crammed with glossy coloured pictures of birds, insects and wild flowers, the names printed underneath. He had a superb collection of birds' eggs. On one wall was a framed photograph of himself, in knickerbockers, holding a great fish—his father, a noted angler, frequently took him to Loch Lomond, and the previous autumn, Gavin, not yet nine, had brought to the gaff a twelve-pound grilse.

Yet these magnificent accomplishments were as nothing beside that inner fibre, that spiritual substance for which no words suitable can be found. He was a silent boy, silent and Spartan. The firm line of his mouth, the small resolute chin, seemed to say to life, quietly: "I will never give in."

On the Friday following our encounter he had waited for me after class and, without words, with only a shy smile, fell into step beside me, along the High Street. After weeks of fleeing down the back ways, how I thrilled to this distinction! We stopped for half an hour at his father's warehouse, where, in the stables at the back, we watched Tom Drin, the head vanman, dose a sick horse, recovering from the hives. Provost Blair beckoned us, on our way out through the big storerooms full of forage and cornbins, piled sacks of meal, beans, and oats, with white-aproned handymen bustling about.

"You two came together the right way." He gave us his dark smile, an Olympian, godlike smile—and a double handful of the sweet carob pods which we called "locusts."

As we ate our "locusts" together, on our way home in the dusk I tried to tell Gavin how wonderful, how lucky, it was to have a father like his, which made him flush with pride—the best thing I could have said. Then, as we stood at the gate of Lomond View, he gazed towards his boots, gently kicking the pavement edge.

"When it's spring I'm going nesting ... in the Winton Hills ... for a golden plover's egg, if you'd like to come ..."

Oh, the joy of being chosen, the picked companion of Gavin for these promised rambles amongst the Winton Hills! And a golden plover's egg! That night I could scarcely sleep for thinking of it. A prospect of tremulous wonder was opening out before me. ...

But wait.... Before I pass to these delights I must record, dutifully, a visit which introduced me to the last member of the Leckie family.

At the beginning of January, Mama, on her evening pilgrimage to the letterbox, gave a cry of joy, as if she had received a message from the archangels.

"From Adam." She bore the letter into the kitchen, where we sat at high tea. "He's coming Saturday at one o'clock. A flying visit. On business."

Reluctantly, she surrendered the letter as Papa jealously reached out. It went round the house. Only Grandpa, who seemed to set little store by the news, and Kate, whose forehead was again sulkily gathering, remained unmoved.

I found myself growing excited as Mama related what a boy Adam had been for winning marbles; how his "head was screwed on the right way," how he bought and sold a bicycle at a profit of ten shillings before he was thirteen; how a year later he went into Mr. McKellar's office with no advantages whatsoever; how, after hours, he did evening collecting work for the Rock Assurance Company, how he saved all his money; how, not yet twenty-seven, he was himself established in the insurance business, representing both the Caledonia Company and the Rock, with an office in the Fidelity Building in Winton, and earning at least four hundred pounds a year, even more—Mama held her breath—than Papa, himself.

Mama also showed me, proudly, his gift: her very yellow gold brooch which—Adam himself had told her—was worth a great deal of money.

At a few minutes before one o'clock on Saturday a motor car drove up to the door. Let me create no false impressions, no false hopes—it was not Adam's. *Still—a motor car!* An early Argyll model, bright red in colour, having a small brass-bound radiator stamped with the Argyll blue lion, a high wide body with handsome side seats and a door at the back...

Adam entered, confident and smiling, wearing a coat with a brown fur collar. He embraced the waiting Mama, who had been up since dawn preparing for him, shook hands vigorously with

Papa, suitably acknowledged the rest of us. He was dark-haired, of medium height, and already beginning to be burly, with a fine blood in his clean-shaven cheeks from his wintry drive. As he sat down to the steak, cauliflower, and potatoes which Mama, with fervent prodigality, whipped out of the oven and put before him, he explained that Mr. Kay, a partner in the new Argyll works, had given him a lift from Winton on his way to Alexandria. They had done the fifty miles in under two hours.

While we all sat round and watched his solo banquet—we had eaten our dinner of shepherd's pie an hour ago—he told us that he had already spent half an hour in the town, and transacted some insurance business with Mr. McKellar. His eye, small like Papa's, but of a clear brown colour, caught mine, almost jocularly. I blushed with pleasure.

Mama, having stolen out to the hall to examine her son's beautiful new fur-collared coat, was back, serving him adoringly.

"One thing we must discuss." Adam interrupted his talk to smile up at her. "The old man's policy."

"Yes, Adam." Papa, who was taking time off from his work, drew his chair into the table close to Adam's. His voice was confidential, respectful.

"It's about due now." Adam spoke thoughtfully. "February seventeenth ... Four hundred and fifty pounds net, payable, as agreed, to Mama."

"A nice sum," Papa breathed.

"Very tidy." Adam concurred. "But we could do even better."

Smiling a little at Papa's earnest perplexity, he went on to explain. "If we continued the existing policy—which I could easily arrange—the amount, payable at the age of seventy-five or death if earlier, would run, with profits, to something like six hundred."

"Six hundred!" Papa echoed. "But that means we wouldn't touch the cash now."

Adam shrugged. "It's there. The Rock Assurance is safe as the Bank. It's a gilt-edged opportunity. What do you say, Mama?"

Mama was looking very unhappy, her hands fluttering about.

"I've said before ... I don't like making money out of my father ... not that way..."

"Oh, come now, Mama." Adam's smile was indulgent. "We straightened that out long ago. He owes you it for board and lodging. Besides, look at the history of the policy. When Grandpa started it years ago, it was only a miserable five-shillings-a-month collection affair with the old Castle Company. And you know it had lapsed and was lying buried with the Castle Company when I went in with the Rock. It would still be there if I hadn't dug it up, and persuaded McKellar, as a personal favour, to make it the basis of a new endowment on Grandpa's life."

Mama sighed but did not speak.

"Would you want your commission on the extension?" Papa asked guardedly.

"Well, naturally." Adam laughed, not in the least offended. "Business is business all the world over."

There was a reflective pause; then Papa spoke with cautious decision. "Yes ... Yes, Adam. I think we should extend."

Adam nodded approval. "You're wise." He opened the bag at his feet and brought out a folded document. "Here's the policy all drawn. I'll leave it with you, Mama. Get Grandpa to sign before the seventeenth."

"Yes, Adam." There was still a shade of reproach in Mama's voice.

Although it conveyed to me a deep impression of Adam's business acumen, I had not in the least understood this conversation. Afterwards when Papa had returned to the office, Adam found time to have a word with me, alone, before leaving for the two-thirty express.

"I hope you'll see me to the station, Robert." He stood up, using a quill toothpick, his small eyes genial with friendship. "I'd like to make you a little present. Commemorate our first meeting. See this." From the coin case at the end of his watch chain he pressed out a half-sovereign and held it up between his finger and thumb. "Money ... fresh from the Mint ... a fairly useful commodity in spite of the disparaging remarks of those who haven't got it. Not a bad idea to get a notion of the value of money while you're young, Robert. Don't mistake me. I'm not one of your stingy ones. I like to get the good of my money ... eat the best, wear the best, stop at the best hotels, have everybody running after me. That's my side of the picture. For the other ... Well, look at Grandpa ... not a farthing to bless himself with, bread and cheese in the attic, dependent even for his half-ounce of shag ..." He broke off, glancing at his watch, smiling so infectiously I could not help smiling in return.

Waiting for him in the lobby, I found myself in warm agreement with his views on the gravities of life and the importance of money. I longed for that moment when, with jingling pockets, I, too, should walk into a restaurant and, in lordly style, order myself beefsteak, while the waiters scurried at my behest. I trembled, in joyful anticipation of the present he would buy me with that lovely half-sovereign.

"You won't mind carrying my bag?" Adam lightly asked me, as Mama helped him into his coat.

I fervently expressed my desire to serve him and picked up the Gladstone bag, which, showing lumps that could be neither books nor papers, was more burdensome than I had expected. Mama kissed Adam again. We departed for the station, Adam walking with a springy step, while I, half running, continually changing the bag from hand to hand, managed to keep pace with him.

"Now what sort of present would you like?"

"Anything, Adam," I gasped, politely.

"No, no." Adam insisted. "It's to be something you'd like, young fellow my lad."

What generosity! What understanding! Thus encouraged, I dared to express my preference. The Common pond was safely "bearing," covered with four inches of good ice and, on my way to and from the Academy, I had paused to watch the skaters with the regard of one who could not attain such happiness.

"I would be very glad of a pair of skates, Adam. They have them in Langland's window in the High Street."

"Ah! Skates! Well, I don't know. You can't skate in the summer, can you?"

Disappointed, I still had to admit the logic of his argument.

"A football might be better." He went on. "Only trouble is you've got to share it with the other boys. They boot the life out of it, burst it, lose it. The thing isn't really your own. How about a pocket knife?" Adam suggested next, acknowledging a greeting from across the street. "No, you might cut yourself. Dangerous. Think of something else."

The heavy bag was killing me, as I sweated after him, in lopsided fashion, one shoulder weighted to the ground.

"I ... I can't think, Adam."

"I tell you what!" he exclaimed, reflectively. "It would please Mama if I gave you something useful. In fact——" His tone quickened with enthusiasm. "Now I think of it, I have the very thing!"

"Oh, thank you, Adam." I hoped that with this burden I should reach the station alive.

He looked at his watch. "Just two minutes off the half hour. Quick, youngster. And don't bump the bag."

He pressed ahead while I toiled up the station steps behind him. The train was already at the platform. Adam leaped into a first-class smoking compartment, took the bag, which I surrendered with a sob of relief, and burrowed in its depths. Then he leaned from the window and placed in my small damp palms a solid brass calendar, rough-hewn like a nugget, shiny as Mama's brooch, with knobs for turning the days of the week and handsomely engraved:

ROCK ASSURANCE COMPANY

Semper Fidelis

"There," said Adam, as though handing me the crown jewels. "Isn't that handsome?"

"Oh, yes, thank you, Adam!" I answered in a startled voice.

The guard blew his whistle; he was off.

I came away from the station grateful to Adam, yet vaguely disconsolate, a trifle bewildered by this new possession, and the rapid strangeness of the day. When I got home I went upstairs and displayed my trophy to Grandpa, who viewed it in silence, with oddly elevated brows.

"It's not gold, is it, Grandpa?"

"No," he said. "If it's connected with Adam you may be sure it's brass."

A short pause, while I re-read the inscription. "Grandpa, has it anything to do with your policy?"

He turned dark red, his expression wounded, outraged, suffused with anger. In a loud voice he answered:

"Never mention that swindle to me again or I'll wring your neck."

There was a silence. Grandpa rose and began to pace up and down, much upset. Majestic with indignation he declared:

"The worst crime in the calendar ... the unforgivable iniquity ... IS MEANNESS!"

With an expression at first bitter, then ironic, then soothed, he repeated this maxim several times. At last, as though regretting his outburst, he turned and studied my cowed form. "Do you want to go skating?"

My heart sank deeper. "I have no skates, Grandpa."

"Tut! Tut! Don't be so easy beat. We'll see what we can do."

Choosing a moment when the coast was clear, he went down to the cellar, behind the scullery, and brought up a wooden box filled with old nails, bolts, doorknobs and rusty skates which—since nothing, I repeat, nothing, was ever thrown out at Lomond View—had accumulated during many years. Seated in his chair, pipe in mouth, while I sat on the floor in my stocking feet, he fiddled about with a key, trying to adjust the smallest pair of Acme skates to fit my boots. My disappointment was great when I saw he could not succeed. But, when everything seemed lost, he found at the bottom of the box a pair of wooden skates which had been Kate's when she was a child. What joy! Screwed into my boot-heels they fitted exactly. We had no straps, it is true, but Grandpa had plenty of strong string which would serve equally. He unscrewed the skates, I put on my boots, and we set out, with animation, for the pond.

What a pleasant and exciting scene: a sheet of ice perhaps half a mile long and a quarter broad, covered with darting, swooping and wobbling figures, moving gaily, tracing intricate patterns, colliding, falling, rising again, all under a clear blue sky to which ascended the high incessant ring of the ice and the shouts of the skaters.

Grandpa fastened on my skates and began to teach me, patiently, with many scientific explanations, how to keep my balance. He lumbered along beside me, guiding and supporting me until I was able to strike out for myself. Then he retired, joined Mr. Boag and Peter Dickie on the bank, lit his pipe and watched me.

Enchanted by this new form of motion, I floundered over the ice. In a quiet corner of the pond some good skaters had put down an orange, which made a brilliant speck of colour on the grey surface, and were doing figures round it. Miss Julia Blair was amongst them and, to my surprise, Alison Keith and her mother, both of whom skated very neatly indeed. Presently Alison came over and, crossing her arms, took both my hands. By imitation, picking up the rhythm of her strokes as she steered me round the pond, I began to make real progress. At my gratitude she smiled, shook her head slightly, and darted back to her mother and the orange. During our circuit she had not said a word.

Later Grandpa summoned me to the bank, with his enigmatic smile.

"Enjoying yourself?"

"Oh, Grandpa, wonderful, simply wonderful."

Later that evening: an opinion drowsily revised . . . I don't think I want those scurrying waiters after all. What fun it was with these old skates and Grandpa's pieces of string! It was just a pity I did not see Gavin on the pond. Yes, Grandma, I will be a good boy to-morrow. I'm sorry I was ungrateful, I promise faithfully to count my blessings in the future. But now . . . now, I am asleep.

Chapter Eight

Spring came quickly that year and the three chestnut trees in front of the house nodded their white plumes before a boy dazzled by freedom, intoxicated with strange and undreamed-of joys.

On the fifteenth of April Grandma left, according to her custom, to spend a few months with her Ayrshire relatives—as I have indicated, she divided the year pretty equally: autumn and winter in Levenford, spring and summer, "the growing months," at Kilmarnock.

We had progressed, she and I, in our grave private devotions. No one, I must here insist, could have been more restrained than Grandma in her handling of my delicate situation. A fervent member of the small but intense sect into which her husband had led her, her convictions were absolute, yet not once did she attempt to impose these upon me. Her attitude never transgressed the correct limits of patient hopefulness. Her strongest action came after dinner on Sundays, when she drew me to her room, and kept me at her knee reading aloud selections from the Scriptures. Approving my account of the war between Saul and David, she rocked gently in her chair by the window, on which the flies buzzed drowsily, viewing the regular Sunday promenade to the Drumbuck cemetery on the road outside and sucking, not the flat soft oddfellow recklessly preferred by Grandpa, but a hard round imperial which rattled lastingly against her teeth. (It seemed to me that the opposite characteristics of their favourite sweets exactly symbolized the difference between my two great-grandparents.) From time to time she interrupted my reading to give me little homilies on good living and the dangers of constipation, and to exhort me, above all, to stand firm against Satan.

Satan, the Evil One, Lucifer, or, as she also named him, the Beast, was for Grandma a Personal Enemy, perpetually gnashing his teeth at the elbows of the Just; and indeed, as her stern theology imperceptibly reinforced my earlier instruction, the Devil began to assume for me a terrifying reality.

On those winter evenings when Grandma was out upon some Gospel activity it was my duty to take up to our bed a stone hot-water jar, which she named her "jorrie," and if she had not returned by eight o'clock, to undress and retire in solitude. There was never much light upon the upper landing and frequently Grandpa was out also, though not of course at church. As I lay in the dark whispering bedroom, menaced on all sides by the shadowy walls and creaking wainscoting, I knew, with every shrinking nerve, that I was not alone. The Evil One was there, hiding in Grandma's "press," ready to pounce upon me the instant I relaxed.

Long moments of stiff and scarcely breathing anguish passed until at last I could bear it no longer. With that thin courage which streaked my natural timidity I jumped up and faced the awful cupboard. There, with shaking knees, a white small figure barely illuminated by the feeble glimmer which ascended from the street lamp outside, I raised my trembling voice in exorcism.

"Come out, Satan. I have the number of the Beast."

Then, blessing myself three times for good measure, I threw open the door. For a second my heart stood still. . . . But no, there was nothing there, nothing but the dim outlines of Grandma's dresses. With a sob of relief I would turn and fling myself beneath the sheets.

Grandma never knew of these nocturnal conflicts, yet I think she was satisfied with her tactful shaping of my tender and unconscious spirit. As she departed for Kilmarnock, in a new bonnet, she pressed a sixpence into my hand and, having exacted from me a promise to take my physic, after many admonitions and exhortations towards "perseverance" she murmured: "When I come back, my lamb, we'll see what's to be done for you."

My heart had come to brim, like a fountain, for my grandma. Yet, strangely, her absence gave me a queer feeling of relief which was intensified when Mama transferred me to a makeshift cot behind a curtain in the kitchen alcove. Oh, the sweet privacy of this little screened recess: almost a room of my own!

Grandpa seemed liberated too. His first act was to take the big bottle of medicine Grandma had left me and decant it, with an impenetrable smile, out of his window. Almost at once the ferns in the plot beneath yellowed and died, causing Murdoch to gloom and mutter, quite mistakenly, against Grandpa's intimate habits.

But never mind, never mind; the household at Lomond View was finding a momentary tranquillity in the miracle of the grey earth's rebirth. Soothed by the peace on the upper landing, Grandpa went placidly every day to the green to beat Saddler Boag at the marleys. Papa put a smart white cover on his uniform cap and actually took me on a Sunday afternoon to the Waterworks, to admire, over the red spiked railings, the big reservoir and the trim official dwelling which he hoped to inhabit when Mr. Cleghorn, the Superintendent, retired. Mama, less worried, ceased those interminable little calculations dealing, in pence and farthings, with her problem of making ends meet. In the morning, while he whittled his downy chin, Murdoch could be heard intoning sonorously: "I love a lassie, a bonnie Highland lassie." Only Kate seemed disturbed, angered even by the swiftly flowing sap, the swooping of the robins bearing straws to the eaves, the distant enchanting whinny of a stallion at Snoddie's Farm.

Before I reveal my own happiness I must probe, with careful tenderness, into this enigma which is Kate.

With the window open and the fragrance of the lilac bush in the back garden drifting in to us, we are seated at the dessert of our midday dinner in perfect amity. Mama, who hates to see anything left, picks up with the serving spoon the last three stewed prunes remaining forlornly in the dish. "Who will have these?" she inquires. "Very good for the blood in the springtime." She makes a tentative offer to the brooding Kate, then, receiving no response, drops them into Murdoch's plate. Immediately, Kate jumps to her feet, the bumps on her brow, like patches of headache, turning fiery red. She cries hysterically: "I am *nothing* in this house. And I am earning too ... bringing in good money ... teaching these smelly little beasts of infants all day long. I will never, never speak to any of you again." She rushes from the room, followed in consternation by Mama, who returns, a minute later, repulsed, shaking her head, and sighing: "Kate is a strange girl."

Murdoch wishes magnanimously to surrender the prunes; but Mama prepares her universal panacea, a cup of tea, which she bids me take up to Kate in her room. I am chosen because I, surely, cannot have offended her. I find Kate in tears upon her bed, her mood soft and self-commiserating.

"They all hate me, every one of them." She sits up unexpectedly on the bed and turns towards me a tear-ravaged face. "Tell me, dear, do you think I'm terribly plain?"

"No, Kate, no ... far from it." I am startled into the lie.

"Your mother was much prettier than me. Simply lovely." She shakes her head dolefully. "And I have such a horrible name. Think of it ... Kate. Who would take *Kate* on a Moonlight Cruise ... or out to the Minstrels at the Point? If you ever do find me in the company of a strange young man, call me Irene. Promise now."

I promise, dutiful but amazed. Kate, in other ways, is so eminently sensible, a conscientious teacher with a creditable record at the Normal Training College, a good hockey player, a beautiful knitter, a member of the Women's Institute. She exhibits to perfection that wonderful Scots quality—"dourness." In her struggle to keep "nits" from the heads of her poor pupils she, who is violently clean, often picks up vermin on her own person and must stand and shake her clothing in the bath whenever she comes in, pale with disgust, yet grimly uncomplaining. Outsiders remark approvingly of Kate: "Such a *worthy* girl." It is to Kate that I owe my sound teeth, for she took me, without a word, to Mr. Strang the Levenford dentist, when they started to decay the month before. She it is who gives me, from her small library, solid books like *Ivanhoe* and *Hereward the Wake.* Yet I know there exists in the same case, for I have perused them breathlessly, volumes wherein the dark handsome hero kneels, in the last chapter, murmuring brokenly before the sweet, womanly figure in white satin he has hitherto ignored. ...

"Oh, well, Robie," Kate concludes our present interview with a sigh, "I suppose we may as well rot here as anywhere."

When I descend I tell Mama that she is much better. But she is not. She confines her family conversation for a fortnight to scribbled messages on torn-off scraps of paper. She quarrels tempestuously with her best friend, Bessie Ewing, so that Bessie, faithful bespectacled Bessie, comes in late in the evening for long perturbed confidences with Mama in the privacy of the scullery. Bessie, who has supported Kate's temperament since they were schoolgirls together, is the intelligent daughter of a refined Knoxhill family. She works in the local telephone exchange all week and every Saturday night dons the blue-and-scarlet uniform of the Salvation Army. Short and anaemic, but with nice fluffy hair, she has an angelic disposition and a way of looking at Murdoch when they meet in the kitchen.

Now I hear her say, earnestly, to Mama: "Really, Mrs. Leckie, I'm worried. It's lack of interest. Now if only we could get her to take up, say, the mandolin ... or even the banjo ..."

Little talebearer that I am, I run to Grandpa with the news: "Grandpa! Grandpa! I think Kate is going to learn the banjo."

He gazes at me, a faint ironic twist to his golden moustache. "I fear that instrument will do her little good, my boy."

I gaze at him blankly; perhaps he means that Kate must learn the piano in the parlour: McKillop Brothers Upright Iron-framed Grand. But no matter, I toss my head, and dart away, merely for the sake of running. I run errands for everyone: for Mrs. Bosomley, who on my return rewards me with her ripe smile and Bovril-spread toast, a sandwich which makes water run from the very substance of my teeth. Forgetful of my precarious position, a little outcast, barely acknowledged, poised on the edge of the unknown, I am happy ... happy that I love, and am loved by, Gavin.

We had begun, Gavin and I, to comb the uplands together: brave expeditions which made my previous voyagings with Grandpa seem babyish indeed. Gavin sought, ceaselessly, and passionately, the sole specimen lacking to his collection, this egg of the golden plover, rarest of all the Winton birds. Yet, as we traversed the lower woods, bent on this quest, he had the patience to instruct me: finding for me in unseen and impossible places all the commoner nests, parting the branches of a hawthorn bush and calmly murmuring: "Missel thrush with five," while with bright eyes I peered at the neat cup of straw and mud, wherein lay, warmly fragile, the speckled blue eggs. He initiated me in the delicate art of "blowing." He swore me to the oath of the woodsman: never to take more than one egg from a nest, his small face turning white with anger as he spoke of boys who "harried" the nest of all its eggs, causing the mother bird to "desert."

Then we climbed Drumbuck Hill. It was a new country we gained, with a breeze that came cool and sweet as spring water on my cheek. Distantly, beneath us, lay a free and sweeping panorama of the world laced with white roads and split by the estuary of the Clyde, a wide bar of shimmering silver, with tiny ships upon it. The town of Levenford was lost in a merciful haze, out of which reached the rounded hump back of the Castle Rock. The toy houses of Drumbuck village crouched far, far down, at our feet. Swathes of green rolled away to the west, and as my gaze followed this meadowland I started, almost in fear, to see a great high shape towering sharp and blue above the flying white clouds.

"Look, Gavin, look!" I cried shrilly, keeping close to him and pointing to the mountain.

He nodded solemnly. "It's the Ben!"

I could have gazed for ever, but again he drew me on, past a whitewashed farmhouse in the fold of the moor with its byre and steadings grouped in a square around it. There was a smell of cows and straw in the yard; a bush of broom, already flaming yellow, shaded the back porch. The curlews were wheeling overhead and the bees droned amongst the blazing gorse as we crossed the farm lands where the cows lay in the shade, all facing in the same direction, barely troubling to chew their cud, only their ears twitching the flies away as they stared at us sideways with their big liquid eyes.

At the end of the fields we began toiling upwards towards the higher peaks.

The moorland Gavin took me to was almost in the sky, a singing wilderness, swampy in parts and split by limestone peaks. As we advanced, bent forward, our eyes seeking amongst the purple orchis and the spongy bog myrtle of the heath, we seemed to be dodging the woolly clouds which scudded across the blue just above our heads. Now and then Gavin would stop to point out silently some rarity: the sundew plant which stickily entangled and consumed insects, the pure white bee-orchid, scented beyond belief. Once an adder streaked crossa our path and before I could cry out, Gavin crashed his boot heel upon its skull. We ate our picnic lunch on a flat rock, Windy Crag, attained by the dizziest of climbs.

For a month Gavin sought the egg with all his skill and resolution—but fruitlessly. One afternoon as we came back, discouraged, from the farthest horizon we had yet attained, I lagged behind at a rushy swamp. Strangely, my interest had turned to these upland marshes and the teeming life which abounded in their waters. I bent down to cup some tadpoles in my hands. Then, as in a dream, my eyes fell upon a careless litter of coarse straw, dropped upon some adjacent moss. Three eggs lay on the straw, large eggs, golden green with purplish splashes.

The cry which broke from me arrested Gavin's small dark figure against the skyline. He was tired. But my wildly waving arms brought him plodding back. Speechless now, I pointed to the moss. I could not see his face, but I sensed by his sudden immobility that we had found the nest at last.

"That's it." He waded in over his boot-tops and brought back one of the eggs. We sat down on the edge of the marsh while, gently, with the utmost care, having first floated it to see if it were addled, he blew the egg, and placed it in my hand. "There. It's a beauty, isn't it?"

"A perfect beauty." I gloated. "I'm so glad we got it at last." When I had admired my fill I held it out. "Here you are, Gavin."

"No." He gazed straight ahead at the remaining eggs which I knew he would rather die than touch. "It's yours, not mine."

"Don't, Gavin! It's yours."

"No, it's yours." He persisted stoically: "You found it and finding's keeping."

"I wouldn't have found it except for you," I pleaded. "It's yours, absolutely yours."

"Yours." He insisted palely.

"Yours," I cried.

"Yours," he mumbled.

"Yours," I almost wept.

We bandied the word desperately until at last, in a frenzy of surrender, I blurted out the naked truth. "Gavin! Will you believe me? It's a lovely egg. But I don't want it. I've hardly any collection and you have. The things I'm really smitten on are frogs and tadpoles and dragonflies and that! If you don't take the egg I swear I'll ... I'll ... I'll throw it away."

Convinced at last by this awful threat, he turned and faced me, delight flooding his grey eyes. His voice quivered. "I'll take it then, Robie. Not for nothing, that wouldn't be fair. I'll trade you something in exchange for it ... something I have that I know you like." He wrapped the precious egg in cotton wool in his collecting tin and smiled at me, that shy and somewhat sombre smile which came from beneath his half-lowered lashes and filled my heart with joy.

The same evening I carried away from his room a singular article which I had coveted ever since, under Gavin's direction, I had learned to manipulate it. It was an old brass compound microscope, once the possession of his sister Julia who as a girl had taken a course in natural sciences at Winton College. In type it was simple, but it had two eye pieces and two object glasses and the lens, though fixed, was actually a Smith and Beck—even in the little things Provost Blair must have the best. Accompanying the instrument were a few elementary slides and a mildewed book with yellowish pages, the first chapter headed: "What You May See in a Drop of Water"; the second, "Structure of a Fly's Wing."

I set the tube up on the table of Grandpa's room and, while he watched me covertly, began assiduously to examine the slides. Since my friendship with Gavin he had been slightly cold towards me. No one could "take the huff" more readily than Grandpa. I think in his heart he approved of my moorland roamings, but since he was not a party to them he affected an attitude of disdainful reproof. Now, however, his curiosity got the better of him.

"What newfangled nonsense have ye there, Robert?" The use of my formal given name indicated that he was not on the best of terms with me. I explained eagerly and soon he was at my elbow, one eye screwed into the mysterious tube, blundering with the adjustment, yet pretending to a consummate knowledge of the machine. I could see that it fascinated him and when I looked in after supper he was still glued to the tube, with a rapt expression on his face. "By all the powers!" he cried. "Do you see these beasties in the cheese?"

Thus began, for Grandpa and myself, an era of glorious adventure as we beat our wings into the unknown. Soon we exhausted the faded primer of Miss Julia Blair; then Grandpa, marching like a new Huxley to the public library, produced more solid works: Brooke's *Elementary Biology*, Steed's *Living Water Weeds*, and, noblest of all, Grant's *Pond Life with Thirty Coloured Plates*. During the daytime, while I was at school, he foraged amongst the neighbourhood's stagnant pools and at night, when I had finished my homework, we sat down to compare the creatures which strayed across our magic lens with the illustrations in our books. Consider our excitement when we identified a slow amoeba and were dazzled by the whirling of a rotifer. Remember, I was not yet nine, I had not fully mastered the multiplication table.

Oh, I am drunk with the wonder of new life. The nests are full of fledglings, craning their necks for food; a foal stands in the field beyond the chestnut trees; lambs bleat beside the ewes in the pastures of Snoddie's Farm. There is a word in my books I only vaguely understand: it is "reproduction"—certain of my little creatures multiply by simple division, others by a more complex process of joining together. Confusedly, I feel myself upon the threshold of a great discovery. Who will reveal to me this unknown secret? Perhaps, of all persons, Bertie Jamieson. Gavin, has gone to Luss for a week, calmly removed by his omnipotent father to profit by the run of spring salmon up the Loch. I walk home every night with Jamieson and his allies but at his house, near Drumbuck Toll, they leave me, with the remark that I am "too young" to accompany them, and disappear into the washhouse, where they lock the door and shutter the window. Standing outside, disconsolate, I hear sounds and sniggering, in what must be a tenebrous interior. When they emerge, sheepishly, Bertie tells me that, as a great favour, I may come in the following night.

I am overjoyed. I mention it to Grandpa as we sit together at our slides.

"What!" He jumps up, upsetting the precious microscope, banging the table with his fist.

"You will not go into that washhouse. Over my dead body. Never. Never."

The following evening as I emerge from the Academy he is waiting outside. He takes me by the hand and as Jamieson runs past catches the wretched boy a buffet which almost fells him to the ground. As he drags me off angrily I cannot but reflect how strange and incredible are the manifestations of spring.

Chapter Nine

And still the spring continues.

Giving off Drumbuck Road to a blind ending was a short unobtrusive street of smaller cottages which bore the disappointing name of "Banks Lane" and which impaired slightly the starched gentility of its parent thoroughfare inhabited by the notables and officials of the Borough, ranging from the Provost, through the Stationmaster and the Head of the Fire Department, to Health Administrator Leckie himself. In Banks Lane dwelt several men, fitters and engineers, who cast a mild blemish on the surroundings by "working dirty" in the Boilerworks. They were not seen, fortunately, at five o'clock in the morning, when the Works hooter sounded them from their beds; but at the dinner hour, and again in the evening, their hobnail boots resounded inappropriately on the clean pavements, their soiled dungarees and grimy hands and faces seemed sadly out of place beside, for instance, the white uniform cap and shining brass buttons of Mr. Leckie.

They were a quiet lot, for their work was hard, and they succeeded, perhaps because their wages were vexatiously large, in enjoying themselves in their own inoffensive ways. Every Saturday afternoon their bright checked caps could be seen joining the stream which flowed in keen anticipation to Boghead Park, home of the local football team. Spruced and in their best clothes, they frequently took train to the city of Winton for a meat pie tea and an evening at the Palace of Varieties. On fine Sunday evenings they would stroll sedately in little bands along the country roads while one of their number improvised with great skill on a concertina or mouth harmonica—often as I lay in bed, during my early days at Lomond

View, burdened with the darkness and my grandma's heavy breathing, a whiff of cigarette smoke, the waft of a gay and teasing tune, would lift me up and make me smile, unseen, reassured that all was still well with the world.

Amongst these Boilermakers, one named Jamie Nigg had begun to show me signs of his regard. He was a shortish man of about thirty, heavy about the shoulders, with big, dangling hands and large, melancholy eyes. With uncanny prescience I divined that he was sad because of his legs, which were exceedingly bandy; they formed a perfect oval through which clear daylight was visible, and although, in his method of walking, he did all he could to conceal it, the deformity was enough to damp the stoutest heart. As I ran back to school at the dinner hour this bow-legged boilermaker often stopped me, viewing me with his inquiring spaniel's eyes, slowly rubbing his jaw with his calloused palm; though he shaved every day the strength of his growth kept his chin and cheeks in saturnine blue shadow.

"How are ye?"

"I'm fine, thank you, Jamie."

"All well at home?"

"Yes, thank you, Jamie."

"Mr. Leckie and the family?"

"Yes. Jamie."

"Murdoch'll be sitting his examination, soon?"

"That's right, Jamie."

"Your grandma's still away?"

"Oh, yes, Jamie."

"I saw your old grandpa on the green last Sunday."

"Did you, Jamie?"

"He looks well."

"Yes, Jamie."

"It's a bonny day."

"It is that, Jamie."

The conversation broke down at this point. A pause; then, reaching into his pocket, Jamie produced a penny and, scarcely smiling, delivered it to me with one of Levenford's oldest and funniest jokes:

"Don't spend it all in the one shop." As I hopped, stepped and jumped away, clutching the coin, he called after me, standing bandy and motionless. "My best respects to all at home."

In a remote fashion, I attributed Jamie's good will to the fact that, like the Provost and Miss Julia Blair, and others in the town who had shown kindness to me, he had known my mother—this phrase, indeed, "I knew your mother," like a recurrent phrase in a piece of music, minor, yet strangely heart-warming, cropped up often during my childhood, and brought with it always a sense of reassurance, of confidence in the inherent goodness of people and of life.

But usually I was too busy darting towards the shop of Tibbie Minns, and her green glass bottles of pink-striped sweeties, to debate the causes of Jamie's interest. My experiences with Adam's half-sovereign had left me vaguely distrustful: if I did not spend my penny someone was sure to discover it, or it would fall out of my breeches as I took them off at night and roll out of the alcove, along the shiny linoleum, to Papa who would stoop and pick it up, with the righteous intention of "saving it" for me. Besides, my body, that of a young, poorly nourished animal, was crying out for sugar. Beasts of the field and forest will die amidst apparent plenty if they are deprived of certain simple and apparently unimportant substances. When I recollect the half-stilled gnawings, the after-dinner unrest of my childhood, I feel that I too might have perished but for the permeating peace afforded me by Miss Minn's sugar balls.

On the last Saturday in May, I encountered Jamie not by chance: he was actually awaiting me at the corner of Banks Lane, and "dressed," too, wearing his navy-blue suit, light brown boots, flat red-and-black-diced cap.

"Do ye want to come to the football match?"

My heart turned a quick somersault, at this sudden invasion of joy into an afternoon rendered empty and listless by the continued absence of Gavin, with his father, at Luss. The football match! The big grown-up game which I had never seen, and never hoped to see!

"Come on then," Jamie Nigg said, advancing the brown boots circuitously.

With my stomach pressed against the rope which surrounded the Bohgead arena I stood beside Jamie and Jamie's gang of friends, and cheered myself hoarse as the coloured jerseys raced and mingled on the green turf. Levenford was playing its most hated rival, the neighbouring club of Ardfillan. Were there ever such tricksters, such brutes and murderers, as these men of Ardfillan, known derisively as the "Jelly Eaters" because of their contemptible custom of permitting small boys to enter their enclosure on the presentation, not of real money, but of empty jam jars which the club redeemed later, for cash, at the local rag-and-bone yard? Thank God that justice prevailed! Levenford was the victor!

After the match Jamie and I walked home in splendid comradeship; then, as we approached the deviation of our ways, our blood still surging in a rich afterglow, Jamie produced a package which had encumbered him all afternoon. His face was quite red and he had suddenly grown husky.

"Give this to your Kate," he said. "From me."

I stared at him in complete bewilderment. Kate! "Our" Kate! What had she to do with us, and our beautiful new friendship?

"That's right." He was redder than ever. "Just put it in her room."

He turned and left me standing with the package in my arms.

At Lomond View Kate was not visible—only Murdoch sat muttering and groaning at his books in the kitchen—so, obeying Jamie's instructions, I took the large wrapped oblong package to her bedroom and placed it on her chest of drawers. I had never been in Kate's room except at her express invitation, and now, with curiosity, and a sense of privilege conferred by my special mission, I dallied, studying the few bottles of lotion and the jar of face cream beside her mirror. There were a number of paper-covered booklets too. I picked them up. *Facial Beauty without Disfiguring Operations. Madame Bolsover's Method, or How to Improve the Bust in Twelve Lessons*. Another, with the mysterious, yet intriguing title: *Girls! Why Be a Wallflower?*—I was about to probe deeper when the door opened and Kate came in.

Her chapped skin reddened with anger. Her bumps gathered instantaneously. And I only saved myself by exclaiming swiftly and adroitly:

"Oh, Kate. I have something for you, a regular surprise."

She halted, her ears crimson, eyes still angry.

"What is it?" she asked suspiciously.

"A present, Kate!" And I indicated the package on the chest of drawers.

She gazed incredulously; then, pausing only to utter a half-hearted rebuke—"Remember, Robert, you must never, never, enter a lady's bedroom unannounced"—she approached the package, took it up, sat down with it on the bed, and, while I watched, removed the wrappings, revealing a beautiful beribboned box filled with three pounds of expensive chocolates. I was convinced Kate had never had such a lovely present in her life. I congratulated her, bending over the box with an air of complicity.

"Aren't they wonderful, Kate? They're from Jamie. He took me to the match this afternoon. You know, Jamie Nigg."

Kate's face was a study—strange mixture of pleasure, amazement, and disappointment. She said, rather haughtily: "Him, indeed! I'll have to return them."

"Oh, no, Kate. That would hurt Jamie's feelings. Besides . . ." I swallowed a bead of saliva.

Kate smiled, in spite of herself; and when she smiled, even this short dry smile, she was surprisingly agreeable. "All right, then. You may have one. But I couldn't touch them myself."

I did not delay in availing myself of this permission and at once bit into a succulent orange cream which immediately discharged its delicious flavour upon my tongue.

"Are they good?" Kate asked, swallowing, strangely, in her turn.

I made inarticulate noises.

"If only it had been anybody but Jamie Nigg!" Kate exclaimed.

"Why?" I argued loyally. "Jamie's the finest fellow you could meet. You ought to have seen him with all his friends at the match. And he knows the Levenford centre-forward."

"Oh, he's low—only a boilermaker. He works dirty. And besides, they say he takes a wee half."

Recognizing this as the idiom for a little whisky, I quoted Grandpa on the subject, staunchly: "He's none the worse of that, Kate."

"Well, then . . ." Kate reddened again, confusedly. "His legs."

"Never mind about his legs, Kate," I pressed earnestly.

"Legs are too important not to mind. Especially when you are 'walking out.'"

I paused, dismayed. "Do you like anyone else, Kate?"

"Well . . . yes . . ." Kate's gaze slipped dreamily over the pamphlet *Why Be a Wallflower?* into the romantic distance, and I took advantage of her abstraction to select another chocolate.

"Of course I've had lots of proposals, at least several, anyhow a few, I wouldn't boast. But now I'm speaking more or less of my ideal. A man of some maturity, dark, well-bred, eloquent . . . like the Reverend Mr. Sproule, for example."

I stared at Kate with amazement: the Reverend was a middle-aged gentleman with a paunch, poetic locks, a booming voice and four children.

"Oh, Kate, I'd sooner have Jamie any day. . . ." I broke off, blushing hotly, conscious that I, of all people, had no right to criticize her minister.

"Never mind," Kate said with queenly understanding. "Have another chocolate. Go on, don't mind me, I wouldn't defile my lips with them. As a matter of fact, love disgusts me. Yes, disgusts me. The woman always pays. Was that a hard or a soft centre?"

"Hard, Kate," I replied earnestly. "A kind of lovely nougat the like of which you never tasted in your life. Look, there's another exactly the same. Let me get it for you, please, please."

"No, no, I wouldn't dream of it." While Kate protested, she accepted in an absent-minded manner and as a kind of afterthought placed in her mouth the nougat I pressed upon her.

"Aren't they simply delicious, Kate?" I asked eagerly.

"No man can *buy* me, Robert. But I must say they are awfully nice."

"Have another, Kate."

"Well, I know it'll turn my stomach. Still, if you insist. Find me one of the orange kind you ate first."

Sitting on her bed, in the next half hour, we ate the entire top tray between us.

"What am I to tell Jamie, then?" I sighed at last.

Neatly tying up the box with its pink ribbon Kate suddenly began to laugh. It was the oddest experience in the world, hearing this strange, gloomy, and bad-tempered girl give way to natural laughter.

"What a pair of hypocrites we are, Robie. At least, I am. Eating the poor lad's sweeties that must have cost a fortune, and sitting in judgment on him. Just tell him the truth. Tell him we enjoyed his chocolates very much. Thank him kindly for them. And let that be the end of it."

I went down the stairs three at a time, determined that Jamie should have, at least, the first part of Kate's message.

Chapter Ten

July came, with the prospect of the summer holidays and hot winds which swayed the yellowing corn. I ran barefooted with Gavin after the watering cart in the warm, wetted dust of the Drumbuck village roads. I climbed with him to the highest point of Garshake Hill to gather the blue "bilberries" which grew there and which Mama received gratefully and made into jam much nicer than our usual rhubarb preserve. I bathed with him in the milldam and swam my first strokes, threshing the cool water with my arms, across a corner of the deep end, then ducked my head beneath the little waterfall while the stream cascaded into my mouth, my nose, and shoals of darting minnows, rising from the sand, tickled my legs. Transported, I heard my shrill, ecstatic laughter rise. Could water be so wonderful? It seemed to wash the last stains of sorrow from my soul. When we came out we leaped and danced, finally flung ourselves flat on the grass, staring at the bright sky with a kind of burning ecstasy. Joy! Oh, the pure, mild warm air, the light, the green of the trees, and in me those forces which awakened, the joy of breathing, the supreme joy of living!

I was too, too happy in my pagan life. The moorland wind had blown God out of my head; the postcards which Grandma sent me received scant attention; I no longer bade the Evil One emerge from dark corners of the house but fell asleep at once, barely muttering the hastiest of prayers. Ah, I had fallen from grace. The heavens were preparing fresh miseries for me.

First came the news that Gavin must again leave me. Every summer his father rented in Perthshire a lodge with a small moor offering fishing and rough shooting—another extravagance which was later to be cast, like an infamy, upon the Provost's Olympian head!—and of course Gavin would spend the school vacation there, amidst the purple of the heather and the blue of the distant hills.

There was more than a whisper originating from Miss Julia Blair that I might accompany him; but my miserable wardrobe, the cost of the railway fare, a score of chill realities, stilled that warm breath to silence. Gavin and I said good-bye at the railway station, our eyes suspiciously bright, pledging our eternal friendship in a special handclasp which we had adopted, firm as steel, with a special cabalistic interlocking of our thumbs.

Then, as I came home along the High Street, the real bolt came streaking from the sky—I found my progress barred. I glanced up and, with a start of undiluted terror, found myself before the tall dark figure of Canon Roche, who, leaning on his flapping umbrella, now transfixed me—as I might petrify a minute organism beneath my microscope—with his dark, unblinking, basilisk stare.

Though, thus far, I had tactfully avoided him, the Canon was one of the town's most striking figures. He was young, in fact the youngest canon in the diocese. He had thin features, a beaky nose, and a fine brow—his distinguished scholastic career at the Scots College in Rome gave ample evidence of a keen intelligence. On his accession to the pastorate of the Holy Angels Church he had found badly run to seed a parish always unruly because of its admixture of races: Polish, Lithuanian, Slovak and Irish emigrants had been at different times attracted to the town by reason of the work and good wages offered by the Boilerworks. Quickly, the Canon realized that one weapon above all was likely to control this rough and scarcely literate flock. He did not hesitate to use it. With a severity foreign to his nature he thundered at them from the pulpit, flayed them with his satire on the church steps, accosted and denounced them in the public streets. In twelve months he had tamed the congregation, earned the friendship of the Marshall Brothers, owners of the Boilerworks, and won the grudging respect of the more liberal town authorities—a difficult matter in a small Scottish community where "the Catholics" were detested and despised. Strangely, too, he had gained not alone the awe but the admiration of his parish. A terror he was, yes, by God, a holy terror was the Canon, God bless and confound him!

Small wonder, though his present tone was mild, that I trembled to be singled out by such a man.

"You are Robert Shannon, are you not?"

"Yes, Father."

Ah, that "Father"—I had betrayed myself. He smiled faintly.

"And a Catholic, surely?"

"Yes, Father."

He began to furl the flapping umbrella. "I've had a letter about you from a colleague in Dublin ... Father Shanley ... He writes me, asking me to look you up." He shot a glance at me. "You come to Mass on Sundays, don't you?"

I hung my head. I had suffered for my allegiance to the Scarlet Woman; her mark was upon my brow; but, alone and timid, since coming to Levenford, I had not visited her Temple.

"Ah!" What a lot of trouble the umbrella was giving him. "You've made your First Communion, of course."

"No, Father."

"Your first confession, then."

The illness of my parents had got in the way of this tremendous obligation; I wished the earth would open to swallow me and my shame: "'No, Father."

"Dear me. That's a sad omission for a man by the name of Shannon. We must put it right, Robert. Right, right away, if you'll forgive the pun which is, I'm sure you will agree, the lowest form of all wit and more worthy of a worthy Episcopal clergyman than of my unworthy self!"

Why did he smile? Why did he not thunder at me? My eyes, already, were smarting with tears—Gavin gone, and *this*! I knew, too, that we were the object of many curious glances from the passers-by, numerous because it was the dinner hour. Soon the shocking tale of this interview would spread far and wide, damning me once again in the eyes of my schoolfellows, upsetting everything at Lomond View.

"We have a First Communion class beginning next month at the convent. Tuesdays and Thursdays after four. Quite convenient, really. Mother Elizabeth Josephina takes it ... I think you'll like her, if you come." He smiled at me with his compelling black eyes. "Will you come, Robert?"

"Yes, Father." I mumbled out of stiff lips.

"That's a good chap." His umbrella, though frightfully untidy, now seemed to his satisfaction. At least, he studied it amiably and began to make whirligigs with it while giving me a short talk upon my obligations. He concluded with a final injunction: "One point, Robert, not very easy, living with non-Catholic relatives as you do, but most important. It's this. Do not eat meat on Fridays. A strict rule of the Church. Remember now ... no meat on Fridays." A parting gleam from those stern, yet kindly eyes, and he was gone.

I tottered off in the opposite direction, still dazed by the mischance of the encounter. I was crushed, caught and convicted of my crimes. The brightness of the day was dulled. It did not for a moment occur to me that I might disregard the Canon's commands. No, no, his eye was now upon me; he loomed, in all his spiritual and temporal powers, too near and awful to be disobeyed. All Grandma's careful preparation of the vineyard of my spirit was obliterated, as by a hurricane. I felt that the mischance of my origin had finally overtaken me. It only remained for me to suffer and submit.

Then, as I approached the back door of Lomond View, a sudden recollection made the sweat break coldly on my brow. To-day—this very day—was Friday. And in the air I could smell my favourite dish, beef stew. I groaned. Dear God and Canon Roche! What was I to do?

I entered the kitchen with a faltering step, took my place at the table where Kate and Murdoch were already seated. Yes, as I feared, Mama placed before me a plateful of stewed steak which seemed, indeed, a larger portion and, from its steam, more savoury than usual. I viewed it distractedly.

"Mama," I said at last, in a weak voice. "I don't think I want this stew to-day."

I was immediately the centre of inquiring stares. Mama considered me doubtfully. "Are you sick?"

"Well, I don't know. Perhaps a slight headache."

"Take some gravy and potatoes then."

Gravy—ah, that, too, was forbidden. I shook my head with a pale smile. "I think perhaps it would be better if I didn't eat anything."

Mama made a little clicking sound with her tongue as she did when not sure about something. Before I returned to school, where classes were going on for a few final days, she gave me a dose of Gregory's Mixture. Passing through the scullery, I had stuffed a hunk of bread furtively into my breeches pocket, and I devoured it hungrily on my way to the Academy. But all afternoon my stomach made painful empty rumbles.

That evening at the family meal Mama, with a nice air of favouring me and at the same time doing a good deed, placed before me a thin slice of the potted head on Mr. Leckie's plate—at this time he always had some "kitchen," as it was called, for his high tea. She glanced at the others self-accusingly: "Robert has not been very well to-day."

My soul shrank within me. I stared glassily at the tender pieces of meat, visible through the clear jelly which encased the delicacy. Why didn't I come out with the truth? Oh, no, no, a thousand no's. I could not do it. The strange and tragic history of my affiliation with the Church of Rome was too painful a subject in this family. It was veiled, buried. To resurrect it would surely bring about my ears upheaval and catastrophe, comparable only to the havoc wrought by Samson in Grandma's picture upstairs. The thought of Papa's face alone . . .

Yet it was he who, for the present, saved me.

"That boys's been at the green grosets," he suddenly declared crossly. "Get him away early to his bed." He lifted the potted head back from my plate to his own.

I had not been near his unripe gooseberries. But I welcomed the injustice, suffered myself to be sent supperless to my little curtained alcove.

On Sunday, before the family was awake, I crept through the dim lobby and scudded out to the seven o'clock Mass, sitting in the back seat of all, hiding my face as the offertory box went round. It was a fine church—built by Pugin, I afterwards discovered—in a simple Gothic style; and very "devotional," with stained glass windows in excellent taste, the white high altar set well back, a series of high arches giving dignity to the nave. But this morning, reeling off my little incantations breathlessly, I drew no solace from it. My knees knocked together as Canon Roche mounted to the pulpit. Perhaps he would preach against me, this faithless renegade who had not the courage of his belief. What a relief ... he did not! Yet the announcement he made was equally destructive to my peace of mind. The following week was Ember Week: Wednesday, Friday, and Saturday were days of fasting and abstinence; God would have no mercy on those weak and faithless souls who dared indulge themselves with flesh upon these days. I went home, my eyes blinking, stricken to the depths, repeating to myself, in a daze: "Wednesday, Friday *and* Saturday." To offend God was bad enough. Yet it was my terror of the terrible Canon which held me to the impossible task.

On Wednesday I was fortunate. Mama, distracted by the prospect of her "washing day," received without suspicion my whispered excuse that I must spend the dinner hour clearing up my books at the Academy, and, bending over the scullery boiler, absently bade me prepare and take along with me some slices of bread and jam. But on Friday when I tried the same device her mood was different: she sharply commanded me to return for my good hot dinner. It was mince she put before me and she left the kitchen with an air which boded ill for me if I had not cleared the plate on her return.

Oh, God, how I was suffering! No bearded Jew, confronted by a crackling loin of pork before the Inquisition, endured, such tortures as were mine. I glanced desperately across at Murdoch, who, while chewing, watched me curiously. He was studying at home now, and, since Kate was delayed by the "break-up" at the Elementary School, he was the only other occupant of the table.

"Murdoch!" I gasped. "This meat gives me terrible indigestion." Swiftly, I took my plate and transferred all my mince to his.

He goggled at me. But he was a big eater, he made no protest except to remark suspiciously: "Quite a vegetarian these days." Did he guess? Impossible to tell. Trembling, with my head down, I ate up my potatoes, careful not to touch those stained with gravy.

The next day I had reached the end of my resources. Unmanned and starving, there was no invention which I could produce: I simply stayed away from Lomond View at the dinner hour, stayed away altogether, wandering round the harbour in lacklustre style, sniffing the good smells of tar and oil like a dog. As I dragged myself home in the evening I was faint with hunger. Pinched by ravening pangs, I forgot my anxiety as to how I should explain my absence to Mama. I wanted food, food.

At her front gate Mrs. Bosomley was standing with some letters in her hand. She asked me to run to the pillar box and post them. Impossible to run. Yet, weak though I was, I could not refuse a favour to this warm-hearted friend. I posted her letters in the round red pillar at the corner of Banks Lane. When I returned she beckoned me to the open window. My eyes lit up. Yes, she was handing me my usual reward, a great warm double sandwich: Bovril on toast.

I stumbled round the back to the rockery, bearing the thick golden sandwich, the fragrance of which, alone, almost caused me to swoon. I sat down and bared my young fangs from which water already streamed. Then, oh, merciless Heaven, I remembered: Bovril! It was meat, pure meat; there was a poster at the railway bridge showing in bright-colours the enormous ox which went into every bottle!

For a full minute, paralysed with dismay, I stared stonily at the ox, the sublimation of all flesh meat, the occasion of sin, clasped between my small hands. Then, with a cry, I fell ravenously upon it. My teeth bit, tore and devoured. Oh, the goodness of it. I forgot the Avenging Angel and Canon Roche. I sucked in the salty, meaty juice with sinful lips. I licked my fingers in carnal joy. When it was all finished down to the last crumb, I heaved a great appeased, triumphant sigh.

Then, horrified, I realized what I had done. A sin. A mortal sin. A moment of awful silence. Then wave after wave of remorse broke over me. The Canon's dark eyes glittered before me. I could stand it no longer. I broke into tears and ran upstairs to Grandpa.

Chapter Eleven

Grandpa was seated, with his face screwed scientifically to the microscope, when I burst upon him. And in this academic position he heard me, in silence, to the end. It did me good that he did not look at me. I dried my eyes and watched him as he rose and in his burst green slippers began to pace the floor. I felt safe in his hands. How I wished that he, and not the Canon, might ordain my religious future.

"It's very simple, boy, to straighten out your Fridays. A word from me to Mama and it is done. But," he quenched my joy with a shake of his head, "that's just the beginning of it. This thing has been brewing for some time. You're in a difficult position here, there's no denying ... all on your own ... It's a queer kind of legacy your poor mother left ye." He paused, stroking his beard, throwing a peculiar glance at me. "Maybe the easiest solution would be for ye just to row in with the rest of them. I mean ... go to church at Knoxhill with the others."

Inexplicably, my tears spouted hotly again. "Oh, no, I couldn't, Grandpa. A boy's got to be what he's born to be, even if it's difficult..."

He persisted, showing me all the kingdoms of the earth. "Grandma would just love you if ye went to Knoxhill. On my oath I assure ye there is nothing she would not do for you."

"No, Grandpa. I couldn't."

Strange pause. Then he smiled at me, not aloofly, but with his rare, slow, heart-warming smile. He came forward and shook me by the hand. "Well done, Robie, lad!"

Deliberately, he selected two peppermint oddfellows from the small stock in his tin, and pressed them upon me. I could not understand these supreme signs of his approval. He only called me "Robie, lad" on the rarest occasions and as the highest token of his regard.

"I might define my own position." He took an oddfellow himself, enthroned himself loftily in his chair. "I stand for religious freedom. Let a man believe what he likes, provided he doesn't interfere with what I believe. That's all over your head, boy. I'll just say, if ye'd gone to Knoxhill, I'd have disowned ye on the spot."

Philosophical silence while he lit a pipe. "I have nothing against the Catholics, except maybe their Popes. No, boy, I cannot say I approve of your Popes . . . some of these Borgias, with their poisoned rings and sichlike, were not quite the clean potato. However, say no more, you're not to blame. You believe in the same Almighty as your grandma, though she won't let you worship Him with candles and incense. Well, I will, boy. I will. I defend your right to do it. And I'll tell ye this, ye've as much chance of getting through the Pearly Gates, or whatever gates we do go through, with your Mass and vestments as she has with her psalms and Bible-banging."

I had never seen Grandpa so worked-up. He, who despised prosiness in others—who curtly dismissed every speaker he heard as "too prolix"—could, oddly enough, be magnificently long-winded himself. He moralized for half an hour in the most heated and dramatic style: burning and immortal words flowed from his tongue, like "freedom," "liberal," "tolerance," "free-thinker," "imperishable heritage" and "the dignity of man." He expressed such wonderful and high-flown sentiments I knew I must be mistaken in fancying that he several times contradicted himself—as when, for example after extolling the virtues of universal love, he banged his fist fiercely on the table and declared that "we," meaning he and I, would "certainly *do* the old besom," meaning Grandma, "in the eye!"

Nevertheless the general effect of his oration was to bring me comfort. On subsequent Fridays, Mama, without a word, gave me discreet helpings of vegetables and, when Papa was not there, a hard-boiled egg. On the first of August—saying nothing, on Grandpa's recommendation, to anyone—I began to attend the little convent of the Holy Angels and to be prepared for my First Communion.

We were a small class under the care of Mother Elizabeth Josephina, only six or seven sniffing little girls and another little boy, Angelo Antonelli, son of the Italian ice-cream vendor in the town. He was a beautiful child, with a skin like a peach, great dark luminous imploring eyes, and soft curly brown hair. He was exactly like one of Murillo's children, though of course I did not know that then; I only knew that he delighted me and, as he was small, more than a year younger than myself, I immediately took him under my protection.

The class was held sometimes in the still twilight of the church, before the side altar, under a stained-glass window of "Our Lord Carrying His Cross"; occasionally in a prim parlour in the convent; but most frequently, since the weather was warm, on the lawn of the convent garden. Here we children would sit on the grassy bank in the shade of a blossoming syringa bush while the good nun, with the book on her knee, and placid hands in the wide sleeves of her habit, occupied a camp stool in front of us. The high walled garden was exquisitely quiet, it seemed a million miles from the busy town. Now and then one could see another of the Sisters, her face screened by her white wimple, pacing up and down one of the paths, saying her rosary. The sweep of her flowing habit was slow and gracious. Some plump pigeons strutted trustingly, quite near us. There was a low still drone of insects hovering about the white syringa flowers, which, with their delicate scent of orange blossom, seemed strangely appropriate to this enclosed place and to these pious nuns who—each with a plain gold ring on the fourth finger of her right hand—counted themselves espoused to God. Through the waving trees the stone cross of the church—its arms enclosed by a circle, the Saint Andrew's Cross—could be seen against the sky. Then our Sister would raise her forefinger to her lips for silence and, while we gazed at her with round obedient eyes, she began to speak to us of the infant Saviour. It is a moment of innocence to remember; never before, and never since, have I known such peace, such a sense of tranquil happiness.

Mother Elizabeth Josephina was quite elderly, her features lined, inclined to severity. She was a good teacher. She made those days in Palestine live for us. Listening breathlessly, we saw the poor stable, and the Child who lay there. We saw the Holy Family fleeing on a donkey—think, a poor donkey!—before the wickedness of Herod. Perhaps because of my somewhat dubious past, she seemed to devote extra attention to me, and this made me proud: especially when she praised the quickness of my answers. When Canon Roche strolled in to regard us, with surprising benignity, Reverend Mother and he would put their heads together, their eyes directed towards me. Afterwards her kindness increased. She gave me scapulars, and little holy pictures, which I carried underneath my shirt. I began with all my heart to love Jesus, who I thought must have resembled little Angelo, sitting trustingly beside me. I longed for the day when, as Mother Elizabeth Josephina explained, He would come to me in the shape of the shining Host which would be placed upon my tongue.

Then she began to warn us, to speak of the horrors of a bad Communion. She cited many painful instances. There was the little boy who had "broken his fast?" thoughtlessly, by nibbling some crumbs from his pocket before advancing to the altar rails; another careless little fiend who had swallowed drops of water from his toothbrush. These were bad enough; but a third story simply made us shudder. A little girl who, from wicked curiosity, had transferred the host from her tongue to her pocket handkerchief . . . Later she had found this handkerchief soaked with blood!

No one followed the progress of my instruction with more profound attention than Grandpa. He had begun by asking me if Mother Elizabeth Josephina were a good-looking woman; to which I was obliged to answer "No." When I told him of the miracle of the bloodied handkerchief, he did not move an eyelid.

"Remarkable!" he exclaimed, reflectively. "I think I will take Communion with you. A most interesting experience."

"Oh, no no, Grandpa," I cried, aghast. "It would be a sin for you, a mortal sin. And first you would have to make your confession

"... tell Canon Roche all the bad things you have done in your whole life."

"That, Robert," he said mildly, "would be a lengthy interview."

Towards the end of July, the Reverend Mother had a mild indisposition and her place on the camp stool beside the syringa bush was taken by a young, fresh-cheeked nun, Sister Cecilia. She was a sweet and gentle person who taught us even more interestingly than Reverend Mother; her blue eyes grew remote and wistful when she spoke of Our Lord; and she did not frighten us with gruesome stories. She charmed me and I ran home to tell Grandpa the news.

"We have a new teacher, Grandpa. She's a young nun. And terribly pretty."

Grandpa did not immediately answer. He twisted his moustache with that gesture I knew so well. Then: "It seems to me that I have been neglecting my duty, Robert. To-morrow I will take you to the class. I should like to meet your Sister Cecilia."

"But, Grandpa," I said doubtfully, "I do not think gentlemen are allowed inside the convent."

He gave me his calm, confident smile, still twirling his moustaches: "We shall see."

True to his word, on the following afternoon Grandpa brushed himself thoroughly, shone his boots, set his hat sedately on his head, and taking his best bone-handled stick accompanied me to the convent, where, after some hesitation on the part of the young maidservant, who, however, was won over by my grandpa's stately demeanour, we were shown to a reception parlour. Here Grandpa seated himself with his hat at his feet, very upright, like a pillar of the church. He, nodded to me once to indicate that the room had won his approval, that he was not insensitive to its atmosphere. Then he directed a chaste yet inquiring regard towards the blue-and-white statue of the Virgin, in a glass case upon the mantelpiece.

When Sister Cecilia entered he rose and gave her his most distinguished bow.

"I apologize for this intrusion, ma'am. You owe it to the fact that I am so deeply interested in the welfare," he laid his hand benevolently upon the top of my head, "of my young grandson here. My name is Alexander Gow."

"Yes, Mr. Gow," Sister Cecilia murmured a trifle uncertainly: although the order was not enclosed, but a teaching one, she was scarcely accustomed to visitors of Grandpa's calibre. "Won't you sit down?"

"Thank you, ma'am," Grandpa bowed again, waiting till Sister Cecilia had seated herself before reoccupying his chair. "I must first acknowledge, frankly and openly, that I am not of your persuasion. You are probably aware of the exceptional circumstances surrounding my little grandson here." The hand on my head again. "You may not know that it was *I* who sent him to you."

"It does you credit, Mr. Gow."

Grandpa made a deprecating gesture, rather sad. "I wish I felt worthy of your congratulations. But alas, my motives, at least in the beginning, were those of reason, the cold reason of a citizen of the world. Yet, ma'am—or perhaps I may call you Sister?" He paused, while Sister Cecilia inclined her head with slight embarrassment. "Yet, Sister, ever since my little boy began coming here—particularly since you, Sister, took over the class—I have found myself touched ... increasingly attracted to the beautiful and simple truths that have fallen from your lips."

Sister Cecilia blushed with gratification.

"Of course," Grandpa resumed, more sadly, yet in his most winning manner, "my life has not been spotless. I have knocked about the world. My adventures ..." Open-mouthed, I glanced at him, apprehensive that he might be on the verge of again bringing up the Zulus. But no, he did not. "My adventures, Sister Cecilia, have brought me into the face of severe temptation, all the harder to resist when a poor devil—ah, forgive me!—when a poor wretch has no one to care for him. There is no more painful deprivation in the life of any man than the lack of the love of a good woman." He sighed. "Can you wonder that now ... one might have the impulse to come ... in search of peace?"

I could see Sister Cecilia was deeply moved. Her fresh cheeks were still flushed and her swimming eyes expressed a deep concern for Grandpa's soul. Pressing her hands together, she murmured: "It's very edifying. I'm sure, if you have a sincere desire for repentance, Canon Roche would be only too happy to help you."

Grandpa blew his nose; then shook his head with a regretful smile. "The Canon is a fine man, exceptionally fine . . . but perhaps a trifle unsympathetic. No, I felt that if I might come, with Robert, to the class, to sit humbly there and listen . . ."

A flutter of doubt troubled Sister Cecilia's face, like a cloud upon a limpid pool. But she seemed anxious, beyond anything, not to discourage Grandpa or to hurt his feelings.

"I'm afraid it might distract the children, Mr. Gow. However, there must be ways and means. I will certainly speak to Reverend Mother."

Grandpa gave her his most charming smile—yes, I repeat, despite his nose, it was an irresistibly charming smile. He rose and shook her hand, or rather sustained her fingers in his, as though he wished to stoop and reverently salute them. Though he restrained himself, Sister Cecilia's colour remained high long after he had gone, and during instruction, while she told us the story of the Prodigal Son, her earnest eyes were moist.

I found Grandpa waiting for me, walking up and down outside the convent, in the best of moods, swinging his stick and humming. On the way home he gave me a dissertation on the refining influences of good women, interspaced with hummings and sudden exclamations: "Delightful! Delightful!" I heard him with a certain anxiety: for in these last weeks I had come up against a fearful personal difficulty, to which I shall presently refer, on this very subject of women. Still, I was glad Sister Cecilia, and the prim, polished quiet of the convent parlour, had made such an excellent impression upon Grandpa.

He tactfully allowed a week to elapse before his next visit, choosing a sunny day on which, as he remarked, "the garden would be particularly lovely." Already, he saw himself beside me on the lawn. He spruced himself more carefully than ever and spent a long time before his mirror, trimming his beard, as he sometimes did before calling on Mrs. Bosomley. Always partial to clean linen, he wore his best white shirt, which he had starched and ironed himself. He even tucked into his buttonhole a little sprig of forget-me-not, the bright vivacious blue of which exactly matched his eyes. Then, he took my hand, threw out his chest. We set out briskly for the convent.

Alas! It was not Sister Cecilia who came to the little parlour, but Mother Elizabeth Josephina, more severe than ever, and only just recovering from jaundice. Grandpa's face fell, his opening smile was chilled, nipped in the very bud, as quickly, brusquely, Reverend Mother sent me from the room, to take my place in the class upon the lawn.

A moment later, seated on the grassy bank, I heard the sound of the front door—shut with a firm hand. Then, through the trees, I saw Grandpa descend the steps and go down the drive. Though I could scarcely distinguish at that distance, he seemed out of countenance, terribly taken-down. When, after a sharp, short instruction, Reverend Mother released us, he was not outside. Later that evening, I noticed he had removed his blue forget-me-not.

Poor Grandpa! I worried that his repentance should be cut so short, but Corpus Christi, the last Thursday of the month, was not far off and I was now in a state of exaltation alternating between misery and bliss. Before I might taste the rapture of Communion I must undergo the ordeal of my first confession. Several times Canon Roche had taken our little class upon this subject, and though his manner was restrained, I began to perceive, dimly, the horrid pitfalls which nature had prepared for unsuspecting children. A vague recognition of the difference in the sexes was borne upon me. The word "purity" was spoken gently, yet with resolution, by our pastor. Then, out of the mists, came the sudden realization of my sin. Oh, God, how I had sinned: the worst, the unforgivable sin. I could never, never tell it to the Canon.

Yet I must. The damnation attaching to a "bad" confession was worse, even, than that resulting from a "bad" Communion. With a sinking heart I saw that I must reveal my infamy. ... Oh, the torture of knowing there was no escape!

At last the day, the fatal hour approached. From beneath the stained-glass window of "Our Lord Carrying His Cross" I staggered, in a sweat of anguished shame, into the dark confessional where Canon Roche awaited me. My bare knees sank beneath me, hitting the bare board with a hollow thud. I began to weep.

"Father, Father, forgive me. I'm so wicked, so terribly ashamed."

"What is it, my dear child?" The gentle encouragement in the hidden austere voice increased my grief. "Did you say a bad word?"

"No, Father, worse, far worse."

"What, child?"

It came with a rush. "Oh, Father, I slept with my grandmother."

Did I hear a merry laugh behind that mysterious grille? Or was it merely the echo of my sobs?

94

Chapter Twelve

Corpus christi has come and the morning sky is grey, grey as the body of the dead Christ when they took Him from the Cross. I have spent a fitful night on my straw mattress in the kitchen closet: only snatches of rest wherein I dream that the living Christ Child is sleeping beside me, His beautiful head on my pillow, His soft cheek against mine. I awake with a start, hoping my dream is not a sin. Lately I have been tortured by scruples: was I guilty of "immodesty" while undressing? Did I gaze "impurely" at a crucifix, at the statue of Our Lady, at anything? With sealed eyes and lips I stumble over the earth's surface, dreading the accident of sin. I am so desperately anxious to make, not just a "good," but a perfect Communion, I have even fallen to the habit of seeking heavenly signs and portents. I say to myself, gazing towards the sky: "If I see a cloud which resembles Saint Joseph's face I shall make a glorious Communion." I squint upwards, compressing my eyeballs, striving to find a paternal profile, at least a beard, amongst the celestial vapours. Or I take three pebbles from the roadway, one for each person of the Blessed Trinity, and tell myself that if I hit the corner lamp-post once in three slugs, I am sure to communicate superbly. But, no! I desist quickly in fear of sacrilege.

This morning, however, I am strangely at peace, and my thoughts are filled with love, with the secret wonder that I, amongst the people who surround me in this house, clamouring for breakfast, for hot water, for shoes to be brushed, for all the humdrum things of life—that I, alone, am chosen for the sweet and joyful honour of receiving in my breast the Son of God.

Last night I washed my mouth out carefully; it is no trouble for me to forgo my breakfast. Is it possible that Mama is in Grandpa's confidence? She does not press me to eat. Barelegged, I go upstairs and find Grandpa preparing to escort me to church: he is excited and would not dream of missing what he calls "the ceremony." Though he takes the huff quickly, Grandpa does not long harbour a grudge, and he has completely got over his dismissal by Mother Elizabeth Josephina. It has been decided at the convent that I am too "big" for a white suit: a merciful judgment—the white shoes and stockings which I must wear have been hard enough to come by and it has fallen to my wonderful great-grandparent to provide them for me, how I do not know, for he has no money, and when I ask him he merely shrugs his shoulders, hinting that he has made a great sacrifice on my behalf. Later, a pawn ticket was discovered ... for the blue vase in the parlour.

But meanwhile, I put on the new shoes and stockings with pride. I go out with Grandpa and soon we are at the church. The High Altar is adorned with white lilies: beautiful and imposing to me as I sit in the front seat of all, beside Angelo, who wears a white sailor suit, and opposite the six little girls—one of whom, I notice with disgust, is giggling from nervousness beneath her white veil fastened with a chaplet of artificial white flowers. In the seats immediately behind us are the relatives of the First Communicants. Grandpa is there—next to Mr. and Mrs. Antonelli, near Angelo's uncle and sister—interested and, I hope, not too disdainful, although he has done all the wrong things, failing to genuflect and to sign himself with holy water. Still, I am glad of him and I know he wishes to be helpful; I hear him stoop to pick up Mrs. Antonelli's glove ... or her prayer book.

The sanctuary bell rings and the Mass begins. I follow it faithfully, reading my Preparation for Communion, but waiting, waiting only for that moment which will make this Mass different from all others, before, or after. How short the time is getting! I feel an inward tremor. Then the *Domine non sum dignus*. At last, at last! I strike my breast three times; then, with shaking knees, I rise and advance with Angelo and the others to the altar rails. I am conscious of the gaze of the congregation concentrated upon us, my poor head is whirling as I see Canon Roche advance, in his beautiful vestments, bearing the chalice, I try in vain to remember my Act of Adoration, I hope I will not make a fool of myself, I close my eyes and lift my head, opening my trembling lips as Reverend Mother has taught us, whispering in my heart a final prayer, simply the word: "Jesus."

The Host surprises me, so large and dry upon my tongue, when I had expected a moist supernatural offering. In my dry mouth it is difficult to dispose of, to swallow; I am back in my place, flushed, my throbbing temples buried in my hands, before I accomplish this. Nothing has happened to me, no sensible flow of grace, no apparent transfiguration of my soul. A wave of disappointment crashes over me. Have I made a "bad"—No, no, I check my mind from stealing down that dreadful avenue and return passionately to my prayer book, where an act of thanksgiving soothes me. I lift my head, am reassured by Angelo's tender sideways smile, by Grandpa's cough behind me. A sense of proud achievement begins to pervade me. I join with the congregation in the Prayers after Mass.

Outside the church, the sun was now shining and, after a smiling moment with the convent Sisters, I was seized upon, congratulated, shaken hands with, warmly embraced by Grandpa and the Antonellis. My remarkable relative was already bosom friends with the Italian family, which seemed delighted, nay, enchanted with him. He introduced me to Mr. and Mrs. Antonelli, their grown-up daughter Clara, and to Angelo's uncle, Vitaliano, who was about fifty, brown-faced, and with the quiet remoteness of the very deaf. Everyone smiled at me; and Mrs. Antonelli, a stoutish, dark-eyed lady with a swarthy fringe, tiny gold rings in her ears and a green velvet dress, beamed at me maternally, repeating: "Such a nice friend for our little Angelo." Then Mr. Antonelli, who was also dark but shorter than his wife and turning bald, suddenly slapped his fist into his palm and directed towards Grandpa his large soulful eyes, which were exactly like Angelo's except that they had pouches beneath them.

"Meester Gow," he exclaimed fervently yet humbly, "am goin'

to ask you a favour. Da two boys are already good frien's ... If you're nota too proud ... come to breakfast."

Grandpa accepted on the spot. Mr. and Mrs. Antonelli were very pleased. We set off: Angelo and I walking in front, while Grandpa and the others followed behind.

The Antonellis lived above their shop, which was painted primrose and vermilion with a proud and glittering gold-lettered signboard: *Levenford Select Ice Cream Saloon, Antonio Antonelli, Sole Proprietor.* This tropical brilliance was continued upstairs. The carpets were vivid, the hangings a gorgeous shade of yellow-green. Coloured holy pictures were everywhere, for the Antonellis were very devout, but on either side of the tasselled mantelpiece two secular paintings, views of Capri and Naples, dazzled the eye with their shimmering blues. And here, good gracious, was Vesuvius, blazing in eruption. A little statue, dressed brightly in pink and white, like a doll, smiled down on me from a gilt bracket on the wall. I had never entered a house so foreign or so rich in mysterious odours. Strange cooking smells provoked my nostrils, fruity smells, acrid, tart and pungent smells, the smells of onion and perspiration, of boiling fat and damp sawdust, the sweet vanilla scent of ice cream powder rising from the cellar below.

While Mrs. Antonelli and Clara were hurrying, with many excited exclamations, to serve the breakfast, Angelo, who had taken possession of my hand, drew me shyly to the end of the first-floor corridor. Here, at the half-open door of a room which proved later to be his uncle's, he paused, with an air of promise. My heart had already bounded at the vision of a barrel organ, a real hurdy-gurdy inlaid with the name ORFEO ORGANETTO in mother-of-pearl, standing on its peg against the wall. Yet I was unprepared for the surprise which followed.

"Nicolo, Nicolo," Angelo, called softly.

A monkey dressed in a red coat jumped from the bed, pattered along the floor and leaped into Angelo's arms. He was a small neat monkey with pathetic eyes and a little, wrinkled, worried face. He had, exactly, that expression which, many years after, I saw on the faces of newly-born babies: a crushed, surprised, troubled, yet peevish air. Meanwhile Angelo was stroking him affectionately and offering me the same delightful privilege.

"Pet him, Robie. He won't bite you. He knows you are my dear friend. Don't you, Nicolo, Nicolo? And he has no fleas, not a single one. He belongs to my Uncle Vita. Vita loves him the best in all the world. He says he is our good luck. When we first came to Levenford and were very poor my uncle used to go round the streets with his organ and Nicolo. Got a lot of pennies too. But now that we are rich, at least quite rich, though he wishes to go playing the organ Mother will not let him. She says it is not nice, that we are above such common things now. So we keep Nicolo as a pet, a great pet. He was three when my uncle brought him here. Now he is only ten, which is still young, very young for a monkey."

Here, Mrs. Antonelli called us. Enchanted, I followed Angelo, who still carried the monkey, into the front room where the others were assembled.

"Oh, not Nicolo," Mrs. Antonelli protested as we went in. "Not today, Angelo, when we have such nice company."

"Yes, Mother," Angelo insisted; "it's my First Communion."

"Oh, very well." Mrs. Antonelli gave Uncle Vita a cross look, then flashed her teeth at Grandpa. "He's just Angelo's pet!"

When Angelo had said grace, we all sat down at the table covered with an embroidered cloth and loaded with many things which did not appear at breakfast time in Lomond View. There were large platters of meat and rice, of tomato-coloured macaroni, a chicken pie, a galantine of tongue, olives, sardines and anchovies, a dish of fruits, and, guarding a big iced cake inscribed "Bless our Angelo," several tall bottles of wine.

Grandpa, seated between Clara and Mrs. Antonelli, was tucking in with every sign of enjoyment. Beaming, at the head of the table, sat Mr. Antonelli. He looked pleased, honoured by our presence.

"A leeta wine, Mr. Gow, justa leeta. Very special. Naples imported. Frascati."

Glasses were filled, even the glass of dark, silent, smiling Uncle

Vitaliano, who seemed to occupy a slightly subordinate position in the family. Rising to his feet, Grandpa proposed a toast.

"To our little ones. A happy and a holy occasion."

We all drank, even we children, for Angelo and I had each a thimbleful. The wine was sweet and warming to my inside.

"You like the Frascati, Mr. Gow?" Mr. Antonelli bent forward anxiously.

"Most refreshing," Grandpa answered cordially. He added, "Light."

"Yes, yes, verra light. Nice and light. Another glass, Mr. Gow."

"I thank you, Mr. Antonelli."

The monkey, looking rather bored on Angelo's knee, reached out casually and helped himself to a banana. I watched, spellbound, while he peeled and began to eat it—like a little man. Angelo nodded to me proudly and whispered: "He will do more tricks for us, after."

"Allow me to fill your glass again, Mrs. Antonelli," Grandpa pressed. "Yours too, my dear Miss Clara." Though they refused, laughingly covering their glasses with their hands, Grandpa was having a tremendous success with the two ladies. He replenished his own glass and after an aside which made Clara laugh again, gravely resumed the account he was giving our hostess of his recent social activities at the Provost's and other large houses in the Cemetery Road. It was plain that Mrs. Antonelli was enraptured to find herself, even remotely, in touch with such gentility.

The laughter increased; Grandpa was now teasing Clara about her young man. "Not a patch on the older generation, these youngsters," he declared grandly.

As Grandpa and Mr. Antonelli began exchanging toasts—"To Italy!" "To Scotland!"—Angelo and I received permission to leave the table. We slipped into Uncle Vitaliano's room with Nicolo and began, softly, pushing in the stop marked *Piano*, to play the hurdy-gurdy. There were four tunes: "The Bluebells of Scotland," "Onward Christian Soldiers," "God Save the King," and "Oh, Mary, We Crown Thee with Blossoms To-day."

Nicolo enjoyed the music too. "The Bluebells of Scotland" was his favourite piece, and when the familiar trills and tinkles fell upon his ear he began to dance and caper for our benefit. Once he found himself the centre of attention, a stimulus which had been lacking in the other room, he increased his efforts, ran along the corridor and skipped back with a hat—it was Grandpa's. Then, using the hat, he minced up and down, like a great swell, doffing his hat and bowing, from time to time. Our laughter excited him. He began to chatter, to hold the hat up with his tail, to let it drop over his head, extinguishing himself. With a shriek of assumed rage he freed himself, kicked the hat round the room, turned a somersault over it, then curled up and pretended to go to sleep in it.

Angelo and I were rocking with laughter when the door opened and Uncle Vita came in, his grave, silent face displeased. He lifted Nicolo, soothed him and put him in his basket in the corner of the room. Then as he picked up and, with his cuff, brushed Grandpa's hat, he said something in Italian. Angelo turned to me: "He says that even for a deaf man there is too much noise in the room, and here, on such a blessed day as this ... He wants us to sit down and sing a hymn." Angelo added of his own accord: "Uncle Vita is very holy."

"What else did he say?"

"Well ... He said your grandpa has already drunk three bottles of wine ... himself. And that he is squeezing our Clara's hand under the table."

Chastened, I sat down on the floor beside Angelo, while Uncle Vita, with the touch of a true virtuoso, turned the handle of the organ. We sang:

> "*Oh, Mary, we crown thee with blossoms to-day,*
> *Queen of the angels and queen of the May. ...*"

Uncle Vita smiled when we finished. Angelo translated: "He says we must never, never forget how wonderful it is to be in a state of grace. If we drop stone dead, if we are killed, cut into little pieces this very second, it does not matter. We go straight to Heaven."

Then I heard them calling me from below; it was time for me

to go. Grandpa, in the hall, was saying good-bye, shaking hands repeatedly with Mr. and Mrs. Antonelli, placing his arm, in a paternal fashion, round Clara's waist; remarking: "Really, my dear, you must accord a gracious privilege to a man old enough to be your father."

"Good-bye. Good-bye." Everyone smiling, exhilarated, except Clara's young man, Thaddeus Gerrity, who had just come in and who turned very red when Grandpa kissed Clara.

Grandpa and I walked down the street. My head is reeling with the joyful events of this eventful day. Grandpa, too, seems not unmoved: his eye is bright, his cheeks are flushed; and from time to time he seems to have a little trouble, not much, with his equilibrium.

A state of grace! Uncle Vita's words returned to me, like a soaring bird, a bird which bears a message. Is it the Frascati still gurgling in my stomach which lifts me, suddenly, to a moment of blurred white ecstasy? I know. I know I have made a good Communion, yes, perhaps even a perfect Communion. I feel a long rolling platitude gathering like a ball behind Grandpa's tongue. But for once, unable to prevent myself, I forestall him. With a rush of emotion I clasp his hand.

"Oh Grandpa, I love our Blessed Saviour very much ... but don't forget, I love you too."

Chapter Thirteen

We are marooned, in August, amidst fields of scorched stubble and dusty hedgerows, the few vagrant airs which stir the drooping trees producing only a sigh of lassitude, the protest of an earth exhausted by too much fruitfulness. Most of the good burghers of Levenford are at the seaside with their families. The empty town seems unfamiliar and as my footsteps echo across the Market Square a vista of deserted cobblestones, of roofs rising one upon another against the Castle battlements, creates the illusion of a city besieged.

Gavin is still away, his earnest postcards causing me to pine more and more for his return. Really, no drama to record in this period of stagnation; yet, beneath the surface of our household, events still move sluggishly, like fish which, although spent, are still capable of sudden and tumultuous movement.

Every evening, when I went out for a breath of air before my holiday homework—a long essay on "Mary Queen of Scots"—I found Jamie Nigg seated on our low stone garden wall, his back directed, in studied carelessness, towards the house. He had his mouth organ with him, and was playing softly and with complete unconcern a catchy tune which, since he could not tell me either its name or origin, I simply called "Jamie's tune." What an infectious melody it was! He did not stop playing when I sat down in silence beside him, grateful for the cool beads of dew forming around us on the yellow grass, for the low line of mist creeping like a relieving army across the parched fields.

After seven o'clock Kate came out of the front door for her evening visit to her friend, Bessie Ewing, usually wearing her light grey raincoat, bareheaded, collar turned up at the back, hands in her pockets. For more than a week she had taken no notice of us, beyond a small, cool, barely perceptible nod to me. Nor had Jamie, motionless, except for his sliding mouth organ, acknowledged her passing. Only the music growing a little stronger as she disappeared, followed her inexorably down the street. Dimly, though it lacked the lush effects of doublet, balcony, and guitar, I sensed this to be a serenade: a Scottish serenade—slow, persistent, dour.

One evening, unexpectedly, almost reluctantly as if against her better nature, Kate stopped. She gazed at me severely: "You ought to be in at your essay."

Before I could reply Jamie took the mouth organ from his lips, shaking it free of its accumulated moisture with jerks of his wrist. "Ah, the boy's doing no harm."

Kate was forced to look at him. She did so angrily: angry about many things; angry at his persistence, at his sitting there calmly while she stood; angry most of all for being angry. But her eyes were the first to fall. Silence.

"It's a fine night," Jamie said.

"It'll probably rain." Kate spoke with bitterness.

"Maybe, maybe. We need a few good showers."

A pause. "Are you detaining me here to talk about the weather?" She made no movement to go, however. Though her plain face was cloudy, I noticed, for the first time, as she stood there in the dusk with one foot courageously advanced and her hands in her pockets visibly clenched, as in preparation for battle, what a trim sturdy figure she had, a well-turned leg, a good ankle. Perhaps Jamie noticed too. Absently, he ran off a few bars of his tune, shook the harmonica again.

"I was just thinking it was a fine night for a walk."

"Indeed! And where *to*, might I inquire?"

"Oh anywhere, just anywhere at all."

"Thank you, thank you very much indeed." Kate tossed her head, stiffly. "Quite a compliment. But as it so happens I'm going down to see my friend, Miss Ewing." She took a step preparatory to departure.

"That's my way too," Jamie remarked, getting up from the wall and dusting himself. "I'll just dauner down with you as far as her gate."

Kate, completely taken aback, could offer no protest. Her colour remained high, her manner indignant. Yet I felt, oddly enough, that she was not wholly displeased as they departed, together, walking far apart, on the pavement. The gathering darkness was merciful to Jamie's legs.

I am standing alone, enjoying my solitude and a last damp, delicious breath; then, as though pursued, I run into the house, begin, in the kitchen, to take my books from my patched satchel.

Murdoch is already bent studiously, turning few pages, but producing showers of dandruff. I often wonder if Murdoch really studies: he has never made any pretence of scholarship and once or twice I have caught sight of a seed catalogue concealed between his covers, evidence of his secret passion for all things horticultural. Through the day he keeps rising restlessly from his books, belching loudly (although he digests like an ostrich it is an article of faith that he suffers, heroically, from "the bile"), going to the mirror to squeeze blackheads from his chin, or into the garden to potter about, like a soul in limbo. Sometimes he unconsciously permits me to glimpse his thoughts.

"Do you know that in Holland they grow tulips by the square mile? Think of it. Mile after mile of tulips!"

Just now, in the corner chair behind him, silent and erect, exactly like a man driving a horse, sits his father. With the approach of the Post Office Examination next month the reins with which Papa guides the unhappy youth have become tighter; indeed, there are signs of the whip. It is necessary, not only for Murdoch's future, but for the Inspector's prestige, that Murdoch should succeed. With all the intensity of a disliked, frustrated man he wishes to announce to the Provost, to Mr. McKellar, to his chief Dr. Laird, Medical Officer of the borough, of whom he is obsequiously jealous, to announce, in fact, all over the town: "My son, my second son ... in the Civil Service ..."

I put my lesson books on the table opposite Murdoch, very

quietly, not to disturb him. My books, inscribed in Grandpa's hairlike copperplate, are covered with brown paper, sewn on by Mama to save them, "to keep them good"—everything must be preserved, never, never wasted, in this household. For three months I have been in a higher class. My new teacher, Mr. Singer, bald, slow, and methodical, is both gentle and encouraging towards me. Free of the tyranny of Mr. Dalgleish, I no longer blot my exercises or stand like an idiot when questioned. I display, instead, a surprising aptitude. In fact at this moment a card, a certain card which I have retained for my own secret satisfaction, falls out of my history book and flutters to the floor, causing me to blush, guiltily, under Papa's eye. He sees the blush, and the card, and is at once suspicious of both. He makes a silent gesture for me to bring him the incriminating card.

There is a long pause while Papa studies the card, my quarterly report card wherein is written, in Mr. Singer's hand:

R. SHANNON

Arithmetic	1st.
Geography	1st.
History	1st.
English	1st.
French	1st.
Drawing	2nd.
Place in Class	1st.

Signed: GEO. SINGER, M.A.

I can see that Papa is dumbfounded. In fact, at first he glances at me sharply, convinced that it is a trick, a cheap deception. But no, the official heading, the flowing signature... I read his thoughts: It must be true. He is far from pleased. He hands me back the card grudgingly, with an offended air, and I return, still guilty, to my books.

Silence in the kitchen except for the ticking of the clock, the turning of a page, a restive stirring from Papa's chair... and, of course, I had forgotten, the click of Mama's needles, for she has come in from the scullery and is knitting a scarf for Adam. It is always for Adam, her knitting.

At nine o'clock Kate returns, does not enter the kitchen, but goes straight from the front door to her room. Good gracious! I must be mistaken. Yet I think that she is humming, humming a little run from Jamie's tune.

Half an hour later Mama looks at me significantly. I put away my books and, moving with great care, lest I knock against something and annoy Papa, I go to my little curtained closet and begin to undress. I am terribly hungry, it seems ages since my tea, and I long, with sudden ravening, for a hunk of bread and rhubarb jam. That white crust, oh, lovely white crust! Mama would give it me, no doubt, but it is preposterous, such a demand at such an hour. I kneel down, say my prayers, then I am in bed. Through the thin curtain I hear the quiet pulse of this house which harbours me: a word exchanged between Mama and Papa, the rustle of a page, the shudder of the bathroom tap, a step above my head.

Sometimes I lie awake, staring at the dim ceiling, and am only half asleep when Murdoch goes upstairs and there begins one of those long, low-voiced conferences held by Papa and Mama in the kitchen before retiring, muttered words of which reach me in the closet. The Ardfillan Hygienic Society ... invited Papa to address them on "Refuse Disposal" ... What did they charge for that beef to-day? What a price! ... No trip to the Coast, this year ... the money will do better in the Building Society, and when Mama pleads gently: Well, perhaps next year, if Adam "comes forward" ... or if Papa is promoted to the Waterworks ... meanwhile it is necessary to save ... save ... save.

But I no longer marvel, I am habituated to Papa's thrift, this consuming passion which seems daily to gain greater ascendancy over him, sets spinning in his brain schemes for further economizing, gives him an ascetic look of perpetual renunciation, forces Mama to endless household and culinary expedients. Mama would like to shop in the "good" stores like Donaldson's, or Bruce's, whose big plate-glass windows are a perpetual invitation to her. Given "the stuff," she is an excellent cook—her drop pancakes (on the rare occasions when there are eggs to spare) are wonderful. She would enjoy composing nice dishes for us. But instead, with a glance at her black purse, she falls back on barley-bree and sends me to Durgan's in the Vennel for a penny napbone ("And ask him to leave some meat on it, dear"), then on to Logan's, also in that poor quarter, for a halfpennyworth "between" carrot and turnip—in plain English, a farthing's worth of each. Poor Mama! ... Last Monday when you broke the new incandescent mantle you were fitting on the hall "gasolier" (always a delicate operation) you actually gave way to tears.

To-night I am tired, ready to sleep. As I drift into unconsciousness, I think that to-morrow I shall probably go with Grandpa to visit the Antonellis.

During the weeks that Gavin was away, I had played a good deal with little Angelo Antonelli. It was nice to have something to do in such a jaded season; and Angelo was always so touchingly glad to see me. He was like a little girl, vivacious and tender, with his lovely swimming eyes and fetching ways. He held my hand as we ran about his yard, and always cried when it was time for me to go home.

Naturally, he was a very spoiled child, there were twelve years between Clara and him. He perpetually demanded from his fat, gentle, and adoring father—and perpetually received—toys, sweets, fruits, everything. He had the complete run of the Saloon, and would rifle a tin of chocolate biscuits or break open a can of preserved pears with less compunction that I would take a glass of water at Lomond View. His childish treble troubled the air all day long: "Mama, I want a slisa melon"; "Dada, I want a limonade." Once he told me, with a little smirk, that he had made his mother get up in the middle of the night to cook him ham and eggs. Yet he never finished what was on his plate—and was always being sick.

Sometimes, when I thought of the absent Gavin's austere, cold fire, of his determined silences, his contempt for the soft and the paltry, I had an inward qualm. But despite his pampering, Angelo had a sweet side; then there was the monkey, a tremendous attraction, for we played with him continuously. Also Angelo's mother encouraged my visits.

Now that her husband, whom she ruled, had made money, Mrs. Antonelli had turned ambitious for her family, which in its poor beginnings had been scorned in Levenford. The luscious Clara was making a good match with Thaddeus Gerrity, whose father operated a successful furniture-removal company. I am sure she smiled on me—a nice little Academy boy, yet a Catholic—and fêted Grandpa with wine and cake, when he regularly visited her in the afternoon, because we represented the genteel Drumbuck Road district, and town officialdom—always important to the alien mind.

I must confess that, now and again, when I heard Grandpa "spreading himself," over the Frascati, to the eagerly attentive Clara and Mrs. Antonelli, I experienced a mild anxiety. Mrs. Antonelli, caught unawares, had a hard look; and her darkness was such I suspected, despite my innocence, that she had resort, regularly, to the razor. Yet nothing seemed to worry Grandpa; he proceeded, smooth and steady, never in difficulty, like a stately barque before a tranquil breeze.

Reassured, I would run out with Angelo to hear the band play on the Common, to take a rowboat on the pond, or to walk to Benediction at the Holy Angels with Uncle Vita: that strange, humble, simple Vita, who was barely tolerated by the family, who spent half his day in tending his beloved monkey and the other half in prayer.

The month drew to its close. One evening when, at Mama's request, I was turning down the gas in the lobby to the required "peep," Kate came in, rather late.

"Is that you, Robie?" She seemed embarrassed by even the glimmer in the hall, but her voice was warm with friendliness.

"Yes, Kate."

As I got down from the chair on which I had been standing to reach the overhead gasolier, she slipped her hand under my arm.

"Dear boy."

I flushed with pleasure: for a long time now Kate had been especially nice to me.

"Listen, Robie." Kate stopped, laughed, then suddenly went on again. "It's perfectly ridiculous ... Jamie Nigg wants to take me to the Ardfillan Fair." She laughed again, at the preposterous notion. "Of course I can't go with him alone, it would be most unladylike. He admits that himself. So ... he ... that is we ... would be glad to take you with us if you'd like to come."

Like to come! Had I not heard of, dreamed of, the Elysian delights of the Ardfillan Fair—where every kind of show, entertainment, and amusement was congregated once a year for the diversion of the countryside?

"Oh, Kate!" I whispered.

"Then it's settled." She pressed my arm again and as she began to climb the stairs she turned kindly, a sort of afterthought. "Your friend Gavin is home. I just saw him coming from the station."

Gavin home! At last. Two days before his time. So that I would see him to-morrow for certain. The thought surged within me, joined with the thought of the Ardfillan Fair. I breathed quickly. Alive with anticipation, I half-opened the front door and gazed out into the darkness. There were no stars, the sky was blotted out, but the soft cool breeze was filled with promise. Oh, life could be wonderful, simply wonderful.

Chapter Fourteen

The next morning I was out early. I had promised to return to Angelo a bundle of magazines which he had loaned me and I wished to be free, as soon as possible. But as I ran down the Cemetery Road, I met Gavin advancing in the direction of Lomond View.

"Gavin!"

He did not speak, but gave my hand the terrible clasp, still trying to master his eager smile, which he must despise as a sign of weakness. He had not grown much but was very brown and wirier than ever. The sight of him, the feel of his grey eyes searching mine, warmed me through and through. I wanted to tell him, impetuously, how much I had missed him. But this was forbidden. It was necessary to be calm and strong, sparing of all but the most essential speech.

"I was coming up to get you." Explaining his appearance at this early hour, he gazed into the distance, towards our Winton Hills. "I thought we might go up Windy Crag. There's an eagle there. The keeper told Father. We'll get on to the crags before the sun's properly up and watch for him. I have our lunch."

I saw he had his knapsack on his back. An eagle; and Gavin; all day on the hills ... My heart jumped. "Simply grand! But first of all I must take these magazines to Angelo."

"Angelo?" he repeated, uncomprehendingly.

"Angelo Antonelli," I explained hastily. "You know, that little Italian boy. I've seen quite a bit of him while you were away. Of course he's very young ..."

I broke off, confounded by the incredulity, the hurt look in his eyes.

"The only Italians I know of in Levenford are those ice-cream peddlers. One of them actually used to tote a barrel organ and a monkey round the town, cadging for coppers."

My ears were burning now, at this condemnation of Uncle Vita, of Nicolo and my friends. Gavin added: "You don't mean to say you've got mixed up with one of their brats?"

"Angelo has been very decent to me," I said in a queer voice.

"Angelo!" More deeply wounded, he smiled scornfully at the name. "Come on. Let's get on the crags. We can talk about all we've been doing when we're up there."

I hung my head, eyes obstinately on the pavement.

"I promised to take these back. The *Sphere, Graphic,* and *Illustrated London News.*" With dry lips, I defended the magazines, hoping thus to vindicate the Antonellis. "They've some wonderful photographs of the development of the death's-head moth from a chrysalis, this week. Every Saturday Mrs. Antonelli sends them to relatives in Italy. They've got to catch the mail. It's kind of Angelo to let me see them first."

Gavin had turned white. His voice was strained and jealous.

"Of course, if you prefer your tally-wally friends to me . . . that's entirely your affair. It just happens that I'm going up the Longcrags now. If you want to, you can come. If you don't I'll leave you to your Angelo."

He waited for a moment, not looking at me, with quivering lip and proud cold brow. My breast was torn asunder, I wanted to cry out how mistaken he was, to beg him to understand. But a sense of his injustice made me as palely stubborn as he. I remained silent. The next instant he was striding towards the Longcrags.

Sick with dismay, still stunned by the suddenness of the quarrel, I continued towards the town. I resolved simply to leave the magazines and come away. But when I reached the Levenford Select Saloon I found Angelo devastated by a grief perhaps greater than my own.

"Nicolo is sick. Very sick."

Between his sobs, he told me how it had occurred. Clara, wicked Clara, was to blame. Uncle Vita, who went in the evenings to pray at the Holy Angels, often for hours at a time, had the habit of putting Nicolo in the courtyard during his absence to enjoy the cool air during these stifling nights. But always he left his window open, so that if the weather turned bad, Nicolo, for whom the drainpipe was an easy ladder, could immediately regain his room. Two nights ago a heavy thunderstorm had broken and Clara, thinking only to protect the curtains, had hastily shut every window in the house. Uncle Vita was at church, the Saloon closed; poor Nicolo was caught for an hour in the drenching downpour; when Vita returned at half-past ten he found the monkey soaked to the skin, huddled in a corner of the yard.

I followed Angelo upstairs. The house was stricken, deranged. In the kitchen Mrs. Antonelli, with a distraught expression, was wringing out cloths in hot water. Clara lay flat on her face, on the front-room sofa. In Uncle Vita's bedroom Mr. Antonelli stood with a pained expression in his big eyes while Vita, in his shirt sleeves, worked over Nicolo like a man aroused.

The monkey was in bed—not his own basket, but Uncle Vita's big white bed, exactly in the centre, propped up on pillows. He wore his best woolly vest and a soft Neapolitan cap with a woollen tassel. His little worried face, isolated on the vast expanse of bed, looked more worried than ever. From time to time his teeth chattered and he shivered violently, gazing at us anxiously, in turn. Uncle Vita, with some kind of pungent oil, was rubbing his chest. While he worked on the invalid, Vita talked all the time, to himself, to the monkey, but mostly, in a voice of recrimination, to Mr. Antonelli. I glanced at Angelo, who like myself was subdued by the grandeur of the spectacle and had ceased to cry. He translated, in a whisper: "Uncle Vita says it is a judgment upon us for forgetting the good God . . . a visitation upon Father for thinking too much of business, Mother of society, and Clara of men. He says he and Nicolo have laid the foundations of our fortune, working for pennies when we were without bread. He says if Nicolo dies . . . That was when he was crying. We will all never, never have any luck again."

Mrs. Antonelli hurried in with a bowl of steaming cloths, holding them subserviently by the bedside. Clara, drifting like a wraith to the doorway, watched with red eyes while Uncle Vita applied the cloths.

They seemed to do Nicolo little good. And suddenly Vita, the saintly, the humble, threw up his hands and came out with a torrent of words. Angelo hissed in my ear. "He says Nicolo must have a doctor, the best doctor in town. That Clara, the wicked and sinful Clara, must fetch him at once."

Clara began to protest.

"She says no doctor will come to a monkey. She will try to get a veterinarian."

I saw at once from the wildness in Vita's face that a veterinarian would not do. "Yes." Angelo gave me a nod. "It is to be nothing but a doctor. We must pay anything, all the gold we have. The best doctor in town."

Clara put on her hat, weeping, but submissive, and departed with a big handful of money from Mr. Antonelli. We all sat round in chairs, watching the monkey, waiting for the doctor; all but Vita, who, beads in hand, and lips moving, was kneeling by the bed.

In half an hour Clara returned, alone. Vita jumped up and, after an interrogation which again reduced Clara to tears, he gave a terrible cry, seized his hat and rushed out.

"Clara went to four doctors and none would come. Uncle Vita has gone himself."

For nearly an hour we waited in the sickroom, then started, every one of us, as the outer door opened. It was Uncle Vita—a sigh of relief went up as we heard someone accompanying him.

The doctor entered. He was Dr. Galbraith, an elderly dried-up man with a small goatee beard, a physician recognized as skilful in the town, but rather unpopular because of his abrupt manner. What subtle persuasions the deaf, unlettered Vita had brought to bear upon this choleric practitioner remained a mystery; and the wonder of it was, he had not come for money.

For a moment he looked as if he would order us all out of the room. But he abandoned the idea, and turned his attention to the monkey. He took Nicolo's temperature and pulse; felt him all over; looked down his throat; then, for a long time, using a short wooden stethoscope, listened to his chest. The monkey's behaviour was perfect, he kept his wide frightened eyes trustingly upon the doctor, even permitted his mouth to be opened without a spoon.

Tugging at his goatee, Dr. Galbraith stared at his patient with a queer interest and approval, completely forgetful of the roomful of people who, impressed by his thoroughness, hung upon his every movement—Angelo had whispered to me: "Uncle Vita thinks he is a wonderful doctor." Then, recollecting himself, the doctor wrote out two prescriptions, a dry twist to his lips as he inscribed them: *Mr. Nick Antonelli.* He packed up his little black bag. He then said: "The medicine every four hours. Keep him warm in bed, linseed poultices night and morning, nourishing liquid diet only. He's a nice specimen of the North African rhesus, macaque. Unfortunately, as a species, they are weak in the chest. This one has double pneumonia. Good night."

He went out. Though Uncle Vita followed him all the way down the street he would not accept a single penny of a fee. I then perceived his interest to be purely scientific: that strange, beautiful, and wholly disinterested emotion which had already stirred me as I sat at my microscope and which in later years was to afford me some of the rarest joys of my life. At this instant, moved by a kinship of race and ideas, I could not repress a thrill of pride in this taciturn Scots doctor. How perfect had been his behaviour amongst these excitable Southerners!

A sense of optimism succeeded his visit; there were instructions to be carried out. I was sent running to the chemist for the medicine; Mrs. Antonelli and Clara began to mix the poultices; Vita himself set a chicken to simmer, for broth. The monkey consented to swallow some milk. He seemed sleepy after his medicine. We tiptoed from the room.

Already versed, to my sorrow, in the dangers of lung disorders, I felt sure the implications of double pneumonia were not fully understood. And, indeed, next morning Nicolo was less well. Restless and burning with fever, he uttered plaintive cries, tossing about the big bed, at which Uncle Vita knelt. All day he barely touched his chicken broth and that evening his breathing was short and rough.

All that week he grew steadily worse and a distracted hush fell upon the household, broken only by sudden hysterics from the women and by wild determined outbursts from Uncle Vita. Cast off by Gavin, and still on holiday, I threw in my lot with the Antonellis. I became a sort of page boy to the stricken monkey. Every afternoon, at three o'clock, Grandpa called, very dignified and serious, on a visit of condolence. He waited in the front room, hoping, I think, for some sympathetic conversation with Clara and, if necessary, Mrs. Antonelli, perhaps a glass of Frascati wine to restore, to cheer the spirits. But the first faint breath of the mistral was in the air. It was Mr. Antonelli who, with a long face, accepted Grandpa's sonorous commiseration. And there was no Frascati wine.

Worse, still worse. Poor Nicolo could now scarcely breathe, all the flesh had fallen from his little bones. The doctor, again approached, flatly stated that the monkey was doomed. Mr. Antonelli spoke palely of closing the Saloon, of straw spread in the street outside.

On Saturday Uncle Vita looked Mr. Antonelli fiercely in the eye. Angelo translated: "He says only God can save Nicolo. Therefore we must pray, pray terribly for a miracle. Father must go to Canon Roche to have prayers and masses said for the monkey. The convent Sisters must make a novena, and come here, to the house, to pray for Nicolo. Oh, dear, Uncle Vita is saying most awful things to my father."

Mr. Antonelli clearly did not like the commission. But Vita now dominated the household; and the monkey had, in some queer way, become a superstition, a formidable symbol whose life or death represented the collapse or survival of the Antonelli fortunes. Mr. Antonelli took his hat and slowly went out.

The following morning, Sunday, Canon Roche announced from the Holy Angels pulpit that masses would be said for the intention of Mr. Vita Antonelli. A trifle disappointed that he did not mention

Nicolo by name, I was reassured that same afternoon by the arrival of Mother Elizabeth Josephina and another Sister from the convent.

The Antonellis were generous contributors to the convent funds and the two nuns were graciously anxious to do all in their power to help. We all knelt down in the front room and in a low voice, so as not to disturb the dying monkey, repeated the Thirty Days' Prayer, and the *Memorare*.

Next day, a wet and dismal Monday, Nicolo was at his last gasp—he had now been ill for exactly nine days. Uncle Vita would now allow no one in the sickroom but himself, he never for a moment left the monkey's side. But at nine o'clock that morning, shortly after I arrived, he emerged; and, in the front room where we were gathered, pointed his finger, like a madman, at Clara.

"Oh, dear Saint Joseph!" Angelo wailed. "He says Clara, who alone is responsible, must make the three hundred and sixty-five steps, now, immediately. It is our only hope!"

In the midst of the ensuing commotion, while they are reasoning futilely with Uncle Vita, let me offer an explanation. This good, this simple soul, product of sunny Italy, and survival of a mediæval age, who in the midst of the traffic of the busy High Street would suddenly stand stock still and gaze up, from beneath his flapping black hat, at the lovely heaven of Saints and Virgins, had invented for himself on this alien soil a most amazing devotion, I might even say a discipline. Upon the Castle Rock, a historic landmark which I have already mentioned, an old fortress guarding the estuary, with derelict cannon, defended in the past by Bruce and Wallace, and now a forgotten shrine, a public monument, there existed an outside winding, stair, leading steeply from the portcullis below to the ruined ramparts of the Castle above and consisting, to the curiosity of succeeding generations, of precisely three hundred and sixty-five steps, one for every day of the year. Uncle Vita's penance was this: pausing to repeat an *Ave* on each step, he ascended this stairway upon his knees.

Ten minutes later Clara and I set out in the rain for the Castle Rock. Clara, the proud, the wicked, was half fainting at the ordeal, the humiliation, in prospect. But Uncle Vita must be obeyed. It was too wet for Angelo to accompany her; I was sent as an escort, to act as "watcher" for the fair penitent. Should a guide or a party of sightseers appear I was at once to warn her so that she might rise quickly and, leaning upon the ramparts, assume a position of intelligent interest in the scenery.

However, the Castle was deserted, cleared by the rain, not an onlooker in sight. We decided that I too should make the devotion. Side by side, saying our "Hail Marys," swooped upon by inquisitive gulls, we ascended, like crabs, under the dripping skies. Clara, despite her distress, had thoughtfully brought with her a soft cushion, also a small umbrella. But I, without such foresight or protection, soon found myself soaked, my bare knees completely worn out, as up, up we went, fervently, painfully, beneath the swooping gulls, the drenching clouds, the startled shades of Wallace and Bruce, the omnipotent God.

At last, it was over; we reached the top. I could barely stand ... or see. Clara in the final throes had, accidentally but cruelly, poked her umbrella in my eye. Still we had done it, we had made the three hundred and sixty-five steps. We returned, conscious of our worth, to the Saloon.

From her martyred air I sensed that Clara was prepared for some bare acknowledgment of her efforts. But not for the scintillation of joy, of praise, which burst upon her at the threshold. The door swung open, the whole family flung themselves upon her. What gratitude! What rejoicings! During our absence the monkey had passed the crisis of his illness. Later, I was to observe and marvel at the amazing transformation which accompanies the resolution of a pneumonic infection. Abrupt and magical ... No, wonder Uncle Vita cried aloud, with shining eyes, that the good God had intervened on little Nicolo's behalf. At twenty past eleven, a moment which was calculated to coincide with the consummation of our reparation, but which, I subsequently decided, approximated more nearly to the instant when the spoke of Clara's umbrella entered my eye, Nicolo had suddenly ceased to suffocate. A mild benignant sweat had broken on him; he had smiled feebly at his patron; then, breathing quietly, had fallen into a deep sleep.

The monkey's recovery was rapid—there arises a memory of Uncle Vita's face, wreathed in smiles, as he announced: "Nicolo has just eaten his first banana." Vita had returned, already, to his usual position of humility, the equilibrium of the household was swiftly being restored. Clara had several new dresses of a violent hue. The good Sisters received a handsome donation, Canon Roche a contribution to the new side-altar fund. The doctor was presented, at dead of night, with three cases of the best preserved apricots; his housekeeper had acknowledged to Mrs. Antonelli that he was strongly addicted to this fruit; it was judged, too, that he would refuse a more conventional gift.

Only towards me, towards the unimportant yet worthy Robert Shannon, was there a strange and incomprehensible coldness, at least a nullity, a vacuum of regard. Had I not, on my bare bended knees, helped to achieve at least half the miracle? Did I not scour the Drumbuck woods for tender green caterpillars, to which the pampered convalescent was passionately addicted? Yet not a word, not a token of gratitude. Instead, queer looks, conversations between Clara, Mrs. Antonelli, and Clara's young man, significantly interrupted when I came up from the Saloon with Angelo. The mistral was blowing colder than before. I was about to learn, early, one of the bitter truths of life.

Several days later, as Angelo and I took the almost fully restored Nicolo round the courtyard for an outing, I received a push which sent me spinning to the wall.

"Get away from that monkey, you." It was Thaddeus, the young man of Clara, scowling at me vengefully. "We don't want you or your kind around here. Get away. Go."

Paralyzed with dismay, I could not even answer him back. But my blood rose slowly nevertheless. I refused to leave. I waited until I had Angelo to myself in the sunny yard.

"Angelo," I said, with quiet intensity. "Something is the matter. What have I done wrong? Tell me, Angelo?"

He would not meet my gaze. Then suddenly he raised his head. His peachy face had turned yellow, the colour of a duck's foot. There was a waspish look in his soulful eyes.

"We don't like you any more," he cried shrilly. "Mother says I mustn't play with you. She says your grandpa is a drunken person who sponges for wine, who has no money, not a lira, who lies about the grand houses he was never inside, who is, in fact, practically the biggest liar in the world..."

I stared at him, dumbfounded. Was this the child whom I had stood beside at my First Communion, the lovely babe whom I had cherished and indulged, for whom, even, in my loyalty I had sacrificed the friendship of Gavin, dear Gavin, the good, the true?

"Yes," he shrilled. "Thad found out everything. Your grandpa is a cheat, a pauper, a tramp. He is known all over Levenford. He chases ladies, at his age! And worst of all he puts his arm round our sweet Clara to annoy Thaddeus from bad and wicked motives..."

I could stand it no longer. I saw, dumbly, that all was finished between Angelo and me. I turned away. But before I did so I punched him with all my force, on his angelic little nose. A mortal sin, perhaps, to damage such an angel. But the recollection of his howl as he ran towards his mother lived joyously in my memory through many bitter weeks. I can hear it still.

Chapter Fifteen

The week of Murdoch's tests has come and that faithful student of seed catalogues stands in the lobby in his best boots and Sunday clothes being brushed all over by Mama, who plumps down on her knees to get at a spot on the back of his trouser cuff, the brush fairly flying in her work-reddened hand, an intent and proud expression on her worn face. Mama, who slaves herself to the bone for us, cooks and mends, scours, polishes and scrubs, makes every penny do the work of three, rises first and goes to bed last, and all for no apparent recompense; Mama who bears up superhumanly under Papa's increasing economies, who finds time to display the soft corner in her heart for the old man upstairs, and for a wretched boy thrown upon her hands .... But this is Murdoch's week: no time for panegyrics. Now that the fateful days are upon him he is pleasingly confident. He has emerged unscathed from a serious talk with his father the night before. He says to us all: "I can do no more." Yes, surely these eternal fingerings have massaged enough learning beneath that dandruffed scalp. He has his lunch money in his pocket, two pairs of spectacles, in case of breakages, his pen, rubber, set squares, in fine, everything. He sets off ponderously to catch the 9.20 a.m. train for Winton, where the Civil Service tests are held. Mama and I, standing at the door, wave to him and in our hearts we wish him well. ...

Every evening, Murdoch came back on the four o'clock local and his father, home early from the office, was already waiting in suspense.

"How did you get on?"

"Wonderful, Father, really wonderful."

As the days progressed Murdoch's confidence increased. Munching an enormous tea stolidly, while we all hung upon his words, he would throw off calm little comments on his day.

"Really, I was surprised ... found this morning's paper so confoundedly easy. I wrote reams ... had to ask for a second exercise book. Some of the other fellows didn't half fill theirs ..."

"Well done ... well done." His father voiced the rare praise grudgingly, but with a gleaming eye.

Mama, without quailing, bent forward and gave Murdoch as large a helping of potted head as his father. I knew, we all knew, that his success was assured. While this pleased me it also made me sad; I could not help contrasting how miserably I should have done in like circumstances. And I had other reasons for my dejection. The Antonelli debacle, fruit of false friendship and ingratitude, still preyed upon my mind; I had not dared mention it to Grandpa. But worst of all, I had not seen Gavin for a fortnight; once only had we met, passing each other, pale to the lips, eyes straight ahead, in the High Street. I longed for this boy whom I had betrayed, longed for him with all my heart.

One faint gleam alone illuminated the horizon. Next Wednesday was the occasion of the Ardfillan Fair, when I was to accompany Kate and Jamie to the "Shows." Grandpa had, in the past, been a regular patron of the Shows and he described their delights to me in glowing phrases. When I remarked, wistfully, that I thought I might enjoy myself, he replied, emphatically: "We shall, boy. We shall."

Jamie had promised to call for us at two o'clock, in a wagonette. He arrived punctually, but in a different vehicle. Kate and I, waiting at the parlour window, gasped our amazement as a yellow motor car chugged up.

"If your brother Adam can do it, so can I." Jamie, less saturnine than usual, under a new checked cap, gave us his explanation on the spot. He was friendly with Sam Lightbody, a mechanic at the Argyll works. Sam had borrowed a car and would drive us to Ardfillan.

We shook hands with Sam, who remained, goggled, on the driver's seat, holding, somewhat tensely, two vertical levers with handles, as though keeping the machine pulsating with his own life-blood. At his suggestion Kate ran in to get a veil to keep her hat in place. Then, as we circled admiringly, before taking our places, there strolled through the gate, brushed, trimmed, and with his best stick: Grandpa.

"Remarkable ... remarkable," he said, eyeing the car; then to Jamie, sternly: "You don't imagine I'm going to let you take my granddaughter to Ardfillan ... till all hours ... with no one to chaperone her but a mere child."

"Oh, Grandpa," Kate said pettishly. "You're not invited."

But Jamie had broken into a rough laugh. He *knew* Grandpa; I had several times seen them emerging together from the Drumbuck Arms, wiping their mouths with the back of their hands. "Let him come," he said. "The more the merrier. Hop in."

The machine, after a few preliminary shudders, jolted into action, then began to glide in delightful style down the Drumbuck Road. Kate and Jamie sat high beside the driver in front, Kate's feather boa floating gracefully in the breeze; Grandpa and I luxuriated in the large tonneau behind. We had barely started when a hand, Jamie's, slipped backwards bearing a large cigar. Grandpa accepted, lighted it and, placing one leg on his cushion, reclined regally. "This is delightful, Robert." He spoke in his well-bred voice. "I hope he drives through the town. It'll give the bodies a chance to see us."

We were, in fact, sliding under the railway bridge on our way to the High Street. Suddenly a wild shout caused me to sit up. I saw Murdoch, standing at the station exit, waving his arms for us to stop. As we swept past he took off his bowler hat and began to pound heavily after us, still waving one arm.

"Oh, stop, Sam, stop," I cried. "There's our Murdoch!"

The machine drew up with another terrible jerk and, when stationary, began to bounce us all up and down like peas on a drum. Sam, while bouncing, turned with a pained expression: I divined that he felt this excessive stopping and starting to be no part of the duty of a normal automobile. But here was Murdoch, puffing and blowing, in his thick good clothes. He climbed in at the back and collapsing in the tonneau exclaimed: "I'm coming with you."

A pause. Was there to be no end to our self-invited guests? Grandpa, in particular, looked hurt at the intrusion, but Sam solved the difficulty by pushing in a lever and throwing us all forward in a series of short convulsions. Soon we were bowling through the town.

"How did you get on, Murdoch?" I shouted above the wind which flowed deliciously past our ears.

"Wonderful," said Murdoch. "Simply wonderful." Still blown, he crouched in his seat with his mouth partly open, his coat huddled about his ears, which stuck out more than ever. He looked pale; I thought he had run too hard. He was fanning himself, somewhat unnecessarily, with his hat. He opened his mouth wider as if to speak, then half closed it again.

Conversation was now impossible. We were out of the town and coasting down the Lea Brae. Before us, reaching out to the sea, lay the wide estuary, all sequined by the high sun; along the shore, through flat green pastures and sandy dunes, wound a white ribbon—the road we must traverse; to the west, above the blue mist, a bluer outline, watchful, ever present, the Ben. Such loveliness, such still and shimmering delight! Why could I not view it without a pang of sadness stealing round my heart? Ah, wretched boy, to whom beauty must always bring this distant, lingering pain. I sighed and surrendered myself to the sad, sweet rapture of our flight.

The car was functioning to perfection: on the down grades we approached a rapidity of twenty miles an hour. As we swept through the villages the inhabitants ran to their doors to stare after us. Men working in the fields straightened themselves, and brandished their hoes at the novelty. Only the livestock of the district seemed to regard us with resentment. It took all Sam's skill to circumvent a stubborn cow; barking dogs furiously escorted us; hens flew protestingly from beneath our wheels; once there were feathers, but the clouds of white dust rising behind mercifully left the massacre in doubt. A solitary humiliation to be recorded: the brave heart of our machine faltered on the crest of an incline; some country ruffians bound for the Shows walked alongside; ignorant laughter—"Yah! Get out and push!" ...

We sailed into Ardfillan at four o'clock, an hour too early for the delights of the Shows, which did not properly begin until evening. While Kate went across the street to make some purchases for Mama in a special millinery shop of this pleasant seaside resort, Sam stilled his engine, and we gazed at the galaxy of booths, tents, and roundabouts, arranged on a square of green beside the Esplanade, with the beach and plashing waves beyond.

Suddenly, crouched pale and hapless, Murdoch gave a great heave. It shook the structure of our vehicle; I thought we were starting again. But, no, the explosion came from Murdoch's soul.

"I'll commit suicide."

The threat was uttered by Murdoch in such a loud tone, almost a shout, that it instantly drew upon him our united attention. He continued, beating the cushions with his fists, his eyes bulging: "I tell you I'll commit suicide. I wanted no post in no Post Office. It's all Papa's fault. I'll kill myself. And he'll be to blame. A murderer."

"In the name of God, man!" Grandpa sat up. "What's wrong wi'ye?"

Murdoch stared at him, at all of us, with those obtuse, near-sighted eyes. Suddenly he broke down and began to blubber. "I'm plunked. Sent home by the examiners. They took me aside this morning and told me not to come back. Just told me not to come back. Not to come back. It must be a mistake. I've done wonderful, wonderful."

Failed; Murdoch failed! Silence of consternation. His bulky sobs were now shaking us all. A crowd gave evidence of forming.

"Here!" Grandpa took him by the coat collar. "Pull yourself together."

"He needs a stiff'ner." The sombre advice came from Sam.

"By God you're right. He needs something to make a man of him." Grandpa and Jamie got the helpless Murdoch out of the car while Sam held open the swing door of the Esplanade Vaults, immediately opposite. As they disappeared into the cool interior, Jamie called over his shoulder: "Hang about, boy. We'll not be long."

I stood for a while, thinking: "Poor Murdoch!" then I strolled disconsolately across the road. The fair ground was now beginning to fill up as people flocked in from the surrounding countryside. I recognized several Levenford faces. Suddenly I caught sight of a figure—small, sunburned, and resolute. It was Gavin.

He was alone, on the outskirts of a small gathering, watching, with his own particular disdain, the efforts of a cheap-jack to sell genuine gold watches to some awestruck farm hands. Then he turned and across the heads of the meaningless crowd our glances met. He reddened deeply, then went white, yet though he transferred his gaze, he did not move away. Indeed, presently he took a few steps in my direction and began, apart from everyone, to study, with concentrated immobility, a billhead advertising Willmot's Steam Bostons.

I felt the attraction of that billhead also. Though it was crudely printed and contained no information that I did not know by heart, I was soon staring at it too, standing beside Gavin, very pale, my cheek beginning to twitch—a horrible peculiarity which always affected me when I got nervous and overstrung. Impossible to say which of us spoke first. We were breathing with difficulty, our eyes remained riveted on that torn poster with its blurred representation of a swing boat standing on its head.

"It was all my fault."

"No, it was mine."

"No, mine."

"No, Robie, really it was mine. I was jealous that you had another friend. I don't want you to have a single friend in the world but me."

"You are my only friend, Gavin. And you always will be. I swear it. And I swear I was to blame. All my silly fault."

"No, mine."

"Mine."

He let me have the last word, a sublime sacrifice, since I know I am the weaker of the two. The poster had lost its attraction. We dared to look at each other. I read in his eyes that he had been as desolate as I. This moment of reunion, so poignantly desired, broke down the barriers of our restraint, evoked from us a demonstration greater even than our crushing handclasp. I took his arm in mine closely, closely, and thus linked, smiling blindly, and beyond speech, we moved off, merged with and lost ourselves in the multitude.

The brass of the roundabouts began to play, the steam whistles of the Bostons shrilly tooted. Cymbals clashed for the Animated Cakewalk; a fanfare for Cleo, the Fattest Woman upon Earth. Loud-talking gentlemen in high collars and bow ties began to swing little canes on the platforms outside the tents: "Walk up, Ladies and Gentlemen. Walk up for Leo the Leopard Man! Walk up for the Peruvian Pigmies! The one and only Talking Horse! Walk up! Walk up!" The Shows had come to life for us. We pushed our way giddily forward. Jamie had given me a florin for spending money. Gavin was equally well supplied. He had come by train from Levenford; but now he could return with me. We need not be separated. The thought gave us added joy.

We tried the coconut shies and soon had three fine milky nuts apiece; Gavin bored one with his penknife and in turn we let the clear sweet juice trickle down our throats. We visited the molly-dolly stalls, the lab-in-the-tub, the shooting gallery. We were decked with trophies, with pins, buttons, spangles and feather favours. Darkness fell and the naphtha lamps flared out. The crowd increased, the music brayed and quickened. Whoop! Whoop! Whooop! went the Bostons. Once I caught sight of Kate and Jamie, close together, laughing, as they braved the Animated Cakewalk. And again there was a vision of Grandpa, Sam, and Murdoch, bestriding three wooden chargers, whirling giddily abreast, plunging and rearing under the lights, to the bombilation of the band. Murdoch had his bowler hat askew, a cigar braced between his teeth, a glassy jubilation in his eye. He rose in his stirrups from time to time, and yelled inhumanly.

It grows late, very late. And at last, worn out but happy, we are all gathered at the car. Kate especially seems happy, she glances frequently at Jamie and there is a bright tenderness in her eyes. Murdoch glares owlishly at Gavin, declares: "I don't care, I tell you, I simply don't care, the whole thing is a matter of complete indifference to a man of my intelligence." Then shakes him warmly by the hand. While Sam, the indispensable Sam, is beneath the bonnet, starting the car, Murdoch and Grandpa stand by with a melodious duet. "Genevieve ... Gen ... e ... vieve." Halfway through, Murdoch departs hastily to the outer darkness, whence I hear sounds of prolonged and dreadful nausea.

Now we are on our way home, moving through the cool night air away from the glare, the pandemonium. In the tonneau behind, Grandpa is asleep with Murdoch lolling pallidly upon his shoulder. On the other cushion Kate and Jamie sit close together. His arm is round her waist and they are looking at the new moon.

In front I am with Gavin. Our friendship is restored, we will never again be separated. ... At least, not until ...

But we do not know of that, thank God. We are happy, confident. There is no sound but the steady beat of our engine, the brave hiss of our acetylene lamps. Sam, our impenetrable driver, is silent and apart. On, on, into the night. Two boys conquering the darkness, the unknown, together, under the unconquerable stars.

"*This* is what I like," Gavin whispers.

I know exactly what he means.

Chapter Sixteen

Grandpa's philosophy, based no doubt on sad experience, was that we must pay for all our pleasures: he would warn me when I was unduly elated: "Man, ye'll suffer for this the morn." After our expedition to the Fair we suffered dreadfully upon the morn. A fateful calm hung upon the house when, later than usual, I got up. Murdoch still lay abed, Papa had gone to work, Mama was working in the scullery. Grandpa, smoking irritably, his nose redder than usual, seemed not to want me. Then, as I came downstairs, the front door opened and Grandma entered. She had returned, unknown to me, on the previous afternoon; and already, in her good bonnet and beaded cape, had been out to the Boilerworks office to draw her pension.

"Oh, Grandma," I cried. "I didn't know you were back."

She gave no answer to my pleased and excited greeting, but advanced with a strange, strained expression on her face. Opposite me, she paused, and under the dark concern of her eyes a sense of uneasiness, of anxiety descended upon me.

"Robert, Robert," she said in a quiet yet unnatural voice, "I wouldn't have believed it of you."

I shrank against the wall. I saw that she had learned, no doubt from Miss Minns, of my apostasy from all her fervent hours. Vaguely, I had been prepared for her discomfiture. But this bitter grief, that greenish look spread across her cheeks, the distracted drawing back of her lips from her teeth, startled and frightened me.

"One of these days you may be glad enough to turn to your grandma again." She said no more than that, but her tone, both pained and sad, made me tremble. Open-mouthed, I watched her continue on her way upstairs. Having knocked on his door, she firmly entered Grandpa's room.

I ran into the parlour. Why did this religion, into which I had been born, raise in Grandma such dark and savage gall? The answer defeated me. Worthy and exemplary woman, she had spoken to perhaps three members of that faith in all her life, her ignorance and misconceptions regarding it were quite ludicrous. Yet it remained her abomination. She would not lightly forgive Grandpa his connivance at my First Communion.

Indeed, at that moment, I heard voices loudly raised above me and presently, while my knees still shook, there came the sound of Grandpa's footsteps in the lobby. I peeped out—he was putting on his hat with a hasty and uneasy air.

"Come along, boy," he said to me abruptly. "It's time you and I removed ourselves."

Outside, I could see that he was troubled. No doubt she had charged him heavily with my defection, but there was stronger cause for anxiety than that. Sitting up late, at her bedroom window, Grandma had plainly observed Murdoch's "condition" on the night before, and had felt it her duty to tell Papa at breakfast.

Now Grandpa made it a practice to keep out of Papa's way, at all times, for he knew that his son-in-law detested him. Only on one occasion, in my recollection, were they together for any length of time—when Papa, in a fit of magnanimity, skilfully fostered by Mama, showed Grandpa and me over the new Levenford sewage farm—and then the event had terminated disastrously. Papa, full of pride, had talked us round the various oxidization and filtration beds, explaining with hygienic ardour that, irrespective of its beginning, the end product of the system was pure drinking water. He filled a glass and offered it to me.

"Try it and see."

I hesitated over the cloudy fluid.

"I'm afraid I'm not thirsty," I stammered.

Papa then offered the glass to Grandpa, whose well-known smile had flickered all the afternoon.

"I never was addicted to water." Grandpa spoke mildly. "And that beverage appeals to me still less."

"Don't you believe me?" Papa cried.

"I will," Grandpa smiled, "if you drink it yourself."

Papa flung down the glass and walked away.

Ordinarily, the two men rarely met; their paths did not intersect; and if Grandpa saw the Inspector in the town he would at once make a strategic detour. But now a collision was imminent. Viewed in the cold light of morning, though it had seemed fitting at the time, Murdoch's escapade took on a more sinister complexion. Papa was violently teetotal: "drink" was anathema to him—and such a wicked waste of money! Enraged by Murdoch's failure, there was no knowing to what lengths he might go to punish the reprobate who had led his son astray.

When we were well clear of the house, Grandpa slowed his rapid strides and turned to me, rather loftily. "Fortunately we have our own resources, Robie. And friends who'll give us a bite if we ask them. We'll go and call on the Antonellis."

I stopped in great embarrassment. "Oh, no, Grandpa, we can't do that."

"And why not?"

"Because . . ." I paused. Yet I had to tell him. I could not bear that he should suffer the ignominy of a door slammed in his face.

He said nothing, not a word—for all his perorations, he had, at least, the gift of suffering an injury in silence. But this was a sad blow; his face turned a queer mottled colour. I thought he might go back to Drumbuck to foregather with the Saddler and Peter Dickie. But no, he continued down the High Street and over Knoxhill, marching me into unfamiliar territory on the south side of the town.

"Where are we going, Grandpa?"

"To wash in the waters of bitterness," he answered shortly.

Whether he meant what he said, whether the salt breezes of Ardfillan had awakened in him a desire for the beaches, or whether simply he wished to put the greatest distance possible between himself and all that was distressing him, I do not know. But presently we came out through the end of the Knoxhill green and found ourselves on the shore of the estuary just below the harbour. This was no idyllic strand, but a reach of drab, ribbed silt, broken by tufts of green seaweed and flat rocks, greyly crusted with young limpets. The tide was out, such water as we saw was leaden grey; the tall chimneys of the Boilerworks, still visible, the rattle of hammers from the Shipyard, the rushing of an effluent conduit from a laundry—these raw reminders of industry increased, rather than diminished, the desolations of the scene.

Yet there was a tang in the breeze, a brackish tang. And immediately around us was that solitude which Grandpa craved. He sat down, took off his boots and socks, rolled up his trousers to the knee and, having splashed across the damp sand, began to paddle in the shallows. I watched, while the grey wavelets caressed his bony ankles; then I peeled off my own shoes and stockings, followed the wet imprints of his feet, and waded in beside him.

Presently he removed his hat: that marvellous hat which I identify, inseparably, with Grandpa—large, square, and faded, ventilated by three metal-edged holes punched on either side, hardened by age to an iron indestructibility; that hat which had contained so many rarities, from Grandpa's head to a pound of pilfered raspberries, which had served, and was still to serve, so many diverse purposes, and into which now, stooping, he began to place cockles and mussels retrieved from this sad seashore . . .

The cockles were pure white and fluted, only a wavering spot the size of a sixpence revealed their presence beneath the flooding sand. The mussels, of a purple nacreous sheen, grew toughly in bunches in the fissures of the rocks. When we had gathered an assorted hatful, Grandpa straightened himself. "Boy," he remarked—though addressing the melancholy waters—"I may be bad . . . but not *that* bad."

On the dry part of the beach, covered with wrack and driftwood, with staved-in coops and a bunk straw mattress cast off from a ship, we made a crackling fire. While he roasted the mussels Grandpa showed me how to eat the cockles. You held the cockle over the flame until it opened, then quickly gulped the saline contents down.

He judged them delicious, far better than oysters, he said, and he swallowed a great many, sadly, as though their salt astringency suited his present mood. I could not care for them, but I found the mussels exactly to my taste. The shells opened wide, wide, exposing upon pearly plates the frizzled contents, tough as meat, and nut-sweet.

"No dishes to wash," Grandpa commented with a grim smile when we had done. He lit his pipe and lay on his elbow, letting his eyes roam across the scene, still indulging his reverie; he added, to himself, as though the salt fare had given him a thirst: "I could do with a dram."

Here, in the light of what ensues, I must try to establish an important aspect of Grandpa's character. He had a fondness, a weakness, for "the drink"; there were evenings when I heard his uneven footsteps on the stairs, accompanied by fumblings, and the jovial exclamations of a man undisturbed by colliding with objects in the dark; but he was not a drunkard. To dismiss him, in Adam's curt phrase, as "an old soak" was to do the man a grave injustice—he had gone on wild sprees, yet there were long sober spells between, and he never took part in Levenford's Saturday night saturnalia, which thronged the streets with reeling figures. All his life he had wanted to do brave and wonderful things—with an intensity which in his later days made him believe he had actually done them—yet in reality his career had been humdrum. His forebears had at one time been extremely well off—in partnership with two uncles, his father had once owned the well-known distillery of Glen Nevis. In a family album I had come across the yellowish photograph of a youth standing with a gun and two setter dogs on the steps of an imposing country mansion. Imagine my stupefaction when Mama told me it was Grandpa, outside his boyhood home—she had added with a faint smile and a sigh, "The Gows were gey important folks in their day, Robie." It was the malt tax which had destroyed the family fortune; and I now know that as a young man, after the "smash," Grandpa had been forced to begin, in the humble Levenford manner, as an apprentice engineer. Yet he had not "learned his trade." He was too impatient, and an enforced marriage, which he never bemoaned, with a simple girl of the people who idolized him, sent him into the hardware business. When he failed here, in high-spirited fashion, he was in turn clerk, farm hand, cabinetmaker, Scots draper, purser on a Clyde steamboat; until finally, through his Glen Nevis connections, he became, like the poet he so greatly admired, an exciseman in the Bonded Service.

Disappointment with himself and a talent for friendship, together with the fact that he "worked amongst the stuff," made him a drinker; yet he was never a graceless one; his craving was spasmodic, rather than inveterate, and sprang from the peculiarities of his temperament, that strange entanglement of opposites, which would cause him one minute to defend my innocence like a lion and the next—but we shall hear of that much later.

At present, in his dejection, there was reason to believe that his craving was coming to the surface, evoked by a bitter sense of his betrayal by Grandma.

"*A certain person*," he declared suddenly, "has been at my throat from the moment she put foot inside the house. I owe her something for all she's done to me. 'Leading Murdoch to ruin'!" He broke off to point moodily with the moist stem of his pipe. "There's the *Lord of the Isles* coming . . . on her 'Round the Kyles' trip . . . She's a braw boat."

We watched while the crowded pleasure steamer raced down the river with flashing paddles and flying bunting, her two red funnels at a jaunty angle, trailing a plume of smoke, the soft sweet music of the "German band" aboard her drifting towards us and still lingering sadly as the rush of waves came in. Poor beachcombers, downcast and penniless, how we longed to be aboard her!

"At first," Grandpa resumed, bitterly, "when I came to live at Lomond View, after the death of my wife, she pretended to be friendly with me. She mended my socks and laid out my slippers by the fire. Then she asked me to give up smoking—she objected to the smell of it. When I refused, that started it. She's worked against me ever since.

"Of course she has the best end of it. She's independent. She goes downstairs to her meals. She gets the Levenford *Herald* before me. She has the hot water on Saturday night and first use of the bathroom in the morning. I tell you, boy, it's enough to turn milk sour."

Other ships went past: some laden scows, a rusty coastal tramp, the river ferry plying on a chain cable between the harbour and Sandbank, the crack white-funnelled Inveraray steamer, the *Queen Alexandra*. Then came a liner, immeasurably huge, a "beef boat" built by Marshall Brothers for the Argentine trade. She passed slowly, impenetrably, behind a noisy tug, a pilot, Grandpa said, upon her bridge, and I followed her with watering eyes until she was only a dark smudge on the far rim of the widening estuary, behind which the sun was now setting, in purple smoke.

Grandpa meditated darkly. There was nothing like a Marshall boat, the Clyde was the noblest river in the world, Robert Burns the greatest poet ... one Scot could beat three Englishmen ... even with a hand tied behind his back ... but it was hard for any man to get the better of a woman. A longer silence. Suddenly Grandpa sat up and with sombre decision slapped his thigh hard with his hand.

"By God! I'll do it."

Startled, my mind still filled with gentle meditations, with slow and stately images of departure, I turned to Grandpa, whose thoughts I had imagined to be similarly attuned. He was no longer brooding and dejected. A grim determination illuminated all his features, radiated even from his nose. He stood up.

"Come on, boy," he repeated, several times, under his breath, as with a kind of awe at his own invention. "By God, what a bawr!"

While he hurried me back through the town, pausing to check the time on the church steeple, I must impose another explanation. The word "bawr," in the local patois—which, for reasons of intelligibility, I have used sparingly—is expressive, in essence, of a peculiar act of vengeance, a vengeance flavoured with devilish humour. Dismiss from your minds anything so paltry as a practical joke. True, the bawr brings satisfaction to its perpetrator and confusion to its victim. But there the faint resemblance ends. The bawr is dire, traditional, the just explosion of a hatred. Where, in Corsica, in like circumstances, they take to the maquis with a gun, in Levenford they sit on solitary beaches, devise, then execute, a bawr.

"Where are you going, Grandpa?"

"First I am going to call on these fine Antonellis." He tempered the shock by adding, in an indescribable tone, "By the back door."

I remained, in fear, at the corner of the alley while he went round to the Antonelli back yard. He was absent only for a few minutes, yet I could not repress my relief when he reappeared, apparently unscathed, even grimly smiling. We set off into the gathering dusk and Grandpa took the unfrequented "Common way."

From time to time I threw him inquiring side glances, conscious that he moved with a singular rigidity: the strange mobile immobility of those porters who carry a high tower of innumerable baskets upon their heads. Then, as by an act of levitation, I saw his hat lift, revolve, and settle back calmly upon his brow. Still, I did not guess. It was only when a thin tail curled from beneath the brim, and mingled with Grandpa's locks in the manner of a queue, that I realized he had Nicolo inside his hat.

I was too surprised to speak: but Grandpa sensed that I had spotted the monkey. He squinted at me carefully. "He aye liked my hat. No trouble in the world to get him into it."

It was almost dark when, shortly before eight, we reached Lomond View. Then, I realized the full finesse of Grandpa's timing: on Thursday nights at half past seven o'clock it was Papa's custom to attend a meeting of the Building Society. We reached Grandpa's room unseen.

Nicolo was in rude health. He knew us perfectly—a fortunate circumstance, since strange faces always disturbed him. At the same time, the novelty of his new surroundings appeared not displeasing to him. He moved about the room, inspecting things with an air of agreeable surprise. I think he had just been fed, which accounted perhaps for his good humour. He refused the oddfellow which Grandpa offered him.

Grandpa contemplated the monkey dispassionately. He was

reserved, rather on his dignity with animals; he never descended to intimacies; indeed, while he professed great affection for the Mikado in Mrs. Bosomley's presence, I had seen him take a distasteful kick at the cat when we met it, in the dark, alone.

Nine o'clock ... A sound upon the landing indicated the passage of Grandma to the bathroom. Grandpa, waiting, darkly upon the alert, acted at once. With an agility remarkable in a man of his years he took up Nicolo and vanished through the doorway. A few seconds; then he was back—without the monkey.

I turned white. I saw at last the full import of his bawr. Yet, even as I trembled, I was conscious of an awful feeling of expectancy. I sat with Grandpa, who was biting his nails, listening tensely while Grandma heavily recrossed the landing. We heard her re-enter her room, the measured sounds of her disrobing, the groan of her bed as it received her. Silence, terrible silence. Then the air is rent: a scream ... another ... and another.

At this point Grandma herself must relate what happened, and in her own broad Scots—which hitherto, in the interests of lucidity, I have translated—for without this idiom, the recitation loses half its savour. Grandma told this story repeatedly in after years, mostly to her friend Miss Tibbie Minns, and always with a dreadful seriousness. No wonder I have always thought of it as "Grandma's Encounter with the Devil."

This is how it goes:

Weel, Tibbie, on the awfu' nicht when the Thing cam' till me I was in waur nor ordinar' health and speerits. I had ta'en off my cla'es, foldit them decent-like on the rocker and put on my mutch and gownie. I had read my chapter like a Christian, ta'en oot my teeth and lichtit my dip—ye ken I aye keep a wee bit can'le by my in the nicht. Then as I put my heid down on the pillay and composed mysel' tae rest, as I aye do, in the airms o' my Saviour, I felt the Thing loup on till my cheist. I opened my e'en. And there, as I hope to be judged, gazing at me by the flickerin' dip, was the Fiend hissel'.

Na, na, it was nae dream, Tibbie, far from it. I wasna sleepin'.

And forbye I'm no' a fanciful wumman. There he was, Satan, tail an' a', grinnin' and yammerin' and gnashin' his tusks at me like he wad gie a' he had tae drag me to the Pit. I'm not easy daunted, Tibbie, ye'll maybe agree, but for aince my banes turned tae watter, as weel they micht. I hadna the breath tae scream, let alane murmur the Lord's Prayer. I just lay like a corp, starin' at the Brute, while he stared back at me.

A' at yince, he ga'ed a kind o' skirl and began to jounce up and down on my cheist like I was a pouny. I tell ye, Tibbie, if I hadna breath before I had less then. He grippit my lugs in his twa paws and began to joggle my heid like it was a milk kirn. He jounced and waggled and waggled and jounced till I hadna breath in me. And a' the time the sparks was fleein' frae his e'en like cinders. I was feared, Tibbie wumman, my skin was in a grue. And weel the Brute kenned it for he banged and yammered and scarted his will at me till he had a' my hair doun and, though it's no' decent to sae, the gownie haulf off my back.

Oh, if I had juist had the presence o' mind to gi'e him the Name, but my puir wits were fair scattered. A' I could do was to whisper, in a voice ye couldna hear below a meal barrel: "Go, Satan, go!"

Feeble though it was, I think maybe it held the Brute. At ony rate he stoppit his pummelin' and wi' a kind o' girn, he took a haud o' my teeth, at the heid o' the bed, where I aye keep them, beside me. Then, as I hope to meet my Maker, he stood up on the bed and began makin' passes wi' the teeth, mopin' and mowin' at me, like he was puttin' them in and oot his mouth.

I tell ye Tibbie, it was maybe that whit saved me. When I saw the Thing abusin' my guid double set my bluid rose up in me at sic a desecration, I stirred from my dwam, sat up and shook my fist at him. "Ye Brute, ye Brute," I shouted. "God send ye back below."

Nae sooner did the name o' the Almighty strike him, for it couldna' ha' been my mere human fist what hindered him, than he gien a shriek that wad have turned ye tae stane. He louped frae the bed, still skirlin' and screechin'. As luck wad have it I had left my door on the keek, for the nicht was warm and I wanted a breath o' air. Oot the room he went, like a streak o' infernal licht while I lay shakin' in a' my limbs, thankin' Providence for my merciful release. I couldna stir for mony a meenute. But when I did and lichtit the gas and was praisin' Heaven that I had suffered nae ill, I saw, the Lord save and defend me, I saw, God help me tae endure it, I saw, I tell ye, what the Brute had done.

He hadna stole my dentures, na, na, nor smashed them neithers. But oot o' black burning malice and revenge, he had droppit them ablow the bed intil my nicht utensil.

Chapter Seventeen

On the following Tuesday, the summer recess ended: Kate resumed her teaching at the "Elementary" and I went back to the Academy. I remember the day vividly—it marked the climax of that mood of profound dejection which enveloped Grandpa like a cloud, one of those moods which I inherited from him and which afflicted me when I grew older, a mood when life seemed dark and worthless.

The weather continued enervating; Grandma remained closeted in her room; Murdoch kept out of the way—he had begun, secretly, to work for Mr. Dalrymple at the Nursery.

Grandpa evinced no desire for his friends; there was no copying to be done; nothing but to endure the heat and Papa's resentment. The old man was being nagged and persecuted. Only a small mind could have devised the expedient of stopping his tobacco. It was this, I think, which prompted Grandpa's final remark, as he fingered, mournfully, an empty pipe. "What's the use of it all, boy . . . what's the use?"

The next morning, as I dressed behind my curtain, Papa was still grumbling at breakfast, railing against the old man, when Mama came down, and in a voice which was both astonished and distraught, exclaimed: "Grandpa is not upstairs. Where can he have gone?"

A pause while Papa's surprise turned to indignation.

"This is the last straw. Have him here at the dinner hour or I'll know the reason!"

Disturbed, but not yet alarmed, I walked with Gavin to the Academy, where we found that we were not only in the same class, but sitting next to each other. This, and the issue of new books which I brought back carefully for Mama to cover, proved a distraction during the day. But as we all sat down to the high tea that evening, I saw from Mama's red eyes and Papa's repressed manner that something was seriously amiss.

"No sign of him yet?"

Mama, shook her head dolefully.

Papa began to drum his fingers on the tablecloth, crunching his toast, as though biting Grandpa's head off.

Silence. Then Murdoch, who had just come in, suggested in a subdued manner: "Maybe something has happened to him."

Papa glared at the unfortunate youth. "Shut up, you dolt. You've had your chance to be clever."

Murdoch collapsed and a more painful silence followed until irritation drove Papa to speak again.

"I must say it's hard enough, in the ordinary way, to support such an encumbrance. But when he takes to staying out, like as not going on the soak ..."

Mama interrupted, aroused at last, a spot of indignation on her cheek. "How do you know he's doing any such thing?"

Papa gazed at her, taken aback.

"The poor old man hasn't a farthing in the world," Mama went on. "Downtrodden and miscalled by everybody. Soak, indeed. The way he's been treated lately it wouldn't surprise me a bit if he had been driven to something desperate ..." She began to cry.

Murdoch looked justified, in a subdued way, and Kate went over to comfort Mama. "Really, Papa," she said, with a note of warning, "you ought to take some steps; with no money he can't have gone *far*."

Papa's expression was unhappy. "And set all the neighbours talking ... Isn't it bad enough already?" He got up from the table. "I've told my staff to keep their eyes open in the town. That's the most I can do."

Papa's staff consisted of a lanky assistant named Archibald Jupp, who always wore an air of passionate willingness because he hoped to succeed Papa, and a stout boy, who moved so slowly that he was known amongst the Boilermakers and other derisive young men as "The Fast Message." Though I was proved to be wrong, I had not much hope of this co-operation. Remembering the desolation of Grandpa's recent mood I began to feel dreadfully worried.

Next morning: no Grandpa, not a sign of him. A definite air of strain, of suspense, pervaded the household. At noon, when there was still no news, Papa struck the table, but not hard, with the flat of his hand: he said, in the tone of a man making a decisive announcement:

"Telegraph for Adam!"

Yes, yes; send for Adam; that was the good, the logical procedure. But a telegram—Ah, this deadly missive, almost unheard-of in the household, seemed a foreboding, almost a harbinger of doom. Refusing Murdoch's aid, Mama put on her hat and went, herself, with her head on one side, to the Drumbuck sub-office, to send the telegram. In an hour there was a telegram back: WITH YOU TO-MORROW THURSDAY 3 P.M. ADAM.

Insensibly our spirits rose at the promise implied in such promptitude, such businesslike decision. Mama remarked, as she put the telegram away in the private drawer where she kept all Adam's things—his letters, school reports, old pay envelopes, even a beribboned lock of his hair: "Adam's the one."

But the following day, before Adam arrived, there was a terrible development. Papa came back from the office in the middle of the forenoon, while I hung miserably about the house. He was accompanied by Archie Jupp, who stood in the lobby while Papa advanced towards Mama and, after some hesitation, with a grave, even a tender, expression, said:

"Mama! Prepare yourself. Grandpa's hat has been found ... floating on the Common pond."

Before our startled eyes, Jupp, who had discovered it, produced the old man's hat, pitifully battered and sodden.

"It was floating at the deep end, Mrs. Leckie. Opposite the boat-house." He spoke with ingratiating condolence. "I had an awful feeling it might be there."

I gazed with shocked anguish at the dripping relic and, as its full significance struck Mama, tears began to trickle down her cheeks.

"Come now, Mrs. Leckie," Archie Jupp said soothingly. "It may be nothing ... nothing at all."

Papa had actually gone into the scullery to make a cup of tea for Mama. He pressed it upon her affectionately, and waited, consolingly, until she had swallowed it, before departing with Archie Jupp.

That afternoon, Adam, wearing striped trousers and a dark jacket with a pearl pin in his grey tie, took command of the situation immediately he arrived. Seated at the table, effective and calm, he heard all the evidence, even my broken tale of Grandpa's brooding melancholy and his last fateful remark. He said: "We must inform the police."

A hush fell upon us at that sinister word.

"But, Adam ..." Papa protested. "My position ..."

"My dear father," Adam replied coolly, "if an old man takes it into his head to drown himself you can't exactly cover *that* up. Mind you, I don't commit myself. But they'll certainly want to drag the pond."

Mama was trembling all over. "Adam! You don't mean, you don't think ...?"

Adam shrugged his shoulders. "I don't think he floated his hat on the pond for fun."

"Oh, Adam."

"I'm sorry I spoke so bluntly, Mama. I know how you must feel. But after all what had he to live for? I'll go down and see Chief Constable Muir. It's lucky he's a friend of mine."

He had taken to smoking Burma cheroots and now he selected one from his crocodile leather case. I gazed at him in acute distress as he pulled out the yellow straw which traversed its length and accurately lit it. With a glance which included also Papa, he turned impressively to Mama: "A good thing, Mama, a *very* good thing, I induced you to extend the policy. Let's see ... an endowment *with* profits." With his left hand he brought out his silver pencil and began to figure on the tablecloth. "Five years at three ... add twenty-five ... why it makes a clear difference of one hundred and sixteen pounds."

"I don't want the money," Mama wept.

"It'll come in very handy," Papa said in a husky voice.

My grief, my growing sense of loss, was choking me as Adam put away his pencil and stood up.

"I'll look in on McKellar, too, at the Building Society Offices. He could smooth out any little difficulties in the way of immediate payment. In fact, I think I'll bring him back with me. You might whip up a really nice meat tea for us, Mama ... something substantial like poached eggs and mince. McKellar would like that. Don't lay it in the parlour ... not yet." He went out.

Obediently, Mama began to carry out Adam's instructions, scurrying between the kitchen and the scullery as though trying by the intensity of her activity to keep her mind off the worst. She baked several batches of scones. Papa, who could not bear the slightest extravagance, actually encouraged her to make pancakes as well, at the sacrifice of a half-dozen eggs. The unprecedented smell of rich cooking filled the air. The table was set with the best tablecloth and the parlour china.

At five o'clock Adam returned, rubbing his hands with satisfaction.

"They'll start dragging first thing, Monday. Unless he rises over the week end. And the cost will come out of the Humane Society Fund. Muir says that Common pond is getting to be an awful spot. Three drownings and a bad ice accident in the last ten years. McKellar can't come till after seven. He's a dry stick. Let's have our tea, Mama."

We sat down to the best meal I had ever eaten in Lomond View: meat, eggs, scones, pancakes, hot strong tea.

"At a time like this," Papa said, looking generously round the table, "I don't grudge a thing."

"Do you think he will rise, Adam?" Murdoch asked in a voice of morbid fascination.

"Well, now, that's a question," Adam answered with knowledgeable interest. "According to Muir they sometimes come up of their own volition within forty-eight hours. Fill up with gas." Mama shuddered and shut her eyes. "Just float up gently, and always face down—that's the curious thing. Sometimes they're stubborn though and stay down. Or they might be embedded in sand or weeds—there's a lot of weed in the pond—and can't move even though the gas is trying to rise them. In that case I'm told if you float loaves, with quicksilver in them, over the pond you often get a dip at the exact spot."

I could not bear it, this awful vision of my poor grandpa, entangled with green weed, sodden from long immersion. But suddenly, a ring at the front bell. Everyone sat up as Kate went to the door and showed in Archie Jupp.

"Sorry to disturb you—" Archie halted, discreetly, at the sight of the family meal. "But I thought you ought to know ... there's another piece of evidence."

Archie had been hurrying, he wiped his brow; he was excited yet expressing a sense of grave commiseration.

"Mr. Parkin, who keeps the boats on the pond, remembered he heard a distinct splash late Wednesday night, opposite his boathouse, and this afternoon he went out with the boathook. He struck some clothing, a man's jacket. He took it to the police office. I've just seen it. It's Mr. Gow's."

Tears burst anew from my smarting eyes; of course Mama was crying again, gently and silently.

Papa made a noble gesture of invitation. "Sit in and take a bite with us, Archie."

Deferentially, Archie pulled up a chair. While accepting his cup from Mama he murmured, in a low voice, to Papa: "He did it once too often, Mr. Leckie."

To my surprise Papa frowned. "No, I can't allow you to say that, Jupp. It's untimely. We all have our faults. He wasn't a bad old soul. He had a certain dignity, too, when you come to think of it. That way he had of walking down the street, swinging his stick." He leaned forward and patted my shoulder, not rebuking me for my snivelling, but rather approving it as he murmured gently: "Poor boy ... you were fond of him, too."

Another peal of the front bell—startling us, yet in a sense expected, confirming all our fears. A terrible silence; a silence of certainty as Kate rose and again went to the door. When she returned she was whiter than I had ever seen her.

"Oh, Papa," she whispered, "someone from the police station. He wants to see you."

Through the half-open doorway, I perceived in the lobby behind her the terrifying form of a policeman, red-faced and solemn, turning his helmet in his hands.

Papa immediately got up, pale but important, and made a sigh to Adam, who also rose. They both went into the lobby, closing the kitchen door behind them as though, by drawing a veil upon the scene, they wished to spare us. Only the mutter of their lowered voices came to us as we sat absolutely mute, as though we ourselves were stricken by the messenger of death.

After a long time Papa came back into the room. A pause. Then Kate, the bravest of us, mustered enough strength to ask: "Have they found him?"

"Yes." Papa spoke in a low voice; he was paler than before. "They have him."

"In the mortuary?" Murdoch gasped.

"No," said Papa, "in Ardfillan jail."

He surveyed us with a glassy eye; felt his way to his chair; sat down weakly. "He's been out on the spree with the tinkers from the Skeoch wood . . . lost his coat and hat in a fight at the boathouse . . . up to God knows what these last two days . . . landed in jail at Ardfillan . . . charged with drunk and disorderly and contempt of the law. Adam has gone to bail him out."

The shades of night were falling as Adam and Grandpa came up the road. Hatless, wearing an old police tunic open and unbuttoned, in place of his lost jacket, Grandpa looked proud but subdued; there was a gleam in his eye—a chink in his armour which betrayed an inward apprehension. As I crouched at the parlour window in anxious solitude, a glimpse was enough to send me scudding upstairs to the refuge of the old man's room.

There, listening tensely, I heard the sound of the front door, followed by a dreadful chaos, filled with loud recriminations from Adam, Mama's tears and lamentations, Papa's whining abuse, but not a word, not a whisper from Grandpa.

At last he came upstairs, moving slowly, and entered his room. He was sadly tarnished; his beard needed trimming; he exhaled strange and uncomfortable odours.

He threw me a quick glance, began to potter about the room, trying unsuccessfully to hum, pretending not to care. Then he picked up his battered and still sodden hat, which, earlier that day, Mama had placed reverently upon the bed. He considered it for a moment, turned artlessly to me.

"It'll stand reblocking. It was always a grand hat."

Book Two

Book Two

Chapter One

The chestnut trees, spreading more widely, were again in flourish, the setting sun was sending up a faint incense behind the Ben as, full of excitement and pride, I hurried home from the Academy one April afternoon in the year 1910. At least I must assume that it was I, though there were times when I seemed a stranger, an uncouth stranger to myself. The other morning, coming out of Baxter's after my early "round," I had caught a sudden glimpse of a strange apparition in the mirror of the baker's shop—a pale and lanky boy of fifteen who has outgrown his strength, stooping, with thin wrists and unmanageable feet, an unfamiliar profile, absorbed and melancholy, a man's nose on a boyish face—I could not repress a start of surprise, of pained unbelief.

But now I was conscious only of my splendid worth, full of my interview with Mr. Reid, held not five minutes ago, on the eve of the short Easter recess. "Jason" Reid had kept me behind the others, then crooked his forefinger for me to come to his desk. My form master was a young man, thirty-two, his stocky figure brimming over with suppressed vitality, the scar on his upper lip a diagonal white weal with tiny white beads, where the stitches had been, symmetrically alongside. This scar—which I suspected to be the result of a hare-lip operation—seemed to pull his nose down, making it flat and boneless, widening the nostrils, even making his blue eyes more prominent, almost bulging, under his fine soft blond hair. He was fair-complexioned, with a dampish skin, for he perspired easily, and was clean-shaven, disdaining to hide that slightly disfigured upper lip by a moustache, as though he welcomed and despised the cruelty of vulgar curiosity. In any case, his speech would have betrayed him, that imperfect articulation which can be reproduced exactly by placing the tongue flat against the roof of the mouth, which softens all the hard ss sounds to th's, which in fact had given Mr. Reid his nickname on that day when we began the account of the Argonauts in the third ode of Pindar, and he spoke, with emotion, of "Jathon."

"Shannon." He drummed with his fingers, while I gazed at him adoringly. "You are not quite a plate of sour porridge"—his usual designation of the members of his form. "There's something I want to put up to you...."

I was still giddy from his momentous words when I reached Lomond View.

I wanted to be alone, to hug my secret, but upstairs Grandpa was waiting at the open window with the draught board set out before him.

"What has kept you?" he asked impatiently.

"Nothing." I had become intensely secretive. Besides, Grandpa wasn't the Homeric figure he once had been to me and my announcement was much too valuable to "waste" on him.

Actually, Grandpa had altered much less than I, his movements were still charged with vigour, though I discerned less ruddy metal in his beard, a few more careless stains upon his waistcoat. He had not reached that stage in his career, to which I must later refer with pain, when his eccentricities became my bane. Lately his life-long friend, Peter Dickie, had been overtaken by the spectre of unwanted old men and retired to the county poorhouse at Glenwoodie. This had sobered Grandpa, who always shied away from evidence of senility, and who resented, as a personal insult, the very mention of the word "death." Still, he looked quite spry, because he was enjoying his blessed annual respite: Grandma had departed on her visit to Kilmarnock. The period to be reviewed is, actually, Grandpa's Indian summer. Yet just then he was in a bad mood, for he imagined I was trying to "do him out" of his beloved game.

"What's the matter with you? Standing there like a cat on hot bricks?"

I resigned myself and sat down opposite him while he bent over the board with frowning concentration, pondering his move with a terrible deliberation, preparing a pitfall which I could easily see coming, moving his man with a pretence of innocence, enhancing this transparent cunning by tapping out his dottle, examining the stem of his pipe, and beginning to hum.

Naturally my mind was not on the game, but whizzing with that magnificent proposal of Jason's which had given me new hope for the future. Like most boys on the verge of leaving school I had worried a good deal about a career. I was ambitious, I knew what I wanted "to be," yet the circumstances of my life, although they enhanced this longing, did not offer much encouragement for its achievement.

At the Academy I had grown accustomed to finding myself at the top of my form and had passed through the hands of various masters who had prophesied in an impersonal sort of way that I should do well. There was Mr. Irwin, tall, thin, and affected, who suffered dreadfully from colds in his head and fostered in me the belief that I was good at English composition by reading approvingly to the class, in his nasal voice, my high-flown, flowery essays on such subjects as "A Battle at Sea" and "A Day in Spring." Then came Mr. Caldwell, known to the boys as "Pin" because of the short wooden peg which supported his withered leg. Meek and elderly, with gentle gestures and a small grey imperial, dressed always in clerical grey, he lived in the classics, and took me aside to tell me that, with application, I might be a Latinist. Others, equally well-meaning, had confused me with their conflicting advice.

Not until I fell into Jason's hands had I felt the warm touch of personal interest. He was the first to regard my interest in natural history as something more than a joke. How well I remember the beginning, that summer day when a pair of butterflies, common blues, flew through the open window into his classroom and we all stopped work to watch them.

"Why two?" Jason Reid asked the question idly of himself as well as the form.

A silence, then my modest voice was heard.

"Because they're mating, sir."

Jason's bulging, satiric gaze found me.

"Plate of porridge, are you suggesting that butterflies have a love life?"

"Oh, yes, sir. They can find their mate a mile away by a particular fragrance. It comes from their skin glands. It's like verbena."

"The plot thickens." Jason spoke slowly, not yet quite sure of me. "And how do they smell this delicious perfume, pray?"

"They have special knobs on the end of their antennæ." I smiled, carried away by my interest. "Oh, that's nothing, sir. The Red Admiral actually tastes with its feet."

Loud shout of derision from the class. But Jason stilled them. "Quiet, clods. This dish of porridge knows something—which is more than can be said of others. Go on, Shannon. Don't our two blue friends here see each other—without the necessity for verbena?"

"Well, sir," I was blushing now, "the butterfly's eye is rather curious. It consists of about three thousand separate elements, each with a complete cornea, lens and retina. But although they have good discrimination of colours they're extremely short-sighted, a range of only about four feet . . ."

I broke off, and Reid did not press me, but at the end of the hour, as we filed out, he gave me a faint searching smile, the first time he ever smiled at me, murmuring under his breath:

"And strange as it may seem . . . not a prig."

From then, while encouraging my biology, he began to take me far ahead of the form in physics; and a few months later set me off in the laboratory upon a line of original research on the permeability of colloids. No wonder I was devoted to him, listening open-mouthed to every word he said in class, with the doglike devotion of a lonely boy, and even, with a thoughtful frown, copying his lisp and slight stutter during my conversations with Gavin.

A year previously Gavin's father had moved him from the Academy to Larchfield College. It was a sad blow to me. Situated in the neighbouring town of Ardfillan, Larchfield was an exclusive and expensive boarding school, so select as to be almost unattainable to ordinary boys—its headmaster had been to Balliol and had actually captained a famous cricketing club at Lords! In spite of the popularity which he came quickly to enjoy in his new environment, Gavin remained loyal to me. On summer afternoons, when I borrowed Mr. Reid's bicycle and rode fifteen miles to watch him knock up a half-century for the school, he would detach himself from his flattering circle at the pavilion and come openly to the far side of the lovely playing fields where I, the lowly alien, lay hidden; fling himself in his blazer and white flannels beside me, chewing an end of grass, remarking through compressed lips: "What's been happening at home?" Nevertheless, although our friendship burned more brightly, although, when Gavin returned, we did everything together, there were long spells of separation when, rather than content myself with a second-rate companion, I fell back upon my own resources and indulged my morbid talent for solitude.

Alone, I roamed the countryside for miles around. I knew every nest, every crag, every sheeptrack on the Winton Hills. I fished the burns in spate, took dabs and pollack from the mudflats of the estuary. I made maps of the uncharted moorland which stretched, a wilderness of peat and heather, beyond the Windy Peak. All the keepers came to know me and to afford me that rare privilege, an unchallenged right of way. My collections grew. Some of my specimens were extremely rare. I had, for instance, splendid preparations of the proliferating hydra—the queer part-plant which liberates an egg—several unclassified forms of freshwater desmids, and that glorious dragonfly the *Pantala flavescens*, which, so far as I could ascertain, had never before been found in North Britain. Because of these wanderings I never missed the "holidays at the coast" which other boys looked forward to in summer—my imagination took me far beyond these tame resorts, turning the upper moorland into a wild stretch of pampas, or to the plains of Tartary over which I advanced cautiously, scanning the horizon for distant lamas ... and sometimes, alas, for endangered missionaries.

Yes, one must admit the painful fact: I was, at this time, ardently devout. Perhaps my solitary hours had fostered this fervour. More probably it was because, like a horse pulling a load uphill, my peculiar nature strained harder in the face of difficulties. Every other day, at great inconvenience to myself, I served Canon Roche's Mass. On the friendliest terms with the Sisters, I swung the censer in the processions which wound, behind fluttering tapers, in the convent grounds. During Lent I performed prodigies of self-denial. I thanked the Almighty burningly, for having included me in the one true fold, and felt the deepest pity for all those unfortunate boys who had been born into false religions and who would, almost certainly, be lost. I shuddered to think that, but for the goodness of God, I might have come into the world as a Presbyterian or a Mohammedan, with only the thinnest chance of earning my eternal reward!

Although I shall not dwell upon them, my religious tribulations had not ceased and there were days in my calendar which I dreaded—less from physical fear than from the violence they inflicted on my spirit. Let us be honest. Levenford, like most Scottish towns, was a small Vesuvius of intolerance. The Protestants didn't like the Catholics, the Catholics were not fond of the Protestants, and both had little love for the Jews (who were mostly Poles, a small and inoffensive community congregated in the Vennel). On Saint Patrick's Day when shamrocks were sported defiantly and the Ancient Order of Hibernians paraded their banners down the High Street behind the green-sashed pipe band, the rivalry between blue and green erupted in unmentionable execrations and innumerable fights. Still more hectic was the Twelfth of July, and the massed procession of the Orange Lodges, Loyal Orders of the Great and Good King William, also with band and banners, led by a man with a tall hat and a gilt-fringed orange apron, riding a white horse and proclaiming: "Saved from popery, slavery, knavery!" while the crowd sang:

"Oh, dogs and dogs and a-holy dogs,
And a-dogs and a-ho-oly wa-ter.
King a-William slew the papish crew,
At the Battle of-a Boyne-a Wa-ter."

The simple act of lifting my cap as I passed the Holy Angels Church usually brought upon me ridicule or contempt, but on these days of strife, the Twelfth especially, I was lucky if it did not involve me in a running fight.

But do not imagine that I mooned away my days between defending the Faith and chasing butterflies and saints in a beatific state. Papa saw to it that much of my spare time out of school was profitably occupied. Ever since I had attained employable proportions, he had hired me out in various useful directions, my present duty being to rise at six every morning to pedal Baxter's tricycle van round the empty streets, delivering fresh rolls to the half-awakened town. My small wages were received by him with the remark that they would ease the cost of my board and keep, and he would go on to tell Mama, with pale earnestness, that it was necessary to cut down further on expenses, although these had been pared to the vanishing point. Recently, indeed, Papa had taken the monthly bills into his own hands and he exasperated the tradesmen by exacting reductions or, when he set out to purchase articles for the household, by trying to knock a little off the price. When something "useful" was in question he was always anxious to buy, especially if it seemed a bargain; yet more often than not, in the end some instinct made him draw away from the purchase, bringing him back empty-handed, but, as he triumphantly declared, with the money still in his pocket. . . .

At this point an exclamation of triumph from my adversary brought back my errant thoughts. While I was dreaming Grandpa had whipped my last two men from the board.

"I knew I had you," he crowed. "You that's supposed to be the cleverest boy in the town!"

I rose quickly, so that he might not see, and so misunderstand, the look of joy springing to my eyes.

Chapter Two

Still restless and excited, I ran downstairs. I was free until eight o'clock in the evening, when I had a special and unbreakable engagement. I thought of calming myself by going to the bioscope matinee, but I had not a farthing in my pocket, or rather in Murdoch's pocket, for I had reached the size when I could wear his old suits, cast off long ago and faithfully preserved amidst camphor in the attic "kist."

I went into the scullery where Mama was damping clothes at the boiler and laying them on the ironing board, her hair and eyes more faded now, face thinner and more tiredly lined, yet still gentle, and enduring. I stood gazing at her with tremendous meaning, almost with a catch in my breath.

"You wait, Mama," I said softly. "Yes, just wait."

She gave me her queer, frowning smile.

"Wait for what?" she asked, after she had tested the hot iron near her cheek.

"Well," I said, lamely, yet with intensity. "One of these days I'll be able to do something for you ... something big."

"Will you do something for me now? Something small. Take a note over to Kate's?"

"Oh, of course, Mama."

I often carried missives for Mama, and so saved the postage stamp, across the town to Kate, at Barloan Toll, or to Murdoch, who was now solidly established with Mr. Dalrymple at the Nursery, doing extremely well and, to his evident satisfaction, emancipated from Lomond View. These letters were a part of Mama, communications of the spirit, containing news, messages, exhortations, even requests—sent out, in patient persistence, in her unflagging effort to hold the family together.

I waited till her iron was cold. Then she entered the kitchen and brought back a sealed envelope.

"Here you are then. I wish I could send a batch of pancakes with you. But . . ." She removed the lid from the earthenware crock and peered into it in a troubled fashion. "I seem to be out of flour. Give them my love, though."

I went out and along Drumbuck Road, crossed the Common and turned left, skirting the great black shape of the Boilerworks—partly stilled by the impending holiday, yet still glowing in its depths, still alive and menacing.

Kate's house was one of the small new cottages built on a round green knoll near the old Toll-gate, on the western outskirts of the town. And as I came up the hill I suddenly discerned Kate as she came along a level side-street, pushing the perambulator before her. It was a fine navy-blue perambulator and Kate loved to push it. She walked miles with it every week, I am sure, through the town, the shops, round the Knoxhill Park, pausing, proudly to stoop and straighten the navy-blue cover with the white N embroidered on the corner.

I stopped to watch, smiling in sympathy, as she came along, quite unaware of me, her figure a little stouter now, bending over as she walked, smiling, clicking her tongue, her eyes intent upon the baby.

"Hello, Kate," I murmured shyly, when she had almost passed me.

"Why, *Robie*." Her tone was warm with welcome. "You poor boy. And me never looking the road you were on. It's baby. Robie, you would not believe, it, he is cutting his second tooth, and with never a whimper, just as good as gold . . ." She bent again. "The pet, the precious, the mother's lamb . . ."

Ah Kate, dear Kate, you are happy with your incomparable child. And to think that, once, they prescribed for you the mandolin!

Kate's home was bright and neat, with the modern convenience of hot and cold running water, and the sharp smell of paint and polish indicating how houseproud she had become. Her marriage was a success despite the forebodings of Papa who, rent by the loss of her salary, had declared that she was throwing herself, and her career, away. When she had laid the baby in his cot she put a pan on the "main" gas stove and soon the delicious fragrance of frying steak and onions came upon the air.

"You'll wait and have a bite with us," she insisted, turning the steak expertly with a knife, and holding her head away to avoid the spark of the fat. "Jamie's upstairs in the bath. He's been on overtime lately or I'm sure he'd have wanted to take you to the football match." What sublime tact from the once churlish Kate! "He won't be a minute. You must be famished." She gave me a quick look as she said that, but looked away with equal quickness.

Jamie came down well-washed, his hair wetly plastered, and wearing complacently, an outrageous red tartan tie.

"It's yourself, boy." That, and his little nod, had more warmth and more welcome in them, for a sensitive heart, than all the protestations in the world.

We sat down to supper at once. The steak, of which Kate gave me a very large portion, was tender and juicy, its rich substance permeated me like a transfusion. Jamie kept heaping my plate with the crisp frizzled onions. There was thick hot buttered toast and strong, scalding tea.

I think Kate and Jamie knew perfectly how poor and limited the food had become at home. Jamie, in particular, pressed me repeatedly and when I could eat no more he fixed on me a reproachful eye.

"It's there, boy," he said, simply.

All my childhood at Lomond View was dominated by a monstrous law: the necessity for saving money, even at the sacrifice of the very necessities of life. Ah, if only we could have done without money, without this Northern thrift which preferred money in the bank to a good meal in the stomach, which put gentility before generosity, this cursed penuriousness which blighted us.

When this money question bewildered and tormented me, I thought of Jamie Nigg. Jamie was never well off; yet whether he spent it upon a good steak, or on taking a forgotten boy to a football game, Jamie always got good use of his hard-won money and, what was better, he made all the money that he touched seem clean.

As we each drank one last cup of tea Jamie began to rally me, for I am sure he regarded my shy and gawky melancholy not only with compassion, but also with concern. Sensing the suppressed excitement of my mood, he remarked gravely to Kate:

"The professor has something on his mind. These quiet clever ones ... they're the worst."

Kate nodded, then gave me a sideways smile that advised me not to take him too seriously.

"They're deep," Jamie said. "Up to all sorts of devilments. Especially when they're good jumpers."

This delicate reference to my success in the recent Academy sports, when I had won the open high jump, gave me an inward glow and although I lowered my eyes I had again to admit to myself that it was a school record, inch and a quarter above the previous best. But that glow was nothing to the incandescence lit within me when Jamie added in a measured voice: "Of course, if you want my opinion, he's in love."

Ah, the pure white flame of pride, the deep and secret realization of this truth. With eyes still lowered I cherished the warm flush of happiness that bathed my heart.

"What's been happening at home then?" Kate asked, curbing Jamie's humour.

I hurriedly produced and gave to her Mama's letter.

"I'm sorry I forgot about this."

Kate opened the letter and read it through twice, and to my surprise her face darkened and her forehead bumps, which I had imagined gone for ever, filled up angrily. She handed the letter to Jamie, who read it in silence.

"It really is too bad. This thing of Papa's is getting to be a disease." Kate made an effort to free herself from what seemed a highly disagreeable thought. Jamie was glancing at me in a queer sort of way. There was an awkward pause.

Just then the baby woke up and Kate, seeming to welcome the interruption, gave him his bottle on her knee. For an instant, as a sign of their regard, I was allowed to take this priceless burden in my arms.

"He likes you," Kate said encouragingly. "Wait till you have one of your own, man."

I smiled, uncertainly. Terrible paradox: I was in love; but how could I reveal to her that I was morally convinced, from certain unspeakable nocturnal experiences, that I was doomed never to be able to have children?

When the baby was restored to his cot I said that it was time for me to go.

Kate saw me to the door. Now that we were alone she was again examining me intently.

"Mama didn't tell you what was in her letter?"

"No, Kate." I smiled up at her. "As a matter of fact, I'm rather taken up with some news of my own."

"Good or bad?" she inquired, with her head to one side.

"Oh, good, Kate ... extremely good, I think ... You see, Kate ..." I broke off, flushing darkly, staring out at the mysterious night, spangled with misty lights, hearing the far-off whistling of a train, followed, like an echo, by the thrilling sound of a ship's foghorn from the river.

"It's all right, Robie." Now Kate was shaking her head and smiling, almost against her will. "You keep your news and I'll keep mine."

I pressed her hand and, unable to contain myself, started running at full speed down the road. Much as I liked Kate, she could not be the first to know. Again, from the unseen river, there came the slow sounding of that outward ship, making me shiver in sheer delight.

Chapter Three

Quickly, my heart lifting at every step, I returned to Drumbuck Road; then, with a sudden quickening of my pulse, entered Sinclair Drive, a narrow street shaded by young lindens which, lightly shedding their twirling flowers, had spread a yellow carpet upon the pavement. Although there seemed nothing new in this familiar thoroughfare which in my childhood had never deeply stirred me, although its rambling old houses wore the same undisturbed air of having seen better days, now ... ah, now its mysterious and exquisite name was engraved upon my heart. It was almost eight o'clock when my unworthy feet fell again upon the soft strewn linden flowers of that beloved drive and my blood pounded as I saw a light behind the drawn blind of the front-room window of the end house. Even as I drew up, I heard the sound of Alison singing.

It was the hour of her practising: she had begun seriously to develop that talent which was widely spoken of in the town. Tonight, she had finished her scales and exercises, those clear true notes, not woven into melody, yet enchanting of their own accord, like the flutings of a bird. Now, while her mother accompanied her on the piano, she was singing "Lament for Flodden," one of those simple Scottish songs which seemed to me difficult to surpass.

"I've heard them lilting at our ewe-milking,
Lassies a' lilting before dawn o' day;
But now they are moaning on ilka green loaming—
The Flowers of the Forest are a' wede away."

A crystal bell pealed into the night, so true, so sweet, I held my breath. I shut my eyes and saw the singer, not the child whom I had often played with, but a tall, grown girl, who no longer flung her limbs about, but walked quietly, with restraint, as though conscious of a new dignity budding within her. I saw her as, on that astounding day six months ago, she came out of the cloakroom and along the school corridor with some other girls, wearing her short navy-blue drill costume, straps crossed over her white blouse, long firm legs in black stockings, speckled black gym shoes on her feet. How often had I passed her like this, with no more than a briskly casual nod. But, suddenly, as I politely stood against the wall to make way for the advancing group, Alison, still talking to her companions, raised her hand to her brown hair which clustered about her slender neck, moulding by this unconscious gesture her young breasts, and at the same time, as she brushed by, her skin warm with her recent exercise, giving me from her dark brown eyes a friendly, melting smile. Dear God, what had happened to me, all in an instant, at the hands of this heavenly creature whom I had so far practically ignored? Waves of intoxicating warmth surged through me as I leaned, bewildered yet entranced, against the wall in the empty corridor, long after she had gone. Oh, Alison, Alison of the quiet brown eyes, and the white, pure, swelling throat, I am caught up in that same rapture as I stand now, hidden by the night, and the deeper shadow of the linden tree, listening, until the last note wings, tremulous, towards the skies.

When there was silence I gathered myself and pushed through the iron gate. The garden was large, surrounded by a high wall and shaded by thick trees, with wide lawns spreading out from the drive, and rhododendron shrubberies which were straggling, somewhat overgrown. Although Alison's mother had been left comfortably off she was not wealthy, and the property was not maintained with the prim propriety of the villas in Drumbuck Road. On the front doorstep I rang the bell, and a moment later I was admitted by Janet, the elderly maid who had been with Mrs. Keith for over ten years and who always regarded me with that air of distrust peculiar to old and favoured servants, but which I then felt to be directed specially against myself. She showed me into the front room where Alison had already spread her books out on the table while Mrs. Keith, seated in a low chair by the fire, was busy with some crochet work contained in a green linen bag upon her lap.

What a bright and charming room it was, quite dazzling after the darkness—the walls light-coloured, hung with white framed water colours done by Mrs. Keith, white muslin curtains draping the drawn blinds. Two bowls of blue hyacinths perfumed the air; a fringed silk shawl hung over the open piano; the furniture was chintz-covered. In the firelight a brass Benares stand glinted beneath its load of bric-a-brac, mostly ivories, brought home from India by Captain Keith. A procession of white elephants, growing in size, marched steadily across the mantelpiece.

"You're punctual, as usual, Robert." Mrs. Keith, while I stood blinking, was endeavouring to put me at ease. "What sort of night is it?"

"Oh, very nice, Mrs. Keith," I stammered. "Misty. But you can see the stars."

She smiled as I drew up a chair beside Alison at the table. "You will always see the stars, Robert. In fact, you are a regular stargazer."

That lenient smile lingered on her kind, sallow, slightly ironic face; I felt her watching me as I began, confusedly, to work with Alison.

Mrs. Keith was thin and rather tall, in her middle thirties, dressed simply, yet with an air of breeding and good taste. She came from a prominent county family but after the death of her husband she had gone out very little, giving herself up to her daughter's education, content with her music and the friendship of a few intimates, amongst whom were Miss Julia Blair, Mrs. Marshall—mother of Louisa, that tormentor of my childhood—and my form master, Jason Reid. Her retirement was perhaps encouraged by the fact that her health was poor—often I had the odd impression that, under her graciousness, she was suffering from headache. Yet, mainly I think for Alison's sake, she concealed her invalidism or, with a light shrug of her shoulders, gently mocked at it. Her devotion to her daughter was extreme, she was proud of Alison's talent and bent upon developing it, but since she was a clever woman with a clear sense of judgment, she seemed to realize the dangers of indulging her possessiveness. She urged Alison to have "suitable" friends of her own age, and from the beginning, after a penetrating scrutiny which ended, I must confess, in a twitch of suppressed amusement, she had encouraged me to come about the house. In my early childhood I had arrived periodically, rather overawed, burdened by the sorrows of timidity, to play staid and boring games with little Alison. On the sunny lawn, while the thin note of the piano came from the open window, or a carriage rolled up the drive bearing Mrs. Marshall to "take tea" with Alison's mother, we held a picnic for her dolls, or fed the goldfish. If it were showery we went indoors where Janet suspiciously gave us bread and butter spread with chocolate seeds and, seated at the table, the rain drumming on the panes, we engaged in a contest known as "Questions and Answers," played with small round cards which bore ridiculous queries like, "Is backgammon an old game?" and the equally preposterous response, "Yes, it was played by the Ancient Druids." Occasionally Louisa was present at these junketings, winning all the games, withering me with her scorn. Then, as we grew older, Alison and I "did our homework" together. She, a practical person, was weak in mathematics; while I, absurdly fanciful, was good at them. And Mrs. Keith, anxious that Alison should take her Intermediate Certificate, without which she could not enter the College of Music at Winton, had recently suggested that I should come in, regularly, to coach Alison in this subject.

"What are you giving my backward and wayward daughter to-night, Robert?" Mrs. Keith spoke with affectionate irony, her eyes on her work.

"Euclid, Mrs. Keith," I answered awkwardly. "The sum of the squares of the sides of a right-angled triangle ... you know ..."

"I don't know, Robert, but I'm sure you do." She did not smile, still trying to help me over my terrible self-consciousness. She was always helping me, without seeming to do so, giving me ideas which I could not find in the book on etiquette which I had procured from the Public Library for the special purpose of improving my behaviour.

"It does seem silly that I should have to learn this, Mother," Alison remarked tranquilly. "It's all so made-up."

"Oh, no, Alison," I said quickly. "It's really very logical. Once you admit that a straight line is the shortest distance between two points all of the thirteen books of Euclid follow automatically."

"I believe you will write a fourteenth book yourself, one day, Robert," Mrs. Keith said. "Or worse—a Life History of Beetles."

"He will, Mother," Alison exclaimed accusingly. "Do you know, in Mr. Reid's class last week he actually proved that an answer in the algebra book was wrong."

While they both smiled I lowered my head in pride and shyness, grateful to Alison for having brought this up, resuming my explanation of the theorem in a low and husky voice.

Seated close beside her, so that our knees touched under the table, I was conscious of a sweetness that made my heart faint. When our hands came in contact on the page of the book an exquisite thrill passed through me. Her rather untidy hair, which lay upon her shoulders and which, from time to time, she shook impatiently, seemed to me something wonderful and holy. I stole quick glances at her fresh cheeks, noticing the moistness of her lower lip as with a puzzled frown she sucked her pencil. I did not, could not, even contemplate the word "love." I hoped that, perhaps, she liked me. I felt that I was living, talking, smiling in a dream.

The hour passed with unbelievable rapidity. It was almost nine. Already Mrs. Keith had stifled a yawn and I had detected her looking at the clock. I did not dare to speak aloud or even whisper to Alison what was in my mind. Suddenly, with a shaking hand, I took a scrap of paper and wrote:

"Alison, I want to see you. Will you come to the door with me to-night?"

A look of surprise came into Alison's eyes as she read the message. Taking her pencil she wrote:

"What for?"

Trembling in all my limbs I wrote back:

"I have something to tell you."

A pause, then Alison gave me her clear frank smile and firmly inscribed the words:

"Very well."

A shiver of joy passed through me. Fearful that Mrs. Keith should see me, the betrayer of her trust, I took the piece of paper, folded it tight, thrust it in my mouth and swallowed it. At that moment Janet brought in a tray of milk and cracknel biscuits—positive indication that the geometry lesson was over.

Ten minutes later I stood up and said good night to Mrs. Keith. Faithful to her promise Alison accompanied me to the front porch.

"It *is* a nice night." She viewed the dewy night with a calm, untroubled gaze. "I'll come with you to the gate."

As we went down the drive I walked slowly to prolong the warm and choking rapture of being near her. Holding herself erect, Alison looked straight ahead. As we passed a dark yet familiar bush she plucked and crushed a leaf—the smell of flowering currant filled the air.

My brain was swimming, the world wavering before me. With a terrible effort I commanded my disordered breathing.

"I heard you singing to-night, Alison."

The banality of that quavering remark, which brutally parodied my pure yet destroying passion, which, in fact, horrified me the instant it was spoken, seemed lost upon her.

"Yes, I've begun to work in earnest. Miss Cramb has just started me on Schubert's songs. They are simply beautiful."

Schubert's songs: vision of the Rhine, the castles on its banks, Alison and I floating down, beneath arched bridges, on a little river steamer, disembarking at an old inn, a garden with little tables . . . Did I tell her all this? No. I croaked—in my "breaking" voice: "You are getting on terribly well, Alison."

She smiled deprecatingly, dwelling on the vagaries of her music mistress, who was, in fact, an exacting and acidulous spinster. "Miss Cramb is hard to please!"

Silence again. We had reached the gate, that point at which I must leave her. I saw her steal an inquiring glance at me. A weakness was now all over my body, a tremulous warmth was flowing about my heart. I drew a sharp quivering breath. It was the supreme moment of dedication, that moment when knighthood comes to flower.

"Alison ... I don't suppose it matters to you ... but to-day something happened to me ... Mr. Reid told me I might sit the Marshall."

"Robie!"

In her surprise and interest she used, earnestly, my name. With hands clenched, my pale cheeks burning, I saw that she had not failed to appreciate the full significance of the secret which I had at last divulged.

The Marshall was, of course, a tremendous thing, of which the name must never, never be taken in vain. It was a scholarship to the College of Winton, founded by Sir John Marshall a century ago, open to the entire county of Winton and of tremendous monetary value—one hundred pounds per annum for five years. It stood as an expression of the passionate Scottish desire for advancement, for education, the determination to give the poor "lad of parts" his chance. Great men had first displayed their greatness by winning this prize—once, when a famous statesman died, a man from Winton whose name was echoed with respect across the seas to the corners of the world, the highest tribute paid to him was that single grave reflection by one who had been his contemporary at the Academy: "Aye ... I mind the day he carried off the Marshall."

"I'll never win it," I said in a low voice. "But I wanted you to be the first to know I'm going to try."

"I think you have a spendid chance," Alison said generously. "It will make a tremendous difference to you if you win?"

"Yes," I answered. "All the difference in the world."

I gazed at her blindly. Lyrical words lay behind my tongue. But I could not speak them. Growing flustered, I shifted my weight from one foot to another.

"I hope it keeps up over the holiday," I said.

"Oh, I hope so," Alison answered.

"On Monday I'm going on the Loch with Gavin."
"Oh, are you?"
There was a throbbing pause.
"Good night then, Alison."
"Good night, Robie."
We parted stiffly, abruptly. As usual, I had bungled everything. Yet, as I hurried along Drumbuck Road, I felt the world still a splendid place, still rich in splendid promise.

Chapter Four

That sweet parting should have been the ending of my day. But alas, there remained the strange and tortuous process of getting to my bed. And to-night was my "night of the Lion's Bridge." Although unusual emotion had tired me I forced myself relentlessly past Lomond View and on to the dark country road leading to the bridge, two miles away. Have we not studied Grandma in her method of retirement? Why, therefore, should we spare this boy, this Robert Shannon, since our purpose is to reveal him truthfully, to expose him in all his dreams, strivings and follies, with as dispassionate, as merciless, a blade as that with which he dissected poor *Rana temporaria*, the frog?

The evening had turned more chill and unfriendly. When I reached the bridge, damp clouds dulled the half-moon, a gusty wind was troubling the young leaves. Tightly buttoning my jacket, Murdoch's jacket, I advanced. The bridge was an old bridge, spanning the River Leven as it poured down from the hills, bound by a narrow stone coping built out above the torrent in three semicircular bays. At each end of the coping was a masoned gargoyle, weather-worn and mutilated, yet still discernible as a grinning lion's face.

Completely alone, I climbed on to the high coping; then, with a sharp intake of breath, began to work my way across the narrow parapet of the bridge. Far below, as I edged along, I heard the unseen tumbling of the waters. The bays were the worst. There, I seemed poised on a high dark precipice while the coping, the bridge, the whole world swayed and spun about me.

I had no head for heights; the ordeal was the most frightening

I could devise. But at last I had done it—across and back. Returned to the solid road, I leaned faintly, with shut eyes, against the figure of the grinning lion. No wonder the king of beasts was amused at my distress. Madness, yes, madness . . . Yet when one is poor and despised, when one trembles and blushes at a sudden laugh from passing strangers, when one has the nervous affliction of moving one's scalp and ears, it is necessary, ah, yes, it is most necessary, to prove, only to oneself, that one is not a coward.

I went home at least partially appeased. The house was in darkness—now not even a peep of gas was permitted in the lobby. I tiptoed up the stairs to the bathroom, bolted the door silently; and with great caution, since Papa would not permit the waste of a single drop of water, I ran a cold bath.

The water was frigid, even to my fingers, yet when I had removed my clothes I lay in it, motionless, with my teeth clenched, until my body was numb and senseless. This was no proof of valour but a precaution, one might say a prayer, against that wretchedness which might overtake one in the night.

I crept upstairs. I was now occupying Murdoch's old room—during the few winter weeks when Murdoch slept at home he used the larger, better, room which once was Kate's. Icy cold, almost disembodied, I lit the end of tallow candle in the enamel candlestick. Around me, shadowy as myself, were my school prizes, worthless books in pretentious bindings—there were at least three copies of Porter's *Scottish Chiefs*—also my precious microscope and natural history collections, contained in cardboard boxes, cases I had made, all of which had cost nothing. Writing materials stood on the top of the chest of drawers and another book, borrowed from the public library, entitled *The Cure of Self-Consciousness*.

Taking up this volume I opened it at Exercise Ten.

"Place yourself calmly before a looking-glass," I read. "Fold your arms and gaze at your reflection steadily. Then, narrowing your eyes, give yourself a fearless stare. You are strong, composed, cool." Without question I was cool. "Next, take a deep breath, exhale firmly and repeat three times, in a low yet potent voice, 'Julius Caesar and Napoleon! I will! I will!! I will!!!'"

I obeyed the instructions implicitly—although my eyes watered and their green hue disheartened me a little. I even took a torn-out sheet of exercise book, printed in bold letters the words "I WILL" and pinned it on the wall where it would meet my fearless stare whenever I awoke. Then I knelt down by the bed.

My prayers were long and complicated, strainingly kept free from all distractions, not directed towards the vague bearded God of my early childhood, but centred ardently upon the Saviour. Occasionally I would guiltily remember the Father and the Holy Ghost and hasten to placate them. But Jesus, in His infinite love and goodness, was the Custodian of my trusting heart. And when I thought of His Mother, whose face had lately grown suspiciously like Alison's face, tears of yearning welled from my closed eyes. Nor were the Saints forgotten. I was continually running up against new Saints I wanted to pray to; and of course once I had started I could not leave them out for fear of offending them. The newest figure in my growing calendar was Anthony, protector of youth.

The final act is at hand: opportunity for that laugh, that sudden unwanted laugh which one hears often in the theatre at a moment when the author has meant to convey something of quiet pathos, of truth, and has failed or perhaps been misunderstood. Let us laugh together, then, as, looking back, we see this lanky shivering boy, this simpleton barely purified by the ordeal of the bridge and the icy bath, take from a hiding place at the back of the drawer a strange instrument, a piece of rope to which are tied bits of old iron, two heavy door keys, a door handle, a broken piece of skate. Quickly, with the familiarity of custom, he ties this about his waist in such a manner that the disturbing metal bears upon his spine. Thus, if he lies upon his back, the position in which one dreams, he will at once awaken. At last he is beneath the patched sheet, curled stiffly upon his side. He has blown out the candle. He is girded like an anchorite and round his scraggy neck he wears a rosary, four authentic miraculous medals, one blessed by the Holy

Father Himself, also the brown scapulars and the blue scapulars—if there were pink or heliotrope scapulars he would certainly wear these too. He has done everything he can. Comforted by this thought, he invites the little death of sleep, with one final aspiration.

"Dear Lord ... please let me win the Marshall."

Chapter Five

Morning comes early and joyfully upon a holiday. On Monday, before the white sky showed its first signs of brightening, I was out of the house quietly, and waiting at the Levenford Cross for Tom Drin, who was to drop me off at Luss on his lochside delivery round.

Tom was late and in a bad humour. He should not have had to work to-day—even I was exempt from my obligations with the rolls—but they were very short-handed at the Blair warehouse. I climbed into the flat, open van amongst the bags of meal and we set off behind the quiet clop-clopping of the horse.

The empty cobbled streets were fresh with morning. A woman taking in milk, a man in his shirt twitching the blind of an upper window, a girl sleepily banging a bass mat at a half-open door—all this conveyed a shining sense of expedition. I was going fishing with Gavin; my last fling before I settled down to grind for the Marshall.

The sun rose but did not break through. It was one of those still silvery days, full of warmth and soft luminous light, when sounds, though muted, are heard from afar and the intervening silences are filled with the rushing of the sap in the green leaves. As the horse's back rose and fell gently, like a ship, between the shafts, the countryside slipped past—misted woods, glimpses of park land, a grey mansion with tall chimneys, terraces and glasshouses, amongst the steaming trees.

At the back doors of these big country houses I helped Tom to unload the sacks and forage. He was a shaggy, muddling sort of man and was several times hard put to propitiate an angry groom complaining that his "order" had been imperfectly executed. Once, as we lifted a heavy box, we found that the hundredweight bag of meal underneath had burst and discharged its contents through the floorboards of the van. Tom cursed, scratched his head, then said to me with an air of smoothing things over: "Never mind, never mind. It'll not be missed!"

When we jogged into Luss it was afternoon, and Gavin was seated, yet without impatience, on the milestone at the head of the short village street. He wore the restrained outfit of his exclusive school, grey flannel trousers and shirt, a shapeless cricketing hat of the same grey, relieved, or, rather exalted by a thin band of blue and white, the Larchfield colours. Impossible to convey the distinction of this waiting figure—grown, like myself, yet still slight—the restrained unconscious pride of that face, already sunburned, beneath the careless, pulled-down hat. At least I can record the silent joy of our terrible handclasp.

"No fishing until evening, I'm afraid," Gavin murmured, as the van lumbered off. "No wind and too bright."

We walked through the quiet lochside village, passing between a score of cottages, all low, straw-thatched and whitewashed, spaced on the short white road which began at the green hill foot and ended at the silver Loch. Fuchsias and rambler roses grew up the cottages, losing themselves in the yellow thatch. The fuchsias were already in flower, dripping a crimson shower against the whitewashed walls. A brown collie dog lay stretched out, dreaming in the white dust. There came a sweet hum of bees. Through the haze we could see the toy wooden pier with row-boats moored by bleached ropes. At such beauty, we exchanged our rare, our secret glance.

Until the hidden sun went down, Gavin and I sat on an upturned boat, outside his father's fishing hut, sorting out tackle, practising that economy of words to which we were pledged. At seven o'clock, after Mrs. Glen, the woman of the cottage, had given us a fine tea of fresh baked scones and boiled new-laid eggs washed down with creamy milk, we righted the boat, pushed it into the water. It was still too early, but the mauve shimmer on the Loch was giving promise of the dusk. I took the oars, pulling out to the still coolness, then stopped rowing, letting the boat drift out, far out upon the calm between the high hills. As the light faded the mauve deepened to dark purple, our faces grew indistinct, then from the disappearing shore came the slow sound of the bagpipes, like the far voice of a man who has lost everything except his soul. I felt Gavin grow rigid in the boat with an anguish of feeling. Nothing was proof against this moment and that sound, not even our stoic vows. Hidden by the growing darkness, suddenly, and in a low voice, Gavin spoke.

"I understand you are sitting the Marshall, Robie?"

I started, quite taken aback. "Yes. . . . How did you know?"

"Mrs. Keith told my sister." Gavin paused, rather heavily. "I am trying for it too."

I gazed at him dumbly; even the mountains seemed to share my shocked confusion.

"But Gavin . . . you don't need the Bursary!"

His frown was palpable in the darkness.

"You'd be surprised." He spoke slowly, with deep embarrassment. "My father has been worried in the business lately. When you buy in bulk—corn and oats, for instance—sometimes you have to take a heavy loss. It isn't as easy as some people think. . . . I mean these people who envy my father and run him down for keeping up what they call too much style." He paused. "My father doesn't like display, Robie. But he has his position to keep up as Provost." A longer pause. "He's done so much for me . . . now that he's so worried I would like to do something for him."

I was silent. I had known for a long time that Gavin worshipped his father; and I had heard whispers that all was not well with the Provost's business. Yet the knowledge that we must oppose each other for the prize on which I had set my heart came as an unexpected blow. Before I could speak he went on.

"With all the cleverest boys in the county competing, one more won't make much difference. Besides, there's the honour of the town. Do you know, it's twelve years since a Levenford boy took the Bursary." He drew a fierce breath of resolution. "One of us must win it."

"You may be the one, Gavin," I said, in a strained voice, only too well aware that he was a fine scholar.

We did not now engage upon those passionate repudiations which had been a feature of our younger days. Gavin replied broodingly: "I admit I would like to win for my father's sake. But I think you have a better chance ... it's hard for me to say that, for I'm proud ... I suppose it's my Highland blood ... and having so wonderful a father." He paused. "If you win, will you go on to be a doctor? ... Or"—he lowered his voice as though he might be overheard—"do you still want to be a priest?"

Not yet recovered from the shock of his earlier communication, I nevertheless received the question with dignity. Gavin was the only person on earth before whom I would reveal myself.

"I don't think I'm good enough to be a priest," I said. "And I must admit my whole heart is set on being a medical biologist, you know, a doctor who does research. Of course when I think of Father Damien and the Curé d'Ars, especially during benediction, I want to give up everything, even falling in love with some good and beautiful girl." A wave of renunciation swept over me. "Yes, then I simply long to go away and try to be a really great saint, eating mouldy potatoes, treating money like dross—that especially would be wonderful—and living in a rough habit and a kind of trance before the altar. I wish I could make you understand what it means, Gavin, when, at benediction, we have our exposition."

"I have an idea," Gavin murmured, rather shamefaced. "Of course ... it would be awful for you if it wasn't what you thought." He added: "I mean, if after all it was only bread."

"Yes," I agreed. "It would be awful. But by praying you can keep that thought out of your head. Prayer is really wonderful, Gavin. You can't imagine the things I've got by praying, for them. And I could give you hundreds, well, dozens of other cases. You know Mrs. Rourke who keeps the dairy shop. Well, Papa was going to prosecute her for selling deficient milk. I saw her praying and praying in church. And do you know, Gavin, the milk bottle that

Papa had taken the sample in burst. Yes, burst completely during the test. And it was the only time this had ever happened to Papa in all his experience." I got my breath again. "Of course one mustn't pray for unworthy intentions. Although they say that Madame de Pompadour's emerald eyes were lovely, you know I loathe the colour of mine; but one wouldn't pray to have that changed, at least, not overnight."

"Will you pray to win the Marshall?" Gavin asked rather stiffly.

"Yes . . . I'm afraid I shall, Gavin." I hung my head, then added, with a rush of generous enthusiasm: "But if I'm not to be allowed to win I'll pray that you do. You're so decent, Gavin, not like most people in the town, even some of my relatives . . . You know how they look down on Catholics. Isn't it absurd? Why, only the other day Canon Roche showed me in the almanac that all over the world there are thirty-two Catholic dukes, just think of it, thirty-two dukes . . . and all that one hears in Levenford is . . . Well, never mind. But that's why I'd like to succeed, just to show them"—a dramatic note entered my voice—"that someone who is despised could be great . . . could become a wonderful scientist . . . a kind of Saviour of humanity . . . perhaps reconcile science and religion . . . perhaps reconcile all the religions."

Overcome by my own stupendous conception, I was silent.

"Yes," Gavin said slowly. "It's pretty rotten that we've got to fight each other over the Bursary. Nothing will interfere with our friendship of course. But we must take and give no quarter." He smiled palely. "I know some prayers, too. . . ."

Out of the soft darkness the moon began to show behind the Ben, then softly it fell upon the waters, streaking the liquid blackness with a constant play of light. We had drifted inshore and there the trees stood darkly still, like plumes raised for the funeral of a god. No, they were simply trees . . . trees growing in a silent splendid land, bathed in the first twilight of creation.

Suddenly a fish jumped, unseen, in the inky shallows and, in a flash, a new mood was thrust upon us. I saw Gavin dimly, reaching for his rod, heard him whisper: "There's one at last."

I brought the boat gently along the bank, dipping my blades

noiselessly. I held my breath as Gavin began to cast, sitting in the stern, motionless, except for the slow rhythmic sweep of his right forearm. Now and then I caught the gleam of the rod, the shimmer of the wet line as it cut the darkness in a silver arc and fell silently, distantly upon the water.

Suddenly there was another splash, louder than the first; and with a start of excitement, I saw Gavin's rod-tip bend like a drawn bow, felt the quivering vibration of his hands as they clasped the butt. As the reel whirred into the silence, from between his teeth Gavin said: "Keep us away, Robie. Don't let him under the boat."

The fish was now leaping, dashing madly in the liquid blackness, sending up jewels of spray when he broke the surface. Backing from the point of Gavin's throbbing rod, I did my best to keep him from beneath our keel. There was no need of silence now. My oars splashed as wildly as the splashing fish. As he started each rush I dug my blades frantically.

"Well done," Gavin panted. "He's a salmon. And a good one." A moment later, "Ship the oars."

The struggle was tearing the arms from his body, yet, though he well knew the thinness of the thread which bound him to the fish, he dared not yield an inch.

Slowly, carefully, he began to wind his reel. The moon picked out his taut figure, his resolute young face, upon which I burningly fixed my eyes, waiting for his next command.

The salmon was rushing less, Gavin was bringing him nearer.

"I see him," Gavin said in a low, husky voice. "A fresh-run fish. Get the gaff. Under this seat."

I crouched down and stretched my arm for the gaff, but as I fumblingly leaned over, my foot slipped on the wet thwarts, I fell full length across the seat, skinning my shins, almost upsetting the boat.

Not a word from Gavin, not a single reproach for my clumsiness. Only, when I had recovered myself and the rocking boat was still: "Have you got it?"

"Yes, Gavin."

A pause. Still quietly, yet with a growing urgency, Gavin whispered:

"He's lightly hooked. I see the fly outside his mouth. We'll have just one chance with him. Take your gaff, and when I bring him up, don't stab at him, just slide the point under his gills."

I took the gaff with a surge of anxiety, kneeling in the well of the boat. Now I saw the salmon, deep, wide and gleaming, of a size which startled me. I had never gaffed so large a fish in my life. Gaffing was a treacherous business. Gavin, who gaffed for his father, had often told me how many salmon had been lost in this last difficult act. I began to shake, my eyes blinked. My ears, too, started their horrible twitch.

The fish was near ... nearer .. near enough to touch. I had a rush of panic, a frightful impulse to impale this great slippery creature with my lance. But no, pale as death, shivering with ague, I waited till Gavin turned him over, then I slipped the gaff under his jaw and brought him quietly over the gunwale. Now Gavin crouched beside me. The moon, riding serene and high in the night sky, showed two boys, near to each other, peering in silent rapture at the noble fish, curving and glimmering, in the bottom of the boat.

Yet, gazing at the defeated salmon, I felt, suddenly, a sad constriction of my heart. I thought:

"Gavin and I ... One of us must be defeated."

Chapter Six

Next morning we slept late in our bunks at the fishing bothy, and when Mrs. Glen had given us breakfast Gavin took his father's hunting knife and in the bright sunshine outside the cottage divided the salmon cleanly in two. The firm pink flesh, with a darker core and a backbone like a pearl button, showed the fish to be in perfect condition.

"We'll toss," Gavin said. "That's the fair way. I'd say there was six pounds in each piece. But the tail-half is the best."

He spun a sixpence and I guessed right.

Gavin smiled generously. "Remember: Boil for only twenty minutes. It makes grand eating that way."

We wrapped our pieces in green rushes and placed them in the basket carrier of Gavin's bicycle. Then we said good-bye to Mrs. Glen and arranged ourselves on the bicycle—Gavin on the pedals, I perched on the "backstep" of the machine. We took turns in pedalling, dividing our labour as we had divided the fish, all the way to Levenford.

It was the dinner hour when I got to Lomond View. Papa and Mama were seated at the table as I entered the kitchen, aware that I had played truant, yet conscious of my peace offering, this precious half-salmon which would surely "do us," in Mama's phrase, for several days at least.

"Where have you been?" Sunk a little in his chair, Papa spoke in the contained, rather bloodless fashion now habitual with him and which seemed to date from that morning, months ago, when with a strange air he refused his boiled egg at breakfast, remarking steadily to Mama: "I want you to stop giving me 'kitchen.' We all eat far too much. The doctors say that heavy meals are bad for you."

"I told you, Papa," Mama now interposed. "Robie's been up the Loch. He mentioned that he mightn't be back last night."

Quickly, I put my bundle on the table. "Look what I've brought you. Gavin caught it but I gaffed it."

Mama parted the green rushes. She exclaimed, in pleased surprise, "Good for you, Robie."

I drank in her praise, eagerly, hoping also for a word from Papa. He was gazing at the fish, remotely, yet with a curious fascination. He was a man who seldom smiled; as for laughter, it was completely foreign to him; but now a kind of pale gleam lit up his face.

"It's a nice bit fish." He paused. "But what would we do with salmon? Far too rich. It would only upset our stomachs." He added, "Take it down to Donaldson's this afternoon."

"Oh, no, Papa." Mama's eyes became troubled, and her forehead furrowed. "Let us keep a few slices anyway."

"Take it all down," Papa said abstractedly. "Salmon is scarce. It's fetching three and six a pound—apparently there's fools that'll pay such a ransom. Donaldson should give us at least half a crown."

I stood aghast. Take this lovely salmon, which would enrich our meagre table, and sell it to the fishmonger! Papa could not mean it. But he had already resumed eating and Mama, with a nervous constriction of her lips, was saying to me as she spooned out the potato-bake remaining in the ashet: "Here's your lunch then, dear. Sit in."

That afternoon, I carried the fish down to Donaldson's in the High Street. Miserably, I handed my rush-covered burden to stout, red-faced Mr. Donaldson in his blue-striped apron, white jacket, and black straw hat. I was quite incapable of selling, of driving any bargain; but clearly Papa had "looked in" on his way to the office. Mr. Donaldson placed the salmon without a word on the white enamel scales. Six pounds exactly. Gavin's true eye had not lied. The big fishmonger, stroking his moustache, looked at me oddly.

"You caught it up the Loch?"

I nodded.

"Did he put up a good fight?"

"Yes." The memory of last night, the Loch, the moonlight, the comradeship, the splendid struggle, made me lower my eyes.

When Donaldson came back from his till, which was in a little glass-enclosed booth at the back, he said to me: "Six pounds at half a crown the pound makes fifteen shillings neat. Fifteen pieces of silver, boy. Give it to Mr. Leckie with my compliments." He stood watching me as I went out of the shop.

Immediately Papa came in that evening I gave him the money, which had made a heavy lump in my pocket all the afternoon. He nodded and ran it out of his cupped hand into his leather purse: he had a very expert touch with any kind of coins.

During tea he was in an agreeable mood. He told Mama that he had met Mr. Cleghorn on his way home. The Waterworks Superintendent was looking very poorly, quite failed in fact, and it was rumoured he was suffering from a stone in the kidney. There was good reason to believe that, even if this condition did not "carry him off," his retirement must be only a matter of months.

Papa's tone was unusually cheerful as he discussed Mr. Cleghorn's probable demise. As he rose he said: "Come into the parlour, Robert. I want a word with you."

We sat at the window, by the vase of dried esparto grass, behind the lace curtains in the unused room. Outside the green chestnut boughs were prancing, like mettled horses, in the breeze.

Papa studied me with reflective kindness, his pale lips pursed, the tips of his fingers pressed together.

"You're getting quite a big lad now, Robert. You've done well at school. I'm very satisfied with you."

I reddened—Papa did not praise me often. He added: "I hope you feel that we have done the right thing by you."

"Oh, I do, Papa. I'm most grateful for everything."

"Mr. Reid came into the office to-day with a paper he wanted signed. We had a long talk about your future." He cleared his throat. "Have you any views on the subject yourself?"

My heart was full. "Mr. Reid probably told you, Papa, I'd ... I'd give anything to study medicine at Winton University."

Papa seemed to shrink a little, actually to diminish in size. Perhaps he was only settling deeper in his chair. He forced a smile.

"You know we are not made of money, Robert."

"But Papa ... Didn't Mr. Reid speak to you about the Marshall?"

"He did, Robert." A spot of colour showed on Papa's transparent cheek; he looked at me earnestly, as though he were defending me, with indignation, against some deception. "And I told him it was most misguided to have raised your hopes with such a wild idea. Mr. Reid presumes beyond his position, and I don't like his radical views. Any examination is unpredictable—as Murdoch's experience showed. And the Marshall! Why, the competition for that Bursary is tremendous. Frankly—without wishing to offend you—I don't believe you are capable of winning it."

"But you'll let me try." I gulped out the words with sudden anxiety.

The "peaky" look deepened on Papa's thin face. He glanced away from me, out of the window.

"In your own interests, I can't, Robert. It would only put all sorts of wrong notions in your head. Even if you did win, I couldn't afford to let you go another five years without earning a penny piece. A great deal of outlay has been incurred in your behalf. It's high time you started to pay it back."

"But, Papa ..." I pleaded desperately, then broke off, feeling myself turn white and sick. I wanted to explain that I would pay him back twice over if only he would give me my chance, to tell him that what I lacked in brilliance I would make up in solid work. But I sat crushed and speechless. I knew it would be useless—there was no arguing with Papa. Like most weak men he attached the utmost importance to not changing his mind. There was no rancour in his attitude—he never used me harshly; in fact it was his boast that he had not laid a finger on me in his life. Moved by the strange forces which worked within him, he had actually persuaded himself that he was "doing this for the best."

"As a matter of fact," he went on consolingly, "I saw the head timekeeper about you last week. If you go into the Works this summer you'll learn your trade before you're twenty-one. And you'll be earning good wages all the time, contributing to the upkeep of the household. Under the circumstances isn't that the most sensible thing you could do?"

I gave an inarticulate murmur. I did not want to go in for engineering, I suspected that I was unfitted for the three years' apprenticeship in the foundry. Even if he were right, all the reason in the world would not assuage the tearing bitterness in my heart.

Papa stood up. "I've no doubt it's a disappointment." He sighed and patted me on the shoulder as he left the room. "Beggars can't be choosers, my boy."

I remained seated, with bowed head. He had made all arrangements at the Works—that, no doubt, was the news Mama had written Kate the other day. As I thought of my buoyant hopes, my talks with Alison and Gavin, the whole foolish structure I had raised, water ran down the inside of my nose. I groaned.

I wanted to be like Julius Cæsar and Napoleon. But I was still myself.

Chapter Seven

The days dragged on and I was in despair. On Thursday, shortly before the close of the Easter vacation, I was mowing Mrs. Bosomley's back green—Papa had an arrangement with our neighbour whereby, for a shilling a month, I kept her grass cut and tidy. These minor earnings of mine were not paid to Papa, that would have been undignified, but, since Mrs. Bosomley owned our house as well as her own—the double property had been left her by her husband—Papa kept a careful record and deducted the exact amount every quarter from the cheque he wrote her for rent.

This afternoon, when I had finished and was putting away the machine, she came to the window, beckoned me inside and set before me a slice of cold apple dumpling and a cup of tea.

Drinking her own very strong tea, which she took without sugar, she watched me with an expression of lively disapproval. She had become stouter and more matronly, and her face, with its network of fine veins over the cheekbones, had a sort of battered look, like an old-time boxer's; but her eye was bright, and her lips had a humorous twist which showed that she was very much alive.

"Robert," she said at last, "I'm sorry to tell you that you are getting more and more like a horse."

"Am I, Mrs. Bosomley?" I stammered dismally.

She nodded. "It's your face. It grows longer every day. Why in the name of goodness are you such a melancholy boy?"

"I suppose I'm just naturally sad, Mrs. Bosomley."

"Do you enjoy being miserable?"

"No ..." I choked dryly over the dumpling, although it was

lusciously damp with fruit. "Not as a general rule, Mrs. Bosomley. But sometimes I'm sad and happy at the same time."

"Are you sad and happy now?"

"No ... I'm afraid I'm just sad."

Mrs. Bosomley shook her head and lit a cigarette. She smoked so much her fingers were stained with nicotine—that was one of the things which made her different from the more conventional residents of Drumbuck Road. There were all sorts of stories about her but she did not seem to mind public opinion in the slightest. She was original, quick-tempered, kind. Murdoch told me she used to quarrel furiously with her husband and fling dishes at him—Murdoch could hear them through the wall—and the next minute she would be out with him in the garden, calling him pet names, with her arm round his waist.

She reached out abruptly. "Let me read your cup and see if I can't find something cheerful in it."

Revolving my empty cup between her fingers, with the cigarette in the corner of her mouth to keep the smoke out of her eyes, she examined the tea leaves at the bottom. She was an excellent cup reader, understood about dreams and the lines of the hand and could tell fortunes with the cards as well.

"Ve ... ry interesting. Your aura is green ... a delicate shade. You will be most successful in the neighbourhood of fields and woods. But don't linger there after dark until you are a little older. You are fierce and jealous in your attitude towards the weaker sex. Aha! What's this? Yes, indeed! You're going to meet a dark handsome woman with a beautiful figure when you're twenty-one." She raised her head. "Doesn't that buck you up?"

"I'm afraid not, Mrs. Bosomley."

"She will be of an extremely affectionate disposition ... the Spanish type ... and crazy about red hair."

But I merely blushed and she put down the cup and began to laugh.

"Oh, my dear boy, you make me ache all over. What *is* worrying you?"

"Oh, nothing very much, Mrs. Bosomley," I said dully.

"I can't drag it out of you." She collected the tea things and got up. "Why don't you talk things over with your grandpa?" A slightly self-conscious note came into her voice—she seemed always to have a high opinion of Grandpa. "In spite of what they say of him, Mr. Gow is a most remarkable man."

Unfortunately I did not now subscribe to this view. I was fond of Grandpa, but the days when I had run to him with my childish pains were over. Also, I had acquired the faculty of closing, like an oyster, upon a private trouble and of wrestling with it, as that mollusc might strive against its pearly irritant, in stoic solitude. I could not even bring myself to speak to Mama, who looked anxious and unhappy about me—perhaps I realized that anything I could say would only make matters worse.

However, it was apparent that Mrs. Bosomley had "had a word" with Grandpa, for on the following day he took me aside and made me tell him what was wrong.

I shall not readily forget the expression with which he heard me: the pained, bemused wrinkling of his eyes. He was a man of many sins, follies, and evasions, yet he was incapable of petty meanness—he could not understand it. There was a kind of grandeur in his face as he reached out for his hat and stick.

"Come on, boy. We'll go down and see this Mr. Reid of yours."

I did not care to be seen with Grandpa in the streets—his little peculiarities increased my own terrible self-consciousness—yet I was too dejected to offer much resistance; and presently, although I was convinced that nothing could come of his intervention, we were on our way, through streets bathed in Saturday afternoon quiet, to Reid's lodging.

Most of the Academy masters occupied respectable villas in the "good" districts, like Knoxhill and Drumbuck Road. But Jason Reid lived in a tall dingy building near the old Vennel, a far from creditable part of the town, largely inhabited by Polish and working families, by dock labourers, and other humble people. His back room overlooked a sooty court; by throwing up his front window, usually opaque from lack of cleaning, he had an excellent view of the three shining brass balls of the Levenford Mutual Aid Society and of the interesting procession which, every evening, rolled through the swing doors of the Harbour Tavern. Reid liked this dwelling for the complete freedom it afforded him; also because it outraged convention and affirmed his socialistic views.

Reid had come to the Academy two years before as a stop-gap when Mr. Douglas was appointed to the headmastership of Ardfillan High School. Reid himself made it clear that his appointment was temporary—he did not care to remain long in one place—also the Rector was obviously not impressed by Jason's careless dress, unorthodox methods and exasperating lack of deference. Yet Jason remained. He was a brilliant and original teacher; even the Rector came to admit it: and besides running the science side he could, most convenient, take the higher English class—he had both the M.A. and B.Sc. honours degrees from Trinity College. As for Reid himself, when I asked him, many years later, why he had remained so long in the dead-end of Levenford, he replied, with his peculiar flat-nosed, ox-eyed smile: "It was very handy for the pawnshop."

This flippancy was the persistence of a pose forced upon him by the circumstances of his life. He was the son of a North of Ireland clergyman and, despite his slight disfigurement, had been intended for the Church, but halfway through his studies he had fallen under the influence of Huxley and renounced the Book of Genesis. The family estrangement which resulted was something Reid never mentioned, yet I sensed it was this upheaval which had forced on him his mask of indifference, the contempt of conventional conduct which broke through, even in his teaching. On his first appearance before the English class we were following a practice introduced by Mr. Douglas rising in turn to proclaim our views on a chosen subject—which was, that afternoon, "What I Shall Do Next Sunday." Lounging in his chair, with his feet on his desk, which was the unconventional attitude in which he chose to instruct us, Reid heard us out: we were all extremely virtuous and correct. Then, in a considering voice, he declared: "Next Sunday? Why, I think I shall lie in bed and drink beer."

For all his bravado he was an unhappy and lonely soul. He kept apart from the other masters: he had nothing in common with them. Occasionally he attended a meeting of the local Fabian Society; but all the other Levenford clubs, including the famous "Philosophical," he dismissed derisively as mere "drinking dens." He had no apparent interest in women. I never at this time saw him speak, or walk, with one in, the street. Yet, because of his devotion to music, he had become friendly with Mrs. Keith and her little circle. The house in Sinclair Drive was the only one he seemed to care to visit.

Perhaps Reid thought I had the makings of a scientist; more probably it was our common heritage of oddness which led him to take an interest in me. Frequently on Sunday mornings he had me to breakfast and fed me with many delicious fried sausages. He was not a great talker and was never in the smallest degree demonstrative. On the contrary he parodied the emotions. He had an austere taste in literature and did his best to knock my fine phrases out of me. He liked Addison, Locke, Hazlitt and Montaigne. He was an admirer of Schiller. Referring to his own isolation in the narrow-minded town, he would quote that philosopher: "The only relation with the public of which a man never repents, is war." Yet occasionally I surprised in his full eyes a glance which was not warlike, but affectionate.

As Grandpa and I went up the narrow staircase, dark and unhygienic, we heard the strains of music coming from Reid's rooms. Grandpa tapped with his stick on the door. And a voice from behind the panel called out: "Come in."

Jason lay exhausted in a wicker armchair by the window, jacket off, trouser ends clipped round thick socks, his feet—still incased in black lace-up bicycle shoes—resting against the table on which stood a foam-topped glass and a gramophone with a flat revolving disc and a long flower-shaped trumpet. As Grandpa began in his suavest manner to introduce himself, Jason silenced him warningly, and with a sweep of his arm motioned us to seat ourselves. When the disc came to an end he rose quickly and changed it, then flung himself back into the basket chair. From time to time he mopped his brow and drank from the glass. I saw that he had come in from one of his violent bicycle spins—spasmodically, when he felt he needed exercise, he would fling himself upon his machine and scorch furiously, up hill and down dale, head down, legs working madly, rivers of sweat running from his eyes, miles of dust floating in the air behind him. Then, safely returned, he would soothe himself with vast quantities of food and drink, and the symphonies of Beethoven recently produced on Columbia records by the Philharmonic Orchestra of London. Reid loved music, he played the piano quite beautifully, but seldom, for he despised his own talent as inadequate and amateurish.

When the symphony was finished he stopped the machine and restored the discs to an album.

"Well, sir," he addressed Grandpa politely, "what can I do for you?"

Grandpa had been slightly irked by the waiting, the lack of *éclat* in his reception. He said peevishly: "Are you quite free to attend to us?"

"Quite," said Reid.

"Well," Grandpa said, "I wanted to talk to you about this boy and the Marshall Bursary."

Jason gazed from Grandpa to me, then he went to a cupboard below the bookshelves and brought out another bottle of beer. He glanced sideways at Grandpa while he inclined the bottle. "My instructions—and of course, a contemptible usher like myself can only obey his instructions—are to keep our young friend and the Bursary as far apart as possible."

Grandpa smiled, his grim, majestic smile, and leaned forward on the handle of his stick. Waiting with pitiful eagerness, I saw that it was to be a peroration, one of his fruitiest:

"My dear sir, it may be true that you have received these instructions. But I am here to countermand them. Not only in my own name, but in the name of decency, freedom, and justice. There are, after all, sir, even in this unenlightened age, certain essential liberties permitted to the humblest individual. Liberty of religion, liberty of speech, liberty to develop the gifts with which the Great Artificer has endowed him. Now, sir, if there is anyone low enough, and mean enough, to deny these liberties, I, for one, will not stand by and countenance it."

Grandpa's voice was rising magnificently and Jason was listening with delight, the faint smile which had appeared when Grandpa used the words "Great Artificer" still stretching the scar on his upper lip.

"Hear! Hear!" he said admiringly. "Take this, old boy, you must be dry."

He handed the glass of beer to Grandpa, and added: "Rhetoric apart, I don't in the least see how it can be done."

Grandpa sucked in the foam from his moustache, and said quickly, in a different voice:

"Enter him on the quiet. Don't say a word to anyone."

Reid shook his head. "It couldn't be done. I have enough trouble on my hands already. Besides, the entry must be signed by his guardian."

"I'll sign it," Grandpa said.

Jason received this oddly, and began presently to pace up and down the room in his soft cycling shoes, his brows knitted, lips no longer smiling. Following him with intent eyes, I saw that he was turning over in his mind the idea presented by Grandpa; and, with an almost painful undersurge of hope, I discerned in him signs of a mounting enthusiasm.

"By Jove!" He stopped suddenly, staring straight ahead, thinking out loud. "It would be rather splendid if we could pull it off. Keep the whole thing mum. Work like fury on the quiet. And then ... if we could do it ... the look on all their faces, from the Rector's to that little runt Leckie's ... at the surprise result." He spun round to me. "If you did get it, they couldn't possibly prevent you from going on to college. Good Lord! It would be something. Like a dark horse winning the Derby."

He studied me, with his full eyes, as though weighing up my points, while I flushed vividly and, turning my cap nervously in my hands, tried to sustain his stare. Whatever Mrs. Bosomley's opinion of my equine propensities, I did not feel like a Derby winner. Mama, who always cut my hair to save the barber's fee, had given me the day before a crop which made my scalp gleam through and reduced the size of my head to most unintellectual dimensions. But Jason, always, from the beginning, was my friend. And now, his Irish blood was quickening, quickening to this new and sporting flavour of the event. He struck the air with his closed fist.

"By God!" he exclaimed, his own cheeks now flushed with excitement. "We'll have a shot at it. Might as well be killed for a sheep as a lamb. You know I always wanted you to try, Shannon. And now I do, more than ever. We'll not say a word. *We'll just tear in and win!*"

That moment can never be repeated—the lifting of my insufferable disappointment—the splendour of a re-opened future, of knowing that Reid believed in me—all this created in my heart a sense of singing joy. Grandpa was offering his hand to Jason; in fact we shook hands excitedly all round. Ah, it was, truly, a splendid moment. But Reid, wisely, cut it short.

"Don't let's make fools of ourselves." He drew up a chair close to us. "This thing is going to be damned difficult for you, Shannon. You're only fifteen and you'll be competing against fellows two and even three years your senior. Then you're full of faults. You know how you rush at things, jump to conclusions without proper deductions. You've got to correct all that."

I gazed at him with parted lips and shining eyes, not daring to speak, but conveying everything by my silence.

"I've a good idea of the lie of the land," Reid resumed in a tone so confidential it thrilled me through and through. "The picture for this year, as I see it, is this: A less than average entry in numbers, but high, quite high in quality. There are three boys in particular that I'm afraid of . . ." He enumerated on his fingers. "Blair of Larchfield, Allardyce of Ardfillan High, and a youngster named McEwan who's been educated privately. Blair you know—he's first-rate, a good all-rounder. Allardyce is eighteen and has been up before, which gives him a tremendous advantage. But the danger, the real danger is McEwan." Jason paused impressively—and oh, how I hated the unknown McEwan! "He's young, about your own age, the son of the classics master at Undershaws, and his father has been tutoring him specially for years. I understand he could speak Greek fluently when he was twelve years old. Knows half a dozen languages now. Quite the child prodigy, all high forehead and large spectacles. In fact, it's believed by those who know him that the Marshall is as good as in his pocket."

The slight bitterness in Reid's tone, his inflection of satire, could not disguise the fact that he was seriously afraid of this horrible boy who at breakfast probably asked his parent to pass the toast in Sanskrit. I could do no more than grit my teeth in silence.

"So you see, young Shannon," Jason concluded in a gentler tone, "we'll have to work genuinely hard. Oh, I won't kill you, not quite. You shall have an hour off every day, for exercise. You won't want to take it, once you get to the really hysterical stage, but I shall insist. You can cool your brain—God help you—walking in the country—or you can take out my bicycle—and mind you don't puncture it. I shall have quite a number of books to give you. Keep them in your bedroom. You'd better study there too. Nothing like a good blank wall for keeping you at it. I'll work out our schedule. I've got all the examination papers for the last ten years in my desk at school. We'll go over every question. We start work to-morrow ... I think that's everything. Any comments?"

I gazed at him, my eyes lit by a white flame of ardour, my whole body quivering with the intensity of my feeling. How could I thank him? How could I tell him that I would work, fight, and die for him?

"Well, sir," I stammered, "I promise you ..."

No use; but I am sure he understood. He rose, with alacrity, and began to select books for me from his shelves.

Grandpa helped me to carry them home. I was between heaven and earth, treading upon air.

Chapter Eight

At the beginning of June an event occurred, trivial in itself, yet so helpful to my purpose I felt it as an intervention of Providence upon my behalf, a direct answer to the petitions with which I was bombarding the Heavenly Throne.

Not long after our great decision in Mr. Reid's room I had come in from my morning "roll delivery" to find Adam, who seemed always to reach the house in the early hours, seated at breakfast, fresh and well-groomed, talking to Papa and Mama, having stepped out of his first-class "sleeper" on the night express from London—whenever Adam travelled on his expense sheet he did so in slap-up style. Although his Winton business connections required these periodic returns to the North, Adam was now in London: he had been appointed Southern representative of the Caledonia Insurance Company. While this change had brought him no increase in salary, Adam insisted it was a tribute to his business acumen and a step towards great things. He was living, at this time, in a residential hotel in Hanger Hill, Ealing.

As I began my own breakfast, of porridge and buttermilk, he resumed his remarks, having broken off to give me his usual hearty greeting.

"Yes, Mama, I think it would interest you to see the house."

"What house, dear?" Mama asked.

Adam smiled. "Why, the house I've just bought..."

"You've bought a house?" Papa spoke with the acute, almost professional interest of a member of the Levenford Building Society, in which, as a matter of fact, all his hard-wrung savings lay. "Where?"

"On the Bayswater Road," Adam said easily. "A first-class situation overlooking the Park. It's a first-class house, too, cream-painted stucco, seven floors high, mahogany staircase, marble piazza, very dignified, and a freehold. But there, you don't want to hear about it."

"But we do, dear," Mama breathed. "It's the most exciting news."

Adam laughed, holding out his cup for more tea. "Well, I'd had my eye on this property for some time, passed it every day on my way to the office. The 'For Sale' board had been up six months when one morning I saw a notice pasted across it: 'Auction. Next Week.' Ha! I thought. Might be interesting! I'd been looking out for a suitable real estate investment ever since I came South. So I dropped in the following Monday at the Auction Rooms. Usual sort of place, fine panelling, lots of gents in top hats. The auctioneer had a top hat too." Adam gave his bacon and eggs an amused glance. "After announcing that the house had cost six thousand, which incidentally is true, he started the bidding with his eye on me, at three thousand pounds. Up it went, up, up, all the top hats bidding against one-another, until it reached five thousand five hundred, where it hung a long, long time before it was knocked down to the shiniest top hat of all. I sat back, never said a word; it was funny the way they'd tried to get a rise out of me. I'd made my inquiries, you see. I knew the bank had a mortgage of two thousand and was threatening to foreclose. The very next day I had a letter from shiny top hat offering to sacrifice the property for four thousand. I threw it in my wastepaper basket. Then . . ."

He took us, step by step, down the devious yet unhurried ways which had made him, only a week before, absolute owner of this magnificent mansion for the cash payment of nineteen hundred pounds.

"My goodness." Mama gave a little gasp, enthralled yet fearful—although the bargain had been great the sum involved was, to her, colossal, terrifying, and indeed it represented most of Adam's capital, saved over the last ten years. "You certainly got the better of them . . . and London men, too. What will you do with the house now, dear? Live in it?"

"Well, no, Mama." Adam received the naïve suggestion, enough to make the angels laugh, with a nice consideration. "The thing's a white elephant in its present form. My idea is to convert it. Eight self-contained flats at rents varying from seventy to one hundred and fifty pounds. I calculate on a net six hundred after paying taxes and the caretaker's wages. Let's say a twenty per cent. return. Not bad for my first real venture outside my own business."

Papa had been listening with strained attention. He moistened his lips. "Twenty per cent. And the Building Society pays me three."

Adam smiled carelessly. "Private enterprise pays higher dividends. And of course the conversion will take money. Probably another nine hundred. It's a nuisance having to find it. I'm not anxious to let all and sundry in on such a good thing."

A faint colour had crept over Papa's forehead. Always his respect for Adam had been tinged by a vague distrust, the distrust of a cautious man for the intangible operations of finance. But now, this house, solid mahogany and marble, offering a princely income—he spoke with difficulty.

"I've always believed in bricks and mortar. It's a pity I couldn't take a look at it with you, Adam."

"I don't see why you shouldn't . . . you might do worse." Adam paused thoughtfully. "Why don't you and Mama come down and spend a couple of weeks with me this summer? Take a month if necessary, combine business with pleasure. I can put you up at Ealing. You owe yourselves a holiday."

"Oh, Adam," Mama exclaimed, clasping her hands at this long-hoped-for invitation.

A great deal of discussion followed: Papa, intensely cautious, never made a decision lightly. But before Adam took his departure it was settled. And I realized, with a thrill of joy, that they would be away, leaving me free of all observation and restraint, during the final stages of my study, during the Bursary examination. Nothing could have been more blessedly opportune.

The days rushed on and soon, while I worked in my room, I heard a strange sound in the house. I had to think for several minutes before I understood that it was Mama singing—low and unmusical to be sure, but still singing. Papa's good clothes hung all pressed and ready, the two Gladstone bags were polished till they shone. Somehow, Mama had managed to buy herself, from Miss Dobbie's, the small millinery shop which dealt in "remnants," a length of dark brown voile and, with flying needle, had "run herself up" a summer dress. But her greatest adventures were with fur—a stringy necklet which she had possessed for at least a quarter of a century, yet which she produced proudly each spring from its camphored hibernation. Mama's fur! One never knew what animal had died to give it being: although there was always, at the back of my mind, the unmentionable vision of some unfortunate cat, flattened by such a prodigious weight as had destroyed poor Samuel Leckie. Mama relined it with a strip of voile, saved from the dress length, reshaped it slightly to bring it up to date. I could see her on the back green, airing it on the clothes-line, shaking it, happily, blowing into it to raise its meagre pile. ... She had not had a holiday in five years.

Whenever she was in danger of "getting above herself," Papa brought her back to earth, with these words of warning: "Think of the fares!"

He felt that if she was not restrained there would be, in her present mood, no end to the expense, the deadly excesses, into which she might entrap him. The thought of eating in restaurants, of being forced, through some misadventure, to spend the night at a hotel, became his nightmare. He planned with redoubled care. Enough food would be taken in a cardboard hatbox to sustain them on the journey, they would sit up, third class, through the night, all the way to London. Already, Papa carried in his vest pocket a little notebook marked *Expenses of Visit to Adam*. He had, I think, the illusory hope that Adam would reimburse him. On the first line was written: "To two railway tickets ... £-7-9-6"; and to this amount Papa returned, time and again, with the gloomy air of a man who had made a ruinous outlay. Later, I learned from Murdoch that Papa, by obsequious representations, had managed to secure "privilege tickets," which were issued to certain officials entirely free of charge.

On the eve of their departure Mama came to my room, sat down on the bed and watched me in silence.

"You're quite busy these days, dear boy." Her faint smile deepened as she added: "And no doubt you will be, while we're in London."

Did Mama know? Had Grandpa whispered a word to her? I hung my head as she continued:

"Your boots aren't in too good a state. They'll not stand soling. If they give out before . . . well, before we come back, there's that nice strong brown pair of Kate's in the cupboard under the stairs."

"Yes, Mamma." I masked my discomposure at the mention of those long narrow boots, once used by Kate for hockey, in colour a jaundiced yellow, lacing halfway up the leg, and so manifestly feminine the very thought of them gave me gooseflesh.

"They've kept their shape well," Mama murmured, persuasively. "I had a look at them the other day."

"I think I'll manage, Mama," I said.

There was a pause.

"You usually manage, don't you, Robie?" Mama smiled gently. She rose, rubbed her hand over my head. Her eyes lingered a little upon me as she went out. She whispered:

"Good luck to you . . . my own boy."

Chapter Nine

Immediately Papa and Mama departed, Grandpa moved my table and all my books into the parlour, which was never used, maintained solely as a patent of gentility. How well I remember that sacred room! It had a round marble fireplace with a gilt mirror overmantel and an aspidistra in the black-leaded grate. Against one wall was a chiffonier covered by lace doilies upon which lay a Japanese fan, three cowrie shells, and a glass paperweight inscribed "a Present from Ardfillan." On the round table in the centre was a red drugget cover with a gilt-clasped copy of *Pilgrim's Progress* laid out at a tasteful angle beside a vase of esparto grass. Near by was the upright piano with a revolving stool. A green plush-framed photograph of Mama and Papa in their wedding attire stood on top. There was one picture, an oil painting entitled "The Monarch of the Glen."

The wide bay formed by the window made a splendid study for me. Here I sat, alone, and with Reid, who could now come and go with freedom. The house was very silent, intensified by the exaggerated care of Grandpa's movements. Mama had arranged that Mrs. Bosomley should come in occasionally to help us; but Grandpa, to my surprise, proved himself a resourceful housekeeper—during those periods in his life when he had been obliged to fend for himself he had picked up the knack of certain dishes, especially soups. No apparent eccentricities, not a single misdemeanour. He seemed to enjoy the freedom of the vacant house, where he was able to potter about without fear of nagging and restraint. As might be surmised, severe restrictions had been placed upon us. Most of the china and cutlery had been locked away, also the good cooking utensils, since Mama was afraid Grandpa would "singe" the pots. She had written out precise instructions for our meals, based upon a small supply of groceries delivered to us every Monday from the stores. A bare pittance had been left behind in ready cash. Nevertheless, Grandpa managed to circumvent these difficulties. He developed a habit of dropping in at the Nursery and, although Murdoch's attitude towards Grandpa could scarcely be described as amiable, we often had a fine cauliflower which did not figure on Mama's menu, or a great pot of floury potatoes which Grandpa boiled perfectly and which I particularly loved. Once or twice, as twilight fell, he departed with a dreamy air in the direction of Snoddie's Farm, and on the next day we would have for dinner a boiled chicken which could only have come from God.

Although he tried to hide it, Grandpa displayed a profound respect for my studies. He had a high regard for "book learning" and indeed for books—which was strange, for he himself possessed no more than three volumes. I must not fail, in passing, to mention these faithful friends. The first was the *Poems* of Robert Burns, most of which he knew by heart; the second, a tattered book over which Grandpa chuckled repeatedly, *The Adventures of Hajji Baba;* the third, in a broken red binding, with a frontispiece of a grimy tramp writing, "Dear Sirs, ten years ago I used your soap, since then I have used no other," was *Pears' Shilling Encyclopedia*—I can still see Grandpa in our early days reaching out with an air of erudition for that wonderful compendium—"We'll see what Pears has to say about it."

Now, inevitably, the stage of his omniscience was over, but he still maintained a lofty air of piloting me through the shoals, and was delighted when I asked him to "hear" my equations or Latin verses. At the end of our first week he made me give up my early morning delivery work, which, by cutting into the best hours, when my head was clear, was proving a serious handicap. We were already deeply committed, nothing would redeem us but success; I went into the parlour and took my place at my books in the grey light of dawn, offering myself to the anguish of unremitting study. Reid had completely exempted me from the class, and all day long I laboured alone in white and burning solitude, in that front room, bent over my small table with passionate application. Time was growing short. My rivals were working, incessantly, far harder than I. There was only one prize. How could I hope to gain it if for an instant, even, I lifted my eyes from the page?

Every evening at six o'clock Reid arrived: with a short greeting and a long look to see how I was standing it, he took a chair beside me. He tutored me until ten, when Grandpa brought in cups of cocoa, which sometimes grew cold, unnoticed, amongst the papers, at our elbows. My stability was renewed by Jason's considered sanity, by his solid figure smelling of tobacco, chalk, and perspiration, by his familiar mannerism of touching back his light blond hair that always looked newly washed, and by the human warmth of his rather "bad" breath which, mingled with the odour of his person, seemed like the exudation of an inexhaustible vitality.

When, at last, Reid has gone—having urged me to go to bed, yet knowing that I will not do so—I draw up more closely to my table fighting my lassitude, my terrible desire for sleep. Perhaps, for a moment, I go to the bathroom to dash my head in water which, since the tank lies immediately beneath the roof, is, in summer, merely tepid. I return, flagging, yet compelled by an inner force to go on, to exact from myself the last ounce of effort. Always, I murmur a prayer before resuming, offering up all my work. To keep awake I jab my leg with a pen-nib, or knock my dull forehead with my knuckles, as if entreating it to understand. The minutes fall away, silently, into the silent night; and still my immovable figure, with coat discarded and sleeves rolled up for coolness, bare elbows on the table, hands clasping the reeling head, remains beneath the gaslight.

Two o'clock strikes. I rise and stagger to my room. Usually I sleep as though stunned the moment I fall upon my bed. But sometimes there are nightmares of my unpreparedness for the examination, of questions I cannot answer. And there are other nights when, worst of all, though dead with weariness, my brain refuses to rest, but continues to function with a hard unnatural lucidity, solving difficult quadratics, intricate problems in advanced trigonometry which normally require pages of calculations—all nothing, mere child's play to this poor brain of mine, whirling and rocketing over the fields of learning while my body lies helpless, as in a catalepsy, waiting for the first streaks of light beneath the blind that will usher me again to the tyranny of my ambition.

My sole respite came in the afternoon when towards five o'clock Grandpa forced me out for my short relaxation. On these evenings when Gavin returned home from Larchfield I employed this hour to meet him at Dalreoch stop, which was more convenient than the main Levenford station; and there, as he left the train and crossed the "goods" yard, I stood waiting at the big white gate, ready to fall into step beside him and compare despondent notes on the progress we had made.

Upon other days I went down to the Academy yard, where there was a high wall with a convenient buttress, to play a game of hand ball with Mr. Reid. Jason was good at fives and had performed, as he put it, in the Public Schools Championship at Queens Club. Our game was scarcely orthodox, for the court was not right, but it gave us lots of running about and I always felt the better for it.

Then, on my lucky afternoons, I saw Alison. Usually I met her at the end of Drumbuck Road as she returned slowly from her singing lesson, hatless, and carrying a rolled patent-leather music case under her arm. In the warm weather she wore a light dress which made her shape bud in the quiet breeze. We did not look at each other and we talked only of the most ordinary things. She would tell me what was happening at school, what Mr. Reid—for whom she had a great admiration—had said that day. Yet from time to time, despite her calmness, her eyes seemed to grow larger and softer, and her lips glowed with colour. When our ways diverged at the corner of Sinclair Drive I raced home, pausing only to pick up a stone and throw it hard. With my blood warm in my cheeks, I flung myself down at my books. Everything was going well with me. And Grandpa, who now brought to my table a cup of tea, was the best, the finest old man ever born.

No, no, I am quite wrong. It was he, the monster, who a week later plunged me to the abyss.

Chapter Ten

It was a hot, still afternoon, with a threat of thunder in the air. Only four days remained before the examination and I was overwrought, my nerves painfully on edge. I had gone to dip my head in water; then, as I stood drying my face, I heard the echo of Grandpa's laugh. I came out from the bathroom to the landing and called to him; but I received no answer. Was this an hallucination? Good heavens, surely my exertions had not brought me to the point of "hearing things." I went slowly upstairs to the open door of Mama's room from which the sound, muffled though it was, had seemed to come. I entered the room, which was quite empty, and immediately heard Mrs. Bosomley's voice followed again by Grandpa's laugh.

I started, then realized that, on this still afternoon, sounds were travelling through the dividing wall; they came from the house next door. Of course! ... I recollected seeing Grandpa trim his beard immediately after lunch.

I was on the point of turning away, when another sound brought me up short. In bewildered yet scared suspense, I gazed at the blank wall patterned with climbing roses, aware that the room through the wall was Mrs. Bosomley's bedroom. Grandpa and Mrs. Bosomley were both there, together.

Against my will, rooted by the consternation rising within me, I listened. Oh, God, surely not ... I tried to free myself from the thought. But there was no mistake, none whatever.

Convulsively, I tore myself away, ran out of the room, straight out of the house. I was shaking all over as I hurried blindly up the road. What was the use of struggling, of fighting, the use of anything? One might make mistakes in spite of a pure and beautiful love. But then one surrendered to evil only at the last ditch, the last gasp, and with an anguished cry. To trim one's beard, before the mirror, and depart whistling, with a look of pleased anticipation—oh, God, that betrayal, by a man whom I had loved and trusted—it ground me to the dust.

Bent only on escaping the images tormenting me, I did not look where I was going. But I had taken, instinctively, the hill road, and as I passed the Nursery a shout recalled me from the tumult of my thoughts. Murdoch was pruning the hedge which flanked the entrance to the garden. I stopped, hesitated, then went over.

"What's the matter?" He had stopped pruning and was eyeing me as he wiped his brow with the back of his big brown hand. "Have you joined the harriers?"

I did not answer this horrible facetiousness—in fact I was quite unable to speak.

"Something gone wrong with the work?"

I shook my head abjectly, my breast still too full for words. Murdoch gazed at me speculatively, his curiosity aroused.

"I know what," he said at last. "The old boy has gone on the booze again." He read my face. "No? Well then, it's another of his tricks?"

"Tricks!" Enraged by the lightness of the word, I was shaken by a fresh spasm. "You wouldn't say 'tricks' if you knew. Oh, Murdoch!" I almost burst into tears. "If people can't at least try to live decently ... and at his age ..."

"Ah!" exclaimed Murdoch, enlightened, placidly pleased with his own powers of deduction. He belched, took a piece of liquorice root from his pocket, bit off a piece, and began to chew it with every appearance of enjoyment.

I turned my pale face sideways, staring fixedly at a cart which was moving along the road. For some peculiar reason this solitary cart, crawling across the summer landscape, made me feel that life was endless in its monotony, that all that I now experienced was the repetition of something which had happened to me hundreds of years ago.

"You know, young fellow," Murdoch said after a pause, "it's about time you grew up. You're clever, and I was always a dunce at everything but gardening—still, at your age, I wasn't so simple. Grandpa has always been that way. A regular lady-killer all his life. Even when his wife, who I must say was very fond of him, was alive."

Silence of despair from me.

"It's just him," Murdoch went on. "And now, even though he's a good age, he can't help, himself. I don't think it's anything to lose your shirt about."

"It's awful," I said faintly.

"Well, there's nothing we can do about it." Murdoch, who seemed trying not to laugh at me, clapped me upon the shoulder companionably. "The world isn't coming to an end. You'll get over all this when you're a bit older. Come along and I'll show you my new carnation. It's budding a treat."

He put the shears under his arm and opened the gate. After a moment of hesitation. I went in and accompanied him, drearily, to the new greenhouse. Here he showed me half a dozen pots of milky-green shoots which were beginning to throw out buds, and explained, with pride, the method he had employed to produce the hybrid. There was something obscurely comforting in the steady movements of his large capable hands arranging the earthy pots, reaching for his clasp knife and deftly snicking off an errant shoot, binding the stems tenderly with raffia.

"If it's a success I shall call it the Murdoch Leckie! Isn't that something? More worth thinking about than . . ." He conveyed his meaning with another kindly slap upon the back.

I was calmer when I left Murdoch, but my outraged state—as ludicrous as the breaking voice that was another symptom of my age—would not let me return immediately to my books. As was to be expected, I dragged myself back, along the High Street to the church.

Here it was cool and quiet. Attending to the flowers on the side altar, the dim shape of Mother Elizabeth Josephina sent little chinking noises down the silent aisle. As she passed into the sacristy she gave me a smile of recognition and approval. I went on my knees in the still twilight, under the high window which had always solaced me, before that figure also carrying a burden, the face drawn by a spasm of pain.

Now, in this ecclesiastical atmosphere impregnated with incense and candle wax, I began to burn with a deep and just resentment against Grandpa, violator of the only virtue which really mattered. I thought of Alison, in her white dress, Alison, whom my love, this first love of puberty, had elevated to sublime and angelic heights. My face burned with shame. How would she regard a boy whose grandfather behaved like mine? Anger entered my heart, and recollecting how Christ had cast the wicked men from the temple, I rose determined to have it out with Grandpa, to finish with him once and for all.

When I reached home it was he who met me in the lobby, greeting me with every appearance of welcome. From behind him there came an excellent aroma of cooking.

"I'm glad you decided to take a walk. You'll work the better for it."

I gave him a cold and scornful glance, the kind of glance with which the archangel transfixed the writhing Lucifer. "What did you do this afternoon?"

He smiled with perfect nonchalance, answered airily: "Just my usual. A game of marleys at the cemetery."

Ah! He was a liar too. Liar and lecher both! But before I could confront him he moved out of the lobby.

"Come away into the kitchen." He was rubbing his hands, full of calm, kindness, and peace of mind. "I have a vegetable soup that'll draw the teeth out your head."

I entered the kitchen and, while he was absent in the scullery, sat down at the table. In spite of my wrongs I was extremely hungry.

A moment later he entered and served me with a big bowl of steaming broth. To divert me, to add point to his culinary achievements, he had put on one of Mama's aprons, and wound a napkin, like a chef's cap, around his depraved and venerable locks. So he was a clown, a pitiful buffoon as well, this fiend who had almost, but not quite, spoiled everything.

I put my spoon in the thick soup, which was filled with peas, chopped-up carrots, and shredded pieces of chicken. I lifted it to my lips, while he watched with an expression of affectionate expectancy.

"Good?" he inquired.

It was delicious. I finished it to the last drop. Then I gazed at this absurd and abominable old man who had earned my loathing and contempt, who betrayed the sacred beliefs of youth, whom I must shun as the cause and occasion of sin. The moment of denunciation had arrived.

"Can I have another helping, Grandpa?" I asked meekly.

Chapter Eleven

The morning of the examination was wet. On the afternoon of Thursday, the day before, Jason had taken all my books away and hidden them.

"Only the second-raters cram up to the last minute," he said. "You see them mucking over notes before they go in. They never win."

What I had learned seemed part of me. Nothing more to be assimilated. At present a mental blackness. But it is there, in the marrow of my bones. Outside my core of desperate resolution I was pale but quite calm as I dressed in the best of Murdoch's cast-offs: not a bad blue suit, though shiny at the elbows and seat. With measured strokes I shone and prepared my boots—which had caused Mama anxiety and which I must speak of later. Grandpa, hovering around, had picked me a buttonhole, to give me courage. Ah, those famous buttonholes of Grandpa's! I remember, distinctly: it was a pink moss-rosebud, with raindrops still upon it.

When he had handed it to me he produced, with a distinct "air," a small square envelope.

"Someone left this for you."

"Who?"

He shrugged his shoulders as though to say: "My dear boy, I am a gentlemen, I don't spy on your affairs." But out of the corner of his eye he watched me, with a pleased expression, as though I were conforming to a pattern he approved, while with nervous figures I opened the letter.

It was from Alison, a short note sending me her good wishes. A glow expanded round my heart . . . I reddened and put the letter in my pocket while Grandpa, whistling, smiling to himself, served my breakfast.

Jason was coming up with me to the College on this first morning. His frivolous pretext: that he did not wish me to get ensnared in the toils of a great city. Jason's kindness to me, all masked by flippancy, his unsparing generosity—for you must not imagine that three months' tutoring, given gladly and for nothing, is a natural phenomenon in a small Scots town—his support, his friendship, above all his complete understanding of my difficulties—all this, in recollection, clouds the eyes, gives one greater hope for the future of the human race than all the ideologies.

At the station we were joined by Gavin, a little pale, like myself, but calm, even smiling. He, too, had been working hard; I had not seen him for at least ten days. Now there was no sense of rivalry between us, we were partners in a tremendous enterprise. I felt a warm lush of comradeship as we exchanged our handclasp and I murmured now, so that Jason might not hear: "One of us, Gavin."

I knew now that it must be I, but if it were not ... dear God, that was an awful thought! ... then let it be Gavin.

The train of destiny rushed in. Our compartment was empty, smelling of cigarette and tunnel smoke, strewn with spent matches, the wooden partition scrawled with the crude wit of the apprentice engineers who travelled on this line. Reid, who did not wish us to dissipate our energies in conversation, had bought us each a *Strand Magazine* which, with a pretence of interest, we held before our faces in our corners. My copy made an excellent shield for my silently moving lips, for I was praying all the time, beseeching Heaven not to lose interest at the last ditch. Reid sat next to me, quite close, staring at the shipyards, chimney-stacks, and gasometers which sped past us in the rain, giving me courage by the communicative pressure of his thick shoulders, not withdrawing when the train threw us together, but trying, it almost seemed, to impart to me, as a final gift, his own strength, spirit, and intellectual power. Although from time to time he made desultory efforts to bring my attention back to Mr. Sherlock Holmes, a character whom he admired greatly, he was excited, yes, tensely overwrought. I could feel this, despite the check he imposed upon himself. He wanted me to win, desired it with every vital fibre of his stocky, vital frame.

The College buildings, washed by the rain as they stood ancient, spired, and grey on an eminence overlooking the Park on the west side of the city, were impressive to a boy of fifteen who had only seen them in his dreams. My old weakness, my inveterate curse, began to afflict me. I felt humble and intimidated as we left the yellow tram which had borne us from Central Station to the foot of Gilmore Hill, and, as we went up the quiet road with the professors' houses on either side, and entered a lovely quadrangle through the low cloisters, I began to question the right of a shabby and contemptible boy to penetrate such sacred precincts. Do not wholly despise me, however. Though my buttonhole and the small square note in my inside pocket should have sustained me, my left boot was already giving me concern, causing me to walk in a fashion so flat-footed that Jason asked:

"Have you hurt your leg?"

I flushed. "Perhaps I've strained my knee."

But we were there now, on the battle ground. The other candidates were grouped round the door of the Bute Hall.

"Plates of sour porridge!" Jason, our ally, holding us apart, gave the comment as much conviction as he dared, yet I could not agree with him. They looked a fine bright crowd of boys, full of life and intelligence. I thought I discerned McEwan, a smallish, bespectacled figure leaning against a pillar, with his hands in his pockets and laughing, yes, dear God, laughing as if he did not care.

At last, a low kind of rumble, which might be from my own heart: the oak doors swung open, the boys began filing through. Suddenly, as I moved, I felt Jason grip my arm in a vice. He bent down, putting his head close to mine, so that I could feel on my cheek his warm, "bad" breath. "Take my watch, Shannon. Don't trust their old clock. And keep cool." His whisper became hoarse, his bulging eyes fastened on mine with terrible intensity. "I know you can win."

The Bute Hall is very large, with stained-glass windows like a church, organ pipes shining dully on a balcony, tattered flags round the walls, newer, brighter flags hanging from the high beams. This morning, however, at the top end, a familiar sight: varnished yellow desks, about a hundred of them, numbered and arranged before the examiner's dais. My number is nine, in the centre of the front row; several buff-covered exercise books, pen, pencil, ink and blotting sheet, all laid out for me. I add Jason's silver watch which shows three minutes to ten. Around me, the creaking and rustling has ceased. The examiner, a heavy, slow man in a faded gown, is already handing out the first paper: Trigonometry. I close my eyes, in a last desperate prayer, and when I open them the paper, printed in small clear type, lies before me. I pick it up and with a start of joy perceive that the first question is one which Jason, with unbelievable cunning, has anticipated. I know the answer almost by heart. With compressed lips and fingers that tremble slightly, I pick up my pen and draw the first virgin exercise book towards me. Then oblivion descends ... nothing exists but that steady outflowing which comes from my bowed figure, wrapped in a pale trance.

Late that afternoon, when Gavin and I returned to Levenford, the train was so full we had little chance to compare notes, though we agreed that the Algebra and Solid Geometry papers had been horribly stiff. Now, worrying about things that perhaps I had missed, I was depressed, spent and cold. My feet especially were cold, and at this point I had better admit, not only that my boots leaked abominably, but that one of them, the left, was worn completely through in the sole, leaving a hole into which three fingers could be comfortably inserted. Still, in my vanity, I had preferred these ruins to Kate's pointed boots, which, although sound, laced halfway up the leg. With considerable ingenuity I had covered the most gaping wound by an inner sole of brown cardboard, cut from an old hatbox taken from beneath Mama's bed. However, the rain and the hard pavements soon uncovered the futility of this subterfuge. In ten minutes I had worn through the cardboard and my stocking as well, and was walking on my bare foot. No wonder

I felt a little damp as I sat in the steamy compartment, crushed between workmen in dripping oilskins.

Jason met the train at Levenford station and immediately took possession of me. In his rooms, while I sat down to a hot dinner of chops and potatoes, he asked me in a queer voice, urgent yet anxious, for the papers. Seated at the desk, beneath his metal reading lamp, using logarithms and books of tables, he worked out every answer; then came over, placed them before me without a word. I compared his results with my own, then glanced up at his strained face.

"Yes," I said.

"Every one?"

"Yes," I said again, humbly, yet exalted by the long breath which broke from him.

The next day, Saturday, we had French, English and Applied Chemistry; for the final subject, which was Physics, we must wait till Monday. I put thicker cardboard in my boot and inked the sole of my foot as a precaution against the worst. Curiously enough, my chief concern was that I should be discovered, in full view of all the candidates, with this indecent, half-naked extremity. As we came up from the tramway terminus a heavy shower caught us. Gavin shared his mackintosh with me, but, of course, he could not share his boots.

What matter? Once in the examination hall all such trivialities were forgotten, lost in the throbbing sweep of my endeavour. I thought nothing of my wet feet until I was again in the train, when, indeed, I shivered and put my hand to my brow, suddenly aware that I had a frightful headache. I was alone. Gavin had remained in Winton to meet his sister, and, during the journey, I stuck my head out of the window into the rushing air to try to cure it.

At Levenford station Jason's faithful, waiting face danced before me; I smiled, to show him that I had not completely disgraced him. He gripped my arm again, protective rather than importunate, and guided me down the steps to the cab rank.

"You're done up ... and no wonder. Thank heaven you have all to-morrow to rest."

He took me home in the splendid luxury of a cab, and Grandpa provided us with dinner, at which, so to speak, I was the guest of honour. During the meal, contrary to my custom, I talked without reserve. Pressed by Jason, I went over the French paper and related almost word for word the English essay I had written.

"Good ... good," Jason kept muttering, moving his hands restlessly, growing more excited every moment. "It was excellent to bring in those quotations. You did well ... very well to say that." There was actually, on Jason's lips, a dry white spume of excitement. Grandpa was equally affected: rarely had I seen him so worked-up. He ate nothing, hung upon my words. He was not only my patron and protector, but rejuvenated, living his youth again through me; he was actually sitting the examination, and winning it, himself. He beamed at me as Reid at last declared:

"I don't want to say things I'll regret, Shannon. But you haven't exactly made a fool of yourself. Monday's paper is your best subject. Unless God turns you into a raving lunatic over the week-end—and that is quite possible—for I myself already feel like one—you cannot fail to score less than ninety-five per cent., deaf, dumb, and blindfolded. Off you go now, for heaven's sake, and sleep your head off."

As I went slowly upstairs I distinctly heard Reid add to Grandpa, as though scarcely able to trust himself:

"He hasn't put a foot wrong. Better ... far better than I expected."

Oh, joy, supreme and blessed transport, making me close my eyes and cling, weak with praise, to the banister of the stairs.

Next morning, Sunday, I awakened at half-past seven and got up to attend church at eight o'clock—an act so completely automatic I was halfway along Drumbuck Road before I realized how very queer I felt. My head still ached dizzily, my throat was painfully dry, and, although the grey day gave promise of being mild, I couldn't stop shivering. Still, I knew that the strain of the examination had played havoc with my nerves. And I must go to Communion this morning, not only out of profound gratitude for favours received, but also because it was part of a solemn vow which I had made to ensure my success.

When I returned from church I found it difficult to swallow my breakfast, I was chillier than ever.

"Grandpa," I said. "I'm awfully cold. It seems silly, but I wish I could have a fire."

He had been studying me from beneath his brows, and although his face expressed some surprise he offered no objection. He remarked, slowly, "I should think you've earned a fire. And you'll have one. In the best room in the house."

He laid and lit a fire in the parlour which, recently, we had used so considerably—the only period, to my knowledge, when this useless mausoleum achieved the status of a human habitation. I felt more comfortable in the armchair by the fire, much warmer; indeed I was soon burning all over.

"What do you fancy for dinner?" Grandpa had been in and out of the room all the forenoon, attending to the fire, glancing at me.

"I don't think I'll bother with anything. I'm not in the least hungry."

"Just as you wish, boy." He hesitated, but said no more. The next time he appeared he was wearing his hat and a casual air which would have deceived no one. "I'm away out for a stroll. I won't be long."

He came back, in half an hour, with Reid. As they entered, the room, I looked up from the position into which I had sunk in the chair. Jason seemed both angry and disturbed.

"Hello, hello! What's all this?" he exclaimed in a brusque voice, utterly foreign to him. "Trying to make out you're sick, eh? Well, it won't work, my good fellow. If you think you're going to run out at the last hurdle, you're very much mistaken."

He blustered forward, drew a stool up to my armchair and took my hand in his, roughly, like a man who is going to stand no nonsense. "Yes, you might have some fever. But we shan't take your temperature. I haven't got a thermometer. And I don't want to put stupid notions in your head. You've simply caught a cold."

"Yes, sir," I said, with difficulty. "I'll be all right to-morrow."

"I should hope so. Don't look so damned sorry for yourself. I warned you you'd get hysterical. Pull yourself together and try to eat something." He turned to Grandpa. "Bring him in some of that milk pudding and fruit you had last night." As Grandpa went out he resumed: "After what we've been through together, I'll get you to that examination hall if I've got to fill you to the ears with brandy. Is your head clear?"

"Fairly clear, sir . . . just a little dizzy."

Grandpa had come back with a saucer of stewed apples and custard. I sat up, determined to do my best, but after I had attempted a few spoonfuls I gazed mournfully at Reid.

"It's my throat, sir."

"Your throat, eh?" There was a pause. "Well, at least we can have a look at that. Come over here."

He led me to the window and adjusted my head none too gently, so that the light fell into my mouth—which, with an effort, I held wide open. He peered for a moment; then, by the immediate change in his attitude, conveyed to me by a lessening of the pressure of his hands, I sensed the presence of disaster.

"What is it, sir?"

"Nothing . . . . I'm not sure." He turned his face away, his tone was flat, absolutely crushed. "We'll fetch the doctor."

While he went out I reeled back to my chair. I knew now that I was very sick. Worst of all was the terrible dread, growing upon me, filling my throbbing head—the dread that I might not be well enough to complete my examination next day. Grandpa was sitting erect, motionless and silent, opposite me.

Within the hour Jason was back with Dr. Galbraith. The doctor took one practised look at my throat, then nodded to Jason.

"Get him up to bed," he said.

Chapter Twelve

Once the acute inflammation has subsided, and the membrane begins to slough from the throat, diphtheria is neither painful nor prolonged. Following the first few days of fever, a dreamy state: the pulse beats slowly and the nerves are pleasantly relaxed. Sometimes this goes too far and the larynx, or even the heart, refuses to function, causing the physician to advance, hurriedly, with a charged hypodermic. But in my case there was no such drama. It was not a severe attack and Dr. Galbraith promised that I should be up in less than two weeks. After months of agonizing effort it was restful simply to be at peace, absolutely motionless upon one's back, hands limp upon the counterpane, eyes upon the shaft of sunlight which penetrated the narrow bedroom window and swung slowly round, filled with dancing motes, as the day advanced.

Do not imagine a mind tortured by disappointment and despair—far, far from it. Yes, I had the firm belief, born of my enfeeblement and the close communion which I still maintained with things celestial, the unshakable belief that God in His infinite goodness would not wilfully destroy the future of a boy who loved Him, who had propitiated Him, day and night, upon bended knees. No miracle was required, no thunderous manifestation of the divine power—simply justice, a little act of justice. The examiners need only, in fairness, allow me an average mark for the paper I had missed. Even Jason had hinted that such a thing was not impossible. When the results were announced ... I closed my eyes, with a faint and confident smile, murmured another tranquil prayer.

Papa and Mama had not yet returned. From postcards which

Mama sent to Grandpa we judged the London visit a success. Mama hinted proudly that Papa had "put money into Adam's house," and, on the strength of this investment, which seemed almost to have gone to Papa's head, they were breaking their journey on the way home to spend an extra week with Grandma's cousins at Kilmarnock. They would return, with Grandma, in about ten days. Grandpa and I calculated, looking at the calendar, that I might just be up before they got back, a stroke of good fortune which pleased us both.

Grandpa made a pretty fair nurse. During my early delirium I was aware of him, as through a veil, moving about my room in his slippers, at all hours of the night, bending to give me my medicine, to swab my throat. I heard Mrs. Bosomley's voice, too, beyond the carbolic sheet which hung outside my door, as she handed in a jelly or a blancmange "shape" she had made. I did not feel like a destroying angel towards her.

Although I lay in isolation I was not without visitors. Dr. Galbraith, dry, uncommunicative and a little rough, arrived every day—if he recognized me as a spectator of that strange episode at the Antonellis' he did not once refer to it. Kate came several times to the front door, but not beyond, for fear of carrying the infection to her child. Murdoch had less reason to take precautions; even so, the frequency of his visits pleased and flattered me; I began to look forward to his lumbering step, his manufactured conversation, filled with heavy pauses, his ponderous jokes (which I knew by heart), his bulletins upon the progress of the new carnation. Gavin, of course, was eager to visit me, and Grandpa nearly broke my heart by refusing to admit him. However, I was mending fast, I should see him soon.

Now there approaches a day which cannot much longer be held back—the twentieth of July, a day which is unforgettable. At times I have had nothing to relate, except lagging trivialities, the absurdities committed by a boy in the painful process of growing up. But this day—this twentieth of July ... It lives in the memory and must again be referred to, years later—a terrible day.

It was Wednesday, and the forenoon passed, completely

uneventful, except that I was out of my room, dressed, and had actually taken a few paces in the garden. After lunch, since the afternoon was so fine, Grandpa rigged up a camp chair for me on the back green, where I sat with a board under my feet and a rug on my knees, enjoying the goodness of the warm sun. In convalescence one's heart is sometimes lifted by the forgotten brightness of the outside world, lifted as by that sudden burst of bird song which comes when the sky clears after rain. Grandpa was in the house removing the evidence of my illness, which could only upset Papa and which, since Mr. Reid had made himself responsible for the doctor's fees, need not concern him.

Presently I heard a step on the pebble path: Jason's vigorous crunching step. He came round the corner of the house, smiled, and sat down on the grass.

"Felling better?"

"Oh, I'm perfectly all right now."

"Good." He nodded, plucked a blade of grass and threw it away.

There was a silence. Then Reid meditated, his gaze moving, here and there, in a peculiar way.

"You've taken things remarkably well, Shannon. Better than I did. I must admit, that day you got sick, I could have wept tears of blood. But we must get over our disappointments, it's one of the arts of living. By the way, have you read *Candide*?"

"No, sir."

"I must lend it to you. Then you'll find out how, thanks to merciful Providence, everything happens for the best."

I stared at him, unable to penetrate his mood, yet aroused, rather flustered by this apt mention of providential intervention. Suddenly he said:

"The results of the Marshall won't be out for another week yet." He paused, then went on steadily. "But I've just seen Professor Grant. He told me the marks."

My heart, though supported by Dr. Galbraith's strychnine medicine, took a fluttering leap, I was conscious of the clenching of my hands, the start forward, the dry choking in my throat. And, as though understanding this, Reid spoke quickly, dropping his unsuspected bitterness, fixing his large oxlike eyes, almost pathetically, on mine.

"McEwan."

The prodigy had won. These boys always win Bursaries, though occasionally it takes an attack of diphtheria to enable them to do so.

Pierced through and through, I stared at Reid as he went on, plucking more grass and throwing it away. "He only scored nine hundred and twenty marks."

I saw, dimly, that Grandpa had come through the kitchen door and joined us on the back green, saw also that he knew. Reid had told him on the way in. I lowered my head in sudden blinding pain. With pale lips I asked:

"Who was second?"

A pause. "You ... twenty-five marks behind ... even without the physics paper. I tried, I nearly went down on my knees to persuade them to give you an average. I offered to show them your class marks. I told them you'd have made not twenty-five but ninety-five." His voice fell into a twisted bitterness. "No use. They couldn't, or they wouldn't, break the rule."

Again silence. Even yet I could not fully apprehend the certainty of my failure. Some further revelation was surely in store for me. As though wishing to ease the agonizing tumbling of my heart Jason added:

"Blair is third, one mark behind you."

Two boys in a boat on the moonlit Loch: "One of us, one of us must win." Momentarily, I forgot my own misery and confusion in a sudden rush of grief for Gavin.

"Does he know?"

Reid shook his head. "Not yet."

Suddenly Grandpa spoke, in a troubled voice, not the voice of a cheap gossip, but the voice of a man who has himself known misfortune, a voice which tells, unwillingly, something sad that must sooner or later be told. Grandpa could never bring himself to offer me sympathy direct. I think he wanted, at this moment, to distract me from the crushing agony of my own defeat.

"Provost Blair has come an awful smash."

I gazed at him numbly. "What do you mean?"

"He's failed, gone bankrupt in his business at last."

I sat paralysed, wrung with an added dismay. Gavin's father a bankrupt, ruined and disgraced... For Gavin to lose the Marshall was nothing; nothing to this. I suddenly saw, white and proud, the face of this boy who worshipped his father, like a god upon Olympus. I knew I must go to him at once.

I had enough presence of mind not to mention my intention. No one seemed to have anything more to say. I waited until Grandpa and Jason went into the house; then, without asking permission, slipped round the side path to the road. I scarcely noticed how weak and shaky my legs were; I wanted to find Gavin.

He was not at home. There seemed nobody about the Provost's grand house; no maid, or gardener; behind the official lamp-posts an air of upheaval and confusion. After I had knocked three times Miss Julia opened the door a little way, as though afraid of what fresh disaster this might reveal. She told me in a broken voice that Gavin had been for some days with friends in Ardfillan; she had telephoned him; he was returning on the four o'clock train.

I knew he would leave the train at Dalreoch. The sky was white with heat. Men were walking in their shirt sleeves, carrying their jackets, fanning themselves with their hats. I dragged myself along, fighting the weakness in my legs, reached the gate of the station yard as the Ardfillan train came in. I waited there, in my usual place, straining my eyes across the hot dust intersected by shimmering rails.

He was there. I saw him jump from the footboard of the stationary train and begin to cross the yard. He did not see me. His face was whiter than the white sky, his eyes stared straight ahead. He knew.

The guard blew his whistle, waved his bright green flag. A goods engine was shunting waggons slowly in the yard. From a stationary waggon, very leisurely, they were rolling barrels of potatoes on to a horse van. The picture is with me still, burned into memory.

As the passenger train pulled out, Gavin, crossing the net of rail-lines, withdrawn into himself, living in his own pain, appeared unconscious of the slowly shunting train on the other track. He wasn't looking where he was going. He was walking directly in the way of the approaching engine. I started and let out a wild shout of warning. He heard me. He saw the engine. But oh God! He had stopped. His foot seemed caught between the points, he was bending, twisting and tugging with all his strength.

"Gavin! Gavin!" I shouted and ran forward.

His eyes, dark in his white face, met mine across the shimmering yard. He tried frantically to move from the rails and could not. Then the engine was upon him. Before I could cry out again his own cry came and a red haze fell upon me.

When I came to myself the yard was crowded, full of voices and confusion. The engine driver, twisting waste in his agitated hands, was explaining to a police officer that he was not to blame. People were saying in shocked voices: "What a tragedy! His father ..." They were trying to make out that Gavin had killed himself.

I crept home, clinging to the wall, shutting my teeth upon a deathly sickness, longing for the darkness. But when night came I did not sleep. Beneath my anguish a dark resentment began to work in me. How simple, how gullible I had been. My tortured thoughts were not yet clear but, swept by a sullen revulsion of feeling, I was conscious that I had reached a crisis in my life.

Next day Papa and Mama returned with Grandma, and as I remained alone, locked in my bedroom, I heard the stir of their arrival. Grandma was calling for me. But I gave no answer.

Avoiding them, I go out, slowly down the road, past the three chestnut trees, outlined against the sky, to the house where the blinds are drawn as if against the too persistent beauty of the world.

As I walk in staring weariness, hands plunged in my pockets, my fingers encounter a little medal, a "miraculous" medal which has been given me when I sat, a trusting child who believed in fairy tales, beside the convent syringa bush. A great sob swells up in me, thrusting upwards from my breast, into my throat. I take the holy trinket and fling it tremblingly away. So much for this God who destroys children, murders them and breaks their hearts.

There is no God, no justice upon earth. All hope has gone. Nothing remains but a blind defiance of the sky.

Gavin lies on his bed, in his own room, fast asleep—in a dream from which he will not awaken. He is wrapped in his dream, his eyelids closed, his face untouched, untroubled. Still proud and resolute, he is remote, far from everything.

Julia Blair, her eyes red with weeping, shows me in silence Gavin's shoe, the strong heel of which he had almost wrenched away in his effort to free his foot, trapped in the point switch of the rail. No, he did not surrender. In his dream that brave heart still lies, undefeated.

Book Three

Book Three

Chapter One

As I came through the Works gates one February evening, the ground hard under my nailed boots and the street lamps wearing frosty haloes, I caught sight of Kate's little boy, Luke, waiting on his father and wearing his new blue Academy cap with all the pride of a boy who has just gone to school. This sudden evidence of time took me by surprise: almost like a blow. Heavens, I am getting old, I am seventeen!

"Give us a penny, Robie." He ran up to me, sturdy and red-cheeked, bright-eyed with his own importance.

I felt through my soiled dungarees with insensitive fingers and found a coin. "You should say, 'Please.'"

"Please."

"Do you know who used to give me pennies when I was about your age?"

I was speaking like a patriarch and, with eyes on the penny, he was not in the least interested. Never mind. It was one of the consolations of my life, this life already heavy with years, loaded with afflictions, in fact practically over, to give him pennies, to take him on Saturday afternoons to the football match where, forgetting my sombre dignity, I cheered just as madly as he.

"Your father will be out in five minutes," I told him over my shoulder as I moved off. "He let me away early to-night."

"To go to the concert?" he called after me.

My nod was lost in the darkness. But my heart treasured the thought as I trudged less wearily across the wintry Common: the prospect of this evening banished even my overpowering and inevitable fatigue. To-night I should not fall asleep at the table the moment I had eaten my supper. Absorbed, I passed the dark bulk of the Church of the Holy Angels without my usual gesture of defiance—a fist clenched, theatrically, in the darkness.

Soon after Gavin's death, when I was on the point of leaving the Academy, Canon Roche had summoned me to the presbytery. He received me in his room with great friendliness and, after pacing up and down with his hands in the pockets of his soutane, turned to me.

"My dear Shannon." His dark eyes burned sympathetically. "All this may be God's way of proving you, of showing you the road you must go."

I looked down.

"You are thinking of going into the Works?"

"Yes," I said. "It's about the only thing left for me to do."

"There aren't many opportunities in a small town like Levenford." He reflected. "Robert . . . have you ever thought of the priesthood?"

I flushed darkly, my eyes still fixed on the carpet.

"Yes, I have."

"It's a wonderful life, my dear boy. A great joy and privilege to serve God as one of His chosen disciples." His gaze was bent warmly upon me. "I'm not offering you empty promises. There is a diocesan fund devoted to the splendid task of educating poor boys for the priesthood. It isn't a large fund. And naturally the candidates selected are few. But, in your case—I have written about you to the Bishop—if you wish, you will be elected immediately, you can leave for the Seminary next week."

I sat silent and ashamed. I saw that Canon Roche expected me to jump at his offer. Six weeks ago I might have done so. But now everything had changed: all my gushing fervour was replaced by arid bitterness.

"Well . . ." The Canon smiled. "What have you to say?"

"I'm sorry." I choked out the words. "I'd rather not."

An expression of surprise appeared on his face. He said quickly: "But don't you want to be ordained?"

"I did once," I said. "But I don't now."

There was a silence. He seemed for the first time to realize my state of mind. But he was too wise to remonstrate. Instead he concealed his disappointment and in a thoughtful, persuasive voice began to describe the happiness of a life devoted to the service of God. He opened up broad spiritual horizons, spoke of the culture and learning freely dispensed by Holy Mother Church. He fell into a pleasant reverie, touching upon his own student days at the Scots College in Valladolid—where, of course, if I wished, I too could go. He painted a picture of the Seminary buildings, of the Spanish landscape, and wound up, with a disarming smile, by recalling a special vine under which he used to take his siesta, refreshing himself, at the same time, with the delicious sweet grapes which almost dropped into his mouth.

I felt myself carried away. I liked and admired Canon Roche. In my emotional state, his winning kindness was irresistible. But something within me refused to surrender. My lips turned pale and stiff.

"I can't," I said desperately. "I don't want to go."

A much longer silence followed, then Canon Roche spoke in a different voice.

"I have no wish to influence you. You must decide for yourself. But I might point out that such a spiritual and material favour won't come your way every day. And of course we cannot hold it open indefinitely. Pray to Almighty God for guidance, and come and see me again on Saturday."

I went out into the grey afternoon. At the end of the week I did not return to the presbytery. My boldness in defying Canon Roche amazed me. But the seeds of rebellion were growing rapidly in my breast. If God would not permit me to be a scientist I saw no reason I should yield to Him and become a priest. Anything seemed better than that—indeed, under the circumstances, the prospect of entering the Works actually assumed a special attraction. Frustrated and full of bitterness, seething with new and terrible ideas, I wanted, recklessly, to submit to the worst that Fate could do to me. And above all, I wanted to show that I did not care.

To-night, after eighteen months, much of these forces had expended themselves. I still dramatized my situation. Yet underneath

I was growing restless and less heroic. Should I never grasp the rich and glowing future for which I yearned, and which seemed always to elude me?

Preoccupied by these thoughts, I was in no mood for interruption, yet as I turned into Drumbuck Road, a figure, a too familiar figure, detached itself from the dim shelter of the wall at the corner and, with a measured greeting, shuffled into step beside me.

My burden, which I have inherited from poor Mama: Grandpa.

"A trifle snell to-night, Robert."

I answered him under my breath, asking myself what he was up to now. The week before I had found him outside the Fitters' Bar addressing a crowd of apprentices on Woman's Suffrage.

"I was wondering, my boy, if you would care to make me a small advance. A mere nothing. Sixpence. For a postal order."

I trudged on in disapproving silence. These competitions, upon which he spends half his day, are part of what he calls his "New Era." To exact the full resources of his declining years he wants to become rich—a mere bagatelle for a man of his potentialities. In the reading room of the public library he cuts out guilelessly, under the very nose of the prim lady librarian, every advertisement which promises him wealth—and the diversity of these cuttings must be seen to be believed. In his room he initiates a voluminous correspondence, supplies missing words, rhyming phrases, the last lines of limericks, a whole vocabulary manufactured from the six letters of the alphabet thoughtfully supplied by the editor of *Home Weekly*. I cannot even pass him on the stairs without his accosting me and, with a confidential air, producing from his pocket a crumpled paper.

"Will you have the goodness to listen to this one, Robert?" He clears his throat and quotes:

"There was a young lady of Twickenham
Whose boots were too tight to walk quick in 'em.
When she came to a stile
There she rested awhile ..."

Triumphantly he brings out his masterstroke.

"*And then took 'em off and was sick in 'em.*"

His envelopes fall into the red pillar-box like snowflakes into a fire. Enraged at his lack of success, he declared "Limericks" to be an utter swindle and turns, with enthusiasm, to "Bullets"—a cabinetmaker in a neighbouring town has won a thousand pounds at "Bullets." . . .

Now, as we walked through the dusk, his voice held out persuasively the incentive of reward:

"I'll repay you out of my winnings. The post office closes at half-past six, and to-morrow is the last day."

"I won't give you a brass farthing," I answered shortly. "And what's more, you're going straight up to your room. For once I'm going out to-night, and if you upset my arrangements with any of your nonsense, I'll break your neck."

Silence; subdued silence. The worst feature of Grandpa's New Era is the new susceptibility of its initiator to a reprimand. I turned into Lomond View, annoyed with myself, but luckily I had not spoken sharply enough to upset him. I watched him slowly climb the stairs—he was now short of breath, very tremulous on any kind of ascent—and waited until reassured by the click of his door before I entered the kitchen.

Papa, seated at the table, spreading his bread thinly and methodically with margarine, gave me a nod of greeting. But it was Grandma, sustained, mellowed, and reinvigorated by her twelve months of responsibility, who, while I "took the rough off" at the scullery sink, silently yet competently brought my "kept" dinner from the oven.

Mama is gone, she who was the soul of this house—a sudden syncope on that winter night; a year ago, when Papa made the scene over Adam's letter about the money. No one suspected that she was ill, unless it was she, herself; yet looking back, in self-reproach, one remembered that gesture which became more frequent, that flight of her hand to her left breast when she was agitated, as though she were trying by the pressure of her fingers to control some pain, to support a flagging heart.

She was pressing her side like that when I found her, alone, livid and gasping for breath, in the parlour.

"Mama, you're ill. Let me get the doctor."

"No," she gasped. "It'll only upset Papa worse."

"But I must. You're really ill . . ."

There was barely time for me to run for Dr. Galbraith. When I returned with him she had already lapsed into coma.

"Worn out." Galbraith made the brief comment as the feeble thread of the artery was lost beneath his touch.

"Will you be coming to-morrow, doctor?" Papa, bewildered, yet outraged by the unusual expense, put the question feebly.

"No." Dr. Galbraith turned brutally. "She'll not be here to-morrow. And you're lucky I don't let you in for a post-mortem."

I shivered at the thought of the desecration of that defenceless body upon a mortuary slab. But Papa, even after she was gone, weeks after the funeral, while recalling with pride the number of wreaths sent in, still seemed unconvinced that she had dared to leave him.

"She always said I would outlive her," he often remarked, with an air of grievance.

To my surprise, he had not sold Mama's things, and it became a regular feature of Sunday afternoon for him to go to the bedroom, take her few dresses from the wardrobe, brush them carefully, and put them back. He was beginning to miss her.

I, too, had failed to realize how much I owed her as she scurried in timid servitude, trying always to do her best, to hold the family together, to propitiate Papa and temper his awful parsimony, to keep her head up before the town, to please everyone—this weak and colourless bondwoman, this heroic soul. Mama was not perfect, her money worries often made her sharp and cross. In my Academy days she sometimes held back the few shillings for my fee-lines until the Rector came into the class, fixed me with his eyes, and announced to my unbearable shame: "One boy in this form has not paid his dues." Again, when the agent called on her for Grandpa's insurance or when she singed, and so spoiled, the porridge, fits of anguished martyrdom would seize her; and with her head on one side, a wisp of hair almost falling into the pail of soapy water, she would scrub the house from roof to cellar, her lips compressed in terrible resignation. Nevertheless she was the nearest to a saint I have ever known. Only because I had sadness enough did I compel myself, with a love acknowledged too late, to think of her as she shook her fur, before her holiday, and smiled, in the sunshine. . . .

"It is really unbelievable." Papa now took a careful mouthful of his bread and margarine, touching me with his transparent, almost friendly smile—since I had begun to bring good wages into the house he had shown open signs of regard for me and often gave me his confidence at the evening meal. "The price of butter. Eleven-pence halfpenny the pound. I don't know what the world is coming to. Fortunately this new substitute is just as palatable, and even more nutritious."

Grandma was crocheting industriously behind her cup of tea, a model of contained stability. Still an active woman, she was managing the household ably, with the aid of a day girl recommended to her by a welfare organization in the town. She had the force to oppose the more grotesque of Papa's economies and had insisted upon the necessity of this daily help.

"I haven't heard a word from Adam," Papa went on palely. "It simply can't go on. I've asked Kate and Murdoch to come in about it next Sunday. I'd like you to be there also, Robert."

I gave a mutter of acquiescence and went on eating, indicating with my fork to Grandma, who at once complied, that I wished more cabbage. Although the food was poor I had enough; I even had this ready service from the old woman. There now existed, in fact, between Grandma and myself, a steady, uncommunicative alliance. Here, surely, was proof of my advancement. It afforded me as much dark satisfaction as did my calloused hands and broken fingernails, my inveterate fatigue, the cough which had begun to trouble me and which I aggravated, deliberately, by smoking.

When I had finished I went upstairs. Sophie Galt, the daily girl, having taken Grandpa his supper tray, was turning down my bed before going home for the night. Undersized and pasty-faced, with short legs concealed by a sateen dress Grandma had made her, she was about seventeen years old, one of a large family living in the Vennel. She had a slight squint, so that she seemed to be watching one all the time out of the corner of her eye. Her under-privileged manner always made me uncomfortable, a feeling intensified since that afternoon when I had surprised her posturing with terrible coquetry before the mirror in one of Mama's hats, taken from the wardrobe.

"Are you going to the Burgh Hall, to-night, Sophie?"

"Oh, no. Where would the likes of me get a ticket?" She straightened my pillow with a great display of thoroughness. "Father got one though at the Club. I expect you'll see him there."

After a pause, she glanced round the room, then over the top of my head.

"Do you think that's everything?"

"I'm sure it is, Sophie."

She lingered, gave the counterpane a final pat, coughed, sighed, at last went out.

My preparations for the concert were not elaborate. During the past two years my acute consciousness of my own person had changed to a state of studied indifference. As I pulled off my shirt there was a general effect of length, of white skin with the ribs showing through, brown blistered forearms, the ever pale face with its plume of gleaming hair. I decided perversely that I would not wear a collar; many of the workmen affected the type of scarf which I now knotted round my neck; I, myself, was a worker, a Fabian in fact, and, by heavens, I would not be ashamed of it!

When I was ready I went into Grandpa's room. He was reclining in his chair, a large new leather-bound gilt-edged book in one hand, a piece of bread and cheese from his tray in the other.

"Truly remarkable, Robert." He took a bite without raising his eyes from the page. "There are thirty-two feet of bowels inside the human form."

This expensive-looking book, the sight of which raised gooseflesh upon my spine, was one of a large stack of identical volumes, which stood against the wall, and which had arrived, express, one month before, addressed to "Alexander Gow, Esquire, Accredited Agent and Canvasser for Fireside Medical Encyclopedia Ltd." Accompanying the package was a bundle of hand-outs: "*You owe it to your loved ones ... more than one thousand diagrams and drawings ... remedies for forty-four poisons, ladies' ailments, blackheads ... simple everyday language ... sensational, daring, see for yourself. ... don't send us a penny, our accredited agent will call every week ...*"

While Grandpa pursues a house-to-house visitation in the remote parts of the town and continues, with interest, to increase his own store of medical knowledge, I recognize forebodingly that his peculiar talents are adapted to gathering in cash receipts, rather than to accounting for them. Unluckily, although his copying days for Mr. McKellar are positively over, the old man still writes a copper-plate hand, sometimes a little shaky, but deceptively fine. At this moment my eyes fall upon a letter amongst the litter of papers on his table: "*My dear good sir: In answer to your esteemed request for references I hasten to advance the name of my son-in-law, who holds the responsible position of Health Administrator to the Royal and Ancient Borough of Levenford.*" And upon another which begins simply, yet more ominously: "*Madam.*"

Grandpa's hair is now almost white—that absence of colour sentimentally referred to as "silvery"—and his once indomitable figure has shrunk considerably so that his coat and trousers sag in places which were once protuberant. His blue eye is a little brighter than it should be, he changes colour very readily, while his nose, strange symbol of his virility, is paler, less turgescent—alas, quite flaccid. I know that Grandpa has passed a sad milestone in his gay career which may be found under a section, always interesting—and profusely illustrated—in the *Medical Encyclopedia*. Mrs. Bosomley has become merely a nodding acquaintance; and his taste in feminine society has declined to those groups of schoolgirls, and attractive little "junior students," whom he stops in the Cemetery Road and sends into fits of giggles with his gallant conversation. Yet Grandpa blandly refuses to acknowledge his own decay. On the contrary, he is more open in his profession of potency, holding himself as might a stallion, a prolific sire, and frequently, with a glance of proud complacency, thumping his poor old chest with his fist. "An oak, Robert. A guid Scots oak. If I stood for the Borough Council..." Thank goodness his smile admits that he is being humorous. "Why, in a year's time they might even want me for Provost."

"Grandpa..."

"Yes, my boy."

I wait until he looks up inquiringly from the page, regretting my display of temper earlier in the evening, resolved not to bully him but to play upon his new, his absurd susceptibility to flattery, and cajole a promise from him.

"I am going out to the concert. You are too fine a man, too much the soul of honour, to take advantage of that fact. You give me your word you won't move from here till I come back."

He beams at me, well pleased, over his spectacles, still marking his place with his finger. "Of course, my boy, of course. *Nobless oblige.*"

That must satisfy me. I nod, close his door firmly and leave him to "Disorders of the Large Intestine."

Chapter Two

The concert was not one of the ordinary performances given every Thursday during the winter by the Levenford Orchestral Society, but a gala affair arranged under "distinguished patronage" in aid of the new Cottage Hospital.

When I reached the Burgh Hall, which stood next to the Academy in the High Street, scores of people were pressing into the entrance. I joined the crowd and, inside the gaslit auditorium, already warm and humming with voices, I chose a seat deliberately, with proud exclusiveness, in a back row underneath the balcony. No matter that Reid had reserved a front seat for me, beside his own; my place was here. In any case I wished to be alone, so that none might witness the emotions which this evening must bring to me.

With the detachment of one who has failed to be a great man and now prefers, at least for the time being, to be nothing, I watched the hall fill until extra chairs had to be placed amongst the palms that lined the cream-painted, stencilled walls. In the large and quite brilliant assembly I could see Kate and Jamie, settled sedately halfway up the hall; Mr. McKellar, with a legal air of waiting to be convinced; Bertie Jamieson with sleek hair, a high collar, and two smart young ladies.

In the second row, behind Sir. Thomas and Lady Marshall, and an array of town councillors, I made out Reid with his party—Alison's mother, her music teacher Miss Cramb, and a stranger with a narrow head and a pointed iron grey beard who must be Dr. Thomas, the noted producer of "The Messiah" and conductor of the Winton Orpheus Choir.

From time to time Jason turned round as though searching for someone—across the sea of heads I clearly observed his face. Now and then he tugged impatiently at the short blond moustache he had recently grown, and which improved his appearance considerably. A thrill passed through me at his expression—I lowered my head quickly, grateful for his friendship, but determined not to be seen, to remain an outcast, entrenched and proud.

Nevertheless, I received a nod of recognition. It was Sophie's father, squeezing in on his free "Club" ticket, looking out of place, as if this was not at all what he had expected. Galt was a pale, lacklustre man with a damp cowlick plastered on his brow and a small ingratiating eye. He was in Jamie's squad with me and, while not a good workman, he had edged himself on to the committee of the local union. In the boiler shed, I was always running into him; and because of his daughter's presence in Lomond View he seemed to find a peculiar interest in me, as though, tacitly, some kind of bond existed between us.

Fortunately there were no seats vacant in my vicinity. I turned away and almost immediately the sudden dimming of the auditorium lights made me quite safe. Amidst some scattered applause, the curtain went up; my eyes were drawn to the stage.

The opening items of the programme increased my sense of tension, they so far surpassed the ordinary level of provincial entertainment. The orchestra began with some lively selections from "Pinafore." Then came the duet from "Tosca," sung by two well-known members of the Carl Rosa Company, at present appearing in Winton. A Brahms concerto, played beautifully by the organist of the City Cathedral, next filled the hall with noble and inspiring music. Lifted up, burning with eagerness, I trembled for Alison in her ordeal, which, every moment now, was growing nearer. I began to fear that too much would be demanded of her—she was so young to make her first appearance upon a public platform and in such expert company! This audience was discriminating, its interest had been whetted by months of "talk." Now, waiting, as I was waiting, for the event of the evening, it had reached a dangerous pitch of expectancy.

At last, after perhaps an hour, a rustle passed through the hall.

I felt my heart beating louder than ever, beating with fear. Except for the grand piano and the accompanist seated unobtrusively before it, the stage was empty.

Then, quietly, from the wings, Alison came on, so young and unprotected that a hush fell involuntarily. She advanced to the front of the stage, immediately behind the japanned footlights, as though wishing, from the beginning, to place herself in communication with her listeners. She had grown since those days when we knocked our knees together over the geometry book; and her long soft dress of pale blue muslin, moulding her fine strong figure, made her seem tall. She wore a ribbon of that same misty blue in her brown hair, now "put up" for the first time. As she stood there, exposed to all these eyes, I felt a deep and secret pride; yet, at the same time, I caught my breath in jealousy.

She faced the assembly, her expression serious, her hands encased in white gloves, holding a sheet of music before her in the ridiculous fashion of the period. Although she shimmered, in a haze, before my straining vision, I saw that she was composed. She waited until the audience was settled, ready to give her its attention, then she glanced at her accompanist and the first restrained chord of the piano broke the stillness. She raised her head and began to sing.

It was Schubert's "Sylvia," which often had enchanted me as I stood hidden by the darkness under the linden tree outside her window in Sinclair Drive. And now, in this hushed hall, though I must share it with so many others, the joy of listening to the song made me stop trembling. I closed my eyes, surrendering to the delight of the pure, sweet notes, assured that this voice could hold captive, not one unseen listener, but all who were privileged to hear.

A burst of hand-clapping followed the ending of the song, Alison gave no sign; she stood, as though waiting to offer up again, without pride, that gift which had been bestowed upon her. When the hall was quiet she sang, first, Schumann's "Wanderlied," followed by "Hark, Hark the Lark"; then, before the stillness could be destroyed, she began the "Mattinata" of Tosti.

This song, which Melba made so popular, full of exacting runs and high notes, soaring upwards at one dizzy moment, and the next cascading downwards, presents great difficulty; its accomplishment, with ease and perfect trueness, brought the audience, already conquered, to Alison's feet. Even the least musical could realize the quality of this youthful voice. The applause refused to die; instead it grew in volume. I could see the other artists crowding in the wings, clapping and smiling. Alison was forced to return again and again.

At last, as though about to give way to tears—and indeed, tears were making my own eyes smart—she was led back by the accompanist. Her mother had stipulated as the condition of her appearance that she should sing only one group of four songs. Also, it was the rule of these charity concerts not to permit encores. But now all that was forgotten. Alison herself seemed incapable of speech; the accompanist, smiling at her, still holding her by the hand, announced that she would give one extra song. More applause. Absolute silence as the audience, triumphant, settled back.

The piano began, repeated the opening bar, and waited; for now Alison, extremely pale, appeared to hesitate. Only for an instant, however. As though freeing herself from all distraction, she clasped her hands—no longer holding that formal sheet—and filled her breast deep. Even before the first notes broke I guessed that she would offer her vanquished listeners an old Scots song. I had not dared to hope for my favourite amongst all these native airs, "The Banks of Doon." Yet this, with beautiful simplicity, was the song she sang.

> *"Ye banks and braes o' bonny Doon,*
> *How can ye bloom so fresh and fair?*
> *How can ye chant, ye little birds,*
> *And I sae weary fu' o' care?"*

The tender words lifted me to the world of my dreams, a world which Alison and I would one day roam together, hand in hand, not far beneath the sky.

When the last note faded, the silence in the hall was profound.

A rigid spell; a community entranced. Then the storm broke. The Scottish song, so exquisitely sung by this Scottish girl, had set the Scottish audience on fire. Perhaps she had won her little victory by the charm of immaturity, perhaps by a pleasant trick of voice over-estimated by local sentiment. The future alone would tell. For the present everyone stood up to applaud. I was on my feet, hoarse, completely hoarse, with cheering.

When the concert ended and I made my way out of the hall, slowly, impeded by the crowd, everyone spoke of Alison. Then, in the vestibule, as I was about to escape, an arm reached out and detained me.

"Where were you?" Reid's face was flushed as my own, flushed with pleasure, yet his tone was sharply annoyed. "We've been looking out for you all evening."

"I preferred to sit by myself."

I felt him frowning at me, as I stared sideways through the arched doorway.

"I'm beginning to get angry with you, Shannon. Why can't you put on a collar and behave like a decent member of society?"

This, from a man who had prided himself on his unconventional views, brought a smile of amusement to my lips.

"Must one wear a collar to be decent?"

"Really, this pose of yours is becoming a nuisance."

"If I'm so peculiar, why bother with me?"

"Oh, don't be an ass, to-night of all nights. Thomas is delighted with Alison. Come on to the reception room. I want to introduce you to him."

Anticipating my protest, he hustled me through the vestibule, along a corridor that ran parallel to the auditorium. He was in high spirits—his love of music had brought him, long ago, into touch with Mrs. Keith, he took a great interest in Alison's talent, and it was he who had arranged for the Orpheus conductor to attend her first public performance.

He gave me a forgiving smile as we approached the end of the corridor. "Couldn't have gone better. Here we are. For heaven's sake, try to look less like Lord Chesterfield attending his own funeral."

We entered a room, opening to the stage, where a number of the performers, their friends, and the town officials stood talking while tea was served by ladies of the Hospital Committee.

Alison stood in the centre of a large group, restored to calmness, yet silent amidst the chatter, holding stiffly a small presentation bouquet of white flowers. Her gaze wandered about the room, as if searching for some recollection of ordinary events which would help her to preserve her steadiness. When our eyes met she gave me, while her lips formed into a faint smile, a glance of communicative understanding.

Awkwardly, I allowed Reid to introduce me to Dr. Thomas, who gave me his free hand and a smile while continuing his animated lecture to Miss Cramb, who for once didn't look as though she had been sucking lemons. I refused the tea which Mrs. Keith offered me—I was thirsty but I knew that my shaking fingers would never support the cup. While I stood, apart, listening to the conversation, my gaze kept straying back to Alison.

At last, an eddy of the crowd brought me beside her. Near, like this, after the remote vastness of the stage, she created in me a wistful and half-fearful excitement, a darkened joy which brought a lump to my throat and twisted my mouth so that I could scarcely speak. Yet somehow I brought out my fumbling tribute, knowing that she disliked praise and was always disinclined to discuss her singing.

She shook her head to indicate that she had not pleased herself.

"Still," she added, as though continuing that unspoken thought, "they have asked me to sing at the Orpheus Chorale."

"A solo part?"

"Yes."

"Oh, Alison . . . that's wonderful."

She shook her head again, but her round young chin was startlingly firm. "It's a beginning."

There was a silence. People were beginning to leave now, putting on their coats and wraps. Quickly, before my courage failed, I said:

"Alison, may I see you home to-night?"

"Yes, of course," she answered quite calmly, glancing round. "Everyone seems to be going now. I'll just tell Mother."

She went over to where Mrs. Keith, looking extremely nice in a dove-grey frock and antique quaint necklace, stood talking to Reid. I watched her as she surrendered her flowers, drew on her thick tweed coat and wrapped a white shawl with a tasselled edge about her hair. I felt Mrs. Keith giving me a mildly ironic look, less kind than before, a new expression which made me redden and move towards the door. It took Alison a long time to say good-night to everyone, but at last we were outside, walking from the Hall together.

"I'm cross with myself." She spoke thoughtfully, after a silence. "Just think of it. Giving way like that and almost crying. I didn't though, thank goodness."

"But, Alison. Your first concert. It would have been perfect if you had cried a little."

"No, it would have been silly. And I hate people who do silly things."

I did not press the matter to another of our arguments: I was beginning to discover that our viewpoints were quite different. Even-tempered, capable, and contained, Alison was everything that I was not. She wasn't clever perhaps, nor had she much sense of humour, but in spite of her slow way of thinking, she was full of practical common sense. Also, she was ambitious—not in my intense and highflown way, but with a logical desire to make the most of her talent. She recognized, and faced with determination, the fact that to become a singer would require study, work, and sacrifice. Her exercises, those deep breathings which enabled her to sing a "long" scale, or to maintain a phrase lasting twenty seconds, had given her a kind of physical serenity. Yet under her placidity, this smooth-brown Juno had a quiet will of her own.

"Let's go up the hill, Alison." Trembling slightly I came a little closer to her as we walked along, aware that every step was taking us nearer Sinclair Drive. "It's a lovely evening."

She smiled at my appealing tone. "It's damp and cold. I think it's going to rain. Besides, Mother'll expect me in to-night. She may be bringing a few friends home with her."

A hot lump rose in my throat; I was ready, in my intensity, to die for her, yet she calmly allowed "a few friends" to come between us.

"You don't seem to appreciate me very much," I muttered, "considering that you'll be away most of the winter."

Mrs. Keith had lately begun to speak of the old house in Sinclair Drive as being too large for her requirements. With Alison's training ahead of her she wanted to economize. She was closing her home for the cold months and spending that time with her sister-in-law in Ardfillan.

"You sound as though Ardfillan were at the other end of the earth," Alison replied with a touch of asperity. "Can't you come and see me like other people? There'll be dances, Louisa's School Reunion especially."

"You know I can't dance," I answered miserably.

"It's your own fault for not learning."

"Don't worry," I said bitterly, "you'll have plenty of beaus. All Louisa's young men. And your own."

"Thank you. I daresay I shall. And I daresay they'll be more entertaining than someone I know."

My heart was bursting; and suddenly my anger gave way to despair.

"Oh, Alison," I gasped. "Don't let's have another quarrel. I'm so terribly fond of you."

She did not answer at once. When she did her voice was troubled, sympathetic, yet struggling against the unknown.

"You know I like you too." She added, in a lower tone, "Very much."

"Then why won't you stay out with me a little longer?"

"Because I'm hungry, I've had nothing substantial since four o'clock." She laughed at herself. We were now at the entrance to her house. "Why don't you come in? The others will be here any minute. We'll have refreshments and lots of fun."

I tightened my lips in the darkness, repelled by the idea of lights, crowds of people and banal conversation in which I was too stiff and proud to join. Under such circumstances I had no capacity for gaiety, the laughter which I forced, so as not to appear unusual, sounded hollow in my ears.

"Your mother didn't invite me," I said moodily. "It's no use. I don't want to come in."

"What *do* you want?" Alison said.

She stopped and stood facing me beside the currant bush in the drive.

"I want us to be together," I mumbled. "Just you and I alone. All I would want to do would be to hold your hand ... so long as I was near you ..."

I broke off, incoherently. How could I tell her what I wanted when my emotions were so tangled, my desires so agonizingly confused?

She seemed touched; her smile was hesitant.

"You'd soon get tired of holding my hand."

"I swear I wouldn't."

In proof of this I reached out and caught her fingers. Then my heart began to beat madly. "Oh, Alison," I groaned.

She did not draw back. For an instant her lips brushed against my cheek.

"There now." In the darkness she was smiling at me quietly. "Good night."

She broke away and, holding the ends of her shawl beneath her chin, ran towards the front door.

When she had gone I stood for a long time in the shadow, torn between elation and disappointment. I hoped that she would return. Surely she would come to the porch and call me in. I had been a fool to refuse and would gladly go now. But she did not come. Gradually the glow faded inside me and, turning up my coat collar, I walked slowly away, pausing several times to look over my shoulder at the lighted window of her house. The wind caught me sharply at the corner of the drive. Alison had been right. It was a damp and icy evening.

Chapter Three

My work at the boiler shop was not that melodramatic toil one reads of in novels, but I was not cut out for manual labour and I found it hard enough. For the most part we made marine engines which went into the vessels constructed in the shipyard; we also built feed and suction pumps, which were usually crated and shipped abroad. I had begun in the foundry, where my job for months had been to file and clean the rough castings with a steel brush. It was heavy and dirty work. Jamie kept his eyes on me and was kind in many ways, but our relationship forbade his showing me favouritism, the slightest sign of which would have been resented by the whole shop. My bench was near the cupola where the cast iron was melted and poured into sand moulds. Sometimes the heat was extreme and on windy days sand blew about the shed, making me cough. Later on I moved into the machine shop. Here the shaped castings were turned and burnished by innumerable lathes. It stood next to the fitting shop, the place of assembly for all the finished parts, and resounded with the clang of hammers and the whirring of its own machines.

The apprentices were, in the main, a cheerful lot, who took life with a carefree grin, were interested in football and horse-racing, and openly ribald in their attitude towards sex. At the end of four years most of them would become seagoing engineers; while others, like myself, went on to the drawing office. A few had come for more specialized training. There was a young Siamese of noble family who appeared every morning, silent and smilingly polite, in immaculate overalls, and who would no doubt, in due course, carry the benefits of Western civilization back to his own country. At the bench next to mine a Welsh youth named Lewis gracefully idled away his time. Lewis was the son of a wealthy Cardiff shipbuilder and, since the Marshall Works enjoyed a special reputation, he had been sent there for a practical course before entering the parental business. He was a vapid, easy-going youth, with oiled hair and a receding chin, who wore vivid bow ties and equally striking shirts. But he was good-natured and generous. He kept on his bench a huge yellow tin of cigarettes, a miniature trunk in fact, and everyone was free to help himself from it. Bored to tears by his enforced sojourn in Levenford, he spent much of his spare time in Winton, where he was often seen dining at the Bodega Grill, or occupying a box at the Alhambra Music Hall. He fancied himself as a lady-killer and his remarks dealt almost exclusively with his amorous adventures in the neighbouring city.

Amongst my fellow apprentices I had tried, anxiously, to find a congenial companion. But, although I longed for friendship, my advances were clumsy, and inhibited by the fear of a rebuff. When I made the effort and went out with some of the wilder spirits, the level of the conversation, long and vociferous arguments relating to the merits of one whippet over another or to the price paid for the winner of the local pony trot, soon reduced me to a stony impotence. I wanted to find someone with whom I could discuss books and music; who would respond eagerly with his own views when I tried to articulate the new ideas towards which I was reaching out fumblingly. But whenever I brought up such subjects, I felt myself suspect of showing off, and quickly relapsed into silence. Lewis was my closest acquaintance and once or twice I had been to tea at his lodgings. But the story of his conquests could be very boring and its obvious mendacity soon ceased to amuse me. Because of my kinship with Jamie and my capacity for silence—a quality always respected in the North—I was quite well-thought-of by the others. I tried, moreover, to do my work to the best of my ability. But I was dreadfully out of my element. The thought of the years that lay ahead of me made me sick at heart.

On the Saturday following the concert, two o'clock had struck and Papa, Murdoch, Kate, Grandma, and I were seated round the cleared table while Sophie, in the scullery, washed the dishes with such complete absence of noise that one could almost hear the straining of her ear drums.

Papa wore the suppressed and anxious expression which now seldom left him. He was thinner. His face had a grey and careworn quality, his cheeks were sunken, his lips tight over his teeth.

"It's a fortnight after quarter-day." He made the remark in a controlled voice. "And still no word from Adam."

"There's time enough, Papa." Kate spoke placatingly.

"That's what you said before. You know when the conversion fell through he promised faithfully to pay me five per cent. on the nine hundred he borrowed. And there's been not a penny of interest from him for the last six months."

In my childhood I had always thought of Adam as a man who would make a fortune. He seemed earmarked for self-made success. Yet now, although our meetings remained infrequent, I had begun to perceive, underneath that genial confidence in himself, an odd limitation. Perhaps it was the tendency, so common in the Scot who thinks himself a "big man," to underestimate other people and their capacity to resist him. Adam was too sure that he could outwit others. In the private enterprise upon which he had embarked so triumphantly with Papa, he had failed to anticipate that the owners of property adjoining his Kensington house, many of whom were rich and influential, would strenuously contest his right to derange their amenities by a conversion to flats. Under the sharp scrutiny of their lawyers the freehold was not quite so watertight as it had seemed. After placing all his available capital in the venture and inveigling from Papa his entire savings, after entering into commitments with a jobbing builder, he had found himself faced with a court injunction and the threat of a devastating lawsuit. The house still remained on his hands; it was now, indeed, the "white elephant" he had once joked about, and it was only too apparent that the men in the top hats whom he so openly derided had got the better of him in the end.

"What about the school that wanted to buy it?" Kate broke the silence.

"That fell through," Papa answered gloomily. "He'll never get rid of it."

"Oh, Papa, you shouldn't worry so much. Adam has a good position, he'll pay you back eventually. And you're very comfortably off. You get a nice salary, Grandma has her compensation and Robie is bringing in a good weekly wage."

Papa, still pale, could hardly speak for indignation.

"Have you no idea of the value of money? Do you expect folks to throw their earnings away without a word ... and be reduced to beggary in their old age?"

"Nonsense, Papa." Kate spoke soothingly but firmly. "There's your superannuation pension. Besides, you're still saving money. Why, you even have a servant in the house, a thing poor Mama never had."

"I wish your mother was alive to hear you!" Papa's eyes flashed; he dropped his voice, breathing with difficulty. "You wouldn't believe how much that girl eats over and above her wages. Not only that, she's broken two of the best plates since she came here. It's wicked, wicked."

Abandoning Kate as hopeless he turned to Murdoch. "Why don't you say something? Should I go to McKellar and start proceedings against Adam?"

Murdoch, bathed in solemn abstraction, shrugged his shoulders, which his work had made big and heavy.

"I wouldn't get myself into the lawyers' hands."

Papa winced visibly and, after a moment, a pained sigh of agreement was forced from him.

"What am I to do then, what am I to do?"

Murdoch began to speak. Always ponderous, he had, during these past months, become invested with a new profundity.

"No one ever paid much attention to me in this house, Father." With surprise I noted that he had dropped the familiar "Papa." "The fact remains, I've made my own way in spite of everything. I have my partnership with Dalrymple, I'm happy in my work in the garden, I'm doing well. At the Flower Show this spring I mean to bring out my new carnation and, if God wills it," again I started with surprise, "I'll maybe have a chance of the Alexandra Gold Medal for the best exhibit in the Show." Murdoch smiled at us all owlishly through his big glasses. "Adam always made a fool out of me, Father. His ways are not mine. Nevertheless he's my brother and I love him. That's the answer to everything. Love."

"I don't know what you're talking about," Papa burst out. "I want my money back plus the interest."

Sophie had come into the kitchen with a scuttle of coal and was replenishing the fire. Papa kept still while she was in the room, but the moment she returned to the scullery he rose with an outraged air, removed the top lump of coal, and put it back in the scuttle. He was flushed, as though the exasperation in his breast had suddenly flared beyond endurance. "No one knows what I have to contend with. One thing after another. Adam! That old fool upstairs who ought to be in Glenwoodie! Cleghorn coming through his kidney operation! What a man could do about it I don't know."

"You could love, Father," Murdoch said kindly.

"What!" Papa exclaimed.

"Yes, Father," Murdoch continued gently. "I mean exactly what I say. If only you could taste, as I have come to taste, the joy of universal love."

He stood up in a peculiar manner. I knew instinctively that he was going to make one of those pronouncements, majestic and terrible, which reared themselves, like sea serpents from a placid sea—intimations from the depths which stunned by their magnificent unexpectedness, and of which to my knowledge, he actually made three: the first at Ardfillan Fair, when he said "I am going to kill myself"; the third, not yet born, when he declared, after the Flower Show, "I am going to be married"; and the second, now, when, as though breathing the Holy Spirit upon us, he announced:

"I'm saved. I'm now a soldier of the Lord."

No more than that, not a single word. Wearing that same rapt smile, he took his hat and went out.

While Papa sat, stupefied, in the kitchen, Kate and I followed him, equally dazed, to the door. And there, sure enough, was the explanation, the pure fount of his conversion: Bessie Ewing, walking sedately up and down in the road outside, waiting on him. She took his arm with a proud, possessive smile. Neither of them saw us, as they walked off, communing, Murdoch's chest expanded, as if already supporting the big drum of the Salvation Army Band.

A long pause followed.

"Well, that's that," Kate said. "Religion takes this family in funny ways." There was an odd look in her eyes as she turned to me. "We're a queer lot. Why you stay on in this house beats me."

I did not answer.

Seeing my hesitancy, Kate gave a little laugh and slipped her arm about my shoulders, pressing her cheek, still dry and chapped, against mine.

"Oh, dear," she said. "Life's an awful business."

She turned and went back to the kitchen, while I slowly climbed the stairs and, still wearing my dungarees, lay down on my bed, not yet having the energy to change. Kate had persuaded Papa and Grandma to accompany her to Barloan for tea. Presently I heard the sound of the front door as they went out. Sophie had already departed for her half-day. Grandpa and I were alone in the house.

The afternoon was very quiet. With my hands behind my head I tried to conjure those visions which were my splendid avenues of escape—no wonder Reid had named me "the melancholy dreamer." But I was held to earth, bogged in the recollection of that scene which had just taken place downstairs; my mind kept turning back to it, like a dog worrying a dry bone—no hope of nutriment, a kind of nervous persistence.

It was like a conspiracy to destroy what illusions were left to me. Murdoch's conversion simply parodied my past religious fervour. Papa's obsession with money, ludicrous and degrading, had become a mania. Now he took his tea without sugar and milk, practically lived on pease brose, undressed in the dark to save the gas. His manipulations with the ends of soap and candles were unbelievable. When anything broke in the house, he mended it himself. The other day I had caught him with a strip of leather and some nails, resoling his own shoes.

Oh, God, how I hated money, the very thought of it revolted

me. Yet, at the same time, I spent my days longing for enough to take me to the University to pursue the work I loved. Kate's question kept buzzing in my head. Why didn't I leave this house? Perhaps I was weak, afraid to venture into the unknown. Yet there was another reason. Less from affection than from a grinding sense of responsibility, which I inherited no doubt from some Covenanting ancestor on Grandma's side, I felt myself unable to leave Grandpa. He would be sure to meet disaster if I didn't stay to keep an eye on him. Whatever the causes, I seemed doomed to extinction in this small town.

Instinctively I thought of Alison, cut by the cruel injustice of her calmness, and, although I yearned for her, Lewis's stories of his adventures came before my mind. They were cheap enough no doubt, yet I had begun to feel it a sign of lamentable weakness that I had never enjoyed such an experience as he described. In novels which I read, young men in my position were always brought to maturity by some nice woman, separated from her husband, not a raging beauty of course, but usually a charming little creature, with humorous eyes and a wide and generous mouth. But did such a one exist in Levenford? I smiled bitterly at the utter futility of the thought. Several of the girls who worked in the dye-works were well known to the apprentices but the look of their bold red faces, the rough slang which they exchanged as they clattered past in shawls and clogs, were enough to damp even Lewis's ardour, let alone my shrinking heart. I sighed heavily, got up and started to change my working clothes.

Suddenly I heard a ring at the bell. Although the ring was polite it disturbed me: now more than ever it was a formidable business answering the front door.

I went downstairs. It was a woman who stood on the threshold, a decent middle-aged and completely strange woman, dressed in dark grey, with limp grey cotton gloves, a black hat and handbag. She looked as though she worked with her hands, perhaps a housekeeper, yet altogether a superior person and she was, strangely, more nervous than I. She conveyed the impression of having waited for the benevolent cloak of evening before venturing to approach the doorstep of Lomond View.

"Is this Mr. Gow's house?"

My heart, which had been emboldened by her timidity, dropped back into my boots. "Yes, he lives here."

A pause. Was she blushing? At least she was uncertain of how to proceed for, studying me, she went off at a tangent. "Are you his son?"

"No, not exactly ... a relation." While I refused to commit myself I perceived the situation to be altogether too obscure, delicate, and dangerous to be handled on the doormat, in full view of the road. "Won't you come in a moment?"

"Thank you kindly, young man." She spoke with careful gentility, and followed me into the parlour where, since it was dim, I found it necessary to light the gas. Without being asked she took a chair, seated herself upon its edge and let her eyes travel round the chill sanctuary, appraising this object and that with guarded approval.

"Quite right. A nice place you have here. That's a bonny picture."

I waited in mystified silence while, not without coyness, she removed her eyes from "The Monarch of the Glen" and inspected me.

"I believe you *are* his son." She gave a little laugh. "And he told you not to say so. Never mind, I respect your discretion. Is he in?"

"If you will be so kind as to tell me your business..." I suggested.

"Well, I may as well tell you." Again that little laugh quickly subdued. "Mind you, I am a respectable widow woman. I think this will explain."

She opened her bag, produced and handed to me two papers. One I recognized with trepidation as a letter in Grandpa's unmistakable handwriting. The other was a marked advertisement from the *Matrimonial Post*.

> Highly respectable widow, age forty-four, dark, medium build, affectionate nature, artistic, moderate means, would like to hear from gentleman of agreeable disposition, preferably churchgoer, with good home and genuine intentions. Small

family no objection. References given and exchanged. Reply Box 314 M.T.

I was stunned. No need for me to read Grandpa's letter; she herself modestly referred to it.

"I had six good replies ... but your ... Mr. Gow's was so beautiful I just had to see him first."

I could have rocked with laughter, if I had not felt like weeping. I exclaimed, quite wildly: "See him then, madam. Go up straight away. The top floor, first door on the right."

She took back the papers, replaced them tidily in her handbag and stood up, self-conscious as a girl.

"Just tell me one thing. Is he dark or fair? My first husband was dark and I thought it would be a nice change ..."

"Yes, yes," I broke in, waving her on. "He's fair. But go up and see for yourself. ... Go up."

She went upstairs and I stood waiting for the short, sharp sounds of her immediate disillusionment. But there was no scene—a good half-hour passed before she descended, and then her expression, though mystified, was pleased rather than resentful.

"Your uncle is a very nice gentleman," she confided to me in a vaguely puzzled voice. "But scarcely so young as I expected."

When, with a suggestion of reluctance, she had gone, I hastened to Grandpa's room.

He was seated, pen in hand, at his table, absorbed in the composition of his favourite "Bullets."

"Robert," he declared. "I have a sure winner here. Just listen to this ..."

"But your visitor?" I interrupted.

"Oh, her!" He dismissed the lady with disdain. "She would have wearied me to death. Besides, comparatively speaking, she hasn't a curdie to her name."

I could not help myself. I turned away in a fit of laugher that was half hysterical, while he gazed after me over his spectacles, mildly astonished, yet unperturbed, a monument of respectability.

Downstairs, I put on my cap and muffler. The dusk was deepening and it held the promise of lights and Saturday night movement in the town. My spirits, unaccountably, had risen. There would probably be music in Reid's rooms, Alison and her mother might perhaps be there. I decided that I would go and make my peace with Jason. But first there was *The Flying Highlander*.

Every Saturday night at five o'clock the Port Doran-London express made a two-minute stop at Levenford to pick up West Coast passengers. It was a superb train, painted red and gold, complete with sleepers and dining cars where white napery and gleaming silver could be seen, through the windows, beneath shaded electric candles. Simply to watch that shining train pull out slowly for the great city of the South was enough to stir the blood, to raise in my breast the wild, vain, but still undying hope that one day I, too, would take my place upon its rich upholstery, beneath its soft rose lights.

I glanced at the clock. There was just time. I hurried down the dark road.

Chapter Four

That winter the Levenford Philosophical Club was making an effort to recover from the run-down condition which, at an earlier date, had provoked Reid's sarcasm. It had once been a fine club, modelled upon the Edinburgh Speculative Society. Mr. McKellar was the new president, and he had arranged for the resumption of the course of public lectures for which the Philosophical had been famous.

Papa did not now belong to the Club. Overanxious to advance his promotion, he had suffered some sad rebuffs from the other members and had come to regard the annual subscription as an unjustifiable expense.

I knew nothing of the lectures until one day towards the end of November when, passing me in the street, Mr. McKellar handed me a ticket without a word. He was a silent man and this uncommunicative gesture, effected without even stopping, was typical of him. The ticket read:

A Lecture will be Delivered
by
Professor Mark Fleming
on
The Story of Malaria
at
The Philosophical Rooms
Admit one   Nov. 30th.

I went eagerly to the Rooms on the specified evening, yet with the feeling that wounds scarcely healed would be painfully reopened.

I sat wedged incongruously amongst stout red-faced townsmen, sedate and prosperous in their fine broadcloth suits. I reddened when McKellar let his eye drift over me without the slightest recognition. But the moment Professor Fleming began to speak I fell under the fascination of the subject and the man.

Mark Fleming was Professor of Zoology at Winton University, a spare dark figure of about forty, with sharp features, a clipped moustache and bright penetrating eyes. He had done some brilliant research work on the lungfish, Lepidosiren, adventuring into unexplored country on the upper waters of the Amazon. To-night, since he was addressing laymen, his address was semipopular. But there was enough of science in it to stir my blood.

He traced the origin of the disease, discussed its ravages and the earlier mistaken theories regarding its cause. Then he passed to the first really scientific approach to the problem, describing the attempts of Ronald Ross to isolate the parasite, that magnificent and painstaking research which was finally crowned by the discovery of "sporozoites" in the salivary glands of a special mosquito. On the white screen at the end of the room Fleming showed us lantern slides, coloured micro-photographs, demonstrating the exquisitely symmetrical stages of development of the parasite. He revealed its life history, its cycle through the blood of various hosts, of which man was one. He summarized the preventive measures which had exterminated the scourge from large tracts of country and which—he gave the classic example—had made possible the building of the Panama Canal.

When he concluded, I drew a long deep breath. I had questions to ask which would show him my burning interest in his subject. But he was surrounded by important people who, although saying stupid and unimportant things, effectually prevented my approach. And presently, looking at his watch, he departed amidst smiles and many handshakes to catch his train.

The stimulation of this lecture, which revived all my passionate love of science, lingered for a few days. It was followed by a reaction of profound depression. For a week I walked with my eyes on the ground, suffering the desolation of a lost cause. Then, quite suddenly I had a great idea. Usually my great ideas crumbled overnight. Seemingly brilliant, they failed to withstand the remorseless logic which I myself unleashed against them. But this was different—it grew steadily, like a shaft of dawn piercing the haggard gloom. I made my plans excitedly, yet with care.

On the following Saturday, I kept back five shillings of my wages, changed quickly, made a parcel of certain articles upon my chest of drawers, and came down to the kitchen for dinner.

"Hurry, Grandma." I smiled at her. "I want to catch the one-thirty train. Big doings on hand."

The old woman was alone in the room. She brought me a plate of mutton stew, but with no answering smile, which surprised me, in view of the new friendship that had sprung up between us. Then, before sitting down with her crochet work to wait for Papa, who was always late on Saturdays, she handed me silently, with an expression of peculiar reserve, a postcard.

I took it, and read it with a gathering frown. Why couldn't people leave me alone? The interfering card bore the stamped heading, PRESBYTERY OF THE HOLY ANGELS, and it said: *Will you call and see me Sunday afternoon at four o'clock?* It was signed: J. J. ROCHE.

Still frowning, but with a passing uneasiness, I crumpled the card and threw it into the fire.

Grandma seemed very busy with her hook, but a moment later, without looking up, she said:

"So you won't go?"

I shook my head stubbornly.

Grandma's lacework appeared to please her greatly. Yet her tone was cautious.

"Suppose he comes here. What am I to tell him?"

"Tell him I'm not in," I mumbled, red-faced.

She raised her eyes and stared at me. Gradually a smile appeared on her face, a slow smile which deepened, as she got up.

"Let me give you some more stew, my man."

Grandma's flattering approval helped me to recover my self-possession. This communication from the beyond—for so I chose to regard my fervent past—had, to be frank, given me something of a shock. I really liked Canon Roche, and felt that my behaviour towards him had been shabby; also my proud indifference towards religion hadn't saved me some rather bad moments of remorse. However, my spirits were too high to be daunted. I put the matter out of my mind and was soon racing elatedly with my bundle for the Winton train.

My purpose buoyed me during the journey. When I reached Winton at three o'clock I took the green tram to Gilmore Hill and was again confronted by the grey, immovable, inspiring edifice of my dreams. I was older now and less easily intimidated, yet as I entered the University and approached the Zoology Department I felt my heart beating rapidly. I knew my way about here fairly well. I had longingly scanned the exterior of the department when sitting the Marshall with Gavin. Now I took one swift look at the big empty lecture theatre, then knocked on the door, panelled in ground glass, and marked LABORATORY. A moment later I knocked more loudly. Then, as no one answered, I boldly pushed open the door.

It was a long high room, half-tiled and lit by many tall windows. On the low benches there were rows of microscopes, wonderful glittering Zeiss microscopes with triple swing lenses. At each place was a double-tiered rack of reagents: drop bottles of fuchsin and methylene-blue, absolute alcohol, Canada balsam, everything the heart could desire. A large electric centrifuge was whizzing under its protective wire. Some complex apparatus I had never seen before gurgled steadily beside the range of porcelain sinks. At the end of the room I made out a tall man in a buff-coloured drill coat attending to a cage of guinea pigs.

I went slowly forward, my parcel under my arm, intoxicated by the aromatic smell of the balsam mingling with the tang of formalin and the sharp fruity scent of ether. The afternoon sunshine was pouring into this heavenly place. As I came near, the man in the drill coat half turned and let his eyes rest on me inquiringly.

"Well?"

"Could I see Professor Fleming, please?"

He was a tall lean man of fifty, with a bilious complexion and a ragged moustache. His nose was long and his hollow cheeks had deep lines in them. He turned back to the cage, skilfully caught up a guinea pig, and with hypodermic syringe poised between the first and second fingers of his left hand, pressed down his thumb and delicately injected the animal with a few minims of a cloudy solution. While doing this he remarked:

"The Professor isn't here."

A sharp disappointment gripped me.

"When will he be in?"

"He seldom comes here on Saturdays. Goes down to his week-end place at Drymen." Another guinea pig received its injection and was restored to the cage. "Come back Monday."

Now thoroughly cast-down, I exclaimed: "I can only get away on Saturdays."

He had finished the injections and, having dropped the syringe into carbolic, one in twenty, he gazed at me curiously.

"Can I do anything? I'm Smith, the head attendant. What is it you want?"

There was a pause.

"I want a job." My heart took a tremendous bound as I uncovered its secret, but I continued bravely. "I want to work here, in this lab, under Professor Fleming. I saw him last week, in Levenford; that's where I come from. Any kind of job ... even if it's only to feed these guinea pigs."

The attendant smiled dryly—at least his fixed and heavy expression lifted slightly.

"These ones don't get fed. What are you doing now?"

I told him. Then rushed on: "I hate it, though. I love science ... zoology especially ... I always have. I've studied it for years, at school and at home. If only I could get a start here, I'd work my way up, I'd do anything, I'd take five shillings a week and sleep on the floor." I unlimbered my package. "I brought these specimens up to show Professor Fleming. Please look at them. They'll prove to you that I'm not lying."

He was on the point of refusing, his long face had turned

disagreeable again. Then, with a glance at the clock, he seemed to change his mind.

"Come on, then. I've got ten minutes before I draw the sterilizer."

He led the way over to the bench and sat down on a stool watching me while, with trembling fingers, I tore the string and brown paper from my collections. I was anxious, of course, yet eagerness and hope were surging in my breast. I felt that I could convince this dubious and saturnine man of my genuine, my unique qualities. I had brought all my specimens, everything. But I did not trouble to exhibit the commoner varieties. I went straight to my rarities, my special hydra, my unclassified Bryozoa, my incomparable Stentors.

While I nervously described them he listened attentively, scrutinizing everything from beneath his heavy lids. Once or twice he nodded and several times shook his head. When I opened my box of sections he displayed his first signs of interest. Leaning forward he took the box from me, removed the slides and held them one after another against the light. Then, pulling a microscope towards him, much as a virtuoso might tuck a violin beneath his chin, he began, while I scarcely breathed, to examine them under the high-power. His hands were stained and dirty, his wrists bony, protruding, I could see, from cheap frayed shirt cuffs. But his long fingers were incredibly sensitive, manoeuvring the oil-immersion lens with careless, impressive accuracy.

It took him a dismayingly short time to run through all my precious work. He honoured three slides with a second inspection; then, straightening himself, he faced me, tugging at his straggling moustache.

"Is that the lot?"

"Yes," I answered very nervously.

He tapped out some tobacco and rolled himself a cigarette which he lit at a Bunsen flame on the bench. "I had a collection like that when I was your age."

I stared at him in complete surprise: it was the last thing I had expected him to say.

"Maybe not so good on sections. But I think better on Spirogyra.

I'd attended Paxton's night school course at the London Polytechnic and I sweated my guts out every week end on the Surrey Ponds. I thought I'd make another Cuivier of myself. That was more than thirty years ago. Look at me now. I'm fed to the teeth with routine. I get fifty bob a week and I have an invalid wife to support." He inhaled musingly. "I tried to get in by the back door of course—the only one that was open to me. No use, my lad. If you want to be colonel of the regiment don't enlist as a private. I've been stuck as a lab attendant all my life."

I felt a sinking feeling at my heart. "But you think my work shows some promise? You said my sections were good."

He shrugged his shoulders.

"They're all right, considering you cut them with an old hollow-ground Frass." He gave me a quick glance. "You see I know. I did it myself. But now we have electric microtomes. Manual dexterity is at a discount."

"At least it would get me a laboratory job?" I was trembling with anxiety. "In spite of what you say I want that. I'd even come in as a lab boy."

He gave a short laugh.

"Can you make Roux's solution? Can you smoke a hundred and fifty recording drums in half an hour? Can you separate blastomeres at the four-cell stage of cleavage? It takes five years to learn that job properly. D'you know that my lab boy is a man of sixty? I let him off to-day because his rheumatism's bad!" His lips were smiling but his look was bitter and sad. "If you want my advice, young fellow, you'll put the whole idea out your head. I don't deny that you have got a turn for this. But without money and a university degree the door is shut in your face. So go back to your machine, and forget it. It's not a bad life, a marine engineer. I'd give a lot myself to see the world on an old ocean-going tramp."

There was a silence. I began mechanically to put away the specimens in their boxes, to parcel them again with paper and string.

"Don't take it too hard," he said when I had finished. "I meant it for the best." He gave me his hand. "Good-bye and good luck."

I went out of the laboratory and down the deserted hill. Already the round sun was setting, streaking the dove-grey with rose. I did not take the tram, but kept on walking, across the Park. A crisp wind sent the fallen leaves scurrying along the paths, like children running out of school. I did not feel, or see, the lovely twilight. Amidst my disappointment a strange rage was burning within me. I refused to believe what Smith had told me. It was all lies. I would return to see the Professor himself next week. Nothing would stop me from achieving my ambition.

And yet, in my heart, I knew that the attendant was right. He might be soured and disagreeable but he had spoken sincerely. The longer I reflected the more surely I realized that my fine scheme for entering the department as a technician was impracticable. It was a case of the wish being father to the thought. The only way to enter was as a fee-paying student and that, of course, was impossible. What hurt most of all was the indifference with which Smith had dismissed my specimens. True, he had praised them faintly. But having, in my foolishness, expected so much, this mild approval served only to dash my high hopes to the ground. A blast of bitterness fanned the fire within me. Strangely, I was not despondent, but wounded and furious. And, as I reached the central section of the city, becoming conscious of the futile package which I still carried, I was possessed by a sudden fatalistic determination. I had failed again. I was fated never to serve my beloved science. I would finish with it for good.

Making my way down Buchanan Street, I entered the Argyll Arcade, a covered passage leading to Argyll Street and occupied by a number of odd little shops. Next to an establishment which sold model engines I found the place I wanted. In the window goldfish were swimming in a green glass tank surrounded by packets of dog biscuits and ants' eggs, amidst a confusion of mousetraps, butterfly nets, rubber articles and sheets of postage stamps. Above was the sign, NATURALISTS' BAZAAR AND EXCHANGE MART.

Inside I waited, breathing the musty odours, until a small, careworn man in a shiny black suit dipped out from behind a curtain at the back.

"I want to sell my collection."

I undid my package again, this time with vehement fingers.

"It's good stuff," I said when I had laid out the boxes on the counter. "Just look at these dragonflies."

"We're not really buying just now." He spoke in a throaty whisper, putting on a pair of pince-nez and beginning to look carefully at everything, weighing each object with white damp fingers.

"No, there's no demand for that stuff." He said regretfully when he had finished: "I'll give you seventeen and six for the lot."

I gazed at him indignantly. "Why, that yellow *æschna* is worth a pound itself. I've seen it priced in the London catalogues."

"This isn't London, it's the Argyll Arcade." His voice was no more than a husky murmur—either he had a dreadful cold or some affliction of the larynx. And his manner was quite indifferent. "That's the best I can do. Take it or leave it."

I felt angrier than ever. I had never before experienced the difference between buying and selling. Seventeen and six for five years' work, for these wild, difficult and dangerous climbs upon the Longcrags, these long careful hours stretching far into the night ... It was a raging insult. Yet what could I do?

"I'll take it."

When I left the shop, no longer encumbered, my arms seemed light and my head was hot. With the coins he had given me and what remained of my original five shillings, I had more than a pound in my pocket. It was six o'clock, the city was bright with lights. I set out recklessly to enjoy myself.

At the corner of Queen Street I found a small restaurant. It looked Bohemian and in the window a tempting display of white fish and red meat was set out between two giant artichokes. I plunged through the swing door, crossed the soft carpet and sat down in a velvet-cushioned booth.

It was a cosy little place, over-upholstered in an old-fashioned way, discreetly lighted by pink-shaded candles like those I had so often admired in the diner of *The Flying Highlander*. I was nervous with the waiter who had a curly moustache and a tight white apron reaching almost to his feet. But I ordered a good dinner of kidney soup, escalope of veal with mushrooms and a Neapolitan ice cream. Then he put the wine list in my hands. Pale but determined, in a voice which shook only slightly, I ordered a flask of Chianti.

I ate slowly: I had not tasted such rich, delicious food for a long time. The wine drew my tongue and cheeks together at first, but I persevered and gradually got to like its rusty flavour, and the generous warmth which flowed all the way down with every swallow. The restaurant was not very full but one or two couples occupied the booths. Opposite me, a good-looking man was entertaining a plump dark girl in a coquettish little hat. I watched them longingly as they laughed and talked in low tones, their heads very close together.

The bill came to nine shillings. It was a colossal figure but now I simply did not care. I finished the wine, tipped the waiter a shilling, received his bow with satisfaction, and went out.

What a glorious night! Lights glittering, movement and excitement in the streets, delightful, interesting people thronging the pavements. At last I was living, I had buried my obsession, I was free. I bought an *Evening Times* from a newsboy and scanned the amusement column beneath an electric sign. There were two variety shows in town, an Edwards musical comedy, a "positively the last night" appearance of Martin Harvey in "The Only Way." None of these appealed to me. Then, at the foot of the list, I observed with delight that a repertory performance of "The Second Mrs. Tanqueray" was being given at the old Theatre Royal. I proceeded to the Royal, took a pit stall, and went in.

Although I had read considerably, and had vague memories of being taken to "Cinderella" by my mother in Dublin, I had never been to a real play in my life. When the curtain rose I was conscious of a thrill of emotion. And soon I was quite carried away. This was the kind of world I had so often visualized, where people never spoke without being witty, where courageous souls burned away their lives in a pure white flame. With all my impressionable, thirsting senses, I drank in every word.

When I left the theatre I was wildly intoxicated. I too wanted to grasp life with both hands, to experience those joys which had so far eluded me. Glowing and voluptuous images rose sensuously before me.

The theatre had emptied early: it was only half-past ten. The streets were much less crowded now, some were quite deserted as I made my way towards James Square, a small open space in the centre of the city flanked by the General Post Office and a large department store whose plate-glass windows remained illuminated all night. Lewis, with a knowing smile, had dropped hints about James Square.

I began, nervously, to walk up and down the broad pavement of the square. Several members of the opposite sex were doing the same thing, pausing occasionally with an air of abstraction, as though waiting for a bus. One was extremely stout, bursting out in all directions. She wore a big hat covered with feathers and lace-up boots on her pianolike legs.

"Hello, dearie." She murmured to me, maternally, as we passed.

Another was tall, thin, mysteriously veiled, dressed all in black. She walked very slowly, with a slight stoop. Occasionally she coughed, but politely, into her pocket handkerchief. She gave me a weary smile which froze my blood. I halted, mystified and dismayed. I could see no one remotely approaching the lovely visions of my excited fancy. Perhaps I should do better in the centre of the square.

I crossed the street to the small ornamental garden, decorated with statues and intersected by paths. Here it was darker, more romantic. And there were more promenaders. Encouraged by the greater promise of the shadows I strolled up the central path. A girl approached, her figure young, seductive in the darkness. When she passed I drew up and turned round. She had stopped and was looking back at me. When she saw that I was interested in her, she turned, and slowly, with an inviting movement of her head, sauntered on again.

My blood was pounding dizzily in my veins. I stood for a moment. Should I follow or wait until she had again made a circuit of the little garden? It was a blind circle, she must return this way: I sat down tremblingly, on a bench at the edge of the path. I only realized that the seat had another occupant when a man's voice addressed me.

"Got a fag, mate?"

I fumbled in my pocket and brought out a packet of cigarettes. I could see dimly that he was an oldish man, down on his luck, a regular tramp in fact.

"Thanks, pal," he said. "You wouldn't have a match?"

Hurriedly, under the leafless trees, in the dark garden, I struck a match and held it to his cigarette. The cupped flame illumined for an instant the remnants of his face. Then it went out.

I sat on the bench a long time, stiffly. I gave him the rest of my cigarettes. I walked heavily to the station. My legs were so weak I could hardly stand. I just caught the last train.

I was alone in the compartment. I sat staring at the board partition in front of me. There was nothing, after all, nothing in life that was not completely ruined. I had sold my collections, my birthright ... for this.

Suddenly I caught sight of a little peep-hole which some mischievous passenger had cut in the wood of the dividing partition. Crushed, overwhelmed by despondency and horror, I rose nevertheless, impelled by nameless curiosity, and put my eye to the little hole.

But the next compartment was empty, quite empty too.

Chapter Five

The winter continued damp and wet. I was now in charge of a light turning-lathe and, resigned to a future at the Works, I tried to take an interest in the machine. But my mind kept wandering; I made mistakes; I saw that Jamie was becoming annoyed with me.

One day towards the middle of December he came up to my bench, frowning, with a metal connecting rod in his hand.

"Look here, Robie," he said gruffly. "You'll have to buck yourself up a bit."

I flushed to the ears; it was the first time he had ever spoken to me in such a tone.

"What have I done?"

"You've wasted eight hours' skilled time, to say nothing of the material." He held out the steel piece. "I told you to drill this with a number two x. You've used a number four and ruined the whole job."

I saw that I had been guilty of a careless blunder. But instead of feeling sorry I was conscious of a slow resentment. I kept my eyes on the ground.

"What difference does it make? Marshalls won't go bankrupt."

"That's no way to talk," Jamie replied sharply. "I tell you straight it's time you stopped crying for the moon and put your back into your job."

He lectured me heatedly for a few minutes; then, having expended his anger, he growled, before moving away: "Come up and have supper with us next Saturday."

"Thanks." I had turned white and my lips were stiff. "If it's all the same to you, I'd rather not."

He stood for a moment in silence, then walked off. I was furious at Jamie, but most of all at myself. I knew that he was justified. As I stood there, sulking, Galt came over from an adjoining bench.

"I saw his nabs putting the dog on you. He's a bit too given to that sort of thing."

Galt was only too ready to air a grudge against any exercise of authority and in his approach I sensed the sympathy of one incompetent workman for another. He had not shaved for a couple of days and his appearance was particularly slovenly. I could not contain myself.

"Oh, shut up."

He drew back with an offended air. "Don't be so high and mighty about it. Next time I'll think twice before I offer you a kindness."

I resumed my work. In the days which followed I tried to improve. But nothing went right. I handled my tools so recklessly, I gouged my thumb with a cold chisel. The wound became infected and suppurated, causing an ugly abscess which Grandma poulticed for me. I felt Jamie watching me uncomfortably, looking as though he wished to speak.

"That's a sore-looking hand you have," he said at last. "It doesn't seem to heal."

"It's nothing," I answered coldly. "Just a scratch."

I almost welcomed the pain which this festering wound caused me. My mind was as dark as the wintery skies. Alison had gone to Ardfillan. She wrote regularly in answer to my frequent and passionate communications but never at great length. When the post brought a letter from her my heart swelled suffocatingly. I took the letter to my room, locked the door, and opened it with trembling fingers. Her writing was large and round, only three or four words to each line. My eager eyes soon devoured the double sheet. She was working hard at two new songs. Schubert's "Ständchen" and Schumann's "Widmung." She and her mother had gone skating with Louisa on the private pond at Ardfillan House. Dr. Thomas had been to see them once. Mr. Reid had called twice.

Everyone was looking forward to the Reunion Ball. Would I not try to come to it? Again and again I read it through. What I longed for was not there. Quickly, I sat down and began my reply, ardent and reproachful, pouring out my soul.

A week before Christmas, Lewis sauntered towards me at the lunch hour.

"I say, Shannon, there's not a bad dance on in Ardfillan next Saturday. Let's go together."

I took a bite of bread and cheese, trying to maintain a stolid attitude. "I'm afraid I'm not much of a dancer."

"Never mind. You can sit them out." He smiled. "I usually do."

"I don't think I can get away."

He persisted in his good-natured effort to persuade me. "It's quite an affair. The St. Bride's Reunion. Lots of pretty girls and a tophole buffet. I've had a couple of tickets sent me. You really must come."

In spite of my determination not to expose my feelings, an insufferable emotion mastered me. I had no dress suit; I could not dance; it was impossible for me to go. The affability of his manner, the friendliness of his insistence, above all the easy indifference with which he took the dance, like all the other good things in life, for granted, acted on me like a goad.

"Damn it all ... Can't you leave me alone?"

He stared at me in surprise; then, with a shrug of his shoulders, left me. I was immediately ashamed of myself. All afternoon I kept my eyes fixed to my machine, cold and sick inside.

On Saturday evening I took the five o'clock workman's train to Ardfillan. For a couple of hours I wandered about the deserted promenade, now swept by a December gale. As I sheltered behind the bandstand on the vacant esplanade with my coat collar up, memories of Gavin rose from the surrounding darkness to haunt me. It was here at the Fair that we had sworn never to be separated. Such a short time ago ... It seemed a lifetime. Now Gavin was gone, while I stood and shivered, on the very spot where, full of hope and courage, we had pledged ourselves to conquer the world.

Towards eight o'clock I made my way to the Town Hall. Mixing with the small crowd which had collected to see the local gentry arriving for the dance, I waited on the pavement outside. A fine rain began to fall. Presently the cabs and motors began to roll up.

Hidden amongst the other spectators, who were mainly domestic servants, I watched the guests enter, happy people, smiling and talking, the women in evening gowns, the men in tail coats and white ties. I saw Lewis stroll in, groomed and oiled to perfection. A moment later, with a start of surprise, I caught sight of Reid's stocky figure hurrying up the steps. At last, after an interval, Alison and her mother appeared. They came in a large party with Louisa and Mrs. Marshall, My heart stood still at the vision of Alison, in a white dress, her face quietly animated, her eyes bright as she talked to Louisa, moving over the strip of carpet. When she disappeared the first strains of the orchestra came stealing out to me from inside the Hall. My heart seemed crushed in my breast. I clenched my hands in my pockets and walked rapidly away. There was no train for three-quarters of an hour. I went into a fish-and-chip shop in a poor street near the station. I had not eaten since lunch and I ordered myself a twopenny portion of chips. Hunched on a bench in the dark little shop I swilled vinegar on the greasy potatoes and ate them with my fingers. I wished I could get drunk. I wanted to degrade myself to the lowest depths.

On Monday morning at the Works I met Lewis going into the machine shop. A strange impulse made me stop and smile to him, not in apology, but with a man-of-the-world directness.

"Look here, old chap," I said. "I'm sorry I cut up so rusty last week. Did you have a good time on Saturday?"

"Yes," he answered suspiciously. "Not bad."

"The fact is"—my smile broadened—"I had a very special appointment with a lady, a young widow I met in Winton, and I got rather annoyed at you trying to drag me out of it."

His face cleared slowly. "Why didn't you say so, you ass?"

I laughed and nodded knowingly.

"Lucky devil." He looked at me enviously. "Nothing like that at Ardfillan. Very proper and correct. You were wise not to come."

This cheap lie cheered me up momentarily, although soon it

brought a reaction of disgust. I retired more than ever within myself, avoiding people, making a virtue of my loneliness. When Kate asked me to her house I usually made some excuse. I saw very little of Reid. On one occasion when we met he gave me a peculiar smile.

"I'm doing my best for you, Shannon."

"In what way?" I asked, surprised.

"I'm leaving you alone."

I walked off. I could find nothing to say. I was deadeningly tired, and sick of everything. Strangely, the one person whom I turned to was Grandma—perhaps I was attracted by her rocklike stability. Where Grandpa was a mere straw in the wind, with no roots to hold him, she drew sustenance and support deep, deep from her country origins, almost it seemed from the soil from which she had sprung. I sat late at the kitchen table talking with her while she gave me glimpses of her "early days" on her father's Ayrshire farm—at the cheesemaking; bringing fresh baked bannocks to the harvesters in the fields; watching the potato pickers as they danced at night, to the fiddle, in the barn. More and more, I noticed in her little "peasant" tricks—her habit, for instance, of picking out the peas from her broth and arranging them in a neat circle round her soup plate, so that she might eat them afterwards with pepper and salt. She was full of country sayings (like "Beetroots give you lumbago" or "Ne'er cast a clout till May goes oot") and she retained her full fondness for brewing "herbals." Her memory, especially for family dates, was wonderful. With her crochet hook she could still make exquisite, intricate-patterned lace which she wore on her cap and collar and which gave to her a perennial air of freshness. Repeatedly, she assured me that her family was long-lived, that her mother remained in full possession of her faculties up to the age of ninety-six. She was quite sure that she would surpass this record, and remarked often, with a composed sigh, of Grandpa and her friend Miss Minns, "how sadly they had failed."

Christmas was almost at hand. The shops in the town were bright with holly and paper streamers. The festive season made but the slightest difference at Lomond View: Grandma would go out to the Watch Night service, Kate might send us a plum pudding; Grandpa, if unrestrained, would not stay sober. Nevertheless, as Christmas Eve approached I felt myself growing restless and uneasy. To combat this I plunged more deeply into the books which I borrowed from the public library. At night I was often so tired that when I settled to read I drowsed off at once, wakening with a start as my nostrils filled with the smoke of the expiring candlewick. But on most Sundays, during that dismal winter, I lay in bed half the day, poring over Chekhov, Dostoievski, Gorki, and the other Russian novelists. My earlier liking for romantic fiction had yielded to a more sombre and realistic taste. Also I had begun to muddle my head with philosophy: plodding through Descartes, Hume, Schopenhauer and Bergson, far out of my depth yet rewarded, now and then, by a wintery gleam which increased my sense of exclusiveness and my haughtiness towards theology. My sardonic smile crumbled the whole structure of divine revelation. Impossible for a scientist, a savant, to believe that the world had been brought to being overnight, that man was created by a process of clay modelling, and woman by the transformation of a rib. The Garden of Eden with Eve eating her apple beside the grinning serpent was a charming fairy tale. All the evidence pointed to a different conception of the origin of life: the development from primæval scum, through millions of years, of colloidal compounds in the great seas and swamps of the cooling earth, the timeless evolution of these protoplasmic forms, through the amphibians and reptiles, to the birds and mammals, a truly remarkable cycle which—dismal thought!—made Nicolo and me, brothers, practically, under our skin.

Shorn of my illusions, I sought soulful consolation in beauty. From the library I took out works upon the great painters and studied the coloured reproductions of their masterpieces. Then I came upon the Impressionists. Their new ideas of colour and form delighted me. Returning from work, I would pause to stare for a long time at the purple shadows cast by the blue chestnut trees or at the pale streaks of lemon lingering in the evening sky behind the Ben. Foolish and morbid, suffering dreadfully from the "green sickness" of youth, I invested this mountain with a portentous symbolism: it represented to me the unattainable in life. If I could not reach the summit, at last I stood, in an attitude of scornful challenge, at its base.

Although defying the lightning, and everything else, I felt miserable when Christmas Day arrived. The night before I had gone to Barloan with a present for Kate's little boy. I wanted to help fill his stocking and, in my heart, I hoped for an invitation to Christmas dinner. But they were all out when I called: I tied my parcel to the door handle and came away. Amongst the few cards which I received there was one from the convent Sisters; I smiled over it—just the correct kind of smile—but my superiority did not make me happier. When one o'clock drew near I could not face the dismal meal downstairs. I took my cap and went out.

The grey streets were deserted as I wandered through the town. There was no restaurant in Levenford where one could have a real meal. At last, in desperation, I went into the Fitters' Bar. Here I had a glass of beer and some bread and cheese. This cold fare did not make the prospect of returning to the cheerless house any more enticing. There was not even a fireplace in my room.

The public library opened between two and three o'clock, a concession to the fact that the day was not a general holiday. It was warm in the library. I spent most of the hour there, and borrowed another book. Then I set out for home.

A raw fog had come down and darkness was not far off. As I came along Chapel Street I did not see a tall figure looming towards me, but the instant I heard the tap-tap of an umbrella on the pavement beside me I guessed who it was, and I could not repress a start.

"Why, it's you, Shannon." Canon Roche's tone was friendly. "I've been wondering if you'd gone to earth for the winter."

I kept silent, telling myself that I would not be afraid of this man who was, after all, only human and not in the least invested with mystical powers.

"I have a sick call at Drumbuck Toll. Are you going that way?"

"Yes, I'm going home."

There was a pause.

"My card to you the other week probably went astray. The post office is no respecter of postcards. I had a colleague staying with me, a South American father over here from Brazil. Knowing your interest in natural history, I thought you might have cared to meet him."

"I've lost my interest in natural history."

"Ah!" I could almost feel his eyebrows lift. "Has that gone too? Tell me, my dear fellow, has anything been saved from the wreck?"

I walked on with my head down.

"What have you got there?" He slid the book from beneath my arm. "*The Brothers Karamazoff*. Not at all bad. I commend Aloysha to your notice. He's a young man with some grace in him."

He gave me back the book. For a few minutes we continued in silence.

"My dear boy, what's been the matter with you?"

His change of tone took me by surprise. I had expected a severe reprimand for "falling from grace," "missing my Easter duties" and so forth; the mildness of his voice made my eyes smart. Thank heavens it was dark—he would not catch me that way.

"Nothing's the matter."

"Then why don't you turn out as you used to? We've all missed you, the Sisters and I especially."

I gathered all my strength, determined not to remain overawed and mute. I wanted him to know what had been taking place in my mind.

"I don't believe in God any more. I've given up the whole thing."

He received this in silence. In fact he walked on so long without replying that I stole a look at his face. It was thin, tired-looking and discouraged. I realized with a shock what had never struck me before—that he too was burdened with his own sorrows, and the thought that I had probably increased them deepened my compunction. Suddenly he began to speak, gazing straight ahead, as though talking to himself.

"You don't believe in God, you've achieved a triumph of reason.

".... Well, no wonder you're rather proud of it." He paused. "But what do you know about God? For that matter, what do I know of Him? ... I'm afraid the answer is, nothing. He is absolutely unknowable ... incomprehensible ... infinitely beyond the grasp of the imagination, of all the senses. We can't picture Him, or explain His treatment of us, in human terms. Believe me, Shannon, the intellectual approach to God is madness. You cannot fathom the impenetrable. The greatest mistake we can make towards God is to be always arguing when we ought simply to believe in Him blindly."

He was silent for a moment before resuming.

"Do you remember when we once discussed those creatures who live five miles down in the ocean, feeling their way, without eyes, in the blackness ... a sort of eternal night ... only occasionally a faint phosphorescent gleam? And if they're brought up, nearer the light of day, they simply explode. That's us, in our relation to God." Another pause. "The greatest sin of all is intellectual pride. I know pretty well what's in your mind. You've reduced everything to terms of the single cell. You can tell me exactly the chemical composition of protoplasm ... Oh, very simple substances. But can you synthetize these substances into life? Until that happens, there's nothing for it, Shannon, but to go on in humility and faith."

Again there was a silence. We had almost reached the corner of Drumbuck Road. As he turned off towards the Toll, leaving me to continue alone, he gave me a parting glance before vanishing in the fog.

"You may not be seeking God, Robert, but He is seeking you. And He will find you, my dear boy, He will find you in the end."

I went towards Lomond View slowly, in a tangle of emotions. I should have felt proud that I had asserted myself: it was something to have the courage of one's convictions. Instead I felt shaken, afraid, and, at the bottom of my heart, horribly ashamed.

If Canon Roche had used the tricks of his trade, the usual shop-worn phrases about the wiles of the Devil and so forth, I should have felt myself justified. One ill-chosen word on his part would have routed him. If he had wrung me with sentimental allusions to the Babe now lying in the Manger, I might have wept, but I should never have forgiven him.

Instead, he had met me on my own ground and quietly shown me my insignificance. Suppose, after all, that the Supreme Being existed. How absurd I should be, a tiny diatom, a feebly whirling rotifer, presuming to defy Him. And what terrors, what torments would be my punishment—worst of all the torment of knowing that I had denied Him. I had at that moment an overpowering desire to fall on my knees, to yield, in blind humility, to the solace of prayer. But I resisted, shivering and stubborn, unconsciously beginning to walk a little faster. As the outlines of Lomond View appeared, I surrendered only to unconquerable sadness. I groaned inwardly: "Oh, God . . . if there is a God . . . . what kind of Christmas have you given me!"

Chapter Six

In May we had a Late Frost followed by a thaw which turned everything to slush. Yet one evening, two weeks before the Trades Holiday, as I trudged home from the Works through the mud and melting snow, the buds were forming upon the hedgerows, I felt the coming spring stirring in my limbs. Alison was home; and on the Trades Holiday, not so far distant, we had arranged to take a trip to Ardencaple—I was looking forward to our excursion with all my heart.

At Lomond View when I entered the kitchen I immediately sensed something unusual in the air. Grandma was seated at the table with an air of resignation while Papa, his hand on her shoulder, was doing his best to propitiate her.

"Fetch your supper yourself, Robert." He straightened himself and gave me a significantly mournful glance. "Sophie has left."

The news did not strike me as especially momentous. I put down my lunch tin, washed myself in the scullery and came back. As I took my hot covered plate from the oven Grandma turned to me, amplifying Papa's explanation in a "put-out" voice.

"After all I've done for her, to walk out without a word of warning. It's past understanding."

"We'll get somebody else, sooner or later," Papa remarked softly. "After all she was very wasteful . . . and a big eater."

"I can't do it all myself," Grandma protested.

"Robie and I will make things easy for you." Papa gave a dreadful, playful kind of smirk. "I don't mind making my own bed. As a matter of fact, I'm very fond of housework."

I saw that he was secretly overjoyed to be free of the expense of the maid and that he would do his utmost to delay the engagement of another.

When I had finished my meal, to oblige the old woman I took up Grandpa's bread and cheese and cocoa, on my way up to my room. As I turned the handle of his door, and carried in the tray, he was seated by a small fire, with his coat over his shoulders.

"Thank you, Robert." He spoke in a mild and reasonable tone. "Where's Sophie?"

"Gone." I put down the tray in front of him. "Left without notice."

"Well, well!" He looked up with a surprised, slightly injured expression. "You amaze me. You never know where you are with people these days."

"It's a little awkward."

"It is indeed," he agreed. "I must say I liked the girl. Very obliging and young."

It was a relief to find Grandpa in a restrained mood, one of these blessed intermissions which filled him with his old contemplative quiet. I thought he looked frail, to-night, a trifle under the weather; and I stood a moment while he dipped his bread in his cocoa and slowly ate it.

"How's the leg?" I asked. Lately he had begun to drag his left foot as he walked.

"Fine, fine. It's only a sprain. I have a grand constitution, Robert."

Next morning, at the Works, I was conscious of Galt, Sophie's father, watching me with a peculiar air. We were working on a new generator and he kept hanging about in my vicinity, coming over now and then to borrow a wrench or a file. Selecting a moment when Jamie was at the other end of the shed he said:

"I want to see you when we knock off."

I gazed with distaste at his colourless, unshaven face, barely lit by a lustreless eye.

"What for?"

"I'll tell you later. Meet me in the Fitters' Bar."

Before I could refuse Jamie appeared and Galt moved off. I felt puzzled and upset. What on earth did he want with me? I told myself I would not go. Yet, at five minutes past six, driven by an uneasy curiosity, I went into the Bar, immediately opposite the Works Gates, and found Galt already seated at a small table in the corner of the long sawdust-strewn saloon, which was almost empty, not yet lit up for the evening.

He greeted me with an earthy smile. "What'll you have?"

I shook my head stiffly. "I'm in a hurry. What's all this about?"

"I'll have a half first." He called for the drink and when it was brought he said: "It's about my Sophie."

I flushed indignantly.

"That has nothing to do with me."

"Maybe not." He drank his whisky in reflective fashion, his eyes wandering all round me. "But it'll be a proper scandal if it comes out."

It was as if he had dashed a bucket of water in my face. Bewildered and confused, there was no denying the thrill of intimidation which icily traversed my spine.

He gave a nod towards the other chair at the table.

"Sit down and don't be so high and mighty. You can stand me another half, too." He paused, again searching me with his small mean eye. "You've no objection?"

"Have one if you want," I muttered.

"Good health," he said when the second drink came.

Half an hour later I went along Drumbuck Road, white-faced and stiff, burning with rage and misery. The leaves were opening on the sappy chestnut trees, but now I did not see them. When I reached the house I climbed the stairs to Grandpa's room, shut the door behind me, and faced him. At my entrance he had risen with a letter in his hand.

"Look, Robie!" He sounded eager and pleased. "A consolation prize in the last competition. A coloured pencil case and a bound volume of *Good Works*."

"You and your *Good Works*!" In my bitterness I hustled him back, upsetting his books and papers.

He gazed at me, crestfallen.

"What's the matter?"

"Don't pretend you don't know." My wretchedness, rather than my rage, made my voice low and concentrated. "When I think of it, after all your promises ... when I'm surrounded by my own troubles ... Oh, God, it's the last straw."

"I don't understand." His head was beginning to shake.

"Then think." I bent over and shook him. "Think why Sophie left."

He repeated the words, his eyes wearing a look of blankness. Then a light seemed to break over him. He stopped shaking and confronted me with a new expression, no longer wondering but almost apostolic, raising his right hand like Moses about to bring a fountain from the rock.

"Robert, I swear to you we were always the best of friends. No more than that. Nothing."

"Indeed!" Bitterness was choking me. "You expect me to believe that ... with your record!" He looked guilty. "You've landed yourself in a hopeless mess. And I wash my hands of you."

I turned away and went out of the room, leaving him quite frightened, on the hearthrug. While I ate my supper I struggled with the implications of this new worry—one minute it seemed trivial, the next full of limitless disaster. Moodily, I wondered if I had done wrong to conciliate Galt ... to bribe him, in fact, by paying for his drinks. Surely that in itself was an admission of guilt. Yet, if I had taken a firmer stand, there was no knowing what he might have done. Oh, misery of miseries! While I dreamed of love as something warm and glowing, this thing came, sordid and disreputable, to mock at me.

An hour later as I went up to my room I found the old man waiting for me on the landing, a sheet of notepaper in his hand. He held this out to me, with dignity and a hint of triumph.

"I've settled everything, Robert." He placated me with a half-smile. "An open letter to the people of the town. Read it."

Wearily, I let my eyes run through the long epistle, addressed "To the Editor of the *Levenford Herald*." "Sir ... an unwarranted aspersion has been cast against me ... I appeal to my fellow citizens

... nothing to conceal ... a life without blemish ... pure as the lily ... respecter of true womanhood ..."

"Goes to the point." Grandpa watched my face eagerly. "It'll just be in time for next week's issue."

"Yes." I met his gaze. "I'll take care of it for you."

"Good, good!" He patted me tremulously on the shoulder. "I didn't mean to offend you, Robie. The last thing in the world. A friend in need is a friend indeed."

I forced a smile which seemed to comfort him, at least he shook me gratefully by the hand.

As he turned to his room dragging his foot after him, suddenly, as a kind of afterthought, he put his head round the door.

"Robie," he said gravely. "My poor wife was a wonderful woman."

Oh, God, what next? I had not heard him mention her name in ten years. I went to my own room. I began to tear into small pieces his open letter to his fellow citizens.

On the following day Galt approached me as we knocked off work. I had expected this and had braced myself to meet a recriminating attitude. To my surprise his manner was quite affable.

"You're in no hurry to-night. Come on in the Bar with me. If you're not too proud."

I hesitated. Then I realized that it would relieve my mind if some sort of understanding were reached between us. We went into the Bar.

There, with his feet in the sawdust, Galt kept the conversation on his favourite topic, "the rights of man." He was a pertinacious speaker —at the Union meetings it was admitted that he had the "gift of the gab"—with a few high-sounding phrases which he brought out with a triumphant air. He believed that the workers were everywhere exploited and preyed upon, "bled white" by their employers. He wanted the men to rise and take the reins of government in their own hands. "Up with the masses, down with the classes!" was his slogan. He was beginning to use the new word "Comrade" and he spoke with unction of "the dawn of liberty."

"Well, I suppose we'll have to get down to brass tacks." He

shook his head regretfully. "My worst enemy couldn't call me anything but a fair man. But I will have my rights. There's no getting over the fact that Sophie has got to be compensated."

I felt a fluttering in my inside. Long afterwards, when I discovered, in a curious way, that Grandpa had no more than put his arm around the wretched Sophie's waist—last feeble prance of the decrepit stallion—I cursed myself heartily for being such an easy victim. Now I gazed at Galt glassily.

"I'm glad you don't deny it." He approved my silence. "It shows you have the right stuff in you. Now to make no bones about it. I want five pounds. Five pounds and we wash the slate clean, everything forgiven and forgotten. These are my terms. And I can't say fairer."

I stared at him in dismay.

"I couldn't get such an amount to save my life."

"There's money in that house," Galt said accusingly. "If you don't get it, I'll go to Leckie myself. He's an old skinflint but he'll pay up sooner than have this plastered over the town."

What on earth was I to do? I saw clearly enough that he had picked me as the easiest and least resistant line of approach. Yet it seemed equally clear that if I failed to get the money he would take the matter to Papa, who had lately been grumbling horribly against Grandpa, threatening again to send him to the Institution at Glenwoodie.

"Will you give me time?" I asked at last.

Galt answered magnanimously. "I'll give you a week, Comrade. That's reasonable."

I stood up. As I went out he pressed my arm with a peculiar archness.

"You're the one that somebody likes."

I walked home, shamed and outraged, my head in a whirl. In looking for a guiding principle I had turned to the shining idea of the brotherhood of man, attending meetings, studying the pamphlets, thinking feelingly in terms of "suffering humanity." We working men were allies, marching forward under the hostile sky. No one could have been more vehement than Galt in protesting the noble virtues of the downtrodden poor. Yet his own poverty was the result of indolence and shiftlessness. And now he had been given his chance to prove his nobility, he was using it to tread all over me.

During the next few days. I racked my brains for ways and means of finding the money. There was only one person whom I could possibly approach. In the fitting shop, for the rest of that week, while Galt kept looking at me, I kept looking at Jamie. Recently our relations had returned to a happier footing, he seemed to feel that I was making a greater effort to "get on with the job." Several times I almost brought myself to the point of speaking to him, then my courage failed me. But on Saturday forenoon, conscious of a growing importunity in Galt's manner, I went up to the head of the assembly shed.

"Jamie." I spoke breathlessly. "Could you lend me some money?"

"I thought something was on your mind." He threw away his cigarette end and smiled at me, at the same time reaching in his pocket for a handful of cash. "How much?"

"It's more than you think." I swallowed hard. "But I promise I'll pay you back."

"How much?" he repeated, still smiling but a trifle dubious.

"Five pounds."

He stopped smiling, looked at me incredulously.

"In the name of God. Have you gone balmy? I thought you meant a couple of bob."

"I swear I'll make it up to you out of my pay."

"What do you want it for?"

"I can't say. But it's important."

He was looking at me curiously. He let the handful of change fall back into his pocket. His expression was cold, disapproving, and disappointed. He shook his head.

"I thought you were beginning to get your feet on the ground. I'm not the Bank of Scotland. I've a hard enough job to make ends meet."

I retreated, horribly humiliated by this sharp rebuff: I could wear any number of hair shirts without a murmur, but a single disparaging word would reduce me to the depths. For the rest of the shift I kept my head down, avoiding Galt's persistent stare. When the hooter blew I dodged him, bolted for the gate and ran half the way home.

During Sunday I managed to lie low, but all the next week Galt nagged me mercilessly. My first hesitation over, I had assumed, identified myself with this obligation. I had an agonizing desire to discharge it. I was a perfectionist, all my early undertakings were infused with a do-or-die intensity, and this was no exception. I wanted the final feverish satisfaction of "paying Galt off." I actually felt that I, myself, owed this money, that it was a just debt which I must at all costs repay. Galt fostered this illusion. He hinted at police court proceedings. He warned me that I was now mixed up in the affair. Remembrance of thoughts and stirrings which had troubled me when Sophie did my room added to this sense of guilt. Was I not just as bad as the old man?

When Saturday came round I was at my wit's end. I tried to elude my persecutor but Galt was waiting for me at the gates. He delivered his ultimatum. He told me in a surly voice, suggestive of the truth, that he had contracted obligations with the local bookmaker.

"If you don't bring it to-night," he said, "the fat will be in the fire with a vengeance."

As I walked away my mood turned bitter and wounded. I told myself that I was sick to death of carrying other people's burdens on my shoulders. I had done enough. I could do no more.

When I got home Grandma was coming downstairs with an air of quiet complacency, and her "Good Book" in her hands.

"He's been asking for you." She made a movement of her head back and upwards. "He had a queer turn this morning. I stopped with him a bit and read him a chapter." Lately she had adopted this worthy practice—in the face of his manifest decline a new protective attitude had replaced her old enmity towards Grandpa.

I stood, undecided, in the lobby, then against my will I went up, turned the handle of the door. He was dressed but resting on his bed, extremely subdued, and looking quite poorly. I had to say something.

"What's wrong with you?"

He smiled. "Too much spiritual reading maybe. I could do with a bit of *Hajji Baba*." He gazed at me speculatively. "You'll be going to the football match this afternoon?"

"There's no match."

He did not say anything more. He expected nothing. Yet I went down to have my dinner, resentful of his desire for my company. I had said that I would have nothing more to do with him. I meant to keep my word.

After lunch it began to rain. I hung about with my hands in my pockets staring out of the window. Then, I climbed the stairs moodily.

I made up his fire until it burned brightly. We settled ourselves and played three games of draughts, also several hands of "nap," a card game in which our stakes were matches, and to which Grandpa was much addicted. We scarcely talked at all. But afterwards, while he reclined in his chair, I read him the adventure of Hajji in the Sultan's palace, which always caused him to chuckle. At four o'clock I made tea and some hot toast and dripping. Afterwards he lit his pipe and sat back with his eyes half-closed.

"This is like old times, Robie."

I felt like breaking out and slanging him. When he was calm, relaxed, like this, the lapses which had marked his whole life seemed all the more wickedly unnecessary. I was furious with him. Yet while he sat drowsing I could not free myself from memories of his kindness to me when I was a child. Of course it was not all kindness, but in part a manifestation of his temperament. He was always something of an exhibitionist, a great character actor, and the role of benefactor was very near his heart. Still, allowing for all this, how could I resign him to his fate at this late hour? He could never endure Glenwoodie: I had seen the place when we went out to visit Peter Dickie. And to such a man as Grandpa it would be the end.

I sighed and got up. As I left the room it annoyed me horribly to see that he was fast asleep in his chair.

That night I took my microscope, which Gavin had given me—my only possession of any value, in fact a really sacred possession which I had sworn never, never to part with, not even if I were ruined and a beggar in the streets. I pawned it in the town. I got a fair price, five pounds ten shillings—slightly more than I had expected. Then I came along the Vennel and crossed the court to the chipped, chalk-scrawled, brownstone building where Galt lived. He was leaning against his doorway in his shirt sleeves.

"I've brought you the money," I said.

His fingers closed over the notes. He looked up at me. His face broke into a sheepish grin.

"That's us clear then. Come on inside a minute." He indicated an interior which was littered and untidy, the spotted wallpaper covered with his "Brotherhood" certificates, pinned cutouts of footballers and boxers.

I shook my head and began to walk away, my spirits suddenly rising by leaps and bounds. Halfway across the Common I realized that, in my nervous excitement, I had given Galt all the money I had received for the microscope, ten shillings more than he had asked. What did it matter? I was clear of him, clear and free. If I had not been so conscious of my maturity, I would have run and jumped. As it was, I went into the shop at the end of the Common and with the small change in my pocket bought myself a round puff-apple pie. I ate it slowly, going up Drumbuck Road, in the still clear evening savouring every morsel, licking the crumbs from my fingers. How good it was! How pleasant that the evenings were drawing out! The light was limpid and tender. A thrush was singing in the chestnut branches. As I drew near I suddenly apostrophized the inoffensive bird.

"One day I'll show you! Hah! You just wait and see!"

Chapter Seven

Levenford, as Mama had once said, was a smoky old town, but the woods, lochs and mountains round about were beautiful. There were all sorts of local Rambling and Photographic Clubs with nominal subscription fees of about half-a-crown, yet when Kate or Jamie pressed me to join, when Grandma, even, with a shrewd look, suggested that a brisk walk "would do me no harm," I merely shook by head and went up to my bed to read. I, who once lived, practically, upon the high summits of the windy crags, had not seen the real countryside for months. However, on the morning of the Trades Spring Holiday, I felt a swift resurgence of my expeditionary fever.

Unhappily, in Scotland, there is always an enemy to combat—the weather. And on this day of freedom, I saw, from my window, as I dressed, that the skies were grey and dripping. Was it to be one of these incessant downpours rendered more depressing because of the sense of a holiday spoiled? I groaned and hastened to the railway station.

Here a number of excursionists were standing, rather disconsolately, on the damp platform; and as I made my way along, my heart suddenly began to beat furiously. *She* was already there, talking to Jason Reid, wearing a sturdy mackintosh and a navy blue beret pulled over her thick hair. Immediately the entire station was illuminated by her presence. As I approached, Reid gave me a nod of greeting.

"Don't worry, Shannon. I'm not coming with you."

Alison shook the raindrops from her nose, interrogating me with a wry smile. "Isn't this the limit, Robie? Perhaps it's too wet to go?"

"Oh, no," I said hurriedly.

I longed to go, in fact I knew that we must, simply must go, even if it hailed. I was reassured when Reid said cheerily:

"You won't melt. Only see you don't get washed overboard: My barometer registered 'Warm & Dry,' this morning. Sure sign of a typhoon."

In these last two years Reid had lost much of his moroseness. This new capacity for not getting "low" in adverse circumstances was something I envied him immensely—I so sadly lacked that quality myself. He was going to Winton on some business for Mrs. Keith, and after talking to us for a moment he left to get his train on the other side. As he did so it struck me that a look of complicity passed between Alison and him; I could not be sure, I was hurrying to the booking office, in my usual harassed fashion, to see about our tickets.

Presently Alison and I took the train to Ardfillan. After the short railway journey, making a dash from the station to the pier, dodging through stacks of barrels and coils of rope, while the fresh breeze from the sea slanted the rain against us, we boarded the North British Railway Company's paddle boat, the *Lucy Ashton*, which made the run to Ardencaple. After wandering round and viewing the engines we found a place in the lee of the deck house where we could stand in comparative shelter. Soon a bell rang below, the hawsers were cast off, the red paddles began to thrash the water, and the ship throbbed away from the quay.

Dodging the waterspouts which the wind blew round the corner into our faces, I bent forward anxiously:

"If it's too much for you we can go below."

Alison's cheeks were beaten by the wind and the rain, the dark beret which she wore, close down on her head, seemed bejewelled with crystal drops.

"I'm enjoying it." She spoke loudly, against the breeze, smiling back at me. "Besides, I can actually see blue sky."

It was true. I followed her pointing finger and made out a break in the ragged clouds which was followed in a few minutes by another. Scarcely daring to breathe, we watched the two blue patches coalesce, expand, and gradually force back the grey. Then, to our delight, the sun burst forth, hot and brilliant. Soon the entire sky had cleared, steam began to rise from the rapidly drying decks. I saw that, by one of those amazing transformations of our northern climate, we were to have, after all, a perfect day.

"Jason's barometer was right!" I exulted.

Alison agreed warmly. "But Robie . . . please don't say Jason." She hesitated. "Mother hates us to call him that. His own name is such a fine one."

We went to the bow of the little vermilion-funnelled steamer, now gliding up the sea-loch beneath the fiery blue sky, between the high hills, stopping occasionally at a village pier to take on a consignment of early potatoes, or a crofter with a few sheep he was bringing in to market. It was wonderful to be with Alison, simply to be near her. Standing at the rail I could not escape the soft contact of her figure when she stirred. Joy and hope flooded my soul in a kind of tender ecstasy.

We reached Ardencaple, the head of the Loch, at one o'clock. The thought that I had three hours to spend with Alison in this lovely spot enchanted me. Nervously determined to do things in style, I hurried her towards the one large hotel—the West Highland Grand—which stood, with a pretentious and neglected air, amidst the few whitewashed cottages of the tiny village.

"Can we have some lunch, please?"

In the draughty hall beneath intimidating antlers, a Highland waitress, starched, elderly and formidable, opposed us. She met my request by leading us sternly into a long cold dining room, where we appeared to be the only guests. The walls were covered with stag's heads, bull's horns and improbable stuffed fish which gaped at us from varnished boards. On the sideboard a meagre buffet was laid out: sinewy-looking mutton and waxy potatoes; a blancmange shape, pale and shivery; strong cheese and damp biscuits. A Highland major domo, with a long white beard and a tartan waistcoat, stood in the background, voicing his distrust of us in

Gaelic to the waitress, who now presented her severe visage at our table.

"The season hasna' begun. She can give ye the cauld luncheon at fower an' saxpence the heid."

Filled with misgiving, I was preparing to submit to this shameless intimidation, when Alison murmured to me:

"Do you really like this place, Robie?"

I started and reddened to the roots of my hair. I had just enough courage to shake my head.

"I don't either." Alison rose calmly and addressed the startled waitress. "We've changed our minds. We don't require luncheon after all."

Unconscious of the woman's consternation and of the agitation of the white-bearded major domo, who was now entreating us to remain, she walked composedly out of the hotel. I followed.

Across the way, Alison entered the solitary village shop and, having studied its resources carefully, persuaded the storekeeper to cut her half a dozen ham sandwiches. While this was being done she moved about, picking up a couple of apples, some ripe bananas, a bar of milk chocolate and two bottles of that splendid beverage, sustainer of my youth, Barr's Iron Brew. All this cost no more than two and six, and went into a brown paper bag, quite easy to carry.

We now set out to climb the hill, taking a path which led through a coppice of young larches, already showing feathery crimson tufts upon their branches. Following the Ardencaple stream, we pushed steadily upwards, through thick ferns and bushes of wild azalea, until at last we came out to a clearing high on the edge of the moorland. It was a forgotten little field, encroached upon by bracken and protected against the wind by stout stone dykes. Through the centre of the meadow the burn dashed and tumbled over clear rocks into an amber pool, fringed with white sand. The banks were of springy turf with clumps of primroses drooping and trailing with the current, their petals drifting down like little boats. The place held a warm air of secrecy.

We sat down on the dry grass with our backs to the wall, near the pool and amidst the soft green mitres of the new bracken. The mountains rose behind us, the Loch, with our toyish steamer anchored far below, was a mirror at our feet. Sunshine came spilling upon us. Flushed and eager, I steeped the bottles in the running stream, while Alison took off her mackintosh and spread out our picnic.

The sandwiches were made with new bread and country ham and butter; they could not have been surpassed. The Iron Brew fizzed refreshingly down my throat. Alison made me eat almost all the bananas. We scarcely spoke, but as we finished she gave me one of her odd smiles.

"Wasn't that better than the old hotel?"

I nodded inarticulately, realizing that but for her calm and decided action we might still be suffering down below.

With a contented sigh Alison removed her beret, closed her eyes and lay back against the dyke.

"This is lovely," she said. "I could go to sleep."

Her healthy, youthful body was relaxed. Her hair, that long tumbling hair with gleams in it, which always seemed a little untidy, was carelessly unloosed, framing her already sunburned face. The tender effect of her lowered eyelashes against her fair warm skin was strangely accentuated by the tiny mole high on her cheekbone. Her white blouse was open at the neck, showing the firm arch of her throat. A fine dew of perspiration was forming on her upper lip.

That joy and terror which I knew so well swept over me again.

"You aren't comfortable, Alison." I swallowed dryly and came near to her, placing my arm so that it supported her head.

She did not protest, remaining relaxed and peaceful, her eyes still closed, lips half smiling. After a moment she murmured:

"You have a very loud heart, Robie. I can hear it bumping all over the place."

What an opening for a pretty speech! Why did I not make it? And why, oh why, did I not clasp her closely in my arms? Alas, for the tragedy of my innocent intensity! I was too simple and too gauche. Besides, my happiness was so intense, I did not dare to move. Tongue-tied, choking with emotion, I continued to support her head, my cheek close to hers, feeling the slow rise and fall of her breathing which caused her patent-leather belt to creak slightly. The sun beat upon us benevolently, warming the rough material of her skirt, so that it exhaled a perfume of tweed that mingled with the scent of thyme. The air was soft and languid and from the woods below there came the teasing echo of the cuckoo.

Rapture forced a whisper from me at last.

"This is what I meant the other night, Alison. You and I together like this. Always."

"What would happen when it rained?"

"I wouldn't mind the rain," I answered fervently. "So long as ..."

I broke off. Alison had opened her eyes, and was looking at me sideways in a provoked fashion. There was a pause. Then with an air of resolution she sat up.

"Robie! I want to talk to you seriously. I'm worried about you. And so is Mr. Reid."

So I was right this morning at the station. Although distressed that she had drawn away from me, I felt proud to be the object of her concern.

"In the first place," she continued, frowning, "we think it's a dreadful waste that you should be stuck in the Works the way you are. You're forgetting all your biology. Do you know that they wanted to make an engineer out of Caruso? But he broke out of it."

"My dear Alison." I shrugged my shoulders with affected indifference. "I have a perfectly good job."

She was silent, her eyes fixed ahead. Had I been a little too heroic in my disavowal? I stole a glance at her profile.

"Of course I admit I get dreadfully tired ... sometimes gouge my hand with a chisel. Then ... there's my cough, too."

She turned to me, with an expression that perplexed me. She shook her head.

"Robie, dear ... you're an awful boy."

What had I said? A surge of distress filled my breast. Why should she treat me with this reproving kindness? The warm air was alive with the liquid murmurs of the brook. My heart, which had been beating madly, contracted.

"Have I offended you?"

"No, of course not." She bit her lip, struggling with her feelings. "You just make me feel how different we are. I'm so practical, a little too solid perhaps, while you are, and always will be, in the clouds. Goodness knows what you'll do when Mr. Reid goes away from Levenford."

I gazed at her in confused surprise. "Reid? Going away?"

Her eyes were lowered, she was twisting the stem of a primrose in her fingers.

"He has applied for a post in England. A school near Horsham, in Sussex. He's been at the Academy too long. This place is small but it goes in for modern methods and will give him more opportunity."

I exclaimed: "Do you mean that Reid has got the post?"

"Well, yes ... I think it is practically settled. He had made up his mind to let you know this evening."

I felt chilled. Although, from time to time, Reid had thrown out hints, this was a sudden and unexpected blow. And why had it been arranged and settled without a word to me? Perhaps he had not wished to hurt me. Yet an unhappy sense of exclusion took hold of me. Before I could express any of these thoughts, Alison continued in a low voice, avoiding my eyes, her colour coming and going:

"I know you're upset that Mr. Reid is leaving. It's horrid to lose one's friends. Although of course people can keep in touch with each other even when they do leave."

There was a queer silence.

"The fact is, Robie ..." Suddenly Alison raised her head. "Mother and I are going away too."

I must have turned pale, my lips could scarcely form the word. "Where?"

Leaning towards me she went on rapidly, earnestly.

"It's my training, for one thing. You know how important Mother thinks it, how specialized it must be. Miss Cramb can't teach me any more. In Winton there is no one much better. It's been decided I shall go to the Royal Conservatory of Music in London."

"London!" It was the other end of the earth; and it was near, extremely near to Sussex.

Alison's colour was now out of control, she was deeply, almost painfully embarrassed.

"For a boy who is so clever you are terribly blind to what's going on. Everyone has known it but you. Mother and Mr. Reid are going to be married."

Stunned, I could find nothing to say. Of course I had to admit that Mrs. Keith was still an attractive woman, that she and Reid shared the same tastes and interests. But, instead of rejoicing, I was appalled.

There was a long silence.

At last, I said, wretchedly: "If you go, I have nobody."

"I'm not going for ever." Her voice was soft, full of kindness and affection. "You know I must think of my singing. But it isn't the end of the world, Robie. And don't jump to conclusions—remember, there's always another day."

As I stared ahead, mournful and desolate, the sun began to slip behind the mountains and there came three sharp blasts from the steamer at the pier, warning that her departure was not far off.

"We must hurry!" Alison exclaimed. "They'll be casting off quite soon."

She gave me, unexpectedly, a hesitant, almost pleading smile and, rising, extended her hand to help me to my feet. As we hastened down towards the boat, I had the strange impression that, for all her firmness, she was swayed by uncertainty equal to my own. The steamer whistled again—a prolonged note, like the siren at the Works. My holiday was over. Suddenly, with a sinking heart, I saw myself alone and lost. The future rose before me like a wall.

Chapter Eight

The last Saturday in July ... Preoccupied by my own woes, I had forgotten that this was the date of the Flower Show, and only recollected the fact at noon, on my way home from the Works. When I reached Lomond View, I was in no mood for the afternoon's event. But I had promised Murdoch to attend the Show, and at two o'clock I went to my room to get ready. The sound of heavy, if uncertain, footsteps above my head caused me, once or twice, to pause, and in the end I was driven to go up.

The old man, washed and trimmed, was posed before his mirror; attempting, with trembling fingers, and very red in the face, to knot his tie. His clothes had been brushed, his boots polished in the best style of his palmy days. He wore a starched white shirt which was tight around his throat.

"That you, Robert?" In spite of his shakiness, his tone was equable, he did not remove his eyes from the glass.

I remained silent for a moment, chilled, despite the heat, by the signs of his activity.

"Where are you going?"

"Where am I going?" He made the knot, successfully, his neck stretched out. "What a question. I am going to the Flower Show, of course."

"No ... no ... You're not well enough to go."

"I was never better in my life."

"It's terribly hot. Sure to upset you. You ought to rest."

"I've been resting all week. You've no idea how tiresome it is to rest."

"But your leg——" I tried a final argument. "You're much too lame to walk."

He turned from the mirror and, although his head was shaking a little, gave me one of his quiet smiles.

"My dear boy, the difference between you and me is that you give up too easily. How often have I told you not to be so easy beat? You wouldn't expect me, the head of the family, to stay away on Murdoch's big day. Besides, I've always liked flowers. Flowers and pretty women."

I had reddened at his analysis of my character, which I felt to be only too true, and now, dismayed, I watched him get into his jacket and, with an air, shoot out his stiff cuffs. He had been ailing these past weeks; yet, with tremulous indifference, he was preparing to disport himself. It was enough to paralyse all my powers of diplomacy. Impossible to turn him from his purpose ...

"Well!" he said, satisfied at last with his appearance, and taking up his stick. "Am I to have the pleasure of your company? Or do you wish me to go alone?"

Of course I must go with him. How could I let him loose in such a crowd, on such a day as this? I followed him as, holding the banisters rather too tightly, and not very sure of his footing, he descended the stairs.

Outside, numbers of the townspeople, men in straw hats, women in light dresses, were moving along the road to the gardens of Overton House where the Show was being held. As we joined the leisurely stream I reflected that at least we should not meet any of Grandpa's less reputable friends in this gathering. Vaguely relieved, yet afraid of his slight unsteadiness, I offered to take his arm.

It was a horrible blunder. Grandpa repudiated my assistance irritably.

"What do you think I am? A fossil ... a mummy?" Doing his best to disguise his dragging foot, he drew himself up, and tried to inflate his chest in the old manner. "In five years' time perhaps I'll ask you to order my Bath chair. I'm not done yet by any means."

Even the remotest allusion to his waning powers was a dreadful mistake. He hated to think that he was failing, and shut his eyes firmly to the fact that he could not go on for ever. Actually, he was succeeding in carrying himself erect: in spite of my anxiety I was compelled to own it. Turned out better than usual, he was, even admitting his erratic feet, and that slight agitation of his head, a presentable figure. Indeed, his white hair, bushy beneath his hat, made him rather striking—eyes were turned towards him, he felt himself a centre of attraction, preened himself, as we strolled along.

"You observe, Robert," he murmured to me, with restored complacency, "these two ladies on the left. Very elegant. Beautiful sunshine too. I wouldn't have missed this for the world."

As we approached the lodge entrance gates, where temporary wooden turnstiles had been installed, Grandpa produced, with a flourish, two free passes, which he had obtained in advance from Murdoch. He was incorrigible.

It was pleasant within the enclosure, one of the finest and largest gardens in the county, now made festive by half a dozen red-striped marquees for the exhibits, by several tents given over to displays of seeds and garden implements, and an open-air tea-court where, deployed round the fountain, the town band was playing a soft waltz. The trim lawns and shady trees, the bright movement of the ladies' dresses, the scarlet and gold of the bandsmen's uniform, the tinkle of the music and the fountain, the sound of well-bred conversation, all this caused Grandpa to blossom out more. He let his feet sink into the velvet turf. His nostrils expanded.

"I aye had a taste for the genteel, Robert. It's my proper element."

He bowed to several persons who did not seem to recognize him, then, in no way discomposed, he began to hum, limping along in a survey of the scene.

"Handsome, very handsome." The excitement was going to his head a little. He remained polite and restrained. Yet he had begun to accept everything as being in his honour. "Look! Is that not Mrs. Bosomley over there?"

"No, it isn't." He was always mistaking people, the "long sight" of which he had been so proud was gone for ever.

"Well, never mind. A fine woman, too. We'll speak to her later.

Take me to Murdoch's carnations now. I always liked carnations. And I want to see if he's won the prize."

I moved him on with relief. I had made out Alison and her mother in the distance and it was my earnest desire to avoid them. We entered the marquees, which were filled with flowers, hothouse fruits and choice vegetables. It must not be forgotten that the Scots are famous gardeners. In one tent was an array of roses of marvellous scent and colour; in another masses of sweet peas exhaling a fragrance delicate as their own petals. We admired baskets of downy peaches; splendid asparagus tied with blue ribbon; bunches of luscious muscat grapes; a giant pumpkin bursting with its own juice. Grandpa viewed them all with mounting pleasure, barely tempered by his air of a connoisseur, his face redder than ever from the sultry heat beneath the blistering canvas. Seeing him so happy, I felt ashamed of my misgivings and glad that he had not been deprived of this hour.

We reached the display of carnations. Here, amongst the considerable gathering which had assembled to regard, with curiosity and respect, a large bunch of blossoms on the front of the stand, we found Kate and Jamie with little Luke. A moment later Murdoch came over from the booth reserved for exhibitors, accompanied by Miss Ewing. The old man was deeply gratified by this family encounter. He shook hands all round, even with Kate's child, whom he addressed affectionately as "Robie." Then, glancing at the surrounding spectators as though favouring them with his confidence, he whispered to Murdoch loudly, so that all could hear:

"What's the verdict, my boy? Have we won the medal?"

Murdoch gave a self-conscious nod towards the stand. "See for yourself."

Hung on the central bunch of carnations—lovely unusual blossoms of a delicate shade of yellow with tinges of mauve upon the petal edges—was a gilt-edged card with ink barely dry: *Bowers Silver Medal for Best Floral Exhibit. Mr. Murdoch Leckie of Dalrymple and Leckie, Nurserymen, Drumbuck.*

"It's just as good as the Alexandra," Miss Ewing explained quickly. "We're very pleased."

Although he had done well, Murdoch had not quite achieved his ambition. It made no difference to Grandpa, however. To him a medal was a medal. His face was crimson.

"Murdoch, I'm proud of you. You do me honour. If you will permit me the privilege of being the first to wear your bonny flower . . ."

He stretched out his hand, took a carnation from the bunch, snapped the stem and slipped it in his buttonhole.

It was a typical gesture and although Murdoch did not look especially well-pleased the buttonhole undoubtedly made Grandpa complete. His smile went round us all before it wavered.

"Take me to where they'll give out the prizes. I'm not tired, mind you. But I'll sit down there, and wait till they give us the medal."

When he was settled in a garden chair on the lawn in the shade of a tall acacia tree, pleasantly near the band, and beside Kate and Jamie, I felt a temporary lifting of my responsibility and took the opportunity to slip away. He would not miss me for the next half hour—already he had taken Kate's son upon his knee and was asking, with a dim indulgent smile:

"Robie, do you mind that day we went skating on the pond?"

As I crossed the lawn I could hear the little boy's shrill answer:

"Never mind the skating, Grandpa. Tell me about the Zulus."

I wandered through several marquees, aimlessly, yet with the corner of my eye sensitively alert for *them*. Reid was leaving for the South the following week, while Alison and Mrs. Keith would join him a few days later—the wedding would be held quietly in London at the end of the month. Strangely, my distress was increased by the fact that, since I had last seen her, Alison had sung beautifully at the St. Andrew's Hall. Wounded and already alone, I shrank from meeting my friends, yet I felt it necessary to say good-bye to them.

"Please don't look so tragic, Robie. You ought to be proud of Murdoch's success."

Mrs. Keith, standing with Reid near the band, wearing a wide hat of soft straw with a white trimming, was glancing at me sideways, giving me her faint smile, less critical than it had been of late.

"Do I look tragic?" I started, and stammered. "Murdoch didn't win the gold medal."

"How could he," Jason said, "when I've been secretly growing vegetable marrows in my window boxes for months?"

"My dear boy." Mrs. Keith's dark eyes were gay. "You're perfectly all right. Still, it would be nice if you cheered up just for a bit."

Under my breath I made a stiff attempt to defend myself.

"Naturally one can't expect to be grinning all over one's face when certain people one is fond of happen to be going away."

Reid shook his head. "Life's a desperate business, Robert; suppose you come and have strawberries and cream with us. We're meeting Alison in the tea-garden in half an hour."

"Yes, do come," said Mrs. Keith. "We'll be there at four."

"Very well."

When they strolled off I turned and went into another marquee where, for a long time, I stared fixedly at a prime bunch of parsnips. I hated parsnips, and I wasn't really thinking of them. The mild satire which had pervaded the genuine friendship in Jason's tone made me suddenly see myself as I must appear to others. Oh, God! What a fool I was! I knew nothing about life, I didn't understand the first thing about it. I existed in a world of dreams, the pale victim of my own fancies. Pray Heaven for just one thing—that I would not break down and make an idiot of myself before them.

At five minutes to four I set out for the tea-garden.

And then, as I came through the crowd, I became aware of Kate, waving to me from the place where Grandpa had been sitting. Something imperative in her signals broke into my utter desolation, caused me to start and hurry forward.

"Grandpa's taken ill." She spoke breathlessly. "I sent Jamie for the doctor but he's taken worse now. Run down to the lodge and telephone for a cab."

Surrounded by a few good Samaritans, the old man lay on the grass which, an hour ago, he had proudly trodden. He was curled on his side, one arm twisted in, as though contorted. His eyes were fixed and open, one side of his mouth breathed noisily, the other half was still. His white hair was dishevelled. He had the wild, sad look of the dethroned Lear after that night of storm. Though I did not know much about it, I saw that it was a stroke. As I started running for the lodge they were preparing to make the awards. The band, having completed its programme, struck up, with a finality that sounded dreadful in my ears: "God Save the King."

Chapter Nine

Sunday; and nearly midnight. This time there is no mistake; the old man is dying. The consciousness of this pervades his room where I sit watching him, pervades the sleeping house, even the night beyond. All day there has been an air of expectancy, of correct behaviour—Murdoch and Jamie talking with Papa in subdued voices downstairs; Kate hushing the eager cries of her little boy as he plays ball in the back garden; Grandma on tiptoe baking a big batch of scones. This is called "waiting for the end," and the family retires with a sense of respectful disappointment that the old man should be "lingering," despite the three shattering electric strokes he has sustained in quick succession, and Dr. Galbraith's prediction that he cannot last. There are no protests when I claim the privilege of sitting up with him: the rights of my affection are recognized, and they are convenient when one has no desire to miss a good night's sleep.

The stillness is frightening; although I have drawn up the blind and opened the window the invasion of the warm and starless night brings no relief. Grandpa lies on his back, no longer snoring, barely breathing through a mouth drawn open by the recession of all his features. Before retiring Grandma has sponged the sharpened, half-conscious face, brushed the white hair, reviving a shadowy impression of that last magnificent appearance at the Flower Show. Age has reduced this body to ruins but has somehow failed to degrade it.

As I gaze at him, melancholy, yet relieved that he is solving a bad problem in the easiest way, I fall into an involuntary meditation: this, surely, is the moment to assay the value of a life, this awful moment of departure which we all must take. What follies, what sins he has committed! No one knows better than I the weaknesses and obstinacies of the old man's character; for already, with a tinge of horror, I recognize, in that sad and foolish boy, myself, these same traits which have descended to me from him. Yet I defend them, these troubled depths of personality: for already, like Grandpa, I have my doubts of the accepted code. These faint ennobling virtues: never to be mean, to be kind, to inspire affection—perhaps they outweigh a hundred besetting sins.

I must have dozed by the bedside. I am aroused by the old man trying to speak. I bend close and manage to catch the word: "Spirit."

It is no deathbed repentance, no reference to the Holy Ghost. He means that drink to which he has long been addicted, of which he now sorely feels the need. It is not good for him, but neither were his other predilections, and since the doctor had not troubled to impose a ban, I feel my way down to the parlour cupboard, where I find the bottle already purchased, not without disapproval, for those visitors that the bereavement will bring to the house and who, like Mr. McKellar, "partake." I pour a little into a cup, neat—he could never bear water with it—thinking it the final irony that the old man should sip the goblet of his own funeral feast.

He is grateful for the whisky, which he swallows with great difficulty. He mutters: "Meat and drink."

These are his last words. I find in that accidental phrase a strange meaning, a terse evaluation of his philosophy of life.

The clock strikes three, shaking me from my drooping fatigue. I see that the old man is now sinking fast, his instant of greatness is at hand. Suddenly the door opens and Grandma, carrying a candle, wearing her mutch and long white "gownie," comes into the room, drawn by instinct, the peasant's instinct which senses unerringly, and with awe, the approach of death. She does not, on this occasion, read aloud a chapter from her "Book." She glances from the dying man to me, silently accepts my chair, while I move over to the window.

The imminence of dawn can be felt: unseen stirrings, the incautious movement of a bird, vague looming of the three chestnut trees.

Grandma's behaviour is superb. She is afraid of the dark presence now standing in the room with us, this reminder of her own mortality. But she is purged of hatred. The bitterness, the animosity which once dominated that little world wherein we three people lived, now seems childish and remote. During these last months, as he sank, so she has risen; not in pity, but rather in mournful realization of her own worth, she has grown quite fond of her old enemy.

Yes, at last. Something has slipped away. The death of a man in the full height of his vigour is a dreadful business, a wrenching, unwilling orgasm. But this old man is tired. A skiff slips away from the shore easily, without splashing. Grandma looks at me, gives a faint nod of affirmation, and rises.

I watch while she binds up the sagging chin, places pennies—another peasant trick—on the closed eyes. I gaze, with great sadness, at the face fixed in this final rigidity. He has reached a place, whether of light or darkness I do not know, where no more follies can be committed; he has escaped from all his persecutors and pursuers—most of all, from himself.

At Grandma's whispered instruction I turn to pull down the blind. The dawn is coming: the chestnuts taking shape, the fields less huddled, a stain of saffron in the east. I blow out the candle. Suddenly from the farm on the hill, as if in mockery of the extinguished flame, there uprises the loud derisive challenge of a cock.

Chapter Ten

On Tuesday we all sat down in the parlour to a ham-and-egg tea after the funeral, which though not lavish was, at Papa's command, done handsomely, by the second-best undertaker in the town. Papa, rubbing his hands and full of courtesies, had brought back Mr. McKellar from the cemetery. Grandma sat on the lawyer's right and Kate on his left; Murdoch and Jamie were at the bottom end on either side of me; Adam occupied the head of the table, next to Papa.

"Everything passed off very nicely, I think." Papa, eager for approval, interrogated Mr. McKellar with his eyes. "Oh, take two eggs, man. Yes, I didn't want to make a splurge. On the other hand I always like to do the right thing. And besides, in a sense, if you understand me, it was due to him."

Some reply was expected from the lawyer. As he accepted his cup of tea from Kate he said dryly:

"I think the funeral was appropriate to the circumstances."

Papa looked slightly irked: it was one of his annoyances never to have been able to make McKellar like him. He looked grateful as Adam remarked:

"No one could have wished for better."

McKellar shrugged his solid shoulders. "When you get to that stage you don't wish for anything at all."

Papa and Adam exchanged a glance of understanding, of alliance against this surly intruder. Although he had arrived only that morning Adam had already assuaged Papa, reassured him on the question of the house, which, after all, was probably going to be sold to the kindergarten school, had calmly offered and, when Papa vacillated, as calmly torn up a cheque, had, in fact, won him so completely, that in the cab home they had fallen to discussing, in low tones, possible "openings" for Papa's new capital, the insurance money which had come to him at last.

"Try some of my scones, Mr. McKellar," Grandma said.

"I will, indeed." The lawyer was making a good tea and, though taciturn to Papa and Adam, he talked amiably, in his heavy style, to Kate and the old lady. He was an ardent advocate of Home Rule for Scotland and here he met Grandma on common ground. He seemed to crouch over his plate, and his eye went darting about the table, in a disconcerting manner.

I must confess that I avoided this steely glance. At the graveside, raw gash in the greensward, where the dignity of "a cord" was conferred on me, I had in a weak and ridiculous manner made a ghastly fool of myself. As we lowered the coffin my body began to shake, I burst into blubbering tears ... at my age! The recollection of it made me hang my head in shame.

"Have you the exact amount of the policy?" Adam inquired casually.

"Yes, I have." McKellar spoke with formality. There was no love between these two: the city insurance man, dabbler in odd affairs, and the small town solicitor-actuary. An interesting character, this McKellar, who had always given me a nod across the street over a period of years—slow, stolid, firm as a rock, he would die sooner than change one halfpenny in his balance sheet. To say that he was honest is a preposterous understatement. He was a watchdog of probity; for all affairs beyond the solid three per cents. he had a shake of his head and this peculiar phrase: "A bad business. Aye, aye, a bad business." Clearly he distrusted Adam as an opportunist, a young man who left his office at rather short notice and who had always shoved himself up at the expense of others.

"What might the accrued sum be?" Adam was still pressing ahead.

"Seven hundred and eighty-nine pounds, seven shillings and threepence ... precisely."

Adam inclined his head while Papa paled at the magnitude, the luscious magnitude of the sum. I could not help thinking of Grandpa, who hated this policy so much that he had forbidden me ever to mention it in his presence. Thank heaven he was spared Papa's joyful whisper:

"When can you pay it?"

"At once." McKellar placed his knife and fork methodically together and pushed away his plate.

"More tea, Mr. McKellar."

"Thank you no, I've done brawly."

"A drop of spirits, then." Papa, the prim abstainer, actually made the hospitable offering.

"Well, if you insist."

When the full tumbler had been placed before McKellar, I slipped from my chair with the intention of escaping unobserved. But that steady and penetrating orb fell upon me like a searchlight.

"Where are you going?"

Papa came to my rescue. "He's still a bit upset ... Maybe you noticed at the funeral. That's all right, we'll excuse you, Robert."

"Sit down, boy." McKellar took a firm dram of spirits. "It's hardly respectful to the old man's memory to slink out in the middle of the proceedings. If you have any regard for him at all—and you're the only one that pretends to have—you might have the decency to bide till I have finished."

I sank into my chair in confusion. McKellar had never used that tone to me before. It stung and humiliated me.

"Let's get ahead with it then," Adam said sharply.

"As you wish." McKellar took some papers from his inside pocket. "Here is the policy, No. 57430, an endowment assurance in the name of Alexander Gow. And here is the will. I'll read it through."

"What for?" Adam was losing his temper at the lawyer's pedantic slowness. "Why all this rigmarole? I was in your office when you drew it, I witnessed it, and I know it by heart."

McKellar gave the impression of being taken aback. "It'll be more regular if I read it. It won't take me a moment."

"Of course." Papa smoothed things over.

McKellar put on his glasses and in a slow broad voice read out the will. It was a short and simple document. Grandpa left everything to Mama, and, in the event of her decease, to her executor, Papa.

"Well." Papa exhaled a satisfied breath. "That's just as it should be. Now there's nothing to detain us."

"Wait!" McKellar almost shouted the word and at the same time thumped the table with his large fist. In the silence which succeeded he glanced round, crouching over the parchment, that slow grim smile, carefully hidden until now, contracting his bushy brows, tightening his firm mouth. He was like a man free at last to unleash and to enjoy some exquisite secret.

His eye found me again, dwelt upon me with open kindness, as he said: "There is a codicil to this will, a holograph codicil dated July 20th, 1910."

An exclamation from Papa, which I scarcely heard. How clearly I remembered that day: that day of mortal sadness, when I lost the Marshall and Gavin was killed.

McKellar went on, letting every word sink in—yes, as though it afforded him excruciating pleasure to stab Papa with each individual word:

"On that day, the twentieth of July, Dandie Gow came into my office. I called him Dandie because, in spite of all his failings and misfortunes, I'm proud to say he was my friend. He asked me outright if he could divert the proceeds of his policy. We had a long talk, he and I, that afternoon. As a result, every penny of the money, I say every penny, and my God, I mean every penny, is left to the boy here, Robert Shannon, under my trusteeship, to enable him to take his medical degrees at Winton College."

Deathly silence. I had turned white; my throat, my heart constricted; I could not believe it, I was too used to misfortune, too beaten-down—it was just another device of the blind sky to pretend to raise me up so that I could be dashed down again, more cruelly.

"You are trying to impose on me," Papa whimpered. "He couldn't do such a thing. He had no right."

The grim smile deepened. "Every right, under this policy, which could not be mortgaged or compounded during his lifetime, but was his to devise and bequeath, voluntarily."

Papa threw a piteous glance at Adam. "Is that so?"

"It's the only way Mama would have it." Adam glared at McKellar. "He was out of his mind."

"Not when he drew the codicil two years ago. He was as sane as you are."

"I'll contest the will," Papa said in a high strange voice. "I'll take it to law."

"Do so." McKellar ceased to smile. He glanced from Adam to Papa in a very threatening manner. "Yes, do so. And I promise you I'll fight you of my own accord, fight you if need be to the County Court, and the High Court. Fight you to the floor of the Parliament itself. It would be a bad business for you, Leckie. There would be no Waterworks for you then, my man." He paused, relishing to the full this little bit of melodrama which, after years of staid practice, had come his way. "Your wife didn't wish to take out this policy, though she paid most of the premiums herself. As for the old man—he had no chance to get a farthing from it. But he wanted it to serve a good and useful purpose. It will serve that purpose, or my name is not Duncan McKellar."

Oh, God, was it really true then ... this wonderful gift from Grandpa, who had never breathed a word of it to me? I kept my eyes lowered, scarcely breathing, the muscles of my face twitching beneath their fixed rigidity. Suddenly I heard Kate's voice, felt her arm go round my shoulders.

"I don't know what the others think ... in my opinion it's the best use that could be made of this money ... yes, the very best use."

"Hear! Hear!" Jamie added in a loud whisper.

Blessed Kate of the bad tempers and the bumps on her forehead, and Jamie, who makes money seem clean and decent ... I humbly trust their little boy will have less difficulty in growing up than did I. McKellar, folding up the papers, addressed me as he stood up.

"Ten o'clock to-morrow at my office. But meantime you can walk down the road with me. A breath of air will do you no harm."

I left the room with him blindly. There comes a point when nature, strung to the breaking-point, can endure no more.

Chapter Eleven

Late that evening there returns from Lawyer McKellar's house an excited small-town mammal of the genus *Homo sapiens*, in brief, that woeful yet warm-blooded vertebrate, Robert Shannon. Although this peculiar biped is actually eighteen and has not so long ago felt upon his stooping shoulders the awful burden of the years, of an almost unrequited love and of countless other miseries as well, he is still unhardened and immature. Now, while conscious of the calm still beauty of the night, a vast pellucid night singing with stars, beneath which his heart also is singing, he gazes straight ahead, flushed, and intent.

The future is wide and open to him. The dry Scots lawyer, who has talked with him so long, will act as his trustee and counsellor, as his friend. He will never go back to the Works. At the beginning of the new session, next month, he will go to the University, living in the students' hostel there, entering with joy upon his medical studies. Biology ... practical zoology ... these magic names have brought that high colour to his cheeks. Already he sniffs the intoxicating odours of formalin and Canada balsam, views that long line of Zeiss microscopes, each with its wonderful oil-immersion lenses, and one of which will be his—in spite of poor Mr. Smith, whom he will be pleased to see again. To think of it! Why, they will probably let him dissect the dogfish, *mustelus canis*, if he is lucky, in his first term!

There is enough money to see him through: the few loose ends left by Grandpa can be cleared up by McKellar for less than twenty pounds. If unpleasant things are said to him when he goes home—and his expression hardens here—he has been told to take no notice. He will soon leave Lomond View for good.

Ah, yes, the future is open and shining. Reid and Alison may be going, but he is going also. ... He will show them that he is not fated to be a failure. His feelings towards Alison have subtly changed, his passion is more sternly contained. Perhaps there is no place for women in the life of a great zoologist? Or perhaps one day in Vienna, when a famous prima donna is singing the title role in *Carmen*, a grave distinguished doctor with a decoration in his buttonhole and a small trim beard will come quietly into the stage box. ...

No, no, these fancies belong to the phase of adolescence which the boy has put behind him. Ahead there is work to be done ... serious, oh, glorious laboratory work.

But wait ... one last moment, one final inconsistency before we let him go. As he passes along Chapel Street there rises before him on his right the dark despised structure of the Holy Angels Church. He needs nothing, this bright spirit, from that place, which no longer deludes him. Bravely, he has resisted all the wiles of Canon Roche to bring him back to it. Sadness has not brought him to his knees. ... Oh, he's past being hoodwinked; practically, in fact, on the verge of being a freethinker.

And yet at this moment he is caught unawares, seized and strangled, by an overmastering force. Remember—he has read everything, from the *Origin of Species* to Renan's *Life of Jesus*, he has smiled at the fable of Adam's rib, and agreed with the witty French Cardinal, whose name he has forgotten, that Christianity rests upon a charming myth. Yet this is something which surges up, which is in his blood, his bones, his very marrow, something he will never be rid of, which will haunt him till the instant of his death.

We are faced with an anticlimax of the first magnitude. But we have sworn, beyond everything, to be truthful. How many times in the future this Robert Shannon will shuttle between apathy and ardour, rise and be smitten down again, we are not at liberty to predict—or how often he will make, and break, his peace with the

Being towards whom all human impulses ascend. The fact remains that now, uncontrollably, he feels the need of communicating the exaltation of his spirit, in the listening stillness. He feels suddenly that his prayer of gratitude will not fall into the void. And with a shamefaced air, he darts into the dark church.

The least we can say is that he is not absent long. Perhaps he has only stayed to light a penny candle, or murmur some incoherent words before the sombre altar. Yet perhaps it is more than that. When he emerges, dazzled a little by the lucid stars and the Northern Lights now searching the polar sky, he sets off more briskly, his footsteps ringing clear in the empty street.

THE END